Praise for Stella Cameron:

"Her narrative is rich, her style is distinct,
and her characters are wonderfully wicked."
—*Publishers Weekly*

"No one does suspense and sensuality
like Stella Cameron."
—*New York Times* bestselling author
Linda Lael Miller

STELLA CAMERON
Shadows

MURIEL JENSEN
Daddy in Demand

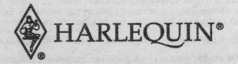

HARLEQUIN®

TORONTO • NEW YORK • LONDON
AMSTERDAM • PARIS • SYDNEY • HAMBURG
STOCKHOLM • ATHENS • TOKYO • MILAN • MADRID
PRAGUE • WARSAW • BUDAPEST • AUCKLAND

ISBN 0-373-83467-5

HARLEQUIN AMERICAN ROMANCE 2-in-1 COLLECTION

Copyright © 2001 by Harlequin Books S.A.

The publisher acknowledges the copyright holders
of the individual works as follows:

SHADOWS
Copyright © 1986 by Stella Cameron

DADDY IN DEMAND
Copyright © 2001 by Muriel Jensen

This edition published by arrangement with Harlequin Books S.A.

® and TM are trademarks of the publisher. Trademarks indicated with
® are registered in the United States Patent and Trademark Office, the
Canadian Trade Marks Office and in other countries.

Visit us at www.eHarlequin.com

Printed in U.S.A.

CONTENTS

SHADOWS
Stella Cameron

For Jerry, with love

The truly generous is the truly wise;
and he who loves not others,
lives unblest.
—Horace

CHAPTER ONE

LEAH. Guy Hamilton concentrated on the white wine he swirled in his glass and tried the woman's name in his mind once more. Then he studied her again. Leah suited her—soft, feminine, yet not easy to forget. She would never be easy to forget.

She leaned and spoke to her husband. "Would you like something else, Charles, dear?" Her voice was low and clear. "A little more of the burnt creme, perhaps?" The man's impatient shake of the head barely acknowledged his wife's question before he returned his attention to a red-faced woman littered with diamonds.

Guy shifted uncomfortably. Leah Cornish was too far away for him to give her an unobtrusive word of comfort and help her over the awkwardness she must feel in front of those observant enough to notice the rejection.

Fortunately, most guests were too absorbed in their own conversations, but a slight flush had risen on Leah's cheeks, and there was an unnatural brightness about her intensely blue eyes. She seemed to be an island—a gorgeous, slightly overdressed island—at one end of the immense dining table. He suppressed an urge to go to her on some pretext. As a total stranger, it wasn't his place to interfere.

"And you come from Phoenix, Mr., ah—"

The deep, masculine voice to Guy's right startled

him. "Hamilton," he said quickly. "Guy Hamilton. Yes, that's right. I'm visiting Wichita Falls from Phoenix."

He remembered this man from the initial introductions. A local congressman. Tall, almost as tall as himself, but thickset and swarthy. Joe Malley, or Marley.

"And the general is your brother, I understand. A fine man. You must be very proud of him," the congressman said effusively.

Guy glanced down the table at his brother, Clark, resplendent in air force dress uniform. "Yes," he agreed genuinely. "Very proud. And glad to have a chance to spend a few days with him. Doesn't happen often." He flexed his own shoulders uncomfortably inside the dinner jacket he'd borrowed from Clark. Too narrow across the back, too much fabric at the waist. It would be a blessing when this evening was over.

"What do you think of Texas?" his companion asked.

"I like it," Guy said. "I like it very much. But I didn't expect it to be this hot in March. Or at least not this humid."

There was more inconsequential prattle that Guy only half heard. He made generic noises to punctuate every short silence. But his attention returned to Leah Cornish. At first he'd thought she was Cornish's daughter rather than his wife. She had to be twenty-five, maybe thirty years younger than her husband, who was an impressive, silver-haired man in a custom-tailored white silk suit.

Charles Cornish clearly gravitated to the flashy, which probably accounted for Leah's too-frilly chiffon dress and sparkling earrings. No doubt the single huge sapphire that hovered provocatively in overly displayed

cleavage was also Cornish's taste. She constantly de-
ferred to the man, and the habit was likely to go beyond
the dining room. Guy would lay a bet that Cornish
chose what she wore. Fortunately, no man could alter
the luster of her dark, shoulder-length hair, gently
waved about an oval face, or the healthy glow of her
olive skin, the perfectly bowed mouth. He blew into a
clenched fist. She would feel silken—

He gritted his teeth and forced himself to face the
congressman. "I'm sorry. What did you say?" Admiring a beautiful woman could be a harmless occupation
but potentially dangerous when she was married. And
he was hardly in a position to allow his imagination
free rein on a woman—any woman.

"I was remarking on how handsome our hostess is,"
the man said lightly, as if reading Guy's thoughts.
"Charles is a lucky devil. She adores him. I'm told she
was only nineteen when he married her, and she's
never looked at anyone but him."

"How old is she now?" The question was out before
Guy could stop it.

"Twenty-nine, thirty, maybe. And Charles must be
close to sixty. I've known them both for some years."
The reply was unperturbed. "Leah seems like a bright
woman from what little she says. Between you and
me—" the deep voice grew more hushed "—I think
Charles prefers to keep her in the background as much
as possible. He's definitely a bit possessive—the age
difference and so on, you know?"

He knew he shouldn't pursue the issue, but Guy
couldn't help himself. "She looks even younger. Do
they have children?"

"No." The man's suggestive laugh chilled Guy.

"But then, maybe good old Charles gets all his kicks from looking. Imagine what that must be like, hmm?"

Guy glanced around uncomfortably, but no one appeared to have overheard the comment. He looked at Leah briefly, and the pit of his stomach tightened. The creep beside him had a point.

"Let's go out on the terrace for coffee and liqueurs, everyone," Charles Cornish boomed abruptly. "Leah, sweet, tell Martin to attend to things."

Dinner had been pronounced over. Guests pushed chairs back over glistening oak floors and began to drift outside. The congressman joined Cornish and the diamond lady, leaving Guy alone, still seated at the table. Clark, laughing at something his wife said, had clearly forgotten him. Guy checked for Leah, but she had already left.

The room was incredible—vast gilt-edged mirrors, dark oils, velvet drapes tied back with gold tassels. It was all too heavy and oppressive for the north Texas climate. He looked at an armoire, fussily inlaid with colored lacquer and gold, then allowed his attention to wander over porcelains crowded on every highly polished surface. One large wall displayed a magnificent Aubusson hanging in shades of rose and magenta. The place was a museum—everything that could be easily recognized as worth a lot was gathered together in one place to impress.

He stood up and headed outside via the hall and the front door rather than the French doors leading to the terrace. A walk by himself would give him the strength to face it all again. He wouldn't be here if he weren't Clark's visiting brother. For Clark's sake and for Miriam's, his charming wife, he'd put on a good face—after a solitary breather.

Extensive grounds surrounded the Spanish-style home. Stucco walls enclosed all that antique European splendor. Guy shook his head and grimaced. The stucco reminded him of Phoenix and his own home, but any similarity ended there. Laughter came to him in muted bursts from the other side of the house, and he set off purposefully in the direction of a shadowy grove of trees.

He passed the edge of the stand and went deeper, enjoying the evening coolness that whispered through swaying branches. Ahead he spotted a faint bluish glow. Guy stopped, squinting, then went on more slowly, noting how the eerie light intensified as he got closer. To his left, something rustled, and he stopped again, close to a tree trunk.

Someone was there, walking in the same direction but much faster and more surefootedly than he. The indistinct figure threaded a path, and Guy followed slowly, unable to overcome his curiosity.

The trees thinned abruptly, cut off in a tidy circle around a large lighted swimming pool. Incongruous. Why would the Cornishes choose to build their pool so far from the house? White chaise longues and several umbrella tables were scattered around. There was a low building, probably for showering and changing, fronted by a wet bar. The layout was traditional, if expensive, but in a very untraditional location.

Then he saw who had preceded him to the clearing. Leah Cornish stood at the pool's edge with her back to him, staring down into the water. A breeze whipped her hair into a darkly flying cloud and plastered her filmy dress to her body. Back lighting turned her curvaceous figure and long legs into a shadowy statue. She might have been nude but for the occasional billow of thin fabric.

Guy's skin turned clammy. He should go back and not intrude. She would be shocked, and probably embarrassed, if he approached her out of the darkness. He closed his eyes for an instant. At least she'd never be aware of the man she'd unknowingly aroused merely by her presence, her aura, to a level he'd chosen to suppress for years.

He stepped back, sensing her need to be alone. All this hubbub, this grandiose posturing, was suffocating her as much as it did him. He felt a sudden, intense sympathy. Unlike himself, she couldn't walk away once the party was over.

A lizard ran over his foot, and he automatically exclaimed, then held still, scarcely breathing.

Too late.

"Who's there?" Leah swung around, one hand at her throat. "Who's there? Charles, is that you? Martin?"

Guy expelled a long breath and moved into the light. "Don't be alarmed, Mrs. Cornish. Just another wanderer from the party. I didn't mean to frighten you." All he could do was approach casually until he stood a few feet away.

"Oh, yes," she said softly when he was close enough to see clearly. "Mr. Hamilton. General Hamilton's brother. I'm sorry I shouted like that." Even in shifting shadow he could tell she had paled.

"You didn't shout. But I shocked you. Sit down a minute." He indicated a chair by one of the umbrella tables. After a fractional hesitation, she did as he suggested and waved Guy down beside her.

"I saw the trees," he continued, "and couldn't resist

exploring. I must admit I didn't expect to find a swimming pool. Not so far from the house.''

"It's secluded," she said. "And Charles prefers me…'' The sentence trailed off, and she made much of smoothing chiffon over her knees.

Guy wondered what to say next. Charles prefers her to what? he wondered. Not to be seen in a swimsuit by anyone else, probably. Or maybe Charles *preferred* her to swim nude; then the necessity for privacy would be even greater. Guy swallowed hard, vaguely shamed by his own sensual musing. Sensual and…jealous? Insanity. The muggy heat of the day must have unhinged him.

"You don't live in Wichita Falls, Mr. Hamilton?"

Strangely, her trying to carry on an exchange surprised Guy. He took a second to recover. "No, ah, no. My brother, Clark, is at Sheppard Air Force Base for a few weeks, as you know. It's the closest he's been to Phoenix, where I live, for years. I decided to make the effort to see him.''

Her blue eyes met his squarely for the first time, and his belly contracted. "Do you and the general have other family?'' she asked, and immediately shifted in her chair, presenting her profile. "That's not my business. I'm sorry.''

"A perfectly normal question." Why was she so timid? "Our parents died some years ago. There's just Clark and me. I'm the baby who wasn't anticipated,'' he said, smiling. "Clark was an only child for nineteen years. And even though I've reached the ripe old age of thirty-two, he still seems to regard me as wet behind the ears.''

"I know how that feels." She laughed, an unaffected, husky sound. "Charles is all I have. I'm thirty, but he definitely thinks I haven't grown up enough to make my own decisions." She pressed her lips together, then went on. "It's good to be cared about, though, isn't it?"

"Yes," Guy replied, cluing in to her need to feel right about her situation. "Of course it is."

She pulled a strand of hair from the corner of her mouth. "This is my favorite place—to hide." A mischievous glimmer took some of the guilelessness from her expression. "Unfortunately, they know where to find me. But if I can get a head start, it takes someone a while to reach me. I don't usually come here at night," she added.

"You like to be alone sometimes?"

Her lengthy indrawn breath was audible. "Frequently."

"Me, too." Guy looked sideways at her. She'd relaxed slightly and was staring at the sky, its velvety blackness pricked by a scattering of distant stars. The color of the dress, azure, suited her, and he began to wish that he, rather than the gentle breeze, could move the scalloped frills at her shoulders and neck.

"How long have you been married?" He could figure out the answer to that one but wanted to keep her talking.

"Eleven years."

"Were you born here, in Wichita Falls?"

One long, pink fingernail made absentminded patterns on the table. "Mmm."

"Your family moved away?" He was asking too many questions. Any minute now she'd replace the protective shield.

"I never had any brothers and sisters—as far as I know." She paused. "My daddy moved on someplace before I ever knew him. Mother worked in a restaurant when I was growing up. She didn't have to after Charles married me. With his help she went South then, just like she'd wanted for so long. Charles has always been so good. My mother had a chance to make a fresh start, and she took it."

Did that mean Charles Cornish paid her mother to get out of the area? "You keep in touch, though?"

"What?" She started and faced him. "Oh, with my mother? No, no. I think maybe she remarried and went to Mexico. I—we haven't corresponded since then."

"I see." But he didn't really.

Leah couldn't take her eyes from his—green eyes that glinted in the lights around the pool, depthless and looking at her as if no one else existed. Charles would wonder where she was. He'd need her to help with their guests. She ought to go.

"Do you work, Mrs. Cornish—Leah? May I call you Leah?"

The stirring inside her was wrong. She shouldn't be here.

"Leah?" he repeated.

"Please," she said. "Yes. Do call me Leah. I've never worked since I was a teenager. That's when I got married, Mr. Hamilton, and since then my husband and home have been my work. I'm not trained, you see. I can't do anything but what I do here except be a waitress. When Charles met me, I was a waitress, like my mother. I didn't even finish high school. I'm—" She stopped, horrified. She'd almost said she was nothing. This had been a difficult, tiring evening. Her defenses were down. She'd already said far too much—all the things Charles insisted she shouldn't discuss with anyone else. What was it about this man that made her want to tell him everything?

He rested his chin on his hands. His face was only inches away. "Everyone can do something, Leah. Particularly someone as bright and special as you."

She felt color rush to her cheeks but wouldn't drop her head. "You don't know me, Mr. Hamilton. I assure you I'm neither very bright nor special. Just lucky."

"Guy," he said. "If you're comfortable using my first name, call me Guy. And you are special. I can feel it. I would say Charles Cornish is the lucky one to have found such a charming woman to spend his life with. Now tell me, what did you *want* to do? Don't you ever dream of something else? This is all very beautiful." He made a wide gesture with one hand. "The house. The grounds. Spectacular, in fact. But you're restless here, incomplete."

"No, Mr. Hamilton—Guy. I have everything a woman could want. I don't dream of anything different, and I'm not restless." She was rushing, too emphatic. "Not restless at all," she said more slowly. "I really don't remember thinking about what I'd do when I was young. There wasn't much choice. Not everyone has a choice, and you have to accept that. What a dull place the world would be if we were all sophisticated and educated, don't you think?"

He was quiet for a long time. Even sitting, he towered over her. A very tall, slender man, with slightly curly blond hair and angular features. Handsome. Too handsome to be wasting time on a married woman.

"I think it would be a shame if you were sophisticated, Leah. You're lovely the way you are. But I don't think I believe you when you say you never dream. You may think you don't, although I doubt that, too.

But I wouldn't be surprised if you were *quite* a dreamer." He dropped one large-boned hand to the table, letting his fingertips rest a fraction of an inch from hers.

Leah twitched. A current seemed to jump from Guy Hamilton's body to her own. For a crazy instant she wanted to twine their fingers together.

"Well," she said at last, hating the slight tremor in her voice, "I guess I always thought I might be good at organizing things. But that sounds like a silly dream."

"No, it doesn't. Go on."

"I used to imagine being some sort of administrator. I'm good with figures and at planning things. Maybe— well, I have thought about it sometimes. Maybe I'd be useful organizing a charity or something—if Charles approved, of course. But even for that I'd have to get some more schooling."

"How old were you when you went to work?" Guy asked levelly.

She hesitated. "Seventeen—almost."

"I see. And now you run this very complicated household, with all these intimidating parties?"

"Yes."

"I suppose you have to plan menus and keep the household accounts—without having had any more education than you'd had by the time you were sixteen. Or does Charles do that, too?"

She must have imagined a sarcastic note in his voice. "No, I do it. I enjoy it—the planning part, I mean. And the accounts." Then she added, "I hate the parties," and without meaning to, laughed self-consciously.

Guy laughed, too, tipping his head, his white teeth glinting, a reflective glow almost turning his pale hair to strawberry blond. His brows were darker, arched; his nose was straight and his mouth wide and mobile.

Suddenly, he stopped laughing and looked at her. "I hate parties, too. My life is pretty quiet, thank God," he said fervently.

"What do you do?" she asked as she checked his left hand for a wedding band and found none. Her nostrils flared with irritation at herself. It wasn't her business. Nothing about him was her business.

Guy didn't answer immediately, and when he did, he seemed slightly awkward. "My work isn't very glamorous, I'm afraid. I'm in public service."

"Oh." Leah didn't know what that meant but couldn't bring herself to pry further. She noted the way his dinner jacket pulled across the shoulders. Probably a loaner from his brother. The cuffs and the collar of his immaculately white shirt were a little worn, too. Intuition told her he was unconscious of his dress rather than too poor to spend more on clothes. This wasn't a man who cared much about impressing people. Unlike Charles. She squashed the disloyal notion at once.

The wind picked up, whisking her skirt high off her thighs. She fought with the dress, loathing its little-girl flounces even more now than when Charles had brought it home and insisted she wear it tonight. A glance at Guy confirmed what she'd suddenly felt—he was looking appreciatively at her legs. The flash of exhilaration that seared her was out of line, but she reveled in the satisfaction it brought.

She shivered, from excitement rather than the unexpectedly chill air, and stood. "Duty calls," she said, pleased with her steady tone. "I must get back."

"I'll come with you," Guy said, immediately at her

side. "You're shivering. Here, put my jacket on. I'm always too hot, and the thing doesn't fit, anyway."

"Thank you." Without a second thought, she let him drape the jacket around her shoulders. He made no attempt to prolong the contact beyond what was absolutely necessary. "Thank you," she repeated, and looked up into those limpid green eyes—gentle but fantastically sexy.

"You're very welcome." He was slightly behind her, his head inclined. She saw the way his lips parted a fraction and felt her own do the same.

"Ah, there you are, Leah. What the hell—"

Charles Cornish, plainly out of breath, broke into the clearing and spoke to Leah, apparently before noticing Guy behind her.

She moved quickly to her husband's side. "I needed a little break, Charles, dear. You know how I get with all those people sometimes. You shouldn't have worried. I was just coming back."

"Yes," he said slowly. "So I see. I'm glad you had company for your *little break*. Mr. Hamilton, isn't it?"

Guy strode confidently in front of the man. "Guy Hamilton, sir. Clark's brother. Your wife was kind enough to allow me to share her oasis for a few minutes." He noted a fine film of sweat on the older man's skin. Pale blue eyes flicked over every inch of him, then darted to the dinner jacket around Leah's shoulders.

"Leah is a perfect hostess. She learned well," he said unctuously. "Cold, my love? Let's get you back to the house for a wrap. Here." He tossed the jacket to Guy. "Thank you for your concern."

In a gesture that was too studied not to be deliberate, he put an arm across Leah's back and under her arm, pulling her to him in such a strong, possessive move that the shaded valley at the neck of her dress deepened.

Guy met Leah's eyes and saw the distress there. Her husband was laying claim to what was his, making sure there could be no misunderstanding. The emotion that shook Guy came as an unfamiliar and totally unexpected jolt—hate. He hated Charles Cornish. For the first time in his adult life he longed to smash a fist into another human being's face.

Their progress back to the terrace was leisurely. Cornish kept his grip on Leah and talked about things of little interest to Guy. Oil, investments, tips on the market—only topics related to money and its accumulation. Guy answered as intelligently as he could and tried not to glance at the woman walking between them.

The rest of the evening passed in an uncomfortable blur. He watched Leah confer often with a white-coated waiter carrying a silver tray who threaded skillfully between groups of guests and artfully placed potted plantings on the red-brick terrace. She moved from one cluster of chairs to another, leaning to ask if her guests were comfortable but never making conversation—more like a waiter herself than the hostess. She avoided Guy. Once or twice their eyes met and held; then she lowered her lids or turned away. She must be exhausted, he thought, and afraid of what that man would say or do later. He ached for her, and the constant inner reminder that he hardly knew Leah Cornish did not help.

"General, Mrs. Hamilton?"

The sound of Leah's husky Southern voice startled him. He was sitting with Clark and Miriam, and Leah had come to stand solicitously at his brother's elbow. "Are you comfortable?" she asked, not looking at Guy. "Can I get you something? Mrs. Hamilton, would you like a wrap?"

Miriam declined, but as Leah turned away, Guy saw how the skin stretched tight around her mouth, the fatigue in every feature.

Disregarding her attempt to pull away, he clasped her wrist and brought her ear to his lips. "We probably won't meet again, little one. But I'll think of you—and your dream. If you ever decide you want to try your hand at some of that organizing you talked about, you can come and organize me. I could sure use it." He let her go, but she didn't move immediately. "Don't lose yourself completely. You *are* special," he added.

Without a word, she straightened and walked away.

CHAPTER TWO

THE CLOCK on Leah's bedside table read six o'clock when she awoke. She rolled to squint through open drapes at a silvery sky streaked with early-morning wisps of lemon and pink. It would be another beautiful May Saturday—too hot for comfort by noon but cool enough now, and cooler again once the sun went down.

Briskly, she climbed from bed and selected aqua shorts and a matching sleeveless polo shirt from her closet. Barefoot, she entered her plant-strewn bathroom with its glass bubble dome open to the sky.

Often, she luxuriated in the circular sunken tub and stared up at the shifting clouds by day or the stars at night. A quick shower would fill her needs now. She intended to spend time in the greenhouse among her orchids before lunching with Charles. Dear Charles. He'd given her all this, and she'd always be grateful.

Deliberately, she chose to keep the shower water invigoratingly tepid. It beat on her upturned face, her shoulders and breasts, making her skin tingle. She soaped vigorously and rinsed, then washed her hair quickly. Only when she twisted off the faucets did she linger. Again, as it had every day for weeks, sometimes many times a day, Guy Hamilton's face came to her mind—and his odd little invitation the night they had met: "...you can come and organize me..."

He'd been joking, and she was a fool. An ungrateful,

dreamy fool, old enough to know better. He'd said she was a dreamer. Damn. Sex, or the lack of it, shouldn't be enough to turn a sensible woman into a preoccupied romantic.

But it wasn't a desire for sex that made her long to see those green eyes. Oh, yes, the thought of that tall, hard body wrapped around hers in the great lonely bed no man entered anymore was appealing. But more than that, Leah yearned to have Guy look at her again, ask questions, listen—just talk to her again. For a while, by the pool, in the soft blue light that paled into a dark sky, she'd felt as if their minds touched. *Forget it*, she ordered herself fiercely.

When she flapped downstairs in her thongs, Leah heard the familiar sounds of Jewel clanging about in the kitchen. The smell of freshly brewed coffee and home-baked cinnamon rolls wafted along the hall.

Leah batted open the swinging kitchen doors. "Morning, Jewel," she said brightly, and went to bend over the dark-haired cook, who worked at the sink. Sun from the high windows shot blue highlights into her long braids.

"Good morning, Mrs. Cornish."

Leah made a face behind the woman's back. The banging pots should have alerted her. Jewel was in a formal mood today. Probably had a fight with her hot-tempered husband, Sam. Leah only became "Mrs. Cornish" to Jewel when the cook was in a sour mood.

Surrounded by brilliant blue-and-green mosaic tiles and light oak cabinets, Leah felt the usual warm glow that inevitably came in this, her favorite room in the house. With satisfaction, she surveyed her hanging plants and the little troughs of cacti along the windowsill. Her green thumb was legendary among the staff. Even Charles seemed to take pride in her ability to grow just about anything.

She returned her attention to Jewel. "The cinnamon rolls smell fantastic, as usual," she tried.

A "Hmmph" was her reward.

"Coffee, too. Join me for a cup?"

Unable to ignore her mistress after a direct question, Jewel withdrew her plump arms from mountains of suds and wiped them on a towel. "I guess," she said flatly. "But I'd better lay off the rolls."

Leah lifted one eyebrow as she filled two brown pottery mugs to their brims with coffee. "On a diet? Not you, Jewel. I didn't think you believed in skinny women." Her own lack of what Jewel termed "extra meat" was a constant battle between them. Even more so in the past few weeks, when Leah had become thinner.

Jewel was Indian, short, well-built, with classic features. Now her high cheekbones flamed. "That Sam. One of these days I'm going to turn *him* in on a new model."

"Meaning?" Leah swallowed a laugh.

"He told me I was dumpy. *Dumpy.* Said I was too young for middle-aged spread but I'd already spread too far to go back. He said if I didn't watch it, he'd find himself some slim young thing instead."

"And?" She was going to laugh. "And what did you say to him, Jewel? *Before* he told you off?"

Jewel dropped into a bentwood chair. "Nothing."

"Jewel—"

"Well, I told him the beer was giving him a belly and no woman finds it sexy to go to bed with a man whose belly hangs over his belt."

Leah sat down with a thump in a peacock-backed

rattan chair and drew up her knees. "You're something," she said through tears of laughter. "You tell that tall, handsome husband of yours he's not attractive, then get mad when he strikes back."

"It's not funny," the cook said icily.

"It certainly is. He wouldn't change you for the world. You go home tonight with a flower behind your ear and a smile on your face and tell him how much he turns you on. And that's an order."

"Miss Leah! I'm old enough to be your mother, and we shouldn't be talking about these things."

Leah got up and threw her arms around the woman's neck, wishing for an instant that this warm soul were her mother. "I always come to you, Jewel, and you give me advice. Why can't I give you some? Particularly when I'm right?" She held up a palm to stop the woman's retort. "I am right, aren't I?"

"I guess so," Jewel said reluctantly. "As usual. But just let that—"

The sound of the doorbell cut off the rest of the sentence. A wire tapped into a box in the kitchen carried the muted ring.

Leah glanced at the clock beside the window. Seven-fifteen. "Who would come to the front door at this hour, Jewel? Are you expecting a delivery?"

"No, miss. And it would be to the back door, anyway. You stay here and I'll get it."

"*You* stay here. It's probably someone with car trouble or something," she finished lamely.

As Leah crossed the wide hall, she glanced upstairs. Charles would still be asleep in the room across the corridor from her own. He always slept late after a night on the town, and there had been more and more of those in the last two years, since he'd been unable—

She shunned finishing the thought and reached the
door. At least she knew her rivals were cards and
booze, not other women, she acknowledged wryly.

She peered through the small peephole and saw two
men in uniform—blue-gray with a stripe down each
well-creased pant leg. Gold badges glinted. Police.

Carefully, she unbolted the door, leaving the chain
in place, and pulled it open a crack. "What do you
want?" she asked, an odd knot in her stomach. Could
it be something to do with her mother?

"Mrs. Cornish?" one man asked politely. She nodded, and he flashed an identification badge at her. "Officers Landon and Garth. State patrol. May we have a
few words with you?"

Leah studied the card until the words ran together.

"Miss Leah, what is it?" Jewel came beside her,
peered out at the two men, then slid off the chain and
opened the door wide. "Is there trouble?" she said,
putting an arm around a trembling Leah. When there
was no reply, she stepped back, waving the officers
inside.

"I'm Officer Garth," the taller man said, taking off
his hat. "Is there someplace private we could talk to
Mrs. Cornish? A place where she could sit down?"

Jewel nodded toward the stairs. "Miss Leah, maybe
I should get—"

"No!" Leah said, suddenly very alert. "Follow me,
please. We'll talk in the kitchen, if you don't mind.
There's less chance of being interrupted out there."
She was already wondering where the police car was
parked and if Charles would see it from his window.
He hated scenes. "Jewel, will you come with me?"

She half expected the policemen to protest about an
audience, but they followed Jewel without a word.

Once in the kitchen, the other officer took charge. "Landon, ma'am." He smoothed thinning red hair with a flattened palm. "When was the last time you spoke with your husband?"

"Spoke with Charles?" Leah said, puzzled. "I—I'm not sure. What are you saying? Please don't drag this out. Just get to the point."

"I will." He remained polite. "But would you sit down, please."

"I'd rather stand."

Landon opened his mouth, but Officer Garth silenced him with a shake of the head. "Very well, Mrs. Cornish," Landon continued. "Do you know where your husband was last night?"

Leah gaped at Jewel, who turned pale under her bronze skin. "Well—I. He was out. But that's not unusual. I can't tell you his exact location. I'm sure he'll be glad to give you that." What had happened? Had Charles gotten drunk again and into some sort of trouble this time? Maybe he'd quibbled with the wrong person over one of his gambling things. Leah knew nothing about gambling.

The policemen were staring at each other, clearly nonplussed. Landon cleared his throat. "I take it you aren't in the habit of waiting up for your husband.

Immediately, Leah felt defensive. *Until four or five or eight in the morning?* she wanted to retort. Loyalty made her study her painted toenails and mumble, "No."

"Does he sometimes not arrive home until after— say, after this time?" Landon checked his watch. "It's almost seven-thirty, ma'am."

"That's not unusual," Leah managed.

Jewel rubbed her back. "Shouldn't I get Mr. Cornish?"

"Mrs. Cornish," Officer Landon interrupted. "I wish I could soften this for you, but I can't. Your husband's car went off the road just outside town sometime last night or early this morning. He drove straight into a river. His body was found around five, facedown in two feet of water. There'll have to be an autopsy, of course, and I shouldn't say this, but I think you deserve to know. There was an open whiskey bottle in the car. It looks pretty obvious he was too drunk to walk to shore and couldn't get up once he fell over. From on-the-spot observation I'd say he probably hit his head trying and that's what killed him."

Leah slid slowly into a chair. "Charles is upstairs—in bed."

She heard Jewel crying, saw the blur of pale blue, the flash of gold and faces bobbing around her. Then, shaking free of hands that tried to restrain her, she leaped from the chair and dashed through the house, up the stairs, along the corridor, and burst into Charles's room. He must be there. He was always there. Charles had been there for her since she was a lost kid, living from hand to mouth with a mother who brought home and slept with every man who had a few dollars in his jeans.

"Charles," she shouted, and ran to his smoothly made bed. "Charles, where are you?" Leah sank to her knees and buried her face in the nubby weave of the spread. "Where are you, damn it?" He'd promised to guard her forever, to keep the past away.

When the sobbing started, she screwed her eyes shut and crawled into a tight ball on the bed. She never remembered how long it took for the blackness to come.

STUCCO WALLS GLISTENED warmly in the midday sun. Leah parked in the driveway and walked around to let herself into the house through the kitchen. There was already a lockbox on the front door.

Several inches of cold coffee still stood in the pot. She poured it into a mug and set it in the microwave to heat. Was it really a month since Charles died? She looked around the kitchen, and her eyes filled with tears. How different this day was from the one she'd begun right here, with Jewel, a few weeks ago.

Jewel was gone. So were the cascading plants—and the glow of life in a prosperous home. Jewel had easily found work in another house on the far side of Wichita Falls. Martin, the butler, too. The plants had died. After her final interview with Charles's lawyers this morning, Leah felt Jewel and Martin were the only ones around here who weren't beyond hope on this baking June day.

In the rosewood-paneled chambers of Lapwood and Enders, her sentence had been delivered by a man who had once played golf with Charles. Her lips had quivered slightly as Max Enders explained her reduced circumstances. He finished, in a voice that broke with mock emotion, by saying how very sorry he was.

The buzzer on the microwave sounded, and Leah straightened. Damn it. She wouldn't give up. So Charles had steadily squandered a huge fortune. So she couldn't even expect more than a very meager inheritance after the sale of the house. So what if Charles had already used his life insurance as collateral against loans. She was Leah Bennett Cornish, survivor. And she *would* survive.

With coffee in hand, she marched into the living room and shoved aside a white sheet to make a space to set down the mug on a shiny black table.

The wall hangings and the paintings were gone. She'd never liked them, anyway. What was left of the furniture had been shrouded. Still. All still. The faint musty odor of disuse sickened her.

Dust motes danced in a shaft of light from the French windows. Leah walked to peer outside. The white iron furniture was stacked around pots of drooping plants. She could have watered those.

For an instant she thought she heard laughter. Closing her eyes, she imagined the groups of animated guests—Martin, in his white jacket, balancing a silver tray, and Charles, immaculately impressive, holding court.

He'd been a good man—most of the time. A laugh bubbled up in her throat. For years he'd been this town's leading light. Most of the fine people of Wichita Falls never knew until after his death that he'd become one of the wildest drinkers and gamblers this side of the county line. They would never know he'd also been impotent for the last two years of his life. Leah would preserve that final dignity for the man who had never once brought up her own shaky beginnings.

Although possessive—sometimes suspicious and jealous—he had loved her. And she would always believe it had been his impotence that finally broke him.

She'd spent her last night in this house. Her own pile of bags and boxes stood in the hall. When she'd finished the coffee, she would pack her possessions into the Porsche, which must be traded for something cheaper, and head for the room she'd rented downtown.

Tomorrow she'd start looking for work. And there

would be no point expecting help from any of the many people who had enjoyed her own and her husband's hospitality or Charles's business influence. They'd disappeared with the discovery that Charles had been on the verge of bankruptcy when he died. A penniless widow was of no interest. She wouldn't even look good on some magnanimous soul's charity record. Leah laughed mirthlessly.

She fumbled in her purse for the keys to her car, and her fingers closed on a stiff envelope. Her scalp prickled as she withdrew the note. "Leah Cornish." Without looking, she visualized the simple script on the envelope—her name and address. She knew by heart the words on the card inside: "I'm so sorry, Leah. I hardly know what else to write. All the stuff in the newspapers shocked and hurt me—for you. But don't let it take everything away from what your husband was. We can all slide off the tracks—too easily. In time he'd have found his way back. If I can help in any way, let me know. Guy Hamilton."

Leah slid out the card and sank slowly onto a covered couch to read it for the hundredth time. A cloud of dust rose around her, tickling her nose. Guy Hamilton, a man who, unlike many, owed Charles nothing, gave him the kindest eulogy. He would help her, too. She was sure of it without knowing why. If only he weren't in another state. He wouldn't pass her by on the street as if she were a stranger, as others had in the past few weeks. And these were the people she'd have to go to for a job.

There were no friends for her in this town, no prospects, nothing. And nothing was what she could easily end up with—again. When Charles died, Leah had also lost the respect his wealth and power had bought. Very few of their acquaintances were unaware of her rocky beginnings. The whispering had already begun. Men looked at her speculatively, women with suspicious contempt. They saw her as an opportunist who married a man many years her senior for his money alone. Now they expected her to hunt for a replacement. A pool of nausea formed in her stomach. Despite his weaknesses, Charles *had* been a good and special man. His memory shouldn't be distorted.

A light crack sounded against the window, and she glanced up, only to see a single locust hover at a pane. Its fat tan body and transparent wings trembled as the creature recovered from the blow; then it flew away.

Leah sighed and stuffed Guy's card back in her bag. She was trembling, too, deep inside and trying to recover. It might be more difficult for her than for the locust.

The bags and boxes filled the trunk and back seat of the Porsche. Leah was sweating, her palms raw, by the time she'd finished hauling everything through the back door and out to the driveway. Eleven years of being Mrs. Charles Cornish, waited on in everything, had made her soft. Those days were over, and she'd have to toughen up once more.

When the last piece of luggage had been stowed, she carefully locked the kitchen and replaced the key under the mat, smiling at how some things never changed. Jewel, Martin, herself—and how many others knew that key was always there?

She hesitated beside her car and shaded her eyes to gaze across an open expanse of flat, sandy ground to the west, where a sullen band of yellow haze hovered above the land. Since her marriage, this had been the view from her bedroom window, and she'd miss its comforting familiarity. Her two-room apartment would overlook a supermarket from the front and a brick wall from the back. She took a last look at the house, feeling for the first time totally separated from its security.

A rhythmic clacking in the scrubby grass nearby sent her scurrying inside the car. A rattlesnake had come out to bask in the pitiless sun its kind loved so much.

She started the powerful engine and swung onto the highway, but only went a few hundred yards before stopping again. "If you ever decide you want to try your hand at some of that organizing..." Had he meant it? Did she dare call his bluff and find out?

Her chest expanded slowly, then she allowed air to hiss through her pursed lips. An almost-breathless sense of daring filled her. She was about to do something she'd never done before, to take an enormous risk on the basis of her own intuition. Too bad the deposit she'd paid on the apartment would be forfeited. She couldn't afford to waste money, but she didn't want to stay in Wichita Falls anymore.

After a swift U-turn, she headed west. Phoenix was almost due west; she knew that much. Organizing was exactly what she felt like. That and some new faces—and a familiar one.

Get there. Check into a motel and call Guy. He'd help her find a job and get started. He'd talked about being in public service—whatever that meant. Maybe there was something in his operation for her. Regardless, she felt deep inside that he wouldn't turn her away flat.

The little car ate miles. Charles had always made sure it was kept in perfect condition, and this was its first really long run. She loved the vehicle. Wistfully, she remembered how Charles had given it to her, making an issue of its being totally hers, her possession, her toy.

Leah drove straight through the rest of the day and into the night, stopping occasionally for large cups of black coffee. Once she pulled into a rest area and dozed for an hour before setting off again.

Sunday's first hour had slid past as she punished the now filthy white Porsche across the state line from New Mexico into Arizona and zeroed in on her destination.

She reached Phoenix at 7:00 A.M.—too early to call anyone, least of all a man who wasn't expecting her.

Too tired and too dirty to search for more than a clean and adequate motel, Leah settled for the Salt River Stopover. She showered, set her travel alarm for ten and crawled gratefully into bed. The chances of catching Guy at home on Sunday should be good. His telephone number had been scribbled on the top of his card. As if he really had hoped she'd contact him, she thought comfortably, when she began to drift.

THE PHONE RANG twelve times. Leah hung up and paced the shabby little room. She'd tried Guy's number twice without success, but it was only eleven-ten. This time she'd force herself to wait longer.

A few minutes after twelve, she dialed again. One, two, three… He wasn't going to be there. For the first time since she left Texas, she felt vague panic. What on earth had made her drive all those miles on nothing more concrete than a chance invitation—probably meant as a joke—and a sympathy card?

''Hello.''

At the sound of his voice, she almost dropped the phone. Her mouth dried out completely.

''Hello,'' he repeated in the same low, soft tone.

Leah cleared her throat. "Guy?" she said in a whisper. "It's me." Immediately, she flushed. She was acting like a silly kid. How was he supposed to know who "me" was?

"Leah?" There was a pause, and she heard him expel a breath. "Leah Cornish, is that you?"

Her heart made a slow roll. He'd remembered her voice. "Yes, Guy," she said breathlessly. "Leah. I'm here in Phoenix. I drove all night. Remember how you said I could come and help you if I wanted to— Well, I need a job, and I know you probably don't have one for me, but I thought maybe—"

"Whoa." He stopped her headlong rush of words. "Back up and start again. No, on second thought, don't. I heard you. Give me time to absorb it all."

Leah felt sick. Sick enough to throw up. He wasn't just surprised to hear her; he was shocked. This was a terrible mistake.

"I shouldn't have done this," she started.

"No—yes," he cut in. "Of course you should. Where are you? I'll come and get you."

"It was a silly thing to do. I just didn't know what I was going to— There wasn't anyone—" Her voice cracked. She mustn't start crying, but she was so tired and alone. "Forget I contacted you, please, Guy. It was good to hear you again. Good—"

"*Don't* hang up," he ordered, suddenly commanding, as if he felt her confusion. "Give me your address and I'll be right over."

Quietly, Leah told him where she was staying and listened while he calculated that it would take him about twenty minutes to get there.

They both hung up, and for several seconds she sat numb, watching the wall. What would he think of her?

What would any man think of a woman who came so obviously chasing after him? How could he possibly understand that she simply needed someone, anyone, who would offer a hand in friendship?

Twenty minutes! In a sudden wild frenzy, Leah went into action. She dragged out a gauzy cotton sundress that didn't show packing wrinkles and slipped it on. The light peach color accentuated her deep tan and the smoothness of her skin. She found matching flat sandals and then turned her attention to a face that showed definite signs of exhaustion.

Makeup helped disguise dark areas of fatigue beneath her eyes. Brighter than usual lip gloss drew attention to her mouth—and, she hoped, away from lines of tiredness. She was brushing her hair, glad of its shimmering quality, when a knock came at the door.

Her heart stopped, and to play for a few more seconds, she rummaged for perfume and sprayed her wrists and throat.

There was another knock, a little louder this time.

With her pulse thundering in her ears, Leah approached the door. "Guy?" she asked, already knowing the answer.

"The same," he replied, and she heard that wonderful hint of laughter in his voice.

She flung open the door and stepped back to let him in.

He came hesitantly, his green eyes, flecked in the daylight with brown, searching her face. "How are you, Leah?" Long, tanned fingers touched her jaw fleetingly.

All she could do was stare.

Guy Hamilton wore black—short-sleeved black shirt and black pants. And at his neck was a stiff white clerical collar.

CHAPTER THREE

HE CLOSED THE DOOR behind him and grasped her shoulders tightly. "Oh, Leah," he said quietly. "This must all have been such a nightmare for you. Let's sit down."

She couldn't move. A priest. Guy Hamilton, the man she now silently admitted to fantasizing about all these weeks, was a priest. A swell of bemused shame mushroomed in her.

"What is it?" he said when she failed to answer. He held her chin between finger and thumb to stop her from turning away.

"Nothing," she lied, avoiding his eyes. "Nothing." Inside she was slowly crumbling.

"I don't believe you. You're tired—exhausted, obviously. And you've been through too much. But there's something else, isn't there? Something I don't know. Are you ill?"

She looked at him squarely, pressing her lips together, and let her gaze travel over his garb. "I'm not ill. I'm fine. What do I call you? Father Hamilton or just plain Father? I guess I should have given more thought to what 'public service' meant."

Guy's brows came together fractionally; then his expression cleared, and he began to laugh. He draped an arm around her shoulders and walked her to the room's only chair before perching himself on the side of the rumpled bed.

As he continued to watch her and laugh, Leah felt a spark of irritation pierce her tired confusion.

"Feel like sharing the joke?" she said at last, running out of patience.

He sobered with visible effort. "It's you." He chuckled, then ran a forefinger around the collar. "And this. You saw the collar, and it immediately spelled priest—Catholic priest. Right?"

"Right," she agreed.

"Well, I'm not."

She stared at him disbelievingly. "You mean you're masquerading as a priest? That's awful."

He threw himself flat on the bed and roared. "No, you naive woman. I'm not masquerading as anything. You happened to catch me in my Sunday best. I'm a minister. Just not Catholic. Is *that* okay? And would it matter to you if I was, anyway?"

With the last question he turned serious eyes on her and waited. Leah felt a dull flush creep up her neck to her cheeks. She could pretend all she liked, but they'd both felt a spark of something more than platonic interest pass between them. In Texas and today.

She sighed deeply. "Of course it's okay. And it shouldn't matter if you were, I suppose. It's just that they seem to have an aura that says, 'Stay away,' and I suddenly felt foolish, as though I'd been too familiar." An insistent pain had begun to nag at both temples. She'd taken about as many shocks as she could handle.

"So. Now that that's out of the way, we can be friends again?" he asked with disarming frankness.

"Friends," Leah said, and immediately wondered

why he should want an albatross like her for a friend. He ought to wish her as far away from him as possible.

He sat up and eyed her critically. "You're beat, friend."

"It shows, huh?" She massaged her temples. "I should never have come bolting in on you like this, Guy. It was just a crazy, spur-of-the-moment urge. I'll have to stick around a day or two to get my wind back. Then I guess I'll head for—" She stopped and frowned.

"You were going to say home?" Guy suggested. "Only you aren't sure where that is anymore, are you?"

The truth hurt. "Texas is home—Wichita Falls. Where else?" Tears stung her eyes, and she tipped her head to stop them from falling.

"No," Guy said softly. "For people like you and me, people with no close family, home is wherever you can make it feel right. Preferably a place where there's a friend or two, or even just a reason to be there—because you're needed, maybe."

She was going to cry, damn it. "And people need you here, Guy. That's why it's your place." She sniffed. Even blinking rapidly wasn't helping.

"And I need you." He was on his knees, pressing her head into his hard shoulder. "Once I said I needed organizing, and boy is it true. You wouldn't believe what a mess I can make of a ledger in no time flat. No one I hire to help stays more than a day or two. They throw up their hands and march off, wild-eyed and muttering. Maybe you're the one who can do the job. Think so?" Leaning away, he glanced at her tear-drenched cheeks before holding her face against his neck. "Cry as much as you need to. Then we'll start sorting things out."

Reluctantly, willing her senses not to riot at the feel, the clean smell of him, Leah eased from his embrace and found a tissue in her bag. "You're just being kind. It's all you know how to be."

"No way." He held up one hand. "Scout's honor, lady. If you hadn't showed up, I'd have had to put an ad in the local paper for a clerical assistant who doubles as a part-time housekeeper and sifted through another raft of applicants. And it would probably be hopeless in the end, just like it always is. Keeping me straight is more than anyone's managed so far."

She tried to smile, then winced. "I've got to get some aspirin." Another search in her voluminous shoulder bag produced a small tin. Guy had brought a glass of water from the bathroom before she'd finished wrestling open the container of pills.

"Just the thought of working for me gives you a headache," he said, smiling ruefully. "I don't blame you. But remember, you'll be free to quit, just like the rest, if I drive you mad."

A tiny shaft of hope began to live in Leah. "You really think I'd be able to help? I can't even type. And I already told you how little schooling I've had."

"You can hunt and peck at the typewriter—you'll soon learn. And if you could run that enormous house and give intimidating parties like—" He stopped. "I'm sorry," he said solicitously. "Bad choice of subjects."

"It's all right. I've got to get used to talking about all that. Just not yet, I guess."

"You need to rest." Suddenly, he was all business. "But not here. We have to find you a place to live—somewhere convenient to the church—and after you've

had a long sleep, I'll help you get settled in. My people
are nice—good people, you'll see. They'll help you as
best they can. They may even help more than you want
sometimes."

He half turned away but faced her again, abruptly.
"I know exactly where you can live. Wally Timmons
has an upstairs apartment in his house. Converted it
after his wife died. He rents it out, and it's empty right
now. Wally's retired, but he does odd jobs for me.
Great old guy. Needs a bit of company more than the
money—just to feel someone else is coming and going.
That'd be perfect, if you like the place." His expression became dubious. "It's not what you're used to,
though. Very small and a bit spartan."

Leah got up on wobbly legs. "I like small," she
insisted. "And I love spartan. Does it have a bed?"

Guy nodded, smiling faintly, and eased her back into
the chair. "We'll go right over. I don't need to call;
he's always around somewhere. If it's okay, even for
a while, you can do what you've got in mind. Sleep
the clock around."

Through drooping eyelids, she watched his tall frame
bend to heft her suitcase onto the bed. He opened it,
toured the room to gather her possessions and tucked
them inside. He glanced around. "Did I get everything?" When she nodded, he closed the case and offered her his hand.

Outside, he settled her in the passenger seat of the
Porsche. His own vehicle was a battered jeep parked
in front of the office. He would come back for it, he
insisted. He also insisted on settling her bill so she
wouldn't have to move again, assuring her, when she
argued, that she could repay him later.

Leah took little notice of the sprawling modern city

they crossed or the mountain Guy pointed out in the distance as Camelback, because it resembled a reclining, blue-gray camel against the cloudless sky. The land was flat, seeming more so as they entered another suburb. Beyond houses that snaked along the road lay sandy plains dotted with pinkish rock outcroppings and plants she couldn't quite make out. Mostly cacti, Guy informed her—interesting but not as spectacular now as they would be when the desert bloomed in early spring.

Bougainvillea, iridescent purple and white, spilled over a nearby wall. Leah sat straighter. Perhaps there'd be a chance to raise unusual plants again. On a corner stood a giant saguaro, its fat arms raised like upturned hooks on a coat stand. She liked Arizona, Leah decided, then slumped back in her seat. What difference did it make whether or not she liked it? She probably wouldn't stay long.

Wally Timmons was at home and delighted at the prospect of a new tenant. A thin, grizzled old man, Wally accepted without comment Guy's explanation that Leah was a good friend, soon to be his own new assistant.

The tiny apartment could be entered via a winding metal staircase at the side of the house and consisted of one large room with a couch that made into a bed, a kitchenette behind folding doors and a turquoise-and-lavender tiled bathroom. Leah instantly loved almost every cramped corner on sight, particularly the jutting bay window and sharply apexed ceiling. She tried not to look too hard at the garish bathroom tile.

They agreed on a rent that seemed ridiculously low to Leah, but at Guy's warning shake of the head, she stopped arguing with Wally. She and Guy hadn't discussed salary yet, but it wasn't likely to be much. She could turn out to be worth nothing as far as either of them knew; then she'd have to find other work. There were restaurants in every town, and she knew she could manage in one of those. Meanwhile, her skimpy funds might have to stretch a long way. In the next few days she'd contact Max Enders with her new address. He'd promised at least a small sum when all Charles's debts were settled. As soon as possible, she must trade the Porsche.

When Wally Timmons had left them alone, Guy carried up all Leah's luggage and stacked it tidily inside the door. He opened the couch, found linen in a closet and started making up the bed.

"I can do that," Leah protested.

Guy waved a dismissive hand. "No, you can't. Sit down. I'll get my pound of flesh out of you later."

"I feel like an absolute pest," Leah said, and yawned. "Absolute pest."

"Right," Guy said in a soothing voice. "A sleepy absolute pest." He finished and checked the air-conditioning thermostat. Apparently satisfied, he pulled out the suitcase she'd taken into the motel. "Can you manage if I open this and leave you?"

A little snuffle made him glance around. She was asleep and gradually sliding sideways in an upright chair. He crossed swiftly to gather her in his arms and deposit her on the sofa bed. The sundress was light enough; it wouldn't hurt if she slept in it. He slipped off her sandals and lifted her head a few inches to settle it more comfortably on the pillow. She sighed but didn't stir.

Guy sat beside her and smoothed damp tendrils of dark hair away from her face. Immediately, he remembered how the breeze had fanned it as he'd watched her beside the pool in Wichita Falls. Since that night, he'd visualized her again and again and made love to her in his mind— He covered his face. Not now. There would probably never be a right time for that. She was a grieving widow who'd come to him for solace, nothing more. Leah had no family, no friends; she'd made that clear. It was up to him to be both if he could.

She moved, rolling over on one side, and pulled up her knees. Guy smiled. She probably always slept like that. His smile slowly faded. Behind her knees, smoothly tanned skin curved over firm muscle. There was something so fascinating about that little area at the back of a beautiful woman's thigh. His gut tightened painfully. If she slept in his arms, she would curl against him that way, their bodies molded together, his hand over her breast.

With more force than he intended, he stood and moved away. This was don't-touch time. It would probably always be that. In her grief and loneliness it was possible she might come to him for physical comfort, but that would be wrong—and out of the question, anyway. It was his responsibility to make sure nothing happened between them.

He studied her carefully. She'd lost weight. She'd been through some tough times. There was an almost-childlike quality to her form, a defenselessness, that made him want to take care of her. But that wasn't what she was going to need. After too many years of suffocating care, Leah Cornish needed to become self-sufficient. If he could help her do that, he'd have been successful. Maybe then there would be a time to think about a different relationship.

Careful not to let the door slam, Guy let himself out.

As usual, it was hot as hell in this almost-seasonless city he'd made his home. He liked it. Fortunately, Leah must like the heat, too—another plus. He grinned in self-derision. Regardless of his fine principles, he wasn't going to find it easy to keep his distance from her.

TWO WEEKS. Leah pushed the creaky old chair away from her desk and surveyed her new domain. She'd already been installed as the new clerical assistant at St. Mark's for two weeks. Unbelievable. And everyone had been so friendly and helpful, just as Guy had predicted.

She stood and stretched. Since eight that morning she'd only left the desk to go to the bathroom. It was four in the afternoon, and she hadn't even had lunch.

Leah didn't care whether or not she'd eaten. A satisfied glow swept over her. In two weeks she'd managed to transform this bulging little room from total confusion into some sort of ordered chaos. Another week or so and it would be totally habitable. Peeling green paint and rickety blinds would have to go eventually. But that would take longer.

Fortunately, Guy worked in a small wing on the far side of the sprawling rambler, and apart from willingly answering her many questions, left her alone to cope. He also lived and slept there, keeping three central rooms free, one for counseling church members and two always ready for anyone who needed a temporary place to stay. Like Leah's office, a big kitchen faced the front of the house.

On her first day at work, Leah had wondered briefly why Guy hadn't immediately suggested she use one of the guest rooms as an interim haven. She blushed at the thought now and pressed her palms to her cheeks. The answer to that question should have been obvious to her. He was unfailingly kind and helpful, clearly grateful for her efforts, no matter how inept, but he kept their contacts to a minimum. The last thing his image needed was a single woman installed in his home.

Guy was determined to maintain a professional basis for their relationship. He had even seemed awkward on the several occasions when she'd noticed how long he'd been shut away working and taken him coffee and a sandwich. When they were in the same room, the air between them was instantly electric.

Absently, Leah started pulling books from a shelf and piling them on the floor. She'd dust each one and replace them in alphabetical order according to author. Every volume was huge and filled with intimidating subject matter. Had Guy read all these? she wondered. He was so intelligent, constantly writing and reading between dealing with the hundreds of small and large problems his parishioners heaped upon him. And he seemed to love his job, to thrive on pressure without sign of strain. He had a kind word and a gentle squeeze of the shoulder for everyone who came to the house.

Was she one more of his good works? Leah supposed so and squelched a spear of disappointment. The important thing was to become useful here and make a place for herself.

The books could wait. With a weary moan, she slumped back into her chair and pulled the dreaded ledger toward her. It was every bit as confusing as Guy had promised. All the small congregation's finances for the year were contained in this miserable black tome filled with chicken-scratch numbers.

She opened the ledger to the last page she'd worked on at the same time as she heard the familiar sound of the jeep's powerful engine roar to a stop outside. It was Guy, back from visiting a hospitalized church member. After a second, she buried her head in her work—at least the calculator he had produced was a help, and so was the natural flair she had for figures. That still surprised her.

"Hi, there."

Leah glanced up to see Guy's head protruding around the door. She smiled a little wanly. "Hi. How was Mrs. Krause?"

"Better." He gave a satisfied nod. "She's recovering nicely from her surgery, and I think a few days in the hospital will do her a world of good, anyway."

"What do you mean?" Leah rested her chin on the heel of a hand.

Guy chuckled. "If you had six children and a husband who rarely worked, you'd be ready for a rest, too. Anywhere, including a hospital after having a hysterectomy."

Leah smiled and swallowed hard at the same time. "I guess you're right." He cared so much about people and had so much empathy.

Earlier she'd seen him working in the garden, surrounded by several small, laughing children from the church nursery. He'd stopped to give each one a piggyback ride, and the sight had warmed her heart. He ought to have a family of his own, and she wondered, yet again, why he didn't.

He was watching her closely. "Are you overdoing it here?" he asked. "You've done wonders, but I don't want *you* laid up with exhaustion." He checked his watch. "You were here early, and it's after four-thirty. Why don't you knock it off for the day and go home?"

To what, she thought, *four walls and a few plants?* "I will when I get a bit farther along with this ledger," she said, hoping her tone didn't betray the emptiness she felt.

"Ah, the beast." Guy came all the way into the room and picked up the ledger. He sat on the edge of the desk and leafed through pages. His strong, tanned throat above an open-necked blue shirt intrigued her. So did his muscular thigh, encased in worn denim, and the long, sensitive fingers. He turned another page and kept reading. The sun was lower now, sending a shaft through the window to turn his hair to molten honey and shade a high cheekbone and the slight cleft in his chin. Guy Hamilton was the most attractive man she'd ever met, and the nicest.

"You're something," he said finally, laying the book back in front of her. "Methodical. It's even start ing to make sense to me, and I detest figures. Can I answer any questions for you?"

"No," she said regretfully, wishing she could think of some excuse to keep him with her a while longer.

He stood. "Then I'd better get to my own work. I'm trying to think of something inspiring to say on Sunday. Unfortunately, there are days when I don't feel very inspired."

His dear, wry grimace remained imprinted on her mind long after he'd left the room. An inner glow emanated from Guy. The result of his faith, she supposed.

Leah braced her chin on one fist. She remembered how, as a child, she'd seen other families going to church on Sundays. *Normal* families, she had tagged them. Often she'd wished she were trotting along as part of a normal family, laughing, secure. Leafing through a battered old bible beneath the covers of her bed had been the closest she got to church. The flyleaf of the tattered volume bore the inscription "For Jack, with love from Grandma." Leah had never dared ask her mother who Jack was, but she liked to believe he was her father. She'd never know now. Shaking her head, she picked up a pen.

The next time Leah looked at her watch, she was shocked. She was also elated. It was ten o'clock and dark outside, but she'd done it—actually done it. Up to this very day the ledger was in order, and it balanced. Her methods were homegrown, and without the calculator she would undoubtedly have taken twice as long, but the wretched black book was in order. She must show Guy.

Without thinking, she snatched up her treasure and ran along the hall. When she turned the corner, a sliver of light showed under his study door.

"Guy!" She knocked and rushed into the cluttered room without waiting for an answer. "Guy, I made the thing balance. I did it—" She halted halfway to his desk, feeling goose bumps dart over her skin. "I'm sorry," she stammered. "I shouldn't interrupt that way."

Guy didn't answer. He was leaning back in the chair, his bare feet crossed on a desk littered with mountains of papers. He wore only a pair of frayed cutoffs and balanced a brandy glass on his flat stomach. But it was the haunted expression in his eyes, and his hair, pushed into a tousled mess, that had made Leah recoil.

"I'm sorry," she repeated falteringly. "I seem to have a habit of barging in when you don't expect or

want me. This—'' She waved the book. ''I was so
excited. It made me feel like I was worth something.''

''Leah,'' he mumbled, moving slowly, swinging his
feet to the floor. He slid the glass among the papers
and stood. ''Got to do something about the air conditioning in this house. It's too hot in here.''

Leah watched, biting her lip and clutching the ledger
to her chest. Guy seemed distant and deeply troubled.
He fumbled for a shirt and shrugged it on. His fingers
hovered over the buttons as if he couldn't decide how
or whether to fasten them. She fought an urge to help
him, touch him, smooth the frown line between his
arched brows. She did nothing. Guy hadn't looked at
her since she first entered the room.

''I'll show you this tomorrow,'' she said quietly, and
took a backward step toward the door.

''No! No.'' Guy faced her, every feature sharply
drawn. ''I was surprised to see you, that's all. I thought
you'd gone home hours ago.'' His voice cracked, and
he dropped his head to rake at his hair again.

Something was wrong. ''Guy...''

He lowered his hand and knocked a stack of note-
books to the floor. ''Hell.'' His gesture was wide, helpless. ''I'm so damn disorganized and clumsy.''

Immediately, Leah knelt to gather the books together
with one hand. The lump in her throat grew larger with
each second. She wanted to share whatever was upsetting him, but how could she when she dare not ask?
He probably wouldn't dream of discussing anything
personal with her.

''Stop, please. I'll do it.'' He was beside her, one
thigh almost touching her hip. ''You don't have to
clean up after me. Or anyone. You're becoming a

whole person now, Leah. You're on your way to a new life you've decided to make for yourself.''

He'd covered her hand and stilled it with his own strong fingers. "Yes" was the only word she could form. Surely he must feel her tremble.

"And you were wrong when you came in and said I didn't want you. You'll never know how much I want you. And you're worth so much—to me and yourself.''

The joy Leah felt was tentative at first. She was afraid to believe he'd really said what she thought he had. All she seemed capable of was to stare up into his face.

He stood, pulling her with him. "You ought to go, Leah.'' Even as he said the words, he stroked her hair. "Please go.''

A small jab of defiance gained strength with the depth of her longing. "I don't want to.'' She stretched to take the glass from his desk and swallowed some of the smooth liquor. "I want you to kiss me.'' The glass wobbled when she set it down. This was madness, and she'd probably regret it. She could ruin everything, and afterward they'd both have to pay the price.

Guy uttered a low, incoherent sound and slowly bent his head to nuzzle her neck with his lips. His jaw was slightly rough, and the sensation it caused made Leah close her eyes. Millimeter by millimeter, his mouth approached hers, touching, feeling every hollow and contour of her face on the way until his lips closed over hers, cool and incredibly sweet, tasting faintly of brandy.

Except to hold her hand, he hadn't touched her, but now he took the ledger, reached blindly behind her to drop it on a chair and held her tightly against his broad chest.

The kiss deepened, and Leah felt the almost-forgotten, heavy heat in her womb. She ran her fingers beneath his shirt and through soft, golden chest hair, smoothed his wide shoulders and locked her wrists behind his neck. His firm hands at her waist heated her flesh and lifted her almost from the ground.

For an instant, he drew back, searching her face before kissing her again, more urgently, his tongue searching for and finding hers as they strained more fiercely against each other.

"Guy," Leah whispered when they paused for breath. "Oh, Guy—" There seemed nothing else to say, but his thumbs went to the soft sides of her breasts. They ached inside her cotton dress, and she yearned to feel her skin naked on his.

He kissed her again, with enough force to rock her head, as he covered each breast and tucked his fingers under her neckline. Her flesh throbbed.

"Leah, Leah," Guy said brokenly. "I knew I shouldn't touch you. That I wouldn't want to stop if I did."

Don't stop. "Kiss me again, Guy." Her lips sought his while he ran his hands over her shoulders and down her back. At her waist he hesitated, then crossed his arms around her, spreading his fingers wide over her ribs.

"Sweetheart," he muttered, and the thrust of his hips into her belly proved he was fully aroused.

Bright, searing desire burst free in Leah. She wanted this man, and he wanted her. Everything was right. Her eyes fluttered shut, and when she opened them again, Guy's were closed, his features darkened with passion. They needed each other.

He pressed hard little kisses along her jaw and down

her neck, then stopped to scan her face. "You are so beautiful," he said. "So perfect. Inside as well as out. I can feel it."

Leah rested her cheek on his shoulder. Somewhere in her brain came the small thought that she'd never known a young man's powerful, stimulating body, never known the exquisite desire that filled her now. For two years she'd scarcely felt a man's touch at all. She shut off her brain. This moment was all that mattered.

"Make love to me," she said quietly, holding his gaze but taking a backward step toward his bedroom. "Take me to bed. I want to lie in your arms."

As she watched, his expression changed. Pure, raw pain slowly replaced passion. He shook his head, his fingers passing fleetingly over her hair, her brow, along the outline of her mouth. His last contact was a brushing, almost-reverent cupping of her chin. Then he turned away.

Leah struggled for composure. When she gripped his arm, he stiffened, making a sound that was a choking groan.

"What have I done?" she asked. "Please, look at me and tell me what's wrong."

His head dropped forward, and he braced his weight on the edge of the desk. "You didn't do anything except be wonderful. And I want you—Lord, how I want you."

"Then what is it?" She was crying now.

"I can't allow myself to make love to you." Guy swung around, his chest heaving. "I'm married."

CHAPTER FOUR

GUY GROUND his back teeth together, willing his heart to slow down. What had he done? What had possessed him? He'd hurt and shamed her—and cut wide open his own torment.

"Leah, listen." He took a deep breath. "Oh, God. Don't look at me like that. I—"

Her face had paled beneath its smooth tan. Every rounded feature seemed drawn and sharp. The blue eyes were huge and dark, tears welling to spill, unchecked, down her cheeks. She pressed her lips together in a trembling line.

"Sit down. I'll pour us both a drink," he said, pleading.

Leah recoiled from his outstretched hand. "No, thank you. I don't want anything. I'm—I'm sorry I pushed myself on you. There was—" She cleared her throat and scrubbed at her damp face. "I never guessed. You didn't say anything. No one did. I—I need a Kleenex."

He took her elbow and guided her into a chair. "Sit there, please. I'll find some tissues."

What a lousy mess. And it was all his fault. He preached, actually preached about honor and truth, to people who stared back at him with self-guilt in their eyes. If only they knew. *Guy Hamilton, minister and fraud.* He slammed through the door to his bedroom and strode into the bathroom. No Kleenex, damn it. Toilet tissue would have to do. He unwound a wad and retraced his steps rapidly, terrified Leah might bolt before he could get there. Why hadn't he explained his situation to her as soon as she showed up in Phoenix? Fear? Yes, fear of losing a woman he had no right to in the first place.

His throat closed when he reentered his office. For seconds he couldn't move. Her body was scrunched in the chair, knees drawn up and tightly wrapped in her full skirt. She was retreating with the wounds he'd inflicted. Small sniffing sounds came irregularly, jerking her body.

Guy pounded one fist against the other palm. He felt absolutely useless to put right the misery he'd caused this woman who'd come to mean so much to him. He'd known she was attracted to him from the outset. Her arrival in Phoenix had proved that. And he'd also been acutely aware of their mutual and growing attachment. If he'd told her...

"Leah." He smoothed her hair until she raised her face. "This was all my fault." With light strokes, he wiped her tears. "Please, don't feel bad or hurt or embarrassed. I'm the one who should feel those things. I gave all the signals—signals I was wrong to give."

She made a visible effort at control, pushing her hair back, taking the tissue to wipe her eyes and nose. "It isn't important. Just a silly reaction. I was excited about the work, I guess, and got carried away. It's late." She glanced at her watch and made a move to stand. "Time I got out of your hair and let you get back to whatever you were doing."

I was thinking about you, sweet lady. All he could do anymore was think about Leah Bennett Cornish.

"Don't go, Leah. Not yet, not like this. Let me explain."

Her fingers made mangled shreds of the tissue. "No need." But she stayed in the chair. "You don't owe me anything, Guy. Least of all the personal details of your life. And you've already given me so much. It was probably natural for me to start dreaming of being closer to you. I've been too alone for too long. You were a convenient outlet for the loneliness, that's all. What happened..." Her voice trailed off, and her next breath shook the length of her body. "It wasn't anything."

"Yes, it was. And we're going to talk about it." Guy dragged another chair close until he could sit immediately in front of Leah. "Will you let me hold your hands?" he asked softly. "I feel like I need to hold on to a friend right now."

Tentatively, she extended shaky fingers, and he grasped them. Her gaze, direct at first, slid away as bright color stained her cheeks. He had embarrassed her deeply.

"I was married while I was still in college," he started. Why did everything he said sound ridiculous? "In California. I was majoring in business—international business. Susan..."

Leah's grip tightened. Guy massaged her cold fingers.

"She was so special. We met at the wrong time and married at the wrong time and for the wrong reasons. Thinking you know where you're going and knowing for sure are very different states. At twenty I only thought I knew what my future held. And boy, was I wrong."

Soft flesh at the neck of Leah's sundress rose and

fell rapidly. Guy tried not to notice nor to acknowledge he'd managed to add to the heap of insecurity her life must have been for months. She made no attempt to answer—or draw away. Inertia seemed to be slowly replacing the emotional riptide of the past half hour.

Sweat stung the corner of his eye, and he blinked. He couldn't risk releasing her hands. "Susan's a psychiatrist," he said. "A very successful one."

"Here?" Leah's voice was a hoarse whisper.

He slid his fingers to her wrists. "No. Oh, no. Still in California."

"But you see her? You get together?"

Guy closed his eyes fractionally. "No, Leah. I haven't seen Susan in six years, since we separated. By the time I graduated, I knew how I had to spend my life. We stayed together through my three years in theological college. She tried, really tried, but she never understood, and I don't blame her—anymore. She married one man, and he turned into someone different. My first posting was to a small California church. For a year Susan commuted to school every day, and every day she came home to a husband too involved in everyone else's problems to be the kind of partner, and lover, she needed."

"She left you?" The effort each question cost Leah was clearly etched in her pinched expression.

"I received an offer of a post here. Susan hadn't finished school."

"You mean you left *her*?"

Guy stood with enough force to topple his chair. He stared at it for a moment, rubbing a hand across the base of his neck. "We decided the time had come for a fresh start for both of us. The decision to part was mutual."

His muscles felt leaden when he bent to right the chair. What he'd just said was yet another lie albeit a half-truth. He hadn't wanted to give up on his marriage. Love died slowly—he'd always believe that. If Susan had asked him to stay in California, even permanently, he'd have done it, because he had loved her. But she didn't ask. In the years when he'd been so preoccupied with his calling, while he'd taken his wife for granted, she'd gone through the process of feeling her love for him die. By the time he realized what had happened, it was too late.

"Why?" The rustle of cotton told him Leah had left the chair. "Why didn't you get a divorce? Six years is a long time to be alone. Maybe you don't accept divorce, or would it be bad for—for Susan in her work? I don't know much about these things."

Again, she was feeling inadequate, overshadowed by what she saw as the shortcomings in her own experience. His fault. "It's complicated," he said. So complicated he wasn't sure he understood himself anymore. Susan had supposedly filed for divorce—at last—but now wasn't the time to discuss his possible freedom with Leah. She'd misunderstand, think he was excusing his earlier behavior, perhaps wonder why he'd rejected her since he was technically almost free.

"What I'm going to ask you is just for me, okay, Guy? I want to understand all this if I can."

The unnaturally tight quality of her voice made him stare at her. Her shoulders were pulled back, rigid, her chin tilted. He nodded, swallowing his apprehension.

"You've been separated from your wife for six years." It was a statement, and he knew he must only listen. "Do you expect me to believe you've lived like a monk—sorry if I'm too personal—for all that time?"

She was gaining momentum. A brittle spark lit her eyes. "I find that hard to believe. So why was it hands off with me? Am I so repulsive?"

The ground felt suddenly insubstantial beneath his feet.

"Guy?"

"Repulsive? Leah, you're beautiful."

"Are you still in love with your wife?"

"No!" he shot back emphatically. "It took a while, but I don't feel anything for her now—except a hope she'll be happy."

"But you don't want me," Leah stated flatly.

"Don't. You'll never know how much I want you at this moment. It would be so easy to be with you, so wonderful. But I told you, I'm still married." Let her leave it at that. He didn't want to say what he knew should be said or get any closer to his own pain of the past years.

"You're married, but you've been alone for a long time," she persisted. "You say you feel nothing for your wife now, but you won't make love with another woman, although you want to. I guess I don't understand any of this."

He touched her cheek, her shoulder, then dropped his hand. Her skin was maddeningly soft. "Adultery isn't acceptable to me." There, he'd said it, and she was bound to think him pious and judgmental. Whatever she thought, there was no way to soften the truth.

The words hung between them. Leah said nothing, but he felt her mind withdrawing, turning inward. She had to believe he'd indicted her with his own values.

Leah opened her mouth but couldn't get enough air. Somehow she must get out of this room, this house, without breaking down again. She'd taken the initiative, asked him to kiss her in a way he'd obviously found brazen. He *had* kissed her—but no one could blame a man who must suffer daily because of his own dedication to fidelity.

"I'm sorry, Guy." The instant she voiced the apology, a shard of anger started its slow burn. He'd taken his own good time to put her off. And he hadn't bothered to tell her the truth about himself when there'd been dozens of opportunities.

A fine film of sweat shone on his brow and upper lip. "I'm the one who should be sorry," he insisted. "The only one. And I am."

She bit back the urge to agree. "Don't work too late." Graceful exits must be one of the few social graces Charles had failed to teach her.

"I won't be able to work tonight, Leah. Surely you know that."

All she knew was that he'd learned almost everything about her and had evidently gained some sort of satisfaction out of playing the crusader. He hadn't considered that sharing his own problems might make her feel more worthwhile or that in doing so, any misunderstandings would have been avoided.

"Forget it, Guy. I intend to." She sounded convincing. "Excuse me." The distance to the door seemed miles.

"Leah—please, don't go like this."

At least he hadn't tried to touch her again. The briefest contact could send her into his arms, reaching, seeking comfort. Then the fire would spark between them again, and if he gave in to it, as he might now—out of guilt—she'd always know it had been for no other reason.

The doorknob slipped in her damp palm, and the

door slammed behind her. The noise echoed dull and throbbing in her ears while she quickly traveled the hallway back to her office. She hesitated on the threshold. This wasn't *her* office anymore. It couldn't be after what had happened tonight.

She'd left the light on. At first she moved sluggishly, turning confused circles, from scattered books on the floor to the disorganized desk and a chair where she'd piled the overflow of papers. Clean up and get out was her immediate and desperate instinct. Yet her fingers fumbled at drawers and knocked stacks of correspondence into confused jumbles.

Leah left the desk and tried to concentrate on the bookshelves. She must at least replace the volumes she'd heaped all over the room. Titles blurred, and author names ran together. All that mattered now was to get everything back in some sort of order and leave.

She picked up the publications, one, two, three, at a time, depending on their weight and thickness, and knelt to stuff them into their shelves. Her hands shook uncontrollably. *Charles.* The old, familiar stab of longing, the yearning for his comforting protection, returned, and she sat on her heels.

Yes, the people who said Charles had filled the place her father should have taken were right in a way. Yes, he'd made her feel safe and wanted and important after she'd grown up feeling like nothing. Was that so wrong? He'd also loved her very much as a wife—until the drink took over. And she had loved him and would never forget that love, or the gratitude that went with it, as long as she lived.

The tears started again, and she swiped at her nose with the back of one hand. Wretched books. She jammed them away as fast as she could. It hadn't been

Charles's fault alcohol made him impotent. Maybe if she could have fulfilled more of his needs, he would never have turned to booze. Maybe he had sensed when she'd started to pine for a young man to fill her life, her arms—her bed.

No! She shoved the thoughts away. He could never have known. Only now did she acknowledge the truth herself. She *had* wanted the excitement and sexual gratification of a lover closer to her own age. But how could Charles have known it when she herself remained unaware at a surface level?

"Leah."

Guy. She couldn't face him again. Not now. Maybe never again. Yet she'd known he'd come—hoped, without forming the wish, that he would.

He took the three books she held. "Please, stop this. You must be exhausted. I am."

"I'm terrific," she lied. "Absolutely terrific. I just wanted to clean up a bit before I left."

Their eyes met, total comprehension of her meaning passing between them, before Leah took the books back and slid them onto a shelf.

"It is time you went home," he said levelly but without conviction. "How's the Bug running?" he asked, referring to the old yellow Volkswagen that had taken the place of her sleek Porsche.

Making conversation, she thought. He was as uncomfortable as she. "Fine. Not the same as my other car, but that wouldn't be possible. Charles always kept it in first-class condition. He worried about me whenever I drove." She swallowed, hating herself for trying to inflict some sort of injury but incapable of resisting the urge to strike back out of her own hurt and debasement.

"He was a good man," Guy said very quietly. "I'm glad he was there when you needed him."

Leah felt the tears prick at her eyes again. Damn. The man would have to be gentle and kind even when she was deliberately spiteful. "Yes," she said, and gulped. "Charles was always there. He was— I still miss him."

"That's natural," Guy replied tonelessly.

"Maybe," she began, tipping her head to breathe. "Maybe if he hadn't had to worry about my loyalty, he'd be alive today."

Nothing could have prepared her for Guy's reaction. He grabbed her shoulders and pulled her upright, shaking hard until she gripped his shirt, gasping. His eyes burned into hers.

"Garbage," he rasped. "What are you saying? I saw the two of you together, remember? You were a perfect wife, irreproachable. Even the crumby papers said so." His grip hurt.

Leah breathed deeply through her mouth. She felt sick. "The crumby papers said a lot of things. What did they know?"

"If you want to punish yourself, fine." Guy held a trembling bottom lip in his teeth before going on. "If that's what it takes to make you feel better, fine. But I don't have to listen to the drivel. Charles was good to you, and I'm glad. I only wish I could have been the one there when he was showing up to play Sir Galahad. Must have been a real penance. Leah, I'd have been glad to pay that penance for you, sweet lady." He averted his face, but not before she saw the moist glitter in his eyes.

She covered his hands for an instant, then carefully disentangled his fingers from her arms. She reached to touch the sharp angle of his jaw but changed her mind and tapped his shoulder lightly instead. "Thank you for being so good to me, Guy. So very kind." Not that he'd know how to be anything else, she thought. "You look tired. Please, don't worry about me. Like you said, I must be tired, too. Sometimes I say things I don't mean when I'm worn out. Get some sleep now. I'll lock up as I go."

He blocked her path to the desk, and for the first time she noticed he held the ledger. "You left this in my office," he said, keeping his head down as he flipped through the pages. She saw his neck jerk. "And you did do it. You made it balance." His sudden glance unnerved her. "How did you manage it?"

Leah turned her back. She'd never learned how to play games—particularly this one of emotional tension, point for point for a prize of what? Ultimate pain and frustration?

"It wasn't so hard," she muttered. "One step at a time. Checks and balances—ordinary stuff by an ordinary brain."

"You aren't ordinary."

If only he would stop making this so difficult. "Guy." She swung to face him. He might be able to handle the stress; she couldn't. "This was a mistake." Her legs shook.

He'd moved between her and the door now. "What was a mistake, Leah?"

"My coming here. I was too impulsive. It's too much for you. Unfair to you. You have enough to cope with without my neurotic inadequacies."

"I want you." He took a step toward her, and she retreated. "I want you right here, and you aren't neurotic. You needed someone, and so did I. The timing wasn't perfect, but it rarely is. Can't we be patient?''

What was he saying? That if she waited, he'd eventually—possibly—be prepared to return some of the passion she'd already displayed so eloquently. Humiliation reddened her face.

Guy set the ledger on the closest chair. ''Can't we?''

''What?'' Her mind blanked.

He came closer until he could run a knuckle along her chin. ''Be patient, Leah. I don't want to lose you. You're needed here. By the people—and by me.''

''Thank you,'' she said stiffly. ''But I'm sure a lot of employees could fill the bill if you look carefully enough.'' If all he needed was a bookkeeper who could also wield a mean duster, he could look elsewhere.

He stuffed both hands in his pockets, and she saw his nostrils flare. ''Why do you choose to misunderstand?'' His mouth came together in a hard line. ''You know perfectly well what I mean.''

She didn't. How could she after his earlier turnoff? ''I've been a real pain to you, Guy.'' Her voice automatically softened. ''You tried to keep your distance— to make sure our relationship was professional. I was the one who misread your signals. I pushed things over the edge for us. There's nothing I can do to change that now—except to remove the irritation.''

''Meaning?'' His tone was steady, still.

Leah avoided his eyes and went to yank open desk drawers. ''I can't believe how much crud one person can collect in a short space of time.''

''I can hardly remember when you weren't here,'' he said, not moving.

She cast around for her purse and opened it on top of the desk. ''Look at the rubbish in this drawer. Pens, most of them useless. Old notes, pencil shavings. Disgusting.'' Without pausing for breath, she dragged the trash can from the corner and scooped grubby debris into it with her fingernails. The broken pens she dropped into the purse, without knowing why.

Finally, she dumped the drawer upside down over the garbage container. "There," she said with hollow triumph, refusing to meet Guy's gaze. His steady regard was a laser on her face.

"Finished?" he asked, too softly.

She moved to the bookcases once more. "Almost." If only he would leave so she could escape without any more fuss.

Rapidly, Leah slid volume after volume back onto the shelves, no longer bothering about alphabetizing. *Keep busy. Don't think for as long as it takes to get out of here* were the only lucid ideas her mind could form. And they meant she must continue working and stay in control, at least until Guy gave up and went away.

"Stop it!"

He almost shouted, and she jumped before continuing her task.

"Stop it, I said. Or I'll stop you. You're overreacting. We both suffered back in that room, but we can get over it and carry on."

Her movements became frenzied. Dim recollections of a man whose face she didn't remember returned, a series of men—and her mother leading them through the house, shouting, "You stop it, Leah. Stop your crying and go to sleep." And her mother's bedroom door would close before the laughter came. Leah never saw her mother's visitors clearly. By morning they were always gone.

That had been long ago, and it had nothing to do with what was happening to Leah now, unless...unless...no, she bore no resemblance to her mother. This was different, and she'd never been drawn to a man purely for sex or money.

Charles had spent eleven years convincing her she was special—her own person, untouched by what her mother had been. "Never allow anyone to make you think you're less than you are," he'd said so often. "We don't know all it took to turn your mother into what she became. She was worth something; remember that. She had you." And he'd smile, softening his cool blue eyes in a way Leah knew only she ever saw. While Charles was with her, it had been easy to believe she wasn't trash. But he was gone now.

The past weeks had been too much. It was time to find a quiet place and regroup—alone. Much as she wanted to be with Guy Hamilton, he had no place for her. He'd made that so very clear.

She squeezed her eyes shut and whispered, "Let me go, Guy."

The sudden, biting grip of his hands on her shoulders, jerking her around and pulling her close, made her stomach plummet. She opened her mouth, but no sound came. His face bent a few inches above her own, every handsome feature dark with fury.

"Will you stop? Will you listen to me? Or do I have to make you? You're hysterical, overreacting—totally out of line."

Something snapped inside Leah. "Maybe," she said with deathly calm. "But whose fault is that? And no one calls me hysterical or out of line anymore. I'm not a kid. You've been good to me, but I earned my way around here." She poked at the ledger. "This mess is straight now, thanks to me. And I thank you for allowing me to find out I *can* do something. Otherwise, I owe you nothing more.''

He lessened his grip, smoothing her arms from shoulder to elbow and back. ''You're right. And I'm sorry for coming on so strong. I can hardly wait to see what else you can do to help set me straight.''

Leah shrugged away, forcing a bright smile. ''Thank you, Guy, but forget it. If there's one thing you don't need, it's me. These past weeks have been good—probably for both of us. But I've had enough of Phoenix. It's too hot here, and I don't like the work.'' Leah whisked her purse straps over her shoulder and made it halfway around the desk before Guy shut the door.

He thrust both hands deep in his pockets and tried a smile that didn't quite come off. ''You grew up in Wichita Falls. The weather's just as hot there, and humid to boot.''

''That's different,'' she said, and took another step toward him.

Blond hair glimmered as he bent to study his bare feet. ''Worse, you mean. Awful. You do like it here, and you like the work. I've seen the thrill in your eyes when you accomplish something. And you like the people—I know you do. You're great with the old folks and wonderful with children. This is a perfect job for you—your slot. Whether you knew it or not, this is where you were always intended to be eventually.''

Leah chewed the corner of her mouth while she decided what to say next.

''You agree, right?'' Guy leaned against the door. ''You wouldn't be happy anywhere else?''

''No wonder you decided to become a minister,'' she said wearily. ''Gives you the perfect excuse to tell other people what to do with their lives. You have a natural flair for being pushy. The bigger the challenge, the pushier you get. I'm not a little lost sheep, Guy. Someone you have to gather up and save. I'm all gathered up together now—by me—and I've got enough sense to figure out when it's time to quit and move on.''

"Leah—"

"No—" She cut him off, one palm raised to reject his next protest. "You can't buffalo me into sticking around until your conscience heals. I mean… Damn, that's not what I meant."

He crossed his ankles, watching her face intently. "I think it's exactly what you meant. You think I'm only trying to get you to stay because I made a mess of things tonight. You're wrong, Leah. Totally, completely wrong. I *do* believe this is the place for you. And I'm very sure no one else will come along to fill your shoes here as well as you do."

"I'm going to take this slowly, point by point," Leah said patiently. "I wasn't suggesting you had a reason to feel guilty about anything that happened between us. What I said simply came out wrong. I intended to explain that I see you as feeling responsible for everyone, including me, and you're trying to make sure you've done all you can before I strike out on my own again. You're a natural caretaker, a collector of lame ducks." She paused for breath.

"But I—"

"Guy, I haven't finished." She would have her say before he could muddle her up yet again. "Second, there is no *one* place in the world for a person. And if there was, you certainly wouldn't be granted some sort of privileged insight into the location." She didn't allow the narrowing of his eyes to deter her. "Finally, I'm flattered to hear how useful I am around here. But I think, if you'll only face it, that neither of us will work as well together from here on. So it's best that I go—without any more fuss." A vague smugness warmed her. She'd finally learned how to take charge of her own life.

His only response was to cross his arms.

Leah approached steadily until one more step would bring her closer than she wanted to get. Desperation mingled with helplessness. Guy Hamilton was mule headed. He'd stop at nothing, including putting his quarry on the defensive, to get his own way. She ran her fingers agitatedly up and down the straps of her purse. "After all," she muttered, "it's not as if I'm leaving you in the lurch. You didn't have someone here before I arrived. You'll get by."

"Don't go."

For several seconds, she watched his mouth as if she'd see the words repeated. Then she met his irresistible eyes. Sticking to a decision was never going to be more difficult than now. "Guy, I'll always be grateful for what you've done for me. You gave me a fresh start and a chance to get my head straight. But I can't stay," she said.

"You can if you want to," he suggested persuasively. "Please want to."

"Guy." She spun away and threw her purse back on the desk. "You can be the most exasperating man. And you take advantage..." *Good grief.*

His laugh was a mellow rumble. "You do have a way with words sometimes, my girl."

"Okay, okay." Leah felt her resolution crumble. He would get his way, at least for now, but she'd be on her guard in future. "I'll continue to work for you until you can find someone to replace me."

"I'm going to be very selective." The laughter was still in his voice. "You're going to be a hard act to follow."

She looked at him over her shoulder, then turned resignedly to slump on the desk. "We'll just have to make sure we advertise in the right places, won't we? And of course I'll be only too happy to weed out unsuitable applicants."

Guy's expression sobered. "We won't find it tough working together—any more than we have until now. I promise you that, Leah. We both know where we stand, and we're both mature. How can we go wrong?"

Leah lowered her eyes, afraid he'd read in them the answer to his question. Guy, the optimist, was forgetting—or choosing to avoid—the obvious. They were healthy members of opposite sexes, and their attraction for each other went beyond a level they'd be able to ignore for very long. He slouched there, rationalizing, while she tried to close out the remembered sensation of his arms around her, his fingers in her hair, her own hands smoothing the broad, hard chest. Her pulse pounded in her ears.

"Leah," he persisted, "we'll be able to do very well, won't we?"

She balled her fists. He wanted her, and not just as a bookkeeper-housekeeper. This man, so determined to fight his natural urges, willed her not to leave because he'd fallen as hard as she. Leah stood and met his inquiring gaze. "Sure, Guy," she said at last. "We'll do just fine—until someone else can take over my job. It's late." She checked her watch and moaned. "If I don't get home, Wally will send out a search party. I'm surprised he hasn't called already.''

Guy raised expressive brows. ''Wally keeps tabs on you?''

Leah couldn't stop a sheepish grimace. ''Not exactly,'' she stalled.

''What does that mean?''

Guy had never allowed any other subject to be glossed over. She might have known he'd pick up on this one. ''I'm supposed to thump on the floor when I get home for the night, that's all. Just so he knows I'm safe. He's a neat old guy.''

''Mmm.'' Guy blew into a fist and moved away from the door. ''He's neat, all right. And I can't remember him really giving a damn about another human being since his wife died. He needed someone to care about. Everyone does. I told you you had a way with old folks.''

''See you in the morning.'' She swept past, skirt swishing, sandals clicking on terrazzo floors in the hall.

Guy listened for the grumble of the Volkswagen's engine, the scrunch of gravel spewing behind rubber, then strained to hear the last possible noise from the little car.

The faint breeze she'd let into the house smelled pungently of fallen oranges—and Leah. Roses and sandalwood, something subtle but hauntingly exotic. He went to sit in her chair and rubbed his fingers over its arms and the worn edge of the desk.

He'd managed to pull it off; he'd bought a little time after what had almost turned into an immediate fiasco. He leaned to rest his forehead on folded arms.

What was he supposed to do? What was right? Sometimes hanging on to old convictions took more *strength* than a man could be expected to have. Strength. Guy laughed bitterly and rolled his head slowly from side to side. He felt weak and insecure—and desperately lonely. After years of believing he'd made peace with his solitary state, he was sickeningly, hopelessly empty.

While he'd prattled on, throwing platitudes and assurances at her, doubt had shone in Leah's blue eyes. He was supposed to be the wise one, the one who had it all together. Laughable. She was honest and true and didn't know how to deceive. And she was gaining confidence with every day. No wonder Charles Cornish had fallen so quickly and completely in love with her—even when she was little more than a child. He must have seen beyond the lovely girl to the beautiful, accomplished woman she was capable of becoming. Too bad Cornish made one fatal mistake—not allowing her to fulfill her potential.

Guy's next thought shook to the core his belief in his own goodness. He was glad Cornish hadn't finished what he started with Leah. Glad because she was still malleable and ripe to succeed completely—with Guy.

He pushed wearily to his feet and left the house, hardly noticing rough, still-warm concrete beneath his bare feet.

The church was cool inside; one small light flickered yellow over whitewashed walls behind the pulpit. Guy hesitated beside the first pew he reached, then walked on. He wasn't ready to pray.

In a storage cupboard where extra hymnals were stored, he fumbled to locate his battered guitar and headed through a side door into the darkened grounds. Leah had never entered the church or shown any interest in what went on there. He wanted to share everything that mattered to him with her, but he mustn't push. At every service, he played his guitar and sang with the congregation. He loved his people and relished the times he felt the little community fuse. Now he wished he could sing for Leah—to Leah.

Crickets sent up a raucous accompaniment to his first gentle chords. Overhead, palm fronds clicked. She was alone, too, and vulnerable. Without meaning to, she'd let slip how little money she had and confessed she didn't even know where her mother was anymore. She had no one—but him. The thought first thrilled, then unnerved him.

Leah might be making strides toward independence, but she wasn't there yet. Even if he could face letting her go, he'd never rest if she did. Experience was the element she lacked most—worldliness. He slid down a tree trunk to sit on a sandy hummock. Worldliness was something he wished she never had to gain.

Guy closed his eyes and ran his fingertips across the guitar strings. He wouldn't let her leave. Somehow he'd keep her with him until he was free to admit his growing attachment—and to accept hers. And she *was* beginning to care for him. She'd tried to explain away her sweet advances as an excited overreaction. A lousy excuse. Leah wasn't the kind of woman who offered herself lightly to a man like some sort of party favor.

God, let him play the cards right, in the right order, perfectly timed. He rested his head on ringed bark, breathed deeply of the night's scents, then listened to the clear, poignant chords he played. Each note came far more from his heart than the guitar.

CHAPTER FIVE

LEAH PARKED in the church lot and walked around the building, its little belfry topped by a simple cross. The red-tiled roof stood out in sharp relief against white stone walls and the pallid early-morning sky.

Sleep had been a fitful waste of time. At five, she'd given up and started assessing and discarding one outfit after another. She hesitated, looking down at the demure navy linen dress and jacket she'd settled upon. Definitely businesslike with its white piping trim and the matching plain navy pumps. From here on, business would be the order of the day, every day. Leah wrinkled her nose. The only drawback was likely to be that she'd probably disintegrate from the heat by midmorning. At least the French braided chignon she'd labored over should help keep her neck cool.

Farther along Fan Lane, the bell on a Catholic church rang out seven dolorous chimes. With any luck, Guy would still be asleep, and she could make a start without having to face him. By the time he put in an appearance, she'd be involved in the task she'd set for herself during the hours of tossing and turning. Then she'd find it easier to appear casual.

The church was separated from Guy's house by a broad expanse of palm-studded grounds. Fan palms—the same kind that lined the street named after them—and in between, some taller, more majestic, date palms.

Guy had filled huge beds on each side of the driveway with multicolored dahlias, in full bloom now. A neat oleander hedge screened the front of the house, and every day brought a fresh crop of pink-and-white blossoms. Leah approached the front door, fishing for her key while she longingly took in every detail. She missed her yard and garden—and most of all, the orchids.

St. Mark's had an extensive vegetable patch behind and beside the house, and she'd considered asking Guy if she could help with its cultivation. That was out of the question now. So was suggesting he fill the pool in the cool courtyard sheltered by his wing. Day after day she'd ogled the blue leaf-strewn pit and tried not to think of her own tree-shaded grotto in Texas. Someone else would be swimming there by now.

An hour later, already sweating, Leah was deeply involved in her self-appointed project for the day cleaning and organizing the kitchen. She'd found a floral wraparound apron in a drawer and donned it without removing her jacket.

The place was passable on the surface. Closer examination revealed grubby corners, a stove that hadn't been cleaned for ages and the most jumbled cupboards Leah had ever encountered.

Leah was adding to a pile of bowls, pots and utensils on the mosaic-tiled table in the middle of the room when she saw the cockroaches. The inch-long monsters chugged contentedly along the baseboard with all the confidence of permanent and very satisfied boarders.

"*That* does it," Leah muttered, poking at strands of escaping hair.

The quantity of disinfectant she dumped into a bucket equaled the scalding water that followed. "First we scrub, then we spray.'' Fury mounted as she remembered Jewel and the flawless running of Charles's house in Wichita Falls. Regular pest control had been automatic there, as it should be in a place like Phoenix. Jewel would have a fit if she saw this mess. ''Penny-pinching skinflint.'' Leah dropped to her knees, ignored the hot liquid in the bucket and scrubbed with both hands. ''Probably thinks he's saving something for God by not paying to keep this joint up. Must be the only house in town where the bugs aren't professionally killed. Figures, though. Empty swimming pool in heat like this. Should have guessed when I saw that. Mean—''

The sound of a foot scuffing behind her stopped Leah in the middle of her tirade. She continued to scrub, her face down and rapidly reddening. If she'd had any sense, she'd have closed the door.

''Penny-pinching skinflint? Mean?'' Guy questioned evenly.

Leah squeezed her eyelids together. All her careful plans to be calm and distant had gone for nothing. She must appear—and sound—about as businesslike as the cockroaches that provoked her outburst.

She pursed her lips and sat on her heels to wring out a cloth. ''I shouldn't have said that.'' Oh, how she hated apologizing again. ''But this kitchen is a disgrace. If someone inspected household kitchens the way they do restaurants, there wouldn't be enough demerits to check off on the evaluation.''

''My,'' he said with mock surprise, ''aren't we testy this morning? Didn't you sleep well?''

That does it. She struggled to stand, arms akimbo, while she glared at him. ''I slept very well, thank you.''

She opened her mouth to ask him the same question and stopped.

His hair, neatly combed and curling forward beneath his ears, was still wet from the shower. He wore the clerical black she'd assumed he reserved for Sundays. Leah hadn't seen him in the garb since she first arrived in Phoenix. She passed the back of one hand over her eyes, closing out the appealing picture he made—green eyes glinting, his lean features deeply tanned against the stiff white collar.

"Cleaning kitchens isn't your job," he spat out suddenly.

Leah's heart flipped over. She'd never heard him speak so sharply. "I—" Her pulse thudded. "The job needs to be done, and I *am* supposed to be the housekeeper around here."

"If you can tidy up a bit here and there, terrific," Guy said far more softly. "But you're invaluable to me in the office. I don't ever want to see you on the floor like that again. Look at your hands." He clasped her wrists and held raw knuckles high enough for her to look at them. "You didn't even put on rubber gloves, Leah."

"I didn't think," she mumbled.

His jaw tightened, and he flattened his lips. Still holding her hands, he stepped back and took her in from head to toe. "What are you wearing?" he asked, amazement tinging his words. "The forecast is for one hundred and sixteen, and you're dressed up like an Eskimo preparing for a blizzard."

She lifted her head defiantly. "You exaggerate. This is a perfectly acceptable outfit for my type of work. Why are you wearing that?" She nodded at his severe shirt.

"We have a wedding today. Young Ben Perez and Sophia Yale are getting married. And what you have on isn't acceptable. It wouldn't be in the office, let alone on the kitchen floor—with that ridiculous apron over the whole thing..." The rest of the sentence trailed away.

"Finished?" Leah pulled away and poked at the bucket with one toe. "Whether you like it or not, I can't leave this mess the way it is."

"You can and you will." Guy rotated his shoulders, exhaling a long breath. "I apologize if I sound ungrateful. I'm not. But this isn't what I had in mind when I asked you to work for me. Call Wally and find out who needs a job for a few hours. That's how I've always gotten by with the cleaning—by calling someone in when I couldn't cope on my own.

"I'm sorry about the bugs. We do have them sprayed. The guy didn't show last month, and I forgot to do anything about it. That's why I need you—to help me keep on track. Call him, too, if you don't mind. The number's written down somewhere. But before you do anything, right now, in fact, please take off that—that *thing* and your jacket. All we need is a case of heat prostration.

"Incidentally, the pool will be filled. I'd forgotten that, too. Feel free to swim whenever you like."

"That's nice of you." She breathed deeply. How easily he turned the tables to make her feel small. "But there's no need to do anything special on my account."

"I want to," he said, then hesitated before adding, "You really shouldn't be bundled up in heat like this."

He remained in the doorway, clearly waiting for her to do as he asked. Leah took off the apron and draped it on top of the pots and pans. She made no attempt to remove her jacket. And she wouldn't until Guy had left and she was good and ready.

"There," she said. "Now may I get on with some work? I will make the calls and get some help after I straighten up what I've started."

He raised both hands in a gesture of exasperated defeat and turned to leave.

"By the way," Leah called to his back, "do you really think brown boat shoes and no socks are appropriate for the occasion?"

Guy swung around and looked down at the same time. "Oh, no," he said. "Thanks—I might have forgotten. It wouldn't be the first time." His attention lifted to her face, and his amused expression faded. "I wish you wouldn't wear your hair up again. It's too lovely to hide."

He disappeared rapidly into the hall, and Leah felt all life go out of the room with him. She touched her chignon thoughtfully before making sure the pins were still secure.

BY EARLY AFTERNOON, Elsie Culver, a garrulous but efficient woman Wally Timmons recommended, had brought the kitchen to shiny perfection. Elsie also cleaned the counseling office and both guest bedrooms before she left, beaming at Leah's praise and delighted with the suggestion of a weekly arrangement.

Guy had been gone all day. He kept his own appointment book, but the arrival of cars and the sound of laughing voices had let her know the wedding took place at eleven. Some time afterward, she'd watched from the window while the bride and groom, followed by their guests, trailed to a reception in the small, separate hall beside the church. She'd smiled at the young

couple's glowing faces and laughed when a minute
flower girl, concentrating too hard on her dignified
walk, landed on her bottom. Guy's appearance, just in
time to scoop up the child and bounce her frown into
giggles, brought a film of tears to Leah's eyes.

That had been an hour ago, and now she could hear
distant strains of guitar music. What would it be like
to dance with Guy at their wedding? Her crazy imagination was treacherous.

She pushed aside several letters from members of
the congregation. They were mostly suggestions or
thank-you notes to Guy and could wait. Physical activity was what she needed, something to obliterate the
little flashes that constantly plagued her—the way
Guy's smile narrowed his eyes, his strong hands forcefully wielding a shovel, gently patting a child's head.
This was all so hopeless.

Restless pacing in front of her desk didn't help. He'd
said he didn't mind her tidying up. Mrs. Culver hadn't
touched his own disorganized study or his bedroom.
Why not make some attempt to straighten them? At
least the study.

Entering the room again took resolution. She let her
eyes travel slowly over his papers, the brandy glass,
still among them, and on to the chairs where they'd sat
facing each other. She would not feel embarrassed
again. Instead, she swept up the glass and headed
through his bedroom to wash it out in the bathroom.

This is a mistake, Leah. The shower tile had dried,
but his towel was still damp and twisted on a bar beside
the sink. His clean scent hung in the air. Tentatively,
she picked up a comb from the shelf and closed her
hand around it while she looked at masculine trappings.
A half-used bottle of after-shave, his razor. He seemed

to surround her, awaken every half-forgotten instinct yet again without even being in the same room. She thought of being here with him, of sharing his shower, watching him shave, leaning against his naked back to fold him in her arms. The next sensation to assail her came close to panic, and she pivoted sharply away.

On the way back to the study, she averted her eyes from his unmade bed and tried not to look at the cutoffs and shirt he'd tossed aside the night before. He probably slept nude. She almost ran through the door, closing it firmly behind her.

Papers on the desk quickly assumed precise positions, shuffled and neatly stacked according to size. Folders, she filed alphabetically in a battered filing cabinet.

The jacket had remained firmly in place all day, but as Leah became more involved in her project, she shed the garment and tossed it on a stool.

By four she was ecstatic. The desk was solid oak, and with a coat of lemon wax, glowed warmly. So did the chairs and an old but venerable-looking credenza. The latter had also been buried with debris that Leah had straightened and placed behind sliding doors below. She'd brought off a transformation, and she could hardly wait for Guy's reaction.

She was admiring her masterpiece when she heard his footsteps in the hall. Her breathing almost stopped as she watched the door handle turn before he entered the room. He seemed not to notice her at first. One hand repeatedly finger combed his hair. His head was slightly lowered, and for the first time she noticed dark streaks beneath his eyes. The man was exhausted. Maybe he hadn't slept so well last night, either.

"Guy," she said softly, "are you okay?"

He started violently and stared at her. "Where were you?" he said sharply. "You weren't in your office, and I thought—" He closed his mouth and rubbed both hands over his face.

He'd been afraid she'd left, Leah thought, not quelling a surge of joy. Her car was on the other side of the church rather than in front of the house, and he'd jumped to the wrong conclusion. "I decided I needed a change of pace," she consoled. "And I remembered you didn't mind if I tidied up a little, so I came back here. What do you think?"

Guy took in the room very slowly. He walked to the desk, then the credenza, running his fingers over each surface. Then he touched the filing cabinet with a look Leah recognized as wonder. She'd really surprised him, she thought happily.

"Good Lord." He turned on her. "What have you done in here? Where are my—my—things? My notes and reference folders? What—" He riffled through a sheaf of paper on the desk. "These aren't in the order I left them. Nothing is. How could you do this to me?"

For several seconds Leah stood mute, goose bumps racing over her skin, her throat tightly closed. Then deep, engulfing heat started somewhere inside and flared to the surface. "You ingrate. There wasn't any order before I started making some. Your things are tidy and easy for you to use. Your reference folders are filed where they belong—in the cabinet. I spent three hours in here, sweating over what must be several years' accumulation of crud, and all I get from you is a bawling out."

"Hardly a bawling out. You surprised me." A white line formed around Guy's compressed lips. He strode to the filing cabinet and wrenched open the top drawer, almost overbalancing the whole unit. "You filed the folders where? Using what system?"

"Alphabetical, of course," she shot back.

"Alphabetical?" Guy's tone was bewildered. He raised a hand, palm up, then dropped it heavily to his side. "Alphabetical? Oh, no. That's the end, then. I'll never find them again. They're filed—when I decide they should be—according to subject. I suppose it never struck you to check how I did it before you started your Suzy Homemaker stunt. When are you going to understand that I don't want you to clean up after me?"

Leah's hurt welled up in her until she could hardly keep from crying. Papers and dull books were all he cared about. The hard work she'd put in to please him meant nothing. She opened and closed her mouth several times like a beached fish, searching unsuccessfully for something scathing to say before racing from the room and back to her office. *Callous, thoughtless ingrate.* She slammed the door and leaned against it for an instant before grabbing the nearest chair and dragging it to the bookshelf closest to the window. *Okay, okay,* she repeated in her head. *Calm down and get on with it. You promised you'd stick this out until someone else could be found for the job, and you're going to make it.*

Not bothering to take off her shoes, she climbed on the seat of the chair. Maybe she should have asked him before tampering with his personal stuff. But the gesture was well-intentioned, and he had to know that. He could simply have thanked her and covered up his feelings. He'd looked desperate. That made twice today he'd disapproved of her efforts. And she was turning into a snapping shrew. Why had she exploded at him that way? She blushed at the memory of her harsh words. There was too much tension between them; altogether too much.

No good putting off the top shelves any longer. She began to pull out pamphlets that had been stuffed between books. Whoever had been here before her must have been a slob. The pile of discards that she dropped on the floor grew rapidly.

"Biles," she read on the spine of one volume, "*Methods of Prayer*." She could rearrange it under B, or perhaps M for method, or would his lordship consider P for prayer a better classification. A footfall sounded outside her door at the same time as Leah balanced precariously on the back of the chair to reach something orange. Her fingers closed on the sheet, and she started to fall.

The room seemed to swing wildly as the bottoms of both slippery shoes slid on the narrow rim of wood. She heard her own scream, then saw Guy running, arms outstretched. His face was a blur.

"Leah!" His yell came a second before the windowsill cracked into her spine and she smacked into an ungainly heap between chair and wall. Several books rained on her hands and forearms as she shielded her head.

She heard the chair scrape aside and instantly felt Guy's arms surround her, his fingers smoothing her loosened hair away from her face. "Are you all right? Leah, say something. Your ankles—" He lowered her carefully to the floor and slid off her shoes, then gently probed each shin and ankle. "No one takes a fall like that and comes out without a broken bone. Speak to me, will you?" he pleaded.

Leah's heart still hadn't returned to its normal place

in her body, but her senses were enough intact to revel in his anxious face and the tender stroking of her limbs. "I'm all in one piece, I think. Just shaken up."

"Does your head hurt?" He peered closely into her eyes. "Do you hurt anywhere at all?"

"N-no. I don't think so. Except for my back where it hit the windowsill," she said, sighing.

Guy must have mistaken the sigh for a moan. "You do hurt. Far more than you're saying. I'm taking you to the emergency room. We'll get some X rays."

"No! No." She had taken a pretty good knock, but being with him, seeing his concern, would soon ease any pain. "If I stay still for a few minutes, I'll be fine."

"I don't think so, Leah. I'll feel better if someone checks you over."

"Guy," she said persuasively, "please believe me. It's not necessary. You just go back to whatever you were doing. I'll rest here quietly for a while."

He stroked two fingers along her cheek. "Have I told you how stubborn you are?" His eyes were close, fathomless.

"Mmm," she whispered, turning her face until her lips brushed his palm. "But not quite so bluntly."

"What are we going to do about us, Leah?" It was a rhetorical question, his own thought spoken almost unconsciously. He followed the question by outlining her bottom lip with a thumb. "Going away wouldn't solve anything. You see that now, don't you?"

She nodded, silently waiting.

When the kiss came, it was infinitely tender, sweetly restrained torture that speared desire into her belly.

Afraid to break the moment, she held still, her head cradled in one of his large hands. Tingling sensations flitted along every nerve as he urgently, repeatedly, pressed his lips to her face and neck. He lifted his head, searching her eyes, and she saw again the agony, the inward battle he was waging.

"Leah, Leah," he groaned, and nuzzled into the hollow of her throat.

He seemed to rest there endlessly, his breath warming her skin. Finally, he stood and took her hands, pulling her up slowly.

Without shoes, Leah felt small. The top of her head was level with Guy's chin. She took a step closer until she could kiss the tanned vee where he'd discarded his collar and opened the neck of his shirt. His arms tightened convulsively around her, and she looked up to find his face tipped back, his eyes squeezed shut.

Leah wanted to smooth away the frown and kiss his mouth into a smile. And she wanted to ask him why he had to suffer, to make them both suffer, when loving and needing couldn't be wrong. Loving. She did love Guy Hamilton and always would. "Guy," she whispered, and waited until their eyes met. She couldn't bring herself to question his motives for disregarding the arousal she felt in his body or the passion she saw in his eyes.

A shuddering sigh rippled through him, and he kissed her again, first deeply, reaching, moving her head from side to side, then softly, his tongue flitting along the membrane inside her lips. His breathing was shallow, and she felt the rapid beat of his heart against her breast. Her own heart leaped erratically.

Leah reached up to touch tiny lines at the corners of his eyes, ran a fingertip along the groove beside his mouth and touched her lips to the dimple that formed there. What would he say if she told him she loved him? She shook her head, clutching him close instead.

"It'll be all right," she said without conviction. "I don't know how yet, but we'll find a way in time." She must believe in what she said and make him believe it, too.

"I hope to God you're right." Guy held her to him. The fingers of his right hand splayed wide over her cheek, then tangled in her hair, and he bent to breathe softly against her ear. "Be patient with me, Leah."

Tears prickled behind her eyelids before a shuffling sound made her crane to see around his shoulder. Everything in her body froze. Elsie Culver stood in the doorway.

CHAPTER SIX

LEAH DUG HER FINGERS into Guy's side. "Elsie," she squeaked. "What a surprise." She bit her lip. What a dumb thing to say.

Guy straightened and turned to face the woman. Leah could see his breathing hadn't returned to normal, but he managed a smile. "Hi, Elsie. What can I do for you?"

"Mrs. Cornish said for me to come back later." Dark eyes moved quickly over Leah, taking in her stockinged feet before settling sharply on Guy's face. Leah didn't fail to notice the use of her married name when the woman had been eager for informality between them earlier.

Guy's arm, lightly circling her shoulders, shocked Leah. She tried not to stiffen. How could he be so nonchalant? "Mrs. Culver's right." The quaver in her voice horrified her. This episode could undermine Guy's position with his congregation. "I've asked her to come in once a week. But I didn't know your policy on payment, so I thought I'd better wait until I could talk to you."

"Ah." He nodded, still smiling at his curious parishioner. "I'm sure you know the going rates, Elsie. Whatever's fair. You two can work it out together, and I'll sign the check. I'm glad you're helping out. I don't want Leah to overdo."

"I see," Elsie Culver said with an emphasis that suggested she saw far more than Guy's words might convey. She spread her feet in their sensible white lace-up shoes and poked at gray sausage-shaped curls. Every second felt interminable to Leah.

Guy cleared his throat and rubbed her shoulder. "Leah's been attempting to pull off the impossible and sort out this place single-handed. Just before you came in, I picked her off the floor. She was trying to do something about these crazy bookshelves—using the back of that chair for a ladder. Perhaps you can help me protect her from herself."

Neat, Leah thought. But not neat enough. Elsie's expression was knowing before she nodded. "I'll be glad to, Guy. Maybe I should wait until tomorrow to get the money and my schedule sorted out. Her being shaken up now."

"Good idea, Elsie." Guy's tone was sober. "She took a hard knock. I tried to persuade her to go the emergency room, but she won't listen."

Elsie was backing away. "Oh," she said, "I'm sure most of us know what's best for us, don't we, Leah? She'll be right as rain before you know it."

Striped polyester swished as Mrs. Culver left.

"Guy," Leah breathed, turning to him. "That was awful. Terrible. I've never felt so embarrassed or vulnerable."

"My congregation trusts me," he said, a distant look in his eyes. "They're good people—the very best. They aren't gossips, and Elsie won't question my explanation of what she saw."

"You mean you expect her to buy that story of my falling?"

Guy absentmindedly rubbed her back. "It wasn't a story. You did fall. How's the bump?"

"I'm probably going to be a bit stiff." Leah slumped into the chair, exasperated. "It'll pass. Right now I have more important things on my mind. You can't brush off what just happened. It could affect your career if a rumor starts."

"It could, but it won't." The windowpane rattled suddenly, and he went to peer outside. "What Elsie saw was hardly a breach of moral ethics. I was holding you. I'd like to hold you again now. If I could figure out a way, I'd hold you all the time."

"I..." Leah swallowed hard and resisted the temptation to go to him, wrap her arms around his tall, lean body and rest her cheek on his shoulder. "Guy, listen to me carefully."

"Weather's changing." The inflection in his voice didn't alter. He crossed his arms on the windowsill. "The wind's picking up."

Avoidance tactics wouldn't help either of them. "Okay, stand there and pretend we haven't said any of the things we've said to each other—or touched each other. Make jokes out of everything. But please be sure you hear every word I say."

His shoulders hunched slightly.

"Guy, do the members of your congregation know you're married?"

"Yes, of course."

Leah winced. He seemed determined to treat possible disaster lightly. "You told them?"

"Of course. When I took this job, I expected Susan to come with me. They thought they were getting a couple." He turned and leaned against the wall, tilting back his head. "I guess we all got a shock."

"All?" Leah's palms were sweating.

"My little flock and me." His toneless voice wrenched her heart. Whether he still loved his wife or not, the thought of his failed marriage continued to hurt him.

She must concentrate. "How did they take it when Susan didn't join you? What did you tell them?" She wanted him to say that he'd explained the complete circumstances of his separation.

He rolled his face toward her, and she saw his gaze center on her lips. His own mouth had set grimly. Guy wasn't as unconcerned as he'd like her to believe. "What was I supposed to say?" he asked tiredly. "That my wife decided going to school was more important than being with me? Or maybe that I'd been a lousy, preoccupied husband and bored her into not giving a damn about me anymore?"

"What did you say, then?"

He sighed and closed his eyes. "You have a way of making me feel so guilty."

"For God's sake, be straight about this, will you?" Leah immediately wished she'd phrased the question differently and had sounded less agitated. "Guy, I'm sorry if—"

"You have nothing to be sorry about, not with me, ever." He began to pace back and forth behind the desk. "I didn't explain. I should have, but I didn't. After I arrived here alone, there were questions about Susan, and I just fielded them. First, what I said was…"

"What?" Leah prompted quietly when he didn't go on.

Guy stared at her. "I said she had to finish up school.

Another of my half-truths. Like the one I told Elsie Culver just now. Some example to my people, right?''

"Don't!" Leah went to stand in front of him and grasped his upper arms. "Why do you think you have to be perfect? You're just a man, Guy. Is that so terrible? Or could it actually make it easier for you to relate to other men's problems, do you think?"

His smile was lopsided as he watched her face. "So serious, and so wise. Sure, I'm only a man. Boy, don't I know I'm only a man." He laughed abruptly, showing beautiful teeth, narrowing his limpid eyes. "But madam, it's a fact that honesty pays in the end. Everyone here knows my marriage is over, although I've never told them. They would probably have liked to help me through the hard times openly, the way I help them through theirs. But I was too proud to admit I was as human and capable of being insured as they are. Also, our Mrs. Culver would have less to report if my permanent separation wasn't a taboo subject.''

The sudden slam of the window made Leah jump. "Keep meaning to have Wally fix that," she muttered. "You are worried about gossip, aren't you?"

"Not really." His biceps flexed beneath her fingers, and he rested his hands lightly at her waist. "Please try believing people mean well. And remember, you can't make much out of a man picking a lady in distress off the floor, particularly when she's narrowly missed killing herself."

Leah slowly shook her head. "I'd better arrive on crutches tomorrow, you naive, trusting man. I know how good all these people are; they've certainly been good to me. But I also know that by the time Elsie Culver's story's been translated a few times, we'll have been making love on the kitchen table.'' She blushed furiously and tried to twist away.

Guy held her fast and stroked her burning cheek. "Everything's going to be okay, I tell you. You're reading too much into a very minor incident.''

"I don't think so. I—''

"Well, I do. And I know these—''

Two of Leah's fingers, firmly placed on his lips, stopped his interruption. "Shh, Guy. Please, don't tell me again how well you know your people. I might scream. You love your work; I know you do. I may not have figured out much about what you do or completely understand everything expected of you, but I do know that a minister, particularly one in a close-knit community, can easily become the focus of speculation.

"If you do stir up controversy and somebody decides to make an issue out of your private life, you could find it hard, maybe impossible, to carry on here. I'm not about to be responsible for upsetting your career. I think we'd better arrange the employment ad we talked about last night.''

"How about a drink?'' Guy said as if she hadn't spoken. "You've had a busy day.''

"Guy—''

"I could certainly use something.'' His eyes met hers briefly, flickered and moved away, but not before she read quiet desperation there. The man was trying to stay inside his own emotional comfort zone.

Someone had to keep a clear head here. "Thanks, but no. I've still got grocery shopping to do before I go home. And I am a bit sore.''

Immediately, Leah regretted the reference to her fall. "You're sore.'' Guy took her hand. "I knew it. You should be lying down. I don't know what I'm thinking about. Come on. You can rest in one of the guest rooms, and I'll get you a cold drink.'' He started for the door. ''And aspirin—you should have aspirin for the inflammation and the pain.''

''Stop.'' Leah stood her ground. ''I'm going home. The sooner someone sees me walk out of here, the better.''

''I think—'' Guy began, then pressed his lips together and sighed. ''I think you're probably right. But Leah, if we can avoid a repeat of today—at least for as long as it's necessary—will you stop talking about leaving?''

''As long as necessary?'' How was she supposed to interpret that comment? ''You mean will I stay on and never interfere with your study again?'' she quipped halfheartedly.

''You know what I mean.'' He dropped her hand and fingered his hair. ''But I'm sorry if I seemed uptight with you about the study. I guess I've been on my own too long. I'm too set in my ways.''

''I'll second that notion,'' Leah retorted heartily enough to make them both laugh.

''Beauty and tact—I'm certainly blessed in my… I'm lucky to have you, Leah. Remember what you said just before Elsie Culver barged in?''

She remembered every detail of the past hour in living color. ''Why don't you tell me?''

''You said we'd work things out somehow.'' He came closer until she had to arch her neck to watch his face. ''I admit today makes that seem like a difficult project.''

''And you asked me to be patient, Guy. But you didn't explain what you meant by that.'' Leah stopped short of mentioning their earlier talk of openness. He was choosing not to risk telling her everything that was on his mind.

For an instant, Guy hesitated, and Leah held her breath, feeling him struggle with his own feelings. He inhaled slowly. "I meant what I said; that's all. Be patient; give us time to be sure what we want and what we should do about it."

She concentrated hard on slipping her shoes back on, keeping her head down. "And while we do that, neither of us will be tempted to push the relationship farther? I hope you're right. Or we may both suffer. I don't want the loss of your job on my conscience." She met his eyes steadily. "Okay, I'll stick around. I like it here. For the first time in my life I'm beginning to feel like a truly useful human being. But I won't live on pins and needles waiting for one of us to take a wrong step. And for the record, I'm not so available you can decide what my future's going to be—even on the short term. I'll make my own decisions about what's good for me." She paused for breath, waiting for his reaction.

The satisfied smile on Guy's wide mouth curled her toes. "I wouldn't have it any other way," he said, and picked up her purse and jacket from the desk. "You're absolutely right. It's best you have an early night. In ten days I'm due to leave for a retreat in Tucson. I'll be away from Monday to Friday, and I'm counting on you to run things around here.

"Tomorrow I thought I'd talk to you about setting up my appointments while I'm gone. If you do it, I'm likely to keep things straight, which I don't always manage by myself. In fact, I think it might be a good idea for you to take over that job permanently. I'll also have to arrange for you to be able to sign checks."

He guided her to the front door and opened it for her. "I'd like to make an early start in the morning, if that's all right with you."

Leah had mumbled an assent and set out for the other side of the church and her car before her mind clicked into full gear. A fiercely hot wind whipped her skirt around her knees, and she walked faster, willing herself not to look back, knowing he stood in the doorway, watching.

Again, she'd been outmaneuvered. All her brave announcements didn't mean a thing. He was steadily making her more deeply entrenched in her job and with him. There was no way she and Guy Hamilton would keep their distance from each other for more than a few days—or hours.

The Volkswagen's door handle burned her fingers. "Damn," she hissed, blowing on her hand. If she didn't watch out, she'd end up with more than burned fingers.

EACH DAY SEEMED WARMER than the one before. It had been a week since Leah and Guy had agreed upon what she knew was a tenuous truce. A hundred times, while poring over papers together, while he gave her instructions or asked his schedule for the day, their eyes met, and in the still seconds that followed, naked desire sprang between them. The prospect of his trip to Tucson next week filled Leah with a mixture of emptiness and relief. At least she'd be able to relax and think her position through for a while.

Today Guy was making sick calls and wouldn't be back before midmorning. Leah rested her chin on one fist. What did he do on sick calls? Speak of faith and God, she supposed. They really had so little in common—almost nothing. She cast about for a shared interest and was about to give up when she remembered his puttering in the garden. They both enjoyed the earth and growing things, although Guy didn't know she loved it, too.

The cranky doorbell reverberated through the house. Only strangers rang the bell. Leah stood and smoothed her cotton shirt and pants before opening the door.

Wally Timmons stood in the shadow of the overhanging roof, hat in one hand, an orchid plant in the other. He opened his mouth several times but seemed to keep changing his mind about what he wanted to say.

Leah took a bony elbow and urged him inside. "Wally, get in out of the heat. You don't have to ring the bell. No one else does. Come on in. I'll find you some iced tea."

He grunted and allowed her to steer him into the big kitchen, immaculate from Elsie's regular ministrations.

"Sit down," Leah insisted. "Set your things on the table and relax. You look beat."

"I'm not staying, Leah. Just came by to ask you a favor. Then I'll be going." His faded check shirt, freshly washed and ironed as always, sported a black string tie with a turquoise clip. Wally wore a string tie no matter what he was doing and was most usually seen with a straw cowboy hat tilted rakishly forward over crew-cut, iron-gray hair. Leah worried that he didn't eat properly, because he was cadaverously thin.

"You'll have some iced tea and some of this meat pie Elsie Culver made or I'll lock the door with you inside," she admonished. "First you eat; then you can ask me your favor."

He flushed, deepening the color in his bronzed and

lined cheeks. His pale blue eyes crinkled at the corners. "If you say so, miss. You're a feisty one, like my Joan."

Tears sprang to Leah's eyes, and she busied herself with the pie. Likening her to his dead wife was the greatest compliment he was ever likely to pay. He'd talked about Joan once when Leah persuaded him to come and eat dinner in her apartment. She'd also learned the couple had lost a daughter when she was nine. The girl had died of complications following a tonsillectomy and would have been about Leah's age if she'd lived. Leah knew that Wally was unconsciously turning her into the daughter he no longer had.

"There." She put a large slice of pie flanked by a peach and some melon balls in front of Wally. "I'll join you in the iced tea. It's a scorcher today, and this house is never cool. Guy keeps hinting about new air conditioning, but he doesn't seem to get beyond hints. Think we'll get thunder again? We could sure use more rain."

"Could be. Leah, I was going to talk—" Wally stopped and fidgeted with his glass back and forth.

She finished a long swallow of her own drink and studied him curiously. Something was bothering Wally. "You were going to talk," she prodded.

He shook his head and speared a large mouthful of pie.

Leah waited, suddenly apprehensive. Could there be something wrong with Wally and he didn't know how to tell her? She drummed her fingers on the table.

He downed half his tea and straightened in his chair. "Would you see what you can do with this?" His voice was tight and crackly as he pushed the plant toward her. "I know you've got a way with the things.

All those plants in your apartment grow apace, and you told me you used to raise orchids.''

Relief, then sweet sadness flooded Leah. She was relieved he hadn't said he was ill and touched that he'd brought the plant. "How nice of you, Wally. I haven't had one in ages.''

"It's nothing,'' he replied hastily. "Had it around for months and the durn thing won't do anything for me. Thought you might know what it needed.''

She stared directly at him until he lowered his face to the plate again and made much of scraping crumbs into a tidy pile. "I'll do my best, Wally,'' she said at last. The pot still had a bright, new price tag on its side, and she'd lay a bet the cash-register receipt was in Wally's pocket.

"You should have a bit of garden to mess with,'' he mumbled gruffly. "It isn't healthy for you to work in that stuffy office all the time. Wish there was more ground around my place.''

The door on the refrigerator didn't latch easily and began to swing open. Leah got up to close it. "I don't spend all my time in the office.'' Wally's suggestion surprised her, but he could be right. "Maybe I should ask Guy if I can help him around the grounds.''

She heard Wally clear his throat and turned to look at him. "You okay, Wally? You don't have a cold or something?''

"Nope. Never better. Just been a bit worried about you lately.''

His comment puzzled Leah. "Why? Because of my back? It's much better.'' She'd told Wally about her fall, and he'd immediately produced a bottle of lotion that smelled like horse liniment.

He made as if to stand, but Leah urged him back

into the chair. "Is there something on your mind you're not telling me, Wally?"

"No." He spoke too loudly. "I reckon I was fussing about nothing. But you don't have any folks to keep an eye on you, so…"

"So you thought you would. Thanks, Wally. And I appreciate it. Everyone needs someone to keep an eye on them. I will do something about getting outside more. I'm sure Guy would let me help in the garden if I asked him."

He shifted and reached for his hat. "That's kind of what I wanted to talk to you about. You and—"

"Wally Timmons, you old goat. What brings you here?" Guy breezed into the kitchen. "Can't remember the last time I managed to get you over the doorstep. Of course—" he winked at Leah "—there didn't used to be a lovely lady to serve you iced tea, and what's that you ate—pie? Good to see you, anyway." He flopped into a chair, slid down and stretched out his long legs.

Leah wondered fleetingly how many ministers did their job in soft cotton shirts and faded jeans that hugged every fascinating male inch. "Tea, Guy?" she asked with an asperity that annoyed her. Around Guy her reactions seemed to take on their own life.

"Thanks." His expression was nonplussed. "You okay, Leah?"

"Yes, I'm okay. I'm terrific. Why is everyone so concerned about my health?" She plopped a glass in front of Guy before remembering Wally was watching. "Will you have some more of this, Wally?" she added more evenly.

"Not for me. I'd better be going."

He felt the tension in the room—who wouldn't? She

and Guy created a charged current the instant they were within yards of each other.

"Who else is concerned about your health, as you put it?" Guy had sat bolt upright and stared intently at Leah.

"She's talking about me," Wally interjected. "I was just saying it isn't healthy for a pretty young woman to be shut away in an office all hours of the day—and night."

Silence hung heavy in the air for seconds while Guy and Leah caught each other's eyes. Was Wally making a point, or was she overreacting out of her insecurity?

Guy recovered quickly, settling back into a more comfortable position. "You think I work my staff too hard, huh? Maybe you're right. But this one's an eager beaver. What do you suggest I do?"

Wally stood and rammed on his hat. "What the heck," he grumbled to no one in particular.

"Wally—" Guy laughed "—I'm asking for suggestions."

Leah watched the old man turn his answer over in his mind before replying. She had the feeling he hadn't managed to tell her exactly what he'd come to say.

"What the heck," Wally repeated, and Leah smothered a laugh. Whatever was troubling him might take time to dig out.

Wally drew himself up to his full, spindly height. "Leah likes to garden. She used to do a lot of it where she came from, and she's got that little apartment of hers full of plants. There's greenery hanging and standing all over the place. But plants aren't the same as digging in the dirt, if that's what you like. You know that, and I know that."

Leah stared, fascinated. Wally's speech was the

longest she'd ever heard him make, and Guy's absorbed attention suggested he was as taken aback as she.

"I didn't know Leah was interested in gardening, Wally. She never told me." Guy glanced at her quickly, then back to Wally. "Is there something I should do about it?"

Wally hooked his thumbs in his belt and slouched. "This wasn't what I came to—" He rubbed agitatedly at the back of his neck. "Oh, what the heck. She wants a piece of garden. Give her one and give her some company while she's working there, too. She's special, this one, unusual. And while you're at it, invite her out. Have her dress up and take her dancing. Young stud like you letting the grass grow under his feet— What's the matter with you? Aw, hell!"

Leah had turned on the faucet before Wally started speaking. Water splashed steadily into the sink as she watched him stalk into the hall. He shut the front door with enough force to make the walls shudder.

Guy remained in his chair, staring at Leah until the sound of running water caught her attention and she turned back to the sink.

She felt Guy come behind her. "That old guy really cares about you," he said.

"I'd never have expected him to explode like that. Or to suggest you should take me out or—" Embarrassment made her stop.

A strong hand gripped her elbow, and Guy turned her to face him. "Beginning to believe not everyone around here is a malicious gossip who doesn't want to see us together?"

"I don't know what I believe anymore." Leah shut her eyes.

He smoothed back her hair. "But you aren't ready to fly away and leave me?"

"I'm not ready to go anywhere, Guy." She met his gaze steadily. "I'm not secure where I am, either."

"I know that, Leah. But I keep telling myself you will be in time, that we both will be."

"Wait and see, right?" She wasn't convinced, but there seemed to be no alternative solution to what they'd started.

"That's it, I guess." Guy rubbed both hands over his face, then looked at her again. "You should have told me you like to garden. Have as much ground as you like. I'll be glad to work with you. It's good to have company out there." He gave a wry grin. "But I think dancing is a little more closeness than either of us should try to handle right now."

After he'd left, Leah picked up the orchid plant Wally had brought and took it to her office. She could still see Guy's face in her mind and feel his presence.

"Wait and see..."

If that was the answer, the way to find herself with him permanently, it would have to do. Life without him would be worthless.

CHAPTER SEVEN

HEAT SCINTILLATED over the highway ahead of the jeep. Guy squinted and arched his neck. Sweat coursed between his shoulder blades. The two-hour drive from Tucson back to Phoenix had felt like two days. He was sticky all over, and a pain niggled at both temples.

When he turned off the Maricopa Freeway at Seventh Street and headed north into the city, a squeezing in his gut joined the headache. Every yard that raced beneath his wheels took him closer to the mushrooming dilemma he must face. The retreat had been different from any other he had experienced. Rather than the healing peace he'd anticipated, the three days he'd managed to stay away had been filled with a series of soul-wrenching revelations. Leah would wonder why he'd decided to return early. One minute he thought he knew exactly why; the next his brain became a confused jumble.

Time to think had been a blessing and a curse. Some of the hurt and frustration he'd never allowed himself to face after the breakup of his marriage had surfaced. There had been moments of panic when he'd deliberately remembered Susan, saw her gray eyes and white-blond hair, imagined her loose-limbed walk and the way she'd had of smiling up at him. They had loved with the abandon of the very young, never considering their happiness wasn't invincible. The vivid return of poignant old feelings had shocked and frightened him. He couldn't go through all that again with another woman.

At the intersection with Van Buren Street, Guy stopped for a light. He'd been unable to feel any rancor toward Susan even when they had parted. She'd been as sad as he, but for different reasons. For her, their love had died, and its passing had left her with an unhappy void. She'd openly explained her reasons for wanting to part, and he'd cried for her loss and for his and for his part in their failed relationship. He didn't know exactly how long he'd continued to love her, certainly for several years. She'd called him once; several times he'd called her. "I'll always care about you, Guy," she'd told him. "I'll always wish the best for you." But she'd stopped loving him, and in time he'd been able to relegate her to the past. In the last three days, he'd finally found a comfortable slot for her. A special but temporary gift, she was a real friend who had come into his life at the wrong time.

A blaring horn startled him into noticing that the light had turned green, and he jerked the vehicle forward. He was tired, and he wanted to see Leah. He checked his watch. Four o'clock. She should still be at the house.

The other clear discovery that had come to him during his quiet hours in Tucson had been the true depth of his growing feelings for Leah Cornish. His admission had brought flashes of intense joy. Until they had met, he'd been convinced he could never love or consider marriage again.

He visualized the official letter he'd received from Susan's lawyer in California a few weeks ago, stating that Susan Hamilton was filing for dissolution of her marriage. Mrs. Hamilton would prefer an uncomplicated proceeding, but if necessary, incompatibility could easily be proved. Cold, legal jargon. Simply, it came down to a bill of divorcement, and that sounded so much sadder to his mind. For Susan to decide on legal action after so long must mean she'd found someone else. Guy smiled faintly and rubbed sweat from the corners of his eyes. He was glad. She deserved to be happy. And when the divorce became final, he could seriously think of doing something about his own future. This time—if there was to be another time to give completely of himself—he had to be sure everything was right.

At McDowell Road, he took a left. Almost home. There were so many gray areas in his understanding of Leah. Two had glared at him persistently and would only become increasingly important if they decided to marry. First, she would be faced with the role of minister's wife, and for them to make a successful team, she'd have to be able to assume her part. Yet he didn't have any idea what she believed or even if she believed in anything at all. He'd waited for her to show some interest in the church, to attend a service, maybe. She had never mentioned faith or even entered the building.

Dust billowed when he turned the wheel at the corner of Fan Lane. The other concern was as big, if not bigger. She must become a complete person, capable of standing alone. Every day she took another step in that direction, but she still had a long way to go. She'd left one insular world for another. As far as he knew, she worked and went home—nothing more. Again, she'd found a safe, enclosed haven and was steadily settling into a pattern. If they married now, he believed their future together would be happy. He also believed

Leah would draw back to resume her place in the shadow of a husband, and he wouldn't allow that to happen. She was too bright, too talented, not to be a person in her own right.

Leah's yellow Volkswagen was parked in the shade of the oleander hedge. Guy sighed with relief and pulled in beside it. There was time to build a foundation for their future. Marriage, or even a consummated relationship, wasn't an issue yet and couldn't be until he was free. In the meantime, he had an idea how to broaden Leah's world. He hoped desperately she'd agree to his suggestion.

She wasn't in her office. The little room still smelled of fresh paint. Her choice of stark white had surprised him, but it opened up the small space. So did matching vertical, slatted shades. The order she'd achieved made him smile appreciatively before he recalled his own reaction to her efforts in his study. Well, she'd spoken of wanting to "organize something," and he'd invited her to try her talents on him. He winced. She'd looked so hurt and puzzled when he hadn't been enthusiastic.

Her perfume lingered in the air. Guy breathed deeply, and the muscles in his thighs contracted. He slung his grip over his shoulder and headed for the other side of the house, glancing into each room he passed. She could be working somewhere outside, he guessed. There hadn't been an opportunity before he left to discuss the piece of ground she wanted; however, he had told her to use as much as she liked.

He'd dropped the bag and stretched out on his bed before he heard the splash of water in the pool. The drape over the sliding-glass door was open. Lying on his side, propping his head, Guy could see sunlight bouncing in silver chips over the blue water and shimmering on the tanned shoulders of the woman who swam there.

Unconsciously, he pulled himself to the edge of the bed. She cut the surface smoothly in easy freestyle strokes. With each angling of an elbow, he saw a flash of her white suit.

At the far end of the pool, she pulled herself up to stand on the edge. Guy also stood and moved closer to the window. He knew she'd been swimming each afternoon since the pool had been filled, and he'd deliberately stayed out of the way until he was certain he wouldn't see her. He should have remembered today and kept his distance. This was what he'd been secretly afraid of, of seeing her, watching her and wanting her until he ached with the wanting.

She flicked water from her face and slicked the long, dark hair close to her head. Smooth limbs gleamed. Against the afternoon's cerulean sky, her slender body stood out in sharp relief. Guy traced each gentle curve and swell beneath the simple one-piece suit. He chewed his bottom lip. Joining her in the water on a blistering day would be perfectly natural, something no one could question—could they? The answer was obvious. Whether or not someone else questioned his motive was irrelevant. He'd know what drove him to her.

Leah made a clean dive, knifing into the water to head back in his direction. She moved with the economy of a practiced swimmer, and Guy closed his eyes. How often had Charles Cornish watched her in the secluded pool he'd probably had built for her alone? Guy detested the idea of the other man being with her and immediately detested himself for envying a man dead.

When Cornish married her, she'd been little more than a child, a beautiful, innocent girl. She'd somehow managed to retain the essence of that innocence and was undoubtedly far more beautiful now. Yet it was the very sense that she was naive and ingenuous that troubled him.

If she were more secure, better equipped to care of herself, would she need him? Would she still choose to be with him if she was exposed to other masculine company? Or had he become a convenient substitute for Charles Cornish, a man who, without her husband's wealth, still represented stability and protection? And was it possible, eventually, that she'd come to long for the luxuries she'd once enjoyed, then resent Guy for not being able to provide them? Thanks to his parents' legacy, he had a comfortable income to supplement his salary, but it didn't allow for many wild excesses.

Guy yanked the drapes closed. The uncertainties were multiplying, and he only hoped they'd both have the strength to face and work them through.

Leah saw Guy a second before he closed his bedroom drapes. She paused, her breath suddenly labored, her heart thundering. He wasn't due back until the day after tomorrow.

She glided to the wall of the pool. His shadow, dark through pale fabric, stayed unmoving until he raised a hand and appeared to rake fingers through his hair. He'd been watching her, and now he was shutting her out. Damn it all.

Leah pulled herself from the water. Was she such a threat to his pure soul? She frowned. Was she unworthy of the good minister, someone who might tempt, then sully him?

A desire to cry passed rapidly and was replaced by simmering fury. If he wanted her, as he repeatedly suggested he did, and he no longer cared for his wife, why

didn't he get a divorce? He'd said his reasons for remaining married were complicated, but he didn't say
why. Could he be clinging to his defunct marriage because it kept him safe from another permanent commitment?

The questions were endless, and Leah wasn't getting
any answers. The only way she'd ever have a chance
to understand this man, to get close enough to him to
win his trust, was to confront him—as often as it took
to get at the truth.

She sucked in a long breath through her mouth and
marched to his door. The shadow had moved away, but
she was certain Guy hadn't left his rooms. Her hard
rap on the glass stung her knuckles. She blew on them,
shook the hand, then stood with feet firmly planted and
elbows akimbo.

Seconds unreeled. Leah could almost hear each one
slip by. Her hand was raised to knock again when Guy
pulled the curtain back a few inches, then opened the
door. He didn't smile, and she saw his throat jerk as
he swallowed.

"Hi," she said brightly. "Thought you weren't coming back from your retreat until Friday."

He rested a forearm on the jamb and pressed his
brow against his fist. "Got all retreated out, I guess."
His eyes held hers for an instant, then lowered to her
mouth and down, slowly, hungrily, taking in her body.
With his visual touch, her skin heated.

"How was it?" Leah managed.

Guy's eyes flicked back to hers. "What?"

"The retreat," she repeated. "How was the retreat?"

"I hated it," he responded flatly.

"Oh." Leah tried to read his closed expression. "Why did you hate it?"

"I think you can work out the answer to that one."

She crossed her arms tightly, willing her heart to slow down. "I think I'd like to hear you tell me."

He lightly traced her bottom lip with his thumb. "Mmm. Three days away from you was too long."

So why don't you find a way for us to be together all the time? "I'm glad."

"Are you?"

"What kind of a question is that?" she asked softly.

"A rhetorical one." Guy's voice was equally gentle. "I hoped you might say you'd missed me, too."

He was rapidly driving her mad. And words weren't going to be enough. She needed tangible proof of his feelings, a sign she could hold on to. "Guy," she said, pushing back wet strands of hair, "it's hot. You must be boiling after that drive. Come and swim with me."

The fist supporting his forehead clenched. A battery of expressions crossed his features before he slowly shook his head. "Thanks, but I don't think so. There must be a stack of work waiting for me, and I might as well get started."

"If you'd stayed in Tucson as long as you planned, you wouldn't be catching up with your work." She felt him drawing back, insulating himself from her.

"That was probably one of the things that made me so edgy while I was away. I knew how far behind I was getting. See you in the morning." He moved to slide the door shut, but Leah grasped the metal rim. "I really would like to get a few things done."

"What you mean is..." Her voice sounded strangled, and she lifted her chin. "What you mean is that you want to do things to keep yourself away from me.

You're afraid to relax with me, to be close to me. Say it, Guy. Admit it.''

His smile was weary. "I probably won't get to my sermon before Friday. Would you mind typing it on Saturday? I'd pay you overtime, of course."

Dull rage expanded in Leah. He refused to meet any issue head-on, and he had the gall to talk about overtime pay as if she were no more to him than casual help. And only a few minutes before he'd admitted to missing her too much to finish his retreat. He confused her, tied her up in knots.

"That'll be fine, Guy," she said, feeling muscles in her jaw tremble. "As long as you pay me, of course." She half turned away, then changed her mind and faced him squarely. "What kind of a God requires a man to prove his belief by living on a mental island?"

Guy said nothing but took a step backward, his complexion paling beneath its deep tan.

Tears stung her eyes once more. "You need someone, Guy. So do I. Doesn't it say somewhere in that famous book of yours that it isn't good for man to live alone?" Her throat burned. He must hear the crying in her voice. "That means you and me, friend."

Several running strides took her back to the pool. A blind forward lunge of her body sent her deep into the water, which surrounded her in its cool, echoing blanket. She swam hard, concentrated on her breathing, the blood pumping through her veins, her limbs pushing against the resistance. She mustn't think. His God. She'd thrown at him the one element that must mean most in his life. If she wanted to kill any chance they had of grabbing a little happiness together, she'd chosen the perfect weapon.

She'd lost count of her laps when she caught sight

of long fingers and strongly muscled arms that matched her strokes entering the water. Guy swam beside her, his broad shoulders dappled with drops of liquid sunshine. She hesitated, trod water an instant, then struck out again. They didn't speak, only kept pace with each other one length after another.

Finally winded, Leah slowed to a lazy sidestroke and watched him. The swimsuit he wore was a brief black slash around his taut body. He passed her again, and powerful legs sent a back-rushing current at her. Muscle and sinew, perfectly toned, stretched and contracted. A thrill of desire flew up her spine.

At the far end, he stopped with both arms spread along the wall while he waited for her. Blond chest hair, turned darker by the water, made a tantalizing pattern. The distance between them narrowed until she could have reached out to touch him. Leah held position, paddling, her eyes questioning his. Guy didn't smile. "Leah," he said, and offered her his left hand.

She felt a beat miss somewhere in some unplayed tune, a step falter in the dance, before she placed her fingers in his and let him pull her near. They swayed, gently bobbed, and he took her other hand. Slowly, they rotated, keeping the distance of their bent arms between them. Leah gazed at long spiky lashes, into his clear eyes, and saw her own longing reflected there.

"It does say man shouldn't be alone," he whispered at last. "Do you read…" The question trailed off, and he pressed his lips together. "I don't want to be alone anymore. But we have a long way to go before we can do anything about it. You see that, don't you, Leah?"

She nodded assent as her brain screamed that she didn't understand anything but her need, their need and the way she felt with him.

Guy steadied her, then pulled himself up on the edge of the pool before hauling her up beside him. They sat, inches separating their legs, and swung their feet in unison. Leah could feel the warmth of his skin radiating into her flesh. Why did her throat have to hurt too much for her to speak? She ought to say something important.

"Neither of us can afford another mistake." Guy spoke low, as if more to himself than her.

"No." Leah glanced up at his clear profile. She wanted to tell him their being together couldn't be a mistake and to make him believe she was right.

He looked at her. "Let's not push this too hard." His hand hovered an inch above hers, then covered and held it on top of his tensed thigh. "Let's not go too far too fast and end up not even being friends."

Leah's heart swooped. His words made her hollow, a shell around the empty space she knew she'd become without him. "I never want us not to be able to see each other. I just… I guess I don't understand you. You won't let me."

His grip tightened. "I want us to understand each other. That's what this is all about. We don't understand each other yet. But we will, Leah, we will."

A stillness closed in around them—silence and warmth and the twin racing of their unspoken thoughts.

Leah turned her palm and lifted his fingers to her lips. She closed her eyes and felt him lean against her, guiding her head into the hollow of his shoulder.

His breathing moved the muscle beneath her cheek. "I feel so peaceful with you like this," he told her.

She wished they could stay as they were forever. "So do I. Guy, I'm sorry I said those things to you about—about—"

"God?" he interjected. "Not so hard to say. And I understand. Forget it. Just let me know if you ever want to talk more on the subject."

Leah didn't know what to say next. She coughed and looked at the sky. How did you admit to a minister, the man you'd fallen in love with, that your religious knowledge was limited to a few semiremembered Bible passages read as a child?

She straightened, suddenly tired. Being here with Guy was precious but tormenting. "It must be getting late. I could go over your appointments with you before I leave if you like." He would know she was running away from a further confrontation, but she needed time alone to think.

"The appointments can wait. I want to talk to you about an idea I had in Tucson." In a purposeful motion, he swiveled to sit cross-legged, facing her. "Have you ever thought about going back to school?"

Leah stared at him blankly.

"I mean to finish your high school requirements. How far from completion were you when you dropped out?"

She wound hair nervously behind one ear. More emotional battering. Now he was dragging up another part of her past she tried never to think about. "Less than a quarter," she mumbled.

"You're kidding," he said, laughing. "Why on earth couldn't you have stuck it out a couple of months longer?"

His incredulous amusement wounded her. He had no idea what her life had been like. "That wasn't a choice I was allowed to make. We needed money immediately, not in a couple of months. There are times, Guy, when eating takes precedence over everything else."

A small internal voice added, *And your mother's drinking habits and her need for cheap, flashy clothes to flaunt in front of her men.* But she kept the thought to herself.

Guy ran a knuckle along her jaw and clasped her shoulder, shaking her gently. "My turn to be sorry. You'd think in my line of work I'd know better than to make sweeping judgments. But how about it?"

"What?" Leah said.

"Going back to school. There are a couple of private colleges right in Phoenix where we could arrange for you to be enrolled for September to polish up and get your diploma. Then you could decide if you want to go farther."

She shook her head. He was going too fast. "You want me to go to school next month? That's only a couple of weeks away—less than that." Why? She'd been inept when she started working for him, but she thought he'd been pleased with her progress.

Guy tilted his head. "Don't you like the idea? There's plenty of time to get you registered as long as you make up your mind quickly."

"I suppose so," Leah said slowly. Another idea was dawning. This could be the next step in some plan to make sure she could make it alone if she had to leave. And she might have to leave eventually if they remained in Guy's self-imposed, don't-touch holding pattern.

"You don't sound very enthusiastic. Frightened?"

"No!" she shot back with a vehemence that jolted her. "No, I'm not afraid. Why should I be? But I'd like to know exactly why you're so keen on the idea." She raised her chin.

He looked puzzled; then his expression cleared. "Do

you think I'm dissatisfied with your work or something?'' When she didn't answer, he added, ''That's exactly the problem, isn't it. Well, you're wrong. I've never had anyone as efficient as you working for me. You're terrific, a miracle. I can't believe what you've accomplished in a few weeks. And neither can I believe the way you taught yourself to type. I know you don't need more training to do what you do for me. But I want to feel you could make it anywhere, and for that you need to finish high school requirements and, possibly, think about something beyond that.'' He paused, watching for her reaction. ''Hey, if you had less than a quarter to go, you must have been a grade ahead.''

''Two,'' she said, and immediately blushed. ''Didn't mean anything, really.''

Guy cupped the side of her face. ''It means, my humble little friend, that you are very bright. But we both know that, don't we?''

She ignored the question. ''I wouldn't mind going back to school, I suppose,'' Leah said, sighing. Silently, she weighed her true feelings on the subject. Whatever happened with Guy, she did need to be able to care for herself. And to survive in a competitive world, she needed training and qualifications. ''I'll do it,'' she announced in a voice that sounded authoritative and foreign to her.

''Great,'' Guy cried, grinning broadly. ''Just great. Come on; this calls for a toast. Let's get some iced tea.''

He dragged Leah to her feet and strode ahead toward the house. She trailed behind, studying his broad back and narrow hips, the long, strong legs. Guy Hamilton was steadily becoming the center of her existence. But his exuberance at her positive response to more schooling provoked a sickening constriction in her stomach.

At the door, his smile brilliant, Guy waited for her to catch up. Leah turned up the corners of her own mouth valiantly. His happiness was out of proportion, born of some much deeper meaning than the obvious one he'd offered. Leah thought she knew the true reason. She was one of his good works. Even though she couldn't deny the conviction that he desired her physically and cared for her in some special way, his consuming mission was to make her whole.

As they parted to change, Leah's nausea became a pain. He intended to patch her and mend her so that, if necessary, he could feel good about setting her free, like a bird after he'd mended its wing.

ON SATURDAY MORNING, Leah got up early. She dressed in lightweight jeans and knotted the tails of a pink checked shirt to leave an inch of midriff bare. Yesterday had been stiflingly muggy, an ominous stillness eventually giving way to lightning that tore the sullen sky into jagged swatches. For an hour Arizona's monsoon warning crackled, and distant thunder rolled before the downpour started. Then hours of sheeting rain in hundred-degree heat left the earth steaming and popping. Although the sun was shining now, today promised more of the same weather.

While she made coffee, she hummed. She wasn't going to spend the day alone, as she had every weekend since she'd arrived in Phoenix. Typing Guy's sermon might not be what most women would look forward to as a treat, but Leah did. She enjoyed working, and she would be near him—unless he had other plans for the day.

Her stomach dipped, and she pushed the thought away. He was bound to be around at least when she arrived.

Since she'd been alone, she'd slipped into the habit of skipping breakfast. The kind of thing people living alone did, she acknowledged, and rummaged in the refrigerator for a container of yogurt. The waistband of her jeans was loose. Time to start eating properly; she was already thin enough.

She glanced around her tiny apartment and smiled. It was the first place she'd ever had that was truly her own. With Wally's permission and aid, hooks had been fastened to the beam at the ceiling apex, and lush hanging ferns tangled their tender shoots with trailing philodendrons. A hoya's shiny leaves snaked jealously down to guard an inverted umbrella of fragrant pink blossoms.

Leah took her coffee and yogurt to a glass-topped bamboo table by the window and settled to watch birds flit noisily about their early-morning business in the ancient sycamore tree outside.

She realized she was still smiling, and a tranquil happiness stole over her. Yesterday, Guy had driven her through the rainstorm to an adult learning center in Scottsdale. The city suburb was a half-hour ride from St. Mark's. Guy had encouraged her to enroll in a private facility nearby and offered to help with the tuition. Leah had been adamant. The Scottsdale program was free, and she didn't want help. She certainly didn't mind traveling the extra distance.

Now that the step had been taken, she felt strangely excited. School had been an exhilarating challenge to her. Having to leave before graduation was a disappointment she'd never forgotten, and now she would

have another chance. She shouldn't have needed someone else to suggest she go back. Too many years of
not thinking for herself had left their mark.

A tentative tap, followed by Wally's distinctive
"Haloo," broke her reverie, and she jumped up to let
him in.

"Morning, Wally." She waved him inside. "Coffee's hot."

He gave her his nervous smile, driving the familiar
deep wrinkles across his thin cheeks. "I had my coffee,
thanks, Leah. Gotta get on the road." He held out a
key, and she took it. "I'm going to be in Mesa for a
week or so. Joan's sister and her family live there."

"I'm glad." Leah patted his arm. "It'll do you good
to have a break. Don't worry about things here. I'll
keep an eye on the place. Was there anything you particularly wanted me to do while you're gone?"

Wally rolled the brim of his straw hat in both hands.
"I guess..." He crossed the room to examine the hoya
blossom. "Darn, but you've got a way with growing
things. I don't think I ever saw one of these bloom
outside a greenhouse before."

Leah watched him, apprehensive without knowing
why. "I don't have too many talents, Wally. I guess
God decided I should have at least one. Was there anything you wanted me to do? You started to say something."

He swung around, a frown puckering his brow.
"This isn't easy, Leah. I've been trying to tell you for
days." The bony brown fingers had unconsciously
worked a piece of straw loose in the hat brim, and now
he studied it closely.

She waited, cold slicking over her skin. The day
Wally visited the rectory, she'd known he wanted to

shed a burden. Guy's arrival had stopped him; then she'd assumed Wally's outburst about her needing recreation was the original purpose for his visit.

"I did get a patch of garden, Wally. I'm still learning how to cultivate the soil here—it's very different from what I'm used to. Thought I might try vegetables, though. You always get more than you can use yourself, and there's certainly plenty of folks to share them with."

He pressed his mouth into a straight line. The length of straw had completely unraveled. "You're one in a million, my girl. Someone who cares. It isn't fair."

Every word he spoke was becoming part of an incomplete puzzle. At last, Leah took a sinewy forearm and led Wally to the chair opposite hers by the window. "Sit. And stop hedging. Say what you came to say."

The thump with which he hit the chair seat spelled reluctance. "You believe in God?" he blurted abruptly, and immediately ran a hand over his reddened face.

"I—yes." Leah frowned. "Never had much time to think about it, but I suppose I do in my own way."

Wally relaxed visibly. "Well, that's that one, then. I told them you did."

"Them?" Leah asked. "Who wanted to know?"

The jerky pulling at his hat brim resumed. She had to resist the temptation to take it from him before he destroyed it completely.

"Wally? Who?"

He rocked his head slowly from side to side. "Just some of the women. And Elsie Culver's husband, George. He's not such a bad stick. Never works, though."

Leah wasn't interested in George Culver's employment record. The cold on her skin had wormed into her belly. "That's all they said? Did I believe in God?"

Wally was on his feet, his features set in an angry mask. "Busybodies, the lot of them. The minister deserves to be happy, and I can't think of anyone I'd rather see him happy with than you."

He stared at her fiercely, but Leah didn't offer any comment. Her heart pounded in her ears.

"They're just jealous. Every one of those women is half in love with the man themselves. But you've got to do something or he's going to get hurt."

She found her voice. "Will you tell me exactly what they're saying and what I ought to do? Please, Wally."

The hat was now a mangled mess. He met her eyes with anguished difficulty. "Guy's still a married man. He should have done something about that a long time ago, but it wasn't my place to talk to him about it. He's always been a private one about his own business. Never talked to a soul about why his wife never came—just stayed to himself. Not healthy for a young man.

"They're saying you two met somewhere else and started— They say you planned to get together even before you were widowed and the job at Guy's house is a cover for—" Wally picked up her coffee cup and took a swallow, apparently without realizing what he'd done. The color in his cheeks had darkened. "What the heck." He backed toward the door. "You and Guy mean a lot to me. There isn't any sin in the pair of you—just a normal need between two young folks. But these biddies can rack it up. Guy could lose his job here if you don't straighten things out."

Leah poked her hair with shaking fingers. "We haven't done anything wrong," she breathed.

"Whatever you do, it won't be wrong." Wally's scratchy voice hardened. "And it's only your business, anyway. But I've got to make sure you know what you're up against. They say the two of you are living in sin. That the married man who's supposed to be their spiritual leader is openly committing adultery."

CHAPTER EIGHT

"Guy!" Leah called. "Guy, where are you?" Her voice bounced, unanswered, through the house. The panic that had started while Wally made his pained announcements swelled to close her throat in a rigid vise.

She reached Guy's empty study and approached his bedroom. "Guy?" she asked tentatively. When he didn't reply, she knocked at the door, and it swung wide beneath her hand. She saw his unmade bed and the covers twisted on the floor; a glimpse beyond revealed a discarded towel and steamy air redolent of his clean, sense-twisting smell. But no Guy. He had showered and left the house.

The bubble in her throat broke into a hiccuping sob. "Where are you, damn it?" The jeep was still parked outside. He couldn't have gone far.

Tears sprang to her eyes, making blurry shapes out of the furniture as she stumbled into the hall and back to her office. She sniffed and dug in her purse for a tissue. He'd asked her to come. If nothing else, he should be here to tell her what he wanted done. And she needed him now. "I need you," she murmured aloud. "I *need* you."

The time... In her anxiety to talk to Guy, she'd left her apartment immediately after Wally. Now the clock on her office wall showed only eight-thirty. She'd agreed to start at ten. Guy wouldn't expect her to be so early.

A loud snap pulled her attention to the window. She saw through the blinds to an ashen sky streaked by a single golden shard of lightning. Thunder roiled, building to a muffled explosion before another crackling glow speared earthward. The rain might not take so long to come today, and Leah was glad. The still pressure in the air around her echoed the mounting tension in her head, and a wild storm would be a relief.

He could be outside working. The lightning was dangerous—he shouldn't be in the open. Leah ran through the front door and around the side of the house. The garden, the grounds, the pool—everywhere she searched was deserted. Her heart jammed against her lungs, and she rushed on, repeating her circuit until she stood, breathless, beside his jeep and her own Volkswagen.

The church... As soon as she thought of it, she noticed that the white building's door stood open. He often went there in the morning—maybe every morning, for all she knew. Several times she'd met him as she arrived for work when he was returning from the church.

Scattered drops of warm rain hit the path. Leah started to walk, watching wet splotches slam pale concrete and spread, faster and faster, until their outlines merged. The top of her hair and her face were damp by the time she inched cautiously through the entrance of the low stucco structure.

Guitar music, played with strong intensity, surprised her. The building was cool and dimly lit. Leah tiptoed along the back wall, squinting. When her eyes adjusted to the gloom, she made out rows of wooden pews be-

tween stone pillars. Several electric candles flickered
in wall sconces toward the front, where a brilliantly
embroidered cloth covered an otherwise-empty altar.
Apart from a blackboard with large numbers chalked
on it and felt banners too far away to make out, Leah
noticed only a plain oak pulpit to one side and the man
who sat in the front pew with his back to her.

Guy was playing a guitar, his body bent to cradle
the instrument, his ear inclined to its strings.

She started forward but halted abruptly, gripping the
cool wood of a pew before sliding in to sit. From here
she could watch him unnoticed. Leah scrunched down,
supporting her chin on the heel of one hand. Guy
played on to the conclusion of the piece and paused,
jaw lifted, the sideways tilt of his face showing his eyes
tightly closed. He nodded slowly, rhythmically, before
strumming again. His deep, mellow voice joined the
notes, and Leah's heart made a somersault. Each unfamiliar word, singing of joy and love, grabbed her
willing, pliant senses and wound them into a desperate
longing. She longed to go to Guy and hold him, but
she couldn't. They were strangers. No, not strangers,
but separated by a world she barely comprehended.

Here he was comfortable and at peace. Here Leah
was an intruder. It was his place, and he was immersed
in something she might never be able to accept as part
of her life. The gentle words, his voice, touching,
reaching, wove a path around her soul. She hadn't
known he sang or played the guitar. How many other
things didn't she know about Guy? And how could she
expect him to be interested in an uneducated, untal-
ented woman such as she for more than a fleeting period when he needed diversion? They shared nothing
but physical attraction.

A final, haunting chord sounded, and Guy rested the guitar between his feet. She saw him sigh, and although she couldn't hear it, felt as if his breath had warmed her face. Leah adjusted her weight, planning to slip back to the house unseen. The muffled squeak of her tennis shoe on linoleum stopped her, but not before Guy's head whipped around.

"Hello?" He searched a moment before sighting her. "Leah! Hi. I didn't hear you arrive. Come sit with me."

He held out a hand and shifted in the pew to make room for her. Leah bit into a trembling lip while she approached. She let him clasp her hand between both of his and sank down beside him. The radiance of his smile and glowing eyes seemed to widen the gulf between their two lives. Had his wife felt the same way, as if she stood outside his serene world, looking in but never able to enter?

Leah studied their fingers, entwined on his knee. "I didn't know you played the guitar or sang. It's beautiful. Your voice is beautiful."

"Shucks, thank you, ma'am." He was laughing, relaxed and glad she was with him. He must have questioned her religious feelings, just as others had, and seeing her in the church probably made him hope she shared his beliefs.

Leah hated destroying his calm moment. "There's a lot we don't know about each other, isn't there?"

He made little circles on the inside of her wrist. "Not so much, I think. Some people spend a lifetime together and know less."

She had to change the subject, to zero in on her real reason for being here. "It doesn't matter, Guy. I've got to talk to you. Wally came to see me this morning. He—he—'' The rest of the sentence wouldn't come.

"What's wrong?" Guy sat straighter. "Look at me."

"Oh, Guy." Slowly, she brought her eyes to his. "I should never have come to Phoenix. You were kind enough to be interested in me and write to me after Charles died. That should have been enough. Why did I try to cling to you? Why did I have to charge in here and mess up your life?"

He frowned. "You've been crying. Sweetheart, please tell me what's happened." Strong but gentle arms wrapped her tightly against him.

"The worst, Guy. That's what's happened." She whispered weakly against his throat. "I've gotten you into deep trouble, just as I knew I would."

He tilted her chin up. "You aren't making a whole lot of sense. How could you cause me any trouble?"

"By giving in to my own selfishness." Leah pushed roughly away, turning her head to avoid the startled look in Guy's eyes. "We can't go on with this," she said. Another tear trickled down her cheek, and she covered her mouth with a shaky hand. "I'm a danger to you, and I won't hurt someone I—I care about."

Guy put an arm around her tense shoulders. "Okay. You've got my undivided attention. And I want to know why you're crying. I can't stand to see you like this."

"The whole parish is buzzing with rumors about us." The air seemed too thin. Leah clenched her teeth to stop them from chattering. "Wally's worried sick you'll lose your job. And so am I."

His sigh made Leah stare at his lifted profile. "You

fuss too much, my friend,'' he told her. "So does good old Wally.''

"No, Guy, no. You aren't a fool or naive; you can't be. Only an innocent would believe this situation isn't as volatile as dry tinder.'' She spread her fingers over his cheek and pulled his face around. "Elsie Culver wasn't fooled when she found us together in my office. Poor Wally almost choked trying to get out what's being said.''

Guy entwined the fingers of one hand with hers and shook his head. "I've heard the same things Wally's heard, and I'm not worried, little one. Not *too* worried. Please, don't let this upset you. These are good people. They're human, that's all. It'll all blow over.''

"Damn it.'' Leah balled both fists against his chest. "Sometimes I wonder if you and I live in the same world.'' She pounded him once, twice, but gently, helplessly. "Don't tell me again how good the malicious gossip mongers in this parish are. I know they are, somewhere underneath. But I also know they're capable of doing you harm by taking away what matters most to you—your work. Your whole world could come crashing down around your ears if whoever runs this joint fires you.''

"Whoever runs this joint?'' Guy's laugh was almost drowned out by an endless bass thunder roll. He bracketed her face in his hands. "You're marvelous. Sounds like the world's coming down around us, anyway. Your hair's wet, my gloomy prophet. Must be raining already. As soon as it passes over, we'd better get to the house so you can dry out.''

"Don't you care?'' Frustration threatened to suffocate Leah. "Or are you so blind you don't really see what's going on here? For goodness' sake, if Wally heard—good old faithful Wally, who doesn't have time for chitchat—the story must just about have traversed the state by now.'' She rallied her courage before adding, ''They think we're having an affair.''

Guy held her shoulders lightly, searching her features, his eyes sparking with some emotion she couldn't read. ''Do you know who really runs this *joint*, as you put it?'' He lowered his lids a fraction before going on. ''God does. And he's not about to allow us to be punished for nothing.''

Leah stiffened. She couldn't get into a theological discussion with him; she didn't want to. She pressed her lips into a firm line.

When Guy looked at her again, she recognized the light in his eyes—fervor and a deep desire for understanding she couldn't give him. ''We aren't having an affair,'' he said. ''As long as we know that's true, there's nothing to fear—from anyone. Trust, Leah. That's all I ask. We don't have to go over why I believe what I believe or whether you agree. Maybe one day, but not now. For now I'm asking you to put the burden on me, because I can handle it, and *I'm* not concerned.''

''But Guy—''

He cut her off. ''No. No buts. I love this congregation, and they love me. We'll work it out. Shall we see how hard it's raining.''

There was no arguing with him. He *was* oblivious of the real world. Leah waited while he stowed the guitar in a cupboard and let him lead her by the hand to the door. She'd intended to insist she get out of his life and out of Phoenix. He made it impossible to push her conviction of impending disaster. If she suggested going, he'd only remind her she'd promised not to and make her feel like a suspicious heel.

"Its not too bad out there." Guy smiled back at her in the entrance. "Let's make a run for it."

TWO HOURS PASSED before Leah finally sat at her typewriter with Guy's sermon. While she'd been in the church, rain had beaten down two hydrangea bushes she'd planted in a corner bed by the pool. Staking and tying hadn't taken long, particularly with Guy's help, but then they'd decided to shore up a row of seedling orange trees as a precautionary measure.

Working beside him, Leah had felt an overwhelmingly poignant closeness. Together they'd scooped at wet mud, their hands touching often, their eyes constantly seeking each other's, their laughter joining while tension steadily ebbed. Afterward they had washed up in the kitchen sink and laughed again at their dirt-streaked faces. Special times—little capsules of happiness she must treasure and guard as memories for the uncertain future, when they might be parted forever.

"Any questions?" Guy loped in and came to stand behind her. "I'm going over to the Krauses'."

Leah glanced quizzically up at him.

"Mrs. Krause is the woman who had a hysterectomy," Guy reminded her. "She's been home a while and insists she's coping, but I doubt it. Her husband may even have taken off—he disappears from time to time. One of these days he'll forget to come back altogether, and that mightn't be such a bad idea. At least she'd have one less mouth to feed and know where she stands.

"Anyway, I'm going to take her kids to the zoo at

Papago Park. The rain's stopped, so we should be okay.''

''Yes,'' Leah replied, disappointed he wouldn't be around as she'd hoped, then guilt-ridden at her own selfish reaction. ''If I have any problems with the sermon we can go over them later.''

He touched her shoulder fleetingly. ''Thank you, Leah. We're beginning to make quite a team, aren't we?''

''I guess.'' Leah rolled paper into the typewriter.

''Nothing else we need to discuss now?''

She bent her head. ''No, you'd better get going.''

''Yes. Leah—'' His words trailed off as her face came up. ''See you later, then.''

Leah felt a nerve in her cheeks twitch. ''Goodbye,'' she said hastily. ''Give those little Krauses a good time. They probably don't get too many.''

He hovered at her elbow. ''Right. I guess I'll go, then.''

''Mmm.'' She nodded, starting to type, her head down again.

''See you later?'' He backed away.

''Later.'' Leah managed not to look up until she heard the front door close. She released a long breath when the jeep's engine turned over and rumbled steadily away.

She slumped in her chair and drove both hands into her windswept hair. Emotional tension scrambled her thoughts and filled her with sweet tumult that threatened to suffocate her. He'd been no more anxious to leave than she was to see him go.

''Trust,'' he'd said. Believe everything would be all right. Leah wanted to believe she and Guy were meant to be together despite each roadblock thrown in their way.

The typing went slowly. Guy's handwriting deteriorated as he became immersed in his topic, and Leah stopped frequently to pore over a sentence.

"Believe." Leah banged out the word and paused. She'd already discovered that reading too closely while she worked slowed down the process. But now she pushed back her chair slowly and reached for the next page of the homily.

"We don't hurt those we love," Guy had written. "We don't see evil in those we love." She slid farther down in her seat and crossed her feet on the desk.

"Love and trust. That's what it's all about—the whole ball of wax." Her eyes skimmed words more and more rapidly. When she reached the bottom, she dropped the sheet to her lap and reached for the next, and the next, until the final page lay crumpled beneath her clenched fingers.

"Believe. Believe in each other's basic goodness. Without charity there's no hope. If we look for crud, expect distrust, we'll find and deserve them. The pure heart trusts, and evil cannot thrive there."

He'd written his message more to her than to his congregation. The conviction grew within Leah and swelled until her pulse pounded the truth in her ears. Guy might not even have realized what he was doing, but he'd said the same words to her earlier, begged her to trust, tried over and over again to assure her his people were good. But he knew she didn't trust, didn't believe, and had left her alone here with his plea for her to change.

She'd never be able to live up to his standards.

CHAPTER NINE

LEAH'S DASHBOARD CLOCK read two minutes to midnight. She'd driven for hours, walked for hours and driven again. Her course had been aimless while she struggled with decisions she could no longer evade. She was exhausted and had no idea exactly how long ago she had left Guy's house and his untyped sermon, trying to run from what she must do now.

She turned into Wally's driveway, and her heart jammed in her throat. Guy's jeep was parked in front of the porch, and she could see his tall, shadowy form leaning on the hood. Too late to keep on going; he'd already seen her.

Before she had time to stop the car completely, Guy pushed upright and strode toward her. The headlights picked up the planes and angles of his strained features and his tousled hair. As she applied the hand brake, he wrenched open the Volkswagen's door and all but hauled her out bodily.

"Leah." He swung her in front of him, and his grip on her arms hurt. "For God's sake, Leah. Where have you been? I've been looking for you for hours."

She had begun to shake, and her jaw ached with the effort to control its quivering. She would not look at him.

"When I got back from the Krauses', I found my sermon on the floor and no sign of you. Nothing. No message. No you.'' His voice broke. "You're shivering. What's happened?"

"Nothing," she whispered, trying to pull free.

Guy shook her and brought his face close. "Tell me what's happened. You look awful."

"Thanks."

"Oh, hell. I'm too beaten for this. At least you could have left a note. I've died over and over in these past hours. You might have been in a hospital—but I checked every one in town, so I knew you weren't. Then I was terrified I'd find you in some ditch—injured or…or dead." Clearly exhausted, he dropped his hands to his sides. "Come on." He recouped visibly and reached for her elbow. "Let's go inside where we can talk. If I don't get coffee, I'm going to keel over, and you've got to need something—sleep above all else, I should think."

She ought to tell him, here and now, that her first instinct of the day had been the right one, that she intended to follow it, to get out of his life immediately. But the lead that seemed to have replaced blood in her veins dragged her down and weakened her resolve. Mutely, she walked with him up the steps to her apartment and let him take her key.

He flipped on the switch to the tiny entryway light and instantly slid a hand beneath her hair to clasp her neck. His piercing appraisal of her made Leah want to hide. She had to be a total wreck. Every pore in her skin felt clogged with grit, and mud from earlier in the day had dried on her tennis shoes and ankles. Her hair, long since dried but unbrushed, was a tangled mass.

"Sit down," he ordered shortly. "Before you fall down. I'll put on a kettle or something." He hadn't been back to her apartment since the day he'd helped her move in but seemed oblivious of his surroundings. "Then we'll talk."

"Guy," she began, not moving. "You're the one who looks as if he needs sleep." Stress had pinched his face and made it appear sharp. White lines ran from each flaring nostril to the corners of his compressed mouth. Guilt at causing him to suffer twisted her insides, but she closed it out and made herself go on. "I'm fine. Please go home and forget about me. It'll be best for both of us, honestly."

His laugh was hollow. "Forget about you? You really don't know a whole lot about me, do you? I'm never going to forget about you. What's the saying…? 'When the going gets tough, the tough get going.' Well, lady, you're looking at a tough man, an obstinate man. You may flag along the way, but be prepared to be picked up and dragged on by me for as long as it takes."

Leah shrugged despondently. She was too tired to argue. Her suitcases and the boxes she'd used to transport her few household necessities from Texas were stored in the coat cupboard. While Guy hovered, she dragged them out and opened the first case on top of the sofa bed.

"What are you doing?"

Leah ignored him and went to the closet. She grabbed an armload of clothes without bothering to remove their hangers.

When she turned toward the couch, Guy blocked her path. "You're going to answer me. What do you think you're doing?"

"If you can't work it out, there's no point in my trying to explain."

"Oh, I can work it out, all right. Only it's not going

to happen. You think I'm going to allow you to run away without even giving us a chance to discuss the sudden change in you since I left this morning. No dice.'' He lifted the clothing from her arms and dumped it over a chair back. ''Why did you stop in the middle of typing my sermon?''

''I *can't* talk about it, Guy. Don't you understand I've had enough of this emotional wringer I've been put through for weeks. Look—'' She met his eyes, then glanced at his mouth and swallowed hard. ''I can't be what you need. When I found you this morning, I intended to tell you I was leaving Phoenix. I should have gone weeks ago, the minute I realized the position you'd be in as long as I stayed. But now I am going, and nothing you can say will change my mind.'' She'd picked up a dress and started stuffing it into the case when he placed a hand very gently over hers.

''How about if I say I think I love you?''

Leah stood quite still. Nothing moved, not Guy, not a muscle in her own body, not a waft of air. Time hung, suspended, before she crumpled, cross-legged onto the floor.

''It isn't fair,'' she mumbled, hunching over.

Guy sank to his knees beside her and stroked her bent head. ''Why, sweet—why isn't it fair? Because I said I thought I loved you?''

''Because every time I try to clear up this chaos and make a fresh start for both of us, you do or say something that muddles me up again.'' She looked at him squarely. ''I can't pretend anymore. I can't be your sexy saint, or whatever you want me to be. Held but never completely possessed. Waiting without knowing what I'm waiting for. Do you have any idea why I couldn't go on with your sermon?''

"No. I asked, but you wouldn't tell me." He swiveled to sit on the rug and lean back against the couch where he could observe her.

"Every word you wrote was aimed at me, wasn't it?" She raised her face. "All the stuff about trust and believing and not hurting people we love— You weren't talking to your congregation but to me."

The green eyes stared back fixedly. "Wrong," he said at last, flatly. "If you had really thought through what I wrote, you'd know exactly what I meant. Aren't you the one who kept telling me my people were gossips—some of them, anyway—'malicious gossip mongers' was the phrase you used yourself only this morning."

Leah rubbed her face hard. "And you told *me* they were good. You've kept telling me they were good. So what was I supposed to think you meant? Who was I supposed to assume you were writing to?"

"My fault again," Guy said bitterly. "Where did you go?"

She buried her eyes on folded arms atop her knees. "I drove around," she said indistinctly. "And walked. I don't know where I went."

Her wrists were gently clasped. He ran his hands up her arms until he could pull her gently onto his lap. Cradled, folded against his faded blue shirt, Leah allowed her tense body to relax slightly. She smelled him, heard his heart, steady beneath her ear, and felt his warmth permeate her flesh.

"I was writing to my parishioners, Leah. The Elsie Culvers who stare up at me every Sunday."

The absentminded grazing of his rough chin across her brow soothed her. "But you said you weren't worried about what anyone else said." She snuggled closer, raising a hand to trace the stubble of his beard from sideburn to neck. "You said you weren't concerned."

He sighed, then tightened his arms around her. "Sometimes I talk a good story. I am worried, and I am concerned. And knowing they'd do this to me hurts like hell."

Leah shifted and slipped from his arms to sit facing him. "You weren't straight with me." She gripped his shoulders. "You pretended. I can't figure out what you want from me, Guy. It's obvious I'm a problem here. I'm willing to go, but you say you want me to stay. *I* want to stay. You say you *think* you love me." After a moment's hesitation, she rested two fingertips on his mouth. "What does it all mean? What do you want me to do?"

Guy kissed her palm, then flattened it against his chest. "Wait for a while. I can't give you some deep, well-thought-out meaning for the way things have happened between us. We met by chance, more by chance than most people do. I was drawn to you then, but you were out of my reach. When you were free, some thread of what we both felt that first night brought you to me. Maybe our paths have been steadily converging all our lives, or maybe we're just two people reaching for each other out of loneliness." He crossed his arms around her back and spoke beside her ear. "It takes time to be sure. And I guess what I'm asking is for you to give us that time and to be willing to wait until I'm free to consider a complete relationship."

"You don't have to be free in the legal sense before I can know if what I feel for you is real. You've been alone for six years. How can it be wrong for us to be together?" She was pleading, but she didn't care.

"It's wrong for me." The timbre of his voice, dipping lower, chilled her. "And it could turn out to be a mistake for you if you discover I was only a convenient man to turn to. There are other men in the world. You need to be sure it's me you want. I need to be sure."

The moment buzzed with the complete absorption that enclosed them. Leah couldn't bring herself to even discuss the possibility of caring for another man.

She straightened until she could see Guy's face. "You're talking as if we were discussing the rest of our lives."

"Aren't we?"

Leah's stomach made a slow roll, and a lump formed in her throat. "Yes." She searched for a way to say everything in her heart but couldn't find the right words. All he had to do was reach out his arms, to take her—as far and as fast as he wanted. Although she'd never be more ready for Guy, she knew they would wait until he was as sure as she.

His face, resting sideways on his knee, was inches from hers. When he spoke, warm breath fanned her cheek. "You start school next week. A whole new world is going to open up for you."

"If I stay." She couldn't look away.

"It's time to face some hard facts, Leah. You should be able to go it on your own. Finishing school will make that easier. Don't run off and start looking for another safe place to hide. You've got too much on the ball to waste yourself."

She moved to grip her shins. "I know I need to be self-sufficient." Defiance rippled through her. "I'm not searching for someone to look after me, if that's what you're afraid of."

His eyes measured her for some time before he replied. "No, I don't really believe you are. But if it's right for us now, it'll be right in a few weeks or months or however long it takes. Let's take our time and be very sure."

Leah let out an uneven breath. "You said you thought you loved me. Didn't that mean anything?"

"You know it does." He smiled and pushed strands of hair behind her ear. "I'm just pointing out that we have to explore all the angles and keep them straight."

"Then..." She pressed finger and thumb into the corners of her eyes. "Then, while we're being logical and analytical, we'd better remember that I'm pretty certain I love you."

"I hope you find out you do," Guy replied softly and without hesitation. "Are you as drained as I am? I could sleep sitting up right now."

Leah nodded. If she wanted him, and she did, there was no choice but to do things his way.

"Do you suppose we could haul out this bed of yours and just lie together?" he asked. "I don't know if I can drive for a while."

She opened her eyes and blinked at him. "I guess we could do that. Sure you're not afraid I'll ravage you?" Her owlish grin brought Guy's answering chuckle as he pulled her to her feet.

"Funny lady. You terrify me. Stand back while I fix this thing."

When they lay side by side on top of the covers, Guy tentatively threaded an arm behind Leah's neck and pulled her head onto his shoulder. She felt so good, so soft. Weary as he was, a flicker of arousal seared him. He closed his eyes and stroked her hair, trying to unwind.

"Guy." Her voice was muffled against his shirt.

"Mmm." One of her jean-clad knees had automatically hooked over his thighs. This might be more than even iron-willed Hamilton could handle. He held very still. "What were you going to say?" he prompted. She'd fallen silent while she fiddled with one of his shirt buttons.

"Can't remember exactly." Her hand went to rest at his throat. "But it was probably something about not wanting anyone else but you."

She sounded fuzzy, thank God. With any luck, she'd fall asleep, and then he'd better get out of here. Tiredness was probably the only thing saving them right now. In the morning, when they were both wide awake, the story was likely to be different.

"Will you promise me something?" Guy whispered into her hair. "The next time you're upset about something, would you please tell me before you decide to drive all over the state? I don't think my blood pressure could take another strain like today."

Regular breathing was Leah's only reply. Her body had gone limp. Her hand slid gradually from his chest, and she half turned onto her back.

The room was dim, lit only by the meager globe in the entryway. Guy waited several minutes before carefully disentangling himself until he could sit on the edge of the bed.

He slid his shoes back on, keeping vigil over Leah's supine form. Heavy lashes flickered, and he held his breath, but she didn't wake.

Her lips parted, and he felt his own do the same and imagined his mouth pressed to hers, to every part of her. Unable not to, he watched the gentle rise and fall of her breasts. The fire in his groin was instant. He wanted to be inside her, surrounded by her.

The air, when he left the apartment, was too warm to cool his heated skin. At the bottom of the steps, he paused to look at a black sky that seemed pinned in place by glittering star tacks.

He gritted his teeth. His damned principles were tearing him, and her, apart. As soon as the divorce was final and he could be certain Leah wanted him for himself, there'd be no more holding back.

FIVE DAYS LATER, on her first night in school, Leah sat doodling in the margin of a notebook sheet. It was five days since she and Guy had lain together and she'd awakened alone, disappointed to find him gone. She smiled to herself. Although nothing direct was mentioned, they were more at ease with each other, and she'd begun to dream of the future—with Guy.

The bell for break rang. Leah filed out of the classroom and followed other students to a commons area. So far, her first night at school had been a snap.

She'd found a math evaluation simple. The ease with which she remembered her facts had both surprised and pleased her. Next would come English, and again she didn't anticipate difficulty.

Along with a teenaged boy, she was one of the youngest class members. Leah scanned the couches and chairs in the room until she located the boy, then grimaced. She hadn't been mistaken when she'd thought he was having difficulty staying awake at his desk. Now he was scrunched down in the corner of an orange plastic couch, his eyes closed.

Leah strolled to sit at the other end of the same couch and poured iced coffee from the thermos she'd brought. Over the rim of the cup, she studied Dan Ingalls. She knew his name from the roll call. He was dozing lightly, his thin wrists and hands twitching occasionally.

Everything about the boy was thin, too thin. Thick, straight black hair fell forward over a broad forehead; his brows were as dark as his hair and finely arched. A handsome kid. She'd noticed the brilliance of his blue eyes when he arrived ten minutes late for class. She'd also noticed the tight line of his wide mouth, the too-old, too-troubled set of his features. Now relaxed, he looked very young and vulnerable.

Leah's attention wandered to shoulder bones, prominently obvious through a clean but threadbare shirt. His knees poked at the worn fabric of corduroy jeans. She drank more coffee and frowned. Something intangible drew her to this boy. Her heart contracted. The something was a sensation that she had something in common with him. At his age, he should be in a regular high school, not trying desperately to keep his eyes open in a roomful of extension students.

She shifted her purse and pile of books to the floor and cleared her throat. The boy started violently, his eyes instantly wide and staring.

"Sorry." Leah smiled. "Did I wake you up?"

His elbows locked, both hands braced on the seat. "No. Just resting my eyes," he lied, and a trace of pink spread over his pallid cheeks.

"That's all right, then," she said matter-of-factly. "Would you like some of my coffee?" It might keep him awake even if it didn't put meat on his bones.

"I…" He slackened his arms. "It's okay, thanks."

"Please," she insisted. "There's an extra cup, and I made too much as usual. I'll only have to throw it away." She poured, then handed him the other cup before he could refuse.

"Thank you." One hand gripped the other biceps tightly while he drank. He showed no sign of speaking again.

"How old are you?" As soon as the words were out, Leah clamped her teeth together, expecting him to withdraw completely.

"Eighteen," he replied flatly, and took another sip of coffee. "You?"

Leah laughed. "I deserved that for prying. It's just that you're obviously so much younger than the rest of us old fogies. But fair play. I'm thirty, soon to be thirty-one."

A suggestion of a smile turned up his mouth. "That's pretty old okay. Next you'll want to know why I don't go to school in the daytime, right?"

She felt her own cheeks redden. "I really wasn't being nosy. I quit high school at seventeen, and tonight I've finally taken the first step toward finishing. Guess I looked at you and saw a bit of myself. Only—" Why would she spill all this to a stranger who couldn't possibly be interested?

"Only?" he repeated, finishing his drink.

Leah refilled the cup and fished some coins from her purse. "Only something tells me you've got more guts than I had." She pushed to her feet, feeling his eyes follow when she crossed to a vending machine.

Deliberately, she made sure he couldn't see her insert her money and receive a granola bar. She moaned and thumped a chrome panel while she surreptitiously dropped in another coin before scooping out the second bar.

Grinning and shaking her head, she returned to her seat. "Here." She tossed one of her purchases to her companion. "My fist must be pretty potent. First I didn't get anything, then I got two."

He glanced sharply from his hand to Leah's eyes. She smiled benignly, guessing she hadn't fooled him. After a moment's hesitation, he tore off the wrapper and demolished its contents in two bites. Again, her hunch had been right. He was hungry.

"So why don't you go to school during the day, Dan?" she ventured when he finished eating.

His blue eyes took on a wary, hooded appearance. She was going too fast, and his life was none of her business, anyway.

He sniffed. "I'm Dan, and you're Leah something or other. You got the name from the roll. I wondered how you knew for a minute."

"Leah Cornish." Her muscles untensed slightly.

"Maybe I like to sleep late and goof off all day—fishing, playing golf, who knows?" The ceiling, with its square white tiles, held his attention.

Leah moved her books fractionally with one foot. "Sure, that's where you get that fantastic tan. I had to go to work, that's why I dropped out of school. There was just my mom and me, and we needed the money. I never thought of carrying on at night and probably couldn't have made it if I did."

"I may not be able to." His eyes shot to her face, and he blushed violently. One slender finger rubbed at the space between his brows. "Fell into that one, didn't I. I guess you and I do have something in common. You can find me at the Serve U Right grocery store, over on Central, any morning between seven and nine. I stock the produce. Then, in case you're into hotels, I park cars at the Benton Plaza until five. Cowboy hat, slick Western gear and all—you wouldn't know me in that uniform. I don't know me in it."

A pang of sad helplessness began its steady procession to Leah's heart. Helplessness and an intense yearning to help Dan. Memories of her own nonexistent childhood flooded in, the years when she'd shone as a student despite total lack of support from a family. Then the sadness at having to walk away a few months before she would have received her diploma.

"Did you do this last year, too?" Her voice sounded tight.

Dan shifted restlessly, and Leah sensed she was getting too close to the walled-off section of his life. She remembered so well her own anger at the world and her unwillingness to accept any kind of interest or understanding from the strangers who were all she had, apart from her mother.

His shoulders hunched, and he seemed to make a decision. "I worked nights last quarter. That didn't cut it for the money we need. I'm with my mom, too—but I've got a brother and two sisters. The girls are pre-school age, so by the time Mom paid for baby-sitting, she wouldn't make anything if she went to work. There, Leah, now you've got the whole scoop on me. Not so interesting, huh?" he finished with a defiant jut of his chin, and picked up his books. "Must be about time to get back in there."

She reached to grip his arm. "You're going to make it, Dan. Let me know if there's anything I can do to help."

"Oh, I'm going to make it, all right." An expressionless mask slid over his face. "I'll end up as chairman of the board somewhere. Thanks for listening.

Guess I was a bit weak tonight. I don't usually spout off my life history.''

Back in the classroom, Leah noticed Dan had moved to a seat closer to the door. By the time she'd gathered her possessions at the end of the session, he'd disappeared, but she couldn't get him out of her mind.

Her heels clipped across the asphalt parking lot on the way to her car. She kept her head down, half immersed in what she'd learned and the prospect of a heavy schedule in the weeks to come and half preoccupied with Dan Ingalls's problems. Intuition told her she was probably the one person he'd ever confided his whole situation to, and then only in a moment of weakness, when she'd caught him off guard.

"Well, how'd it go?"

At the sound of Guy's voice, her face snapped up. He was standing beside her car, both hands sunk deep in his jeans pockets.

"What...oh, very well, thanks. What are you doing here? Where's the jeep?"

Close enough now to see him clearly beneath a lamp standard, his sheepish expression amused her.

"I caught a bus over." He rolled onto his heels. "Thought maybe you'd give me a lift home."

Leah struggled to keep a straight face while sweet warmth suffused her insides. He'd wanted to be here when she got out on her first night. She could hug him. "I'll think about it," she said laughing. "But let's get this clear. You decided, spur of the moment, to take a bus ride that just happened to end up here?"

"Well—"

"Then," she interrupted. "Then, when you were about to catch the bus back again, you remembered I was taking classes here tonight and thought it would be nicer to ride home in my sumptuous Bug than a stinky old bus. Have I got it right?''

He exhaled audibly. "So I'm behaving like the mother of a kindergartner on the first day of school. So I deliberately came to meet you because I wanted to make sure you were okay." His right toe scuffed loose gravel. "And I also wanted to drive you home, because I don't like you wandering around in the dark alone," he finished in a rush.

Several passing students were turning curious faces toward them. Leah hurriedly opened the passenger door and motioned Guy inside. "We're attracting a crowd. Get in. I'll drop you off on my way home."

"I can go all the way with you, then walk back." Guy protested. "It's only a couple of miles."

"Get in," Leah retorted, and walked around to the driver's side. Once settled, she switched on the ignition and studied his face in the glow from the dashboard. "Everything went beautifully tonight, Guy. You don't have to worry about me, because I'm going to love going to school again."

Being cared for with a depth Guy couldn't disguise filled her with deep joy. But tonight she'd acknowledged something else. She wanted to stand on her own feet. If and when she and Guy decided to make a joint life, she would not come to him as little more than a childish dependent.

He grunted as they headed west. "If you hit a rough spot with your studies, will you let me help?"

"Of course. I'm counting on it."

At the church, she drove him all the way to the rectory and waited for him to get out. When he didn't move, she reached across the console and kissed his cheek. "Thanks for caring about me." She gripped the steering wheel. "Night, Guy. See you in the morning."

He opened the door, then turned back and pulled her roughly into his arms. "You're something. Do you know that? And I think I'm crazy about you."

Leah's attempted laugh didn't quite come off. "You think a lot of things, sir. Maybe you should try making up your mind about a few of them."

His mouth came down on hers in a fierce kiss, his tongue reaching far into her mouth. When he drew back to look at her, Leah's heart was a drumroll. She pushed her fingers into his hair. Guy rained a hundred tiny, brushing kisses over her face and neck, ending with another sound possession of her lips before he swung from the car and strode into the house without looking back.

After several seconds, Leah's heart slowed to a normal rhythm, and she drove slowly home. Guy's attempt to excuse his concern had been transparent. He had a protective urge toward her that wouldn't quit, and she loved it.

CHAPTER TEN

THE NEXT ten days sped by. Leah went to school four nights a week and began to find herself wilting earlier in the afternoon as attacking her homework before work in the morning became a routine. But with each class her self-confidence grew, and she looked forward eagerly to every new challenge—and to the shy friendship she was building with Dan Ingalls.

He had gotten into the habit of sitting with her during recesses. Sometimes they hardly talked at all. But occasionally he revealed a little more about his family, and she grew less reserved over her own early life.

Leah was convinced Dan didn't get enough food for his gangly eighteen-year-old frame but knew the granola-bar ruse wouldn't work twice. He'd agreed to share a sandwich she brought one night, then turned up the next time with two overripe peaches Leah knew must have been castoffs from the grocery store. She'd eaten the fruit, fighting back tears as she did so. How did you help a desperate boy without wounding his pride?

Tonight was Friday, and she had a plan. Despite her persistent pleas for him not to, Guy continued to show up after every class session and drive with her as far as the rectory. He had a natural flair for plugging in to other people's problems and for gaining their trust. If she could persuade Dan to go out with them for a hamburger, she might begin solving two obstacles to her peace of mind: Dan's need for more food and the discovery of a solution to his money worries. She hadn't felt right discussing the boy's concerns behind his back, but if she could get Dan to talk himself, Guy was likely to cast around for a solution.

The final bell sounded, and Leah grabbed the bag she'd bought for her books. She scurried up the aisle, searching anxiously for Dan, who had done his usual disappearing trick. Why hadn't she invited him out during recess?

In the hall, she broke into a run, turning the corner in time to see Dan's tall, angular back at the top of the building's front steps. Her shout came as a breathless croak, and by the time she burst into the fresh air, he was gone.

From her vantage point, Leah scoured the lot, watching each moving figure. Then she saw him and froze. *Good Lord.* She knew he lived miles away, at the far end of Indian School Road, but he was pedaling through the side gate on an ancient bicycle.

Now she really would cry if she didn't get a hold on herself. She hid her eyes with one hand and bit into a quivery lower lip. His father had been dead a year. Apart from his mother, he was the only one old enough to be of any real help to his family. He was struggling to work at two jobs, finish school and sandwich homework in between. And to top it off, he must be riding the old bicycle miles and miles every day to save bus fare. There'd been no one to help her out of the pit when she was a struggling teenager—until Charles had come along. Dan's plight was twice as desperate as hers had been. Surely she could find a way out for him.

"Hey, Leah."

At the familiar sound of Guy's voice, Leah uncovered her eyes and watched him jog in her direction. Slowly, she joined him, and as he draped his arm around her shoulders, she knew what she had to do.

"Carry your books?" Guy laughed, reaching for her bag. His smile dissolved as he looked down into her face. "Why so sad? Something go wrong?"

"Nothing's wrong—with me. Can I stand you a hamburger?"

He jolted to a stop. "A hamburger? Didn't you get dinner? You've got to eat—"

"I just want an excuse to go somewhere and talk," she interrupted brusquely. "Not your place, not mine. A bar, anywhere. I need your help—and your full attention."

Guy frowned but didn't ask any more questions while they walked to her car.

THE FOLLOWING AFTERNOON, Guy helped Leah into the jeep and set out to find the Ingallses' house on the far side of town.

"I've watched Dan get more and more exhausted," Leah said when they made the turn to head north on Seventh Street. "And he's irritable. He snapped at the English teacher last night; and I'm starting to worry they'll kick him out."

Guy glanced sideways at her. Wind blew through the open sides of the jeep, whipping her hair into a dark cloud around her face. Her deep blue eyes were shadowed with worry. "You're sure he'll be at work when we get to their place?" he asked, returning his attention to the road. Every time he looked at Leah, he had to quell an urge to touch her, and his condition was getting worse.

"He doesn't get off from the hotel till five. I thought I told you that." Her voice came to him in snatches. So did wafts of her perfume.

The night before, at Oscar Taylor, a trendy bar and grill in the plush Biltmore Fashion Center, she'd poured out Dan's story. Again and again, while wooden fans whirred overhead and her fingers made tight little patterns on a marble-topped table, Leah had gone over points that clearly opened wounds in her own memory. It hadn't taken any time for Guy to recognize that Leah's bond with this boy came from the experiences of her own young life.

Phoenix was having one of the hottest Septembers on record. The thunderstorm season had slowed, but the intense heat continued. Today Guy wondered if he shouldn't consider getting rid of the jeep for an air-conditioned vehicle. He twisted his head toward Leah again and found she'd rested her head back and closed her eyes. Her skirt slid above her knees, revealing long, smooth legs.

He gripped the wheel a little tighter.

"We should be able to talk to Dan's mother before he gets back," Leah said. "I want you to meet him, too, but I think we'll get farther without him at first. From what he's told me she's a very reasonable woman. He told me how she worries about his schooling. Sometimes I think he'd give it up now if it wasn't for her."

The sun blazed white, almost bouncing over the surface of broad Indian School Road, with its low-lying buildings and singed shrubs. Leah had found Dan's address in the telephone book, a tiny house on a small street angling off behind a row of stores.

"Looks like the place." Guy parked at the curb behind a weeping willow, its graceful boughs unmoving over an arid expanse of sand and scrub grass that made up the front yard. "I suppose this isn't what you want to hear, but I'm nervous."

Leah squeezed his hand. "Why shouldn't you be? At least we know we're on the same wave length. But the worst that can happen is that she tells us to get lost."

Guy stared at her for a moment before climbing out. She didn't expect him to be a superman, only himself.

Side by side they walked up the path. Leah rang the bell as Guy righted a toppled red tricycle.

The door opened several inches. "Yes."

Both lowered their eyes to a small face that appeared at handle level in the narrow crack. Guy managed to smile warmly. "We wanted to see your mommie. Is she in?"

A knee wriggled back and forth beneath pink shorts as the little girl considered what to say next. A shock of black curls cascaded to her shoulders and bobbed with the movement of her body. She appeared to be about four. "I've got to ask what you want," she said guilelessly, her blue eyes wide.

Sympathy stabbed at Guy. The mother was probably afraid of debt collectors, or just plain afraid—of everything. He hunkered down to the child's level. "Would you tell your mommie we're friends of Dan and we'd like to talk to her about him?"

Immediately, the door swung wide, and they were confronted by a petite woman with the same shock of black curly hair as the child. On one hip, she carried another little girl, who couldn't have been more than two. Guy's heart twisted. So much unhappiness. So many lonely people no one could reach.

"Dan?" the woman said sharply. "What about Dan? Did something happen to him?" Her face had paled, and her hand rubbed unconsciously, rhythmically, at the baby's leg.

"No, Mrs. Ingalls," Leah reassured quickly. "This is nothing like that. I'm in the same class as Dan over in Scottsdale, and we've gotten to know each other. This—" she hooked an arm through Guy's "—is my friend, Guy Hamilton. I also work for him. Could you spare a few minutes, do you think?"

The woman shifted the child to her other hip and nodded agreement. They followed her into a shabby but clean living room where she sat in an unraveling cane rocker and waited until Guy and Leah perched on mismatched straight-backed chairs.

"What did you say your name was?" Mrs. Ingalls addressed Leah.

"Leah Cornish. Dan's a wonderful boy, Mrs. Ingalls."

"My name's Connie." She smoothed the skirt of a yellow checkered housedress. "What's all this about Dan?"

Guy had deliberately kept quiet while Connie Ingalls gained some ease with Leah. Now he bent forward to rest his elbows on his knees. "This is almost more about you than Dan." He smiled down at the smallest child, who had crawled from her mother's arms and stood staring up into his face. He held out his hands, and she clambered onto his lap.

"That's Mary," Connie said. "She doesn't usually take to strangers."

"Guy has a way with children." A blush flashed up Leah's neck when Guy caught her eye. So, he thought with satisfaction, she watched him when he didn't know it. "But it's children we came to see you about really, isn't it, Guy?" she ended lamely.

While Guy outlined the plan he'd come up with since last night, the other child, Anna, coaxed Leah to a shoe box in the corner and proudly displayed a doll made of a white athletic sock. He kept one eye on Leah's easy manner, the way she sat on the floor to interact with the girl, and quickly explained his own plight at the church nursery.

After Connie absorbed the fact that he was a minister, he told her about his ongoing difficulty in finding and keeping permanent staff and how he needed someone to oversee and manage the facility.

Connie looked blank. "What does this have to do with Dan or me?"

"Well." He coughed. Leah was now tucking a handkerchief blanket around the sock doll as Anna leaned contentedly against her, one thumb in her mouth. "Well, Connie, Leah was telling me how Dan works at two jobs and has a hard time of it getting through his homework. She also explained the obvious; it would cost you more in day care for your children than you could earn most places. So I wondered if you would do us all a favor by running my church nursery."

Worn hands wound and unwound in Connie's lap. "I don't know what to say."

"Say you'll do it," Guy pressed. "You'd bring the girls with you, of course. The pay's not terrific, but you'd all get your food there, and Dan could drop one of his jobs so he'd have a better chance at his schooling. You have another boy—how old is he?"

"Bob's twelve." She leaned forward, hope beginning to dawn in her eyes. "He comes home from school and takes straight off to do his paper route, anyway. He'd be all right till I got home.''

Leah stood up suddenly, holding Anna's hand. "What about transportation? Do you have a car? I could come and get you in the morning, then bring you back.''

Connie shook her head. "You've done enough. We like the bus, don't we, girls? Don't you worry about that.'' She frowned. "Did you already talk to Dan about this?''

Guy and Leah fell silent and looked at each other. Anna wrapped an arm around Leah's leg, and she absently ruffled the girl's shiny curls. *She's got a way with children, too,* Guy thought. *Maybe we'll have—* Not now; it wasn't the time to think about himself.

"Dan doesn't know, does he?'' Connie's delicate brows drew together. "He'll think it's some sort of charity and get mad. He's like his dad…'' The words trailed off.

The child on his lap had knelt to watch Guy's face closely. He tried to look around her, then laughed when she firmly clamped a small hand on each side of his jaw. "Well,'' he started, and Mary touched his moving lips. He kissed the end of her nose and caught her to his chest, where she snuggled happily.

A sniff snapped his attention back to Connie, who swiped impatiently at the corner of one eye. "Stupid,'' she said harshly. "Don't have much time to think about it. But Ed—that's my husband—never had much time to hold Mary before—before he died. I expect Dan told you he had lung cancer. They say children come into the world with needs built in and one of them's love— from more than one parent who's always too uptight to give them enough. Seeing Mary like that—'' she nodded at Guy "—with you, makes me wish I could give them more, get them around more people."

"Oh, Connie, don't." Leah crossed to the older woman and sat on the floor beside the rocker. "Listen. This job will be just what you need. It'll get you out of the house. The girls will have other children their own age to play with. And you'll all be around a lot of good people." Her voice wavered, and she immediately glanced at Guy, smiling self-consciously through tears that welled in her eyes.

He smiled back knowing she'd unconsciously called his parishioners good but that she meant what she said.

"But Dan..." Connie began.

Anna had gone to rest against Leah's back and wrap her arms around her neck. Leah clasped the little hands beneath her own chin. "Dan will come around," she said firmly. "He's proud, but he loves you all too much not to see that this is a perfect situation. Leave it to Guy; he's great with young people. He'll explain everything to him, and Dan will be glad; wait and see."

Guy has a way with children.... He's great with young people. He sat back, still hugging Mary. Leah was excellent with children, and she was the one who had wheedled her way into Dan's confidence, something he'd probably have found more difficult himself. This woman had strengths she refused to recognize, an almost soul-wrenching specialness, yet she was still willing to slip into the background behind a man she cared for.

"Mom! I'm home. Where are you?"

The sound of a door slamming and Dan's voice turned the living room scene into a motionless tableau. Connie fixed a smile on her face, but her hands held the chair arms in a death grip.

"Wait till you see what they were throwing out." Dan strode into the room, head down in a grocery sack. "This bread's still fresh and—" He glanced up, his eyes fastening on Leah. "What are you doing here?" Dull, angry red suffused his face and neck.

"Hi." Leah kept a tight hold on Anna's hands. "I brought a friend of mine over to meet you. Remember I told you about Guy Hamilton, the man I work for?"

The boy's hostile blue stare shifted to Guy's face, then flicked away. "Sure." He was prickly, surly. "How'd you find us?"

"Dan, they…" Connie began.

Dan shook his head sharply, cutting her off. "Let them tell me, please, Mom."

"Telephone book, silly," Leah retorted with artificial lightness. "We decided to go for a drive and ended up coming here."

Guy looked at the ceiling. She was a lousy liar— D-minus variety.

Dan shoved the brown sack on a Formica-topped table and stood stiffly behind his mother. "And I'm Little Bo Peep. I never asked you to come snooping around after me. What is he?" He indicated Guy. "Some sort of do-good social worker?"

Guy flinched. This was going to be tougher than he'd thought. He opened his mouth, but Leah's next move took center stage.

She swung Anna into her arms and stood, feet planted firmly apart. "You listen to me, Dan Ingalls. Pride's one thing. Being a damned fool and making other people suffer because of it is another. I was where you are today once. I found a way out—marriage. It probably wasn't the best escape route, but it was the only one that came along. I've told you all about me, and I know a fair amount about you. I want to help you like someone helped me. Can't you stop being so pigheaded and accept that for what it's worth? Guy's no do-gooder, and neither am I..." She coughed and covered her face with her spare hand.

Guy got up quickly and set Mary down. He went to put an arm around Leah, who turned her face against his shoulder.

"Okay," Guy said quietly. "We're letting this get out of hand. There's nothing going on here that we can't all walk away from, so what do you have to lose by listening?" He hated sounding harsh, but the right effect was produced. Dan visibly subsided. "Let's all sit down and talk," Guy added.

An hour later, mentally whipped, Leah followed Guy from the little house. Mary and Anna had been soundly kissed and hugged by both of them, and Connie stood, glowing, in the doorway. Dan, deflated but smiling, waved from the shadows behind his mother's shoulder.

"Long route home?" Guy asked when they waited at the intersection with Indian School Road. Late-afternoon sun rays turned mica sidewalks to sheets of glitter. "I think maybe we need to unwind."

"Whew," Leah responded, locking her hands behind her head. "Long way home sounds good to me. That was something. When you told him you were a minister, I thought he'd pop a blood vessel."

"Poor kid," Guy snorted. "He's got a lot to work through. Including the fact that despite his father's strong religious beliefs, he died and left his family alone. That didn't help him warm up to me."

"You were magnificent with him." Leah put a hand on his thigh and felt the muscle move as he changed gears and the answering shudder deep inside her own body. She began to withdraw her hand, but Guy held it there, and they drove in silence for several minutes.

"Will it be all right, Guy?"

He looked questioningly at her; then his expression cleared when he must have realized she was talking about the Ingallses rather than their own situation. "*Everything* will be all right." His grin was wry as he applied both hands to the wheel and drove beside the pink mountains that edged Phoenix's Valley of the Sun.

"Connie's going to settle in just fine," Leah continued, trying to sound convinced. "But I can see trouble with Dan if he thinks anyone's doing him a favor or he's not paying back every little kindness we try to show them."

Guy sighed. "You ought to know what I'm going to say next, little one."

She did, at once, but studied the landscape instead of answering him.

"Trust."

She smiled despite herself and punched his shoulder playfully. "I'll try." And she would, but not without constant wariness.

At St. Mark's, Leah declined Guy's invitation to come in for a while. She wanted to get ahead with some of her schoolwork.

He slammed the door of the Volkswagen behind her and crossed his arms on the window rim. "Ma'am," he said solemnly.

Leah met his clear green eyes and felt herself begin to sink. "Yes, sir?"

"Would you do me the honor of accompanying me to dinner one week from tonight. That'll be a Saturday, and I thought we could take a run up to an intimate little place I know on Squaw Peak. Of course, if you're busy, I'll understand.''

His tone was light and bantering, but Leah saw the way his fingers curled tightly into his palms. Her own mouth felt like a dust bowl. "And how do you know about intimate little restaurants," she quipped with a coolness she didn't feel.

Guy wrinkled his nose. "When Wally got back yesterday, I asked him to suggest someplace."

"Our guardian matchmaker?" Leah said. "Wally has to be the world's most unlikely fairy godmother." They both laughed until tears ran down her cheeks and Guy rested his forehead on his arms.

Leah turned on her engine. "Thank you," she managed. "I'd be delighted to have dinner with you. It's time we both broadened our horizons."

She drove away without looking back. Guy had asked her out for dinner. A real date. He was taking the first tentative steps toward a courtship.

CHAPTER ELEVEN

"MEET ME ON THE PATIO." Leah scanned Guy's note quickly. What now? She'd just got back from running errands, and all she wanted was the impossible—a long, cold drink and some sleep. Her schedule was beginning to wear her down.

She slid a box of office supplies on top of the cupboard behind her desk and headed for the back of the house via a sliding-glass door off one of the guest bedrooms. This was the room where she changed when she went swimming, and it had begun to feel almost like her own.

Guy's back was to her, his fair head bent forward over a book. Leah pursed her lips. Guy was always reading something. She wished she had half his brains. Maybe then the new concepts that seemed to come at her faster with every hour in school wouldn't take so long to master.

She allowed herself a selfish moment to feast on his broad shoulders and the way his hair curled at the top of his collar. Then she walked beside him, "You wanted to see me, Guy?"

He started. The book must be engrossing, although it looked vast and dusty to Leah. "Yup. Sit down and have some tea. Made it myself, so it's bound to be fantastic." He'd opened his shirt almost to the waist, and sunlight bronzed the hair on his chest.

Leah deliberately studied the dancing blue water in the pool as she plopped into a chair and accepted a sweating glass. "I can't stay long. I just got back and my in basket looks like I died a month ago."

Guy laughed. "You're too industrious. You've been looking tired. I want to talk about that and find out how you think things are going around here."

More and more, he included her in discussions about parish affairs. She could feel him consciously relegating responsibility to her, allowing her to share in decisions. And he never missed an opportunity to offer help with her studies. They'd started working together regularly in the garden, and Guy always found a way to turn their conversation into a question-and-answer session.

"No comment?" he asked. "Are things that bad?"

She realized her silence had lasted too long. "Sorry. I was thinking. Of course things aren't bad. They're great. Connie Ingalls is as happy as a clam, and I've never seen the kids so well organized and content. Wally told me the parishioners are delighted with the change."

Guy turned his face up to the sun and closed his eyes. "Goes to show. Whatever you give, you get back a hundredfold."

His philosophy again, his faith. Leah inwardly drew back, closed out the worried little voice of doubt and searched his face instead. Vulnerable in relaxation, he looked younger. His beautiful mouth, slightly parted showed a glimpse of white teeth and his silver-tipped lashes cast fanlike shadows on his cheekbones.

"Any problems you think we should be addressing?" He opened one eye to squint at her.

Leah thought a moment before shaking her head.

"None I can think of, except—" She pressed her lips together.

"Except?" Guy sat up and turned his full attention on her. "Except what?"

It was now or never. Might as well get it over with. "My schooling is interfering with my doing the job properly. I'm beginning to think it was a mistake to go back." There, she'd said it.

He snapped the book shut and slid it onto the table. "I was half expecting you to say something like that. I've felt it coming, but I don't understand why, and—" His hand closed around her forearm. "There's nothing wrong with your work. You just said yourself how smoothly everything's running around here."

She ran her tongue over the roof of her mouth, gathering every scrap of courage she possessed. "It's getting tougher and tougher to juggle everything, Guy. I might have to quit the extension program. I need to give my full attention to my responsibilities here." Her heart started to thud hard. Surely he would understand she didn't want to give up, that it was a case of being sensible.

Guy stood and rammed his hands into his pockets. He stared at the sky until Leah thought her head would pop with the waiting. "No," he announced at last. "I know I don't have any right to tell you what to do, but I'll do my damnedest to stop you from quitting. What's the real problem? What aren't you telling me?"

Leah felt like an errant kid called on the headmaster's carpet. "Geometry," she said, and immediately curled up inside. *Dumb excuse; why not be honest?*

His stare bored through her. "Sure, Leah—you're going to give up school because you don't like geometry? Come on."

"Okay." She squeezed her eyes shut. "Okay, you want a blow-by-blow misery list, I'll give it to you. It isn't just geometry or English or any individual subject. I am struggling in some areas, but the main thing is I can't handle my schedule. I get up when it's still dark and work for three hours before I come here. You'll agree I don't have the luxury of deciding whether or not to earn a living. And don't think I regret that—I love it here. But by the middle of the afternoon I'm half asleep, and on four days a week I have to gather up enough energy to go to school *after* I finish work. The nights when I don't go to school I try to catch up with things around the apartment and do *more* homework. I'm whacked, Guy, and I'm not making it."

Guy began to pace, furious concentration furrowing his brow. "I'm sorry." He stopped abruptly in front of her. "I don't know what I've been thinking about. Of course it's too much. I get so involved in other people's problems I forget the one who—" His throat moved convulsively, and a horrified awareness darkened his eyes.

"Don't," Leah cried, knowing he was remembering his neglect of his wife. "This isn't your problem, or your fault; it's mine."

"No, no." The metal chair creaked beneath his weight as he sat and buried his face in his hands. "Please, let me work this through." He lifted his eyes to hers. "You'll be finished with the learning center in a few weeks. For the rest of that time, I want you to pack in the parish business at noon and spend the afternoon doing homework. I'll be around to deal with any problems that come up and to help you."

Leah opened her mouth to protest, but Guy reached to silence her with a quick kiss. "You're more important to me than anything or anyone else. I'm so proud of everything you've accomplished.''

Trembling weightlessness invaded her legs. ''You've already done too much for me. I can't take any more from you.''

His fist came down on the armrest. ''You can, and you will. Think. How would it look to Dan Ingalls if his idol quit? Could you blame the kid if he did the same? He's down to one job, but he does still have to manage that and be the man around the house for Connie and the little kids.''

She covered her eyes. ''If you wanted to make me feel like a creep, that was the way to do it. Why am I so weak?''

Fabric swished, and he was beside her, holding her tightly. ''You aren't weak, my love. Just a perfectionist who's gone on overload. And I *have* been blind in some ways, although I was concerned that you seemed tired. Just say you'll do this my way from here on, please. It'll all work out for the best, believe me.''

Leah wrapped her arms around his shoulders and rested a cheek against his neck. Peace stole over her. She would do anything for this man.

''Is the answer yes?'' he asked against her ear. The wide circles he made over her back began to awaken responses she mustn't allow.

''Yes.'' She pulled away, averting her face. ''But just for once I wish it was me doing something for you instead of the other way around.'' Emotion clogged her throat. ''I've always known the world was made up of givers and takers, and Guy—'' She willed herself to look at him, biting back shame at her own spinelessness. ''I thought one day I'd manage to change sides.

But I'm still a taker, aren't I? I'm sorry, but I am working at it.''

Guy felt blood drain from his veins. If he didn't get out of here now and think, he'd say all the things he was determined not to say—yet. He traced the bridge of her nose with a knuckle and gave her a determinedly cheerful grin. She didn't have to know he was dying inside. ''I can tell you how much you give until I'm blue in the face, lady, and you won't believe me. But I'll say it, anyway. You *give* all the time. If you stop to think, you'll know I'm right.''

Her blue eyes were clear mirrors heavily shadowed by her dark lashes. She held trembling lips tightly closed.

Oh, God. ''Leah, I have to attend to a couple of things. Why don't you swim, or rest? Or start on some schoolwork, if it makes you feel good?'' He bounced to his feet, backing away at the same time. ''We'll touch bases later, all right? Will you do that?''

Her whispered ''Yes'' reached him a second before he reentered the house.

So who did *he* get to talk to? Who did any ''pillar of strength'' talk to when he himself was confused and hurting? Guy paused beside the desk in his study, braced his weight on outstretched hands and hung his head. So far he'd managed to find enough guts to invite Leah out to dinner on Saturday night. Big deal. They were together most of every day, and he hadn't been able to open up and tell her where he stood, his hopes and dreams for them or his hang-ups.

Damn. While he'd been so tied up with his own world, he hadn't even noticed how strung out she was becoming. What did he have to offer a woman on a full-time basis? He'd already blown one marriage; would he do the same if he got another chance?

The room seemed to shut him in, the walls steadily pressing closer. Guy headed for the front door. He'd climbed into the jeep when he noticed Wally raking a fresh load of pea gravel beside the social hall.

The old man saw life clearly and knew where he'd been and where he was headed. When his wife died, he'd come to Guy and stumblingly asked for an ear to listen to his bewilderment. Wally had known, with that wisdom of the honest, that his pain and emptiness must be faced and shared or it would suffocate him.

Guy's walk from the jeep to the social hall seemed one of the longest he'd ever taken. Wally didn't hear him coming and continued to rake, sweat gleaming on the back of his thin, wrinkle-crazed neck.

"Wally—" Guy's voice sounded loud in his own ears. "Got a few minutes?"

The rake stilled instantly, and Wally swung around, shading his eyes. "Hello there, Guy. Didn't hear you. What's up?"

Resolve fled. "Oh, nothing really, ah... Good load of gravel?"

Wally looked puzzled. "Gravel's gravel."

"Well, then—that's good." He scuffed at a clod of dirt. "Hot again today."

"Hot most days," Wally said.

Guy felt sick. "Monsoon season's about over, I guess."

"I guess."

"Wally...how's Joan's sister?"

Wally slowly rested the rake against the wall and hooked his thumbs into his belt. "Same as when you asked me the other day, after I got back from Mesa. She's fine.''

Guy smiled. He was making a fool of himself. "There was something I was going to ask you about."

"I figured there was." The straw hat was shifted to the back of Wally's head. "So why don't you stop horsing around and spit it out."

"Because." He shouted the word, and heat flooded his face. "Because I don't know how, damn it. I need some advice, and I don't know how to ask for it. Go on, have a good laugh about that one. I won't blame you. I might even join in."

Wally indicated a nearby bench, and they walked to sit in silence.

After several minutes, Wally stuck a sharp elbow in Guy's ribs. "How about starting at the beginning. Seems like that might be best."

"I think you already know the beginning." Sweat drizzled down the side of Guy's face. "For six years I've only been a husband on paper. You've got to know my marriage ended in the physical sense even before I came here. My fault. I never learned how to give a woman the attention she needs."

A grumping noise came from Wally as he shifted his weight. Guy sighed; he was probably embarrassing the man.

"An old codger like me doesn't know much about this stuff," Wally began gruffly. "But I'm not blind. I can see when two young folks are all tied up with each other. You're scared; that's your trouble. And all the talk around the parish has got you going in circles. Leah says you reckon it doesn't, but I know better."

Guy draped his elbows over the back of the bench

and stared at the toes of his shoes. No point in arguing against the truth.

"You don't know what to do next, do you?" Wally added.

"I sure don't," Guy muttered, flicking stray pebbles from the seat. "We need some sort of life away from this place, but I've never been good at—at courting a woman, I guess you call it. How do I know when something's right? I can't go through what I went through before. And I can't put Leah through it. Oh, hell." He leaped up and shied a rock against the closest palm trunk. "The best thing I can do is back off and let her find someone else."

Wally's laugh was a bark. "Oh, sure. You'll back off. In the pig's eye you'll back off. You're in too deep, but too thickheaded to admit it. I tried to tell you what to do weeks ago, then figured it was none of my business. Now you've asked me. You just came from her, right?"

"Right." Guy sank back onto the bench, his hands hanging between his knees.

"And you're both miserable?"

"You've got it."

"Then go back in there and do something about it. Take her somewhere and forget all this." He spread his arms wide. "I got a hunch the jawing around here's about died out, so you can forget that."

Guy chewed his lip. "I hope you're right. I am taking Leah to dinner on Saturday night."

"Great," Wally said, and slapped Guy on the back. "Good idea. But take her somewhere *now*. You're both walking around like love-struck kids, and until you sort things out between you, you won't be any good to the rest of us."

"Wally—" Guy sighed. "She was going to quit school because she was so tired. I didn't even notice she was burning out."

"Disgusting," Wally replied solemnly. "A man shouldn't make human mistakes—not you, particularly."

"This is serious."

"Sure it is. So *do* something about it. Take her out of herself. Give her all your attention for a while and you'll see her come alive again."

Guy crossed his arms. Here he was, asking a man more than twice his age how to go about letting a woman know he cared about her. "Shoot," he growled. "I don't know how to do it. I've spent too much of my life tied up with my work."

Wally's characteristic "What the heck" split the air with as much force as any curse. "Think about what she likes," he exploded. "Think, man."

"I am thinking. Nothing's coming, or I wouldn't be here making a fool of myself."

"You don't make a fool of yourself when you show a friend you need help. That takes guts."

Guy shrank inwardly in the face of this man's hard-learned wisdom. "Do you have any idea, anything at all, what I could do?" he asked humbly.

Wally grabbed his elbow and propelled them both to their feet. "She likes plants. The weirder, the better. She's crazy about orchids, and they don't grow well in normal conditions around here. Take her to that desert garden place—over in Papago."

"What if she says no? She's tired."

"Don't take no for an answer. Drag her into that jeep of yours and sweep her away. No woman can resist a little force now and again. Tell her how good she looks. Listen to what she says. And don't talk about church goings-on or school or anything but the two of you." Wally clamped his mouth shut abruptly and tilted his hat back over his eyes. "I gotta get on with spreading that gravel. I've already said too much."

"I BET YOU NEVER SAW a saguaro as big as that?" Guy said, whisking Leah along a path past a jungle of giant cacti. "What's that called—the spiky thing? I see them all over, but I've never known the name."

Leah adjusted her sunglasses and tried not to look aghast. "It's just a yucca." She panted, running to keep up. "Arizona's state plant, remember?"

"Ah, yes," he replied, and paused to stare intently at the speckled, swordlike leaves. "Beautiful."

She quelled the impulse to say she didn't find yucca beautiful; interesting, maybe, but not beautiful. Ever since Guy had rushed back into her office and insisted they were going to the Papago Desert Garden, he'd kept up a steady stream of conversation and constant motion. Tired before they began, she was now drained, mentally and physically. She'd give anything to find out what was in his mind. And it wasn't cacti or yucca.

"The orchids are in those greenhouses." Guy pointed to two identical buildings near the entrance. "Like to see them?"

He was already steering her rapidly to the right. "I'd love to," Leah managed, and immediately felt an infuriating bubble of laughter well in her throat. Hysterical. She must be losing her mind. Or Guy was—or maybe both of them.

Inside the first glassed-in building, the familiar humid air made her stop and breathe deeply. Everywhere she looked, lush foliage had been used to form a natural backdrop for dozens of orchids.

"Like it?" Guy watched her closely. "Are they like the ones you used to raise?"

Leah smiled. "My little greenhouse wasn't quite up to this, but I did have some of these varieties, yes. And I love it in here. Feel that air—and look, birds. They've got tropical birds in here."

Guy followed her glance to where a brilliantly plumed parrot perched on a giant philodendron creeper. "Did you have birds?"

"No!" She threaded an arm beneath his to soften her amused reaction. "No, Guy. This is big-time. Once, Charles took me on a trip to Canada, to British Columbia. We went to a conservatory in a place called Queen Elizabeth Park. There was this huge dome full of tropical shrubs and flowers, and the birds were everywhere. I can still close my eyes and remember the scents. Gorgeous."

Guy became still. "Can you close your eyes and remember Charles?"

She couldn't believe he'd said it. He sounded jealous. Leah pulled her arm away and frowned up at Guy. "Yes," she said slowly. "I still remember Charles, with or without my eyes closed. He was a kind man, the best, and I was married to him for eleven years. Can you still remember Susan?"

Pain washed over his features, and she had to hold back an impulse to comfort him. "That's different," he said.

"Why?" she asked very softly, her stomach plummeting. "Because she was your wife and therefore more important than my husband? You're not making any sense."

"Forget it." He walked on, and Leah had to hurry to catch up.

"I'm not going to forget it, Guy." She dodged in front of him on the narrow pathway. "Don't turn away. Why did you want me to come here with you today?"

His laugh was derisive. "Because I wanted to give us a chance to get closer."

She swallowed and laid a hand on his chest. "Thank you. I want that, too. So what's wrong?"

"Nothing." His eyes were riveted on her. "Except the faraway expression on your face when you spoke about good old Charles just now. You'd think the man had been a saint rather than—"

"Don't," she cut him off. Her breath came in painful jerks. "Please, don't. You didn't know him the way he was when we met. I don't think anyone ever knew him the way I did. And even if he'd been a monster, which he wasn't, he was my husband, and I won't let anyone drag down his memory. He loved me, Guy. He had a lot of faults, but who doesn't? You? Me? I don't think so." She crumpled abruptly onto a huge stone frog. "Forgive me, please. I sound like a righteous boor."

Firm hands grasped her shoulders, and she was pulled against Guy's solid body. "You're the one who needs to forgive me, as usual. I just can't stand the thought of anyone else mattering that much to you."

Leah gritted her teeth. *But you aren't willing to commit yourself to me. You're still too afraid.* "I think we're both pretty worn out. Let's call it a day."

She let him hold her hand, although every inch of her cried out for solitude.

"The place we're going to on Saturday is called Beside the Point.'' Guy's attempt at nonchalance didn't quite make it. ''Should be nice.''

They reached the exit turnstile. Leah clicked her jaw nervously. Hot as it was, her skin was clammy. ''That's something I was going to talk to you about, Guy. I can't make it Saturday.''

He halted, trapping her between the metal railings. ''Can't go? Of course you can go. You said you would.''

His expression was a mixture of male ego incredulous at rebuff and disappointed small boy. Leah panicked. ''I don't have anything to wear, and anyway, it's my birthday.'' Her mouth remained opened. Of all the excuses she could have come up with, that had to be the most ridiculous.

Slowly, Guy pulled her close until she stood toe to toe with him. ''Saturday is your birthday, huh? Great. All the more reason to celebrate.'' His grin was suddenly wicked. ''In fact, instead of just dinner, which would certainly not be enough for the occasion, I suggest we drive up into the mountains for the day. Have you been to Sedona?''

''N-no. I mean—''

''You haven't? Perfect! I'll take you. And you've given me the perfect idea for a birthday present. Come on. The Biltmore Fashion Center will still be open. I'll buy you a new outfit for the occasion.'' His hand at her waist propelled her forcefully across the parking lot.

''I can't let you do that.'' Her voice jarred as he bundled unceremoniously into the jeep.

All the way back to town, he brushed aside her arguments, finishing by telling her how unhappy she'd make him if she wouldn't allow him the small pleasure

of buying her something. By the time she followed him
through the plate-glass doors of Saks, self-consciously
trying to order her windswept hair, she was limp and
beyond further debate.

She stood awkwardly by while he considered the
store directory. "One floor up," he announced, and
grabbed Leah's hand as he resumed his meteoric pace
up the left side of the escalator. He took the steps two
at a time past mildly surprised patrons.

"Guy," Leah hissed at the top. "Where are we going? Everyone's staring at us."

"You, you mean. Don't blame 'em. You're gorgeous."

She shook her head helplessly and followed him
across bottomless carpet, feeling more like someone
who'd come to clean the place than shop there.

"Designer!" Her heart sank. "Guy..." she started
again, but he was already flipping through racks of
wildly expensive creations. Why hadn't she kept her
big mouth shut? She'd shopped in plenty of stores, and
departments, like this. Times had been different then.
No way would she let Guy buy her an outfit, and *she*
certainly couldn't afford anything here. She wasn't sure
she could afford to breathe the rarefied air.

"What do you think of this?" He held up a gauzy
dress with a handkerchief hem and spaghetti straps.
The colors resembled an evening rainbow.

Leah gave him a gentle smile. He was so special, so
gracious and giving—and he had exceptional taste to
boot. The dress was a knockout and would have a
knockout price to match.

"Well?" He opened wide, questioning eyes.

She hooked an arm through his. "Listen," she whispered. "You have spectacular taste. That is absolutely

the most scrumptious creation I've been within miles of for a long time, but—''

"But you don't like it." He cut her off with a frown and started rifling through the rack again. "Maybe this one's the wrong size."

"No, no." She laughed, holding his wrist. "I love it. And it happens to be the right size. But take a look at the price tag. Go on, look at it."

He did, and his frown deepened.

"See?" Leah tried to ease the garment from his grasp. "I don't need anything like that. Anyway, since we're going to Sedona by jeep on Saturday instead of out to some fancy restaurant, I won't need something special to wear."

Guy looked down into her face for a long moment, his dear, slow smile spreading to warm every feature.

He hung the dress back on the rack, and Leah let out a grateful sigh. When he turned back to her, he was still grinning.

Leah narrowed her eyes. "What's the joke?"

"No joke," he shrugged innocently. "I'm glad you can spend the day with me on Saturday, after all."

"I never said—"

Guy tapped her bottom lip. "Oh, but you did. You just said that since we we're going to Sedona, you wouldn't need a fancy new dress. Don't tell me you're the kind of woman who lets a man down twice in one afternoon?"

She tried to think of a snappy comeback, but nothing came. "Let's get out of here, you operator." Leah punched his hard stomach playfully and marched toward the down escalator.

CHAPTER TWELVE

HE TOOK THE BOX from behind his back and laid it quietly on her little table by the window. Arriving an hour early, even on the pretext of getting out of town before the weather heated up, wasn't done, he knew. But he'd hardly slept all night and hadn't been able to wait a minute longer to see Leah.

At least the surprise element of his appearance had distracted her and she hadn't noticed the oversized package, semihidden behind his back. When she'd opened the door, sleepiness still glazed her eyes as she stared at him, disoriented, and clutched a short cotton bathrobe together at her throat. She'd looked soft, so incredibly sexy. Not blurting out his news immediately had taken superhuman control.

She was clattering mugs in the tiny kitchen. "Got to have coffee while I dress, Guy. Can't make it without coffee." She sounded fuzzy, and he smiled affectionately. How would she react when he told her what he'd found among his unopened personal mail after she'd left yesterday afternoon? He was a free man. The official notice in his pocket informed him he no longer had a wife.

"How about you, Guy?" Leah called. "It won't take me long to get ready, but why don't you have a cup of Cornish morning mud while you wait."

"Boy," he said, laughing, "with an endorsement

like that, how can I refuse?'' The perfect moment to break his news would come when they were alone and separated from the mundane trappings of their everyday lives.

"Here you go."

Her voice, behind him, caused Guy to swing around abruptly. Barefoot, her white robe with its ruffled edges barely reaching mid-thigh, she was like some beautiful, exotic butterfly. The robe was all she wore. Its thin fabric clung to her body and molded full breasts, their tips clearly defined and erect.

Leah's eyes met his when they returned to her face, and a rosy glow touched her cheeks and lips. Total understanding of his thoughts passed between them, and she smiled gently when she offered him a mug. "I'll get dressed, and we can hit the road. I'm looking forward to seeing more of the scenery outside town."

Guy surrounded her wrist and set down his mug before taking hers away "I've got something for you. For today." Just the contact of their two skins inflamed his desire. He consciously slowed his breathing. "The box." He indicated the pink-wrapped package. "Open it."

"You—Guy, I told you not to buy me anything. Thirty-one-year-old ladies don't need birthday presents." She went to run a finger over a length of lavender ribbon. "What is it?" She grinned, and the little-girl excitement popped to the surface.

Guy laughed. "You look more like eleven than thirty-one right now. Open the thing and see. No, wait—'' One large hand splayed on top of the box. "I can't resist giving a hint."

Leah tried unsuccessfully to pry his fingers loose. "Guy, don't tease."

He gave a theatrical sigh. "Okay, but the man said you can change them if you don't like them. I bought you a set without pruning shears, since we already have a couple of pairs. But if you want your own—"

"Guy Hamilton, you beast." Her fists, pressed against her hips, made the robe gape, and Guy felt light-headed with the effort not to touch her.

"Open it." His voice caught, and he cupped her jaw, leaning to part her lips gently with a kiss that sent his heart into four-four time. She stood on tiptoe and wrapped her arms around his neck. Their bodies fit together perfectly. Guy squeezed his eyes shut. His response was about to become evident to them both. He set her carefully away from him. "That was instead of a birthday card."

Her mouth, thoroughly kissed now, was moist and dark. After a lingering look, she stroked his jaw, then bent to concentrate on unwrapping the package.

"Oh, Guy, you shouldn't have done this." Her breath escaped in a long sigh as she pulled the rainbow gauze dress from its tissue cocoon. "It's so beautiful. I loved it when you showed it to me the other day. But it cost a fortune, and you can't afford it." She immediately clamped a hand to her mouth, blushing furiously.

Guy choked on his laughter. "I should think you'd be embarrassed. How do you know what I can afford? Just because I don't drive a fancy car and bop around in trendy duds, you think I'm a pauper, is that it?"

She shook her head mutely and gave him a wry grin.

"Good," he retorted. "Because I'm not. Actually I'm an eccentric millionaire. Now, I want to see you in that cheap little number. The saleswoman assured me, it's perfectly casual enough for a day's driving in the mountains." He pinched his nose. "'Actually, sir, this was undoubtedly created with *ultimate* versatility in mind. The lady will feel *utterly* comfortable wherever she wears it.'"

Leah kissed the corner of his mouth quickly and hurried into the bathroom, smiling broadly and fondling her present. He'd pleased her, Guy thought with satisfaction. They were starting off the day on the right foot; he was thinking about her first instead of taking her presence for granted.

He sat down and mulled over the questions that had plagued him all night. One sip of coffee proved Leah hadn't been kidding when she called it mud, but he took several swallows before abandoning it. His tight muscles and nerves began to unwind. She'd always had that effect on him, and here, among her greenery and the evidence of her light and airy touch, he felt her presence even when she wasn't in the room.

His fingers curled around the folded envelope in his pocket. The news had come earlier than he expected—a blessing and a possible curse. It might have been better if he hadn't known until she finished school. He picked up discarded gift wrappings and crumpled them inside the dress box. Now he could do what he'd wanted for so long—ask her to marry him, become her lover. His gut flattened against his spine.

A piece of ribbon had fallen beneath the table. Guy picked it up and rolled and unrolled one end. Familiar slivers of uncertainty gnawed at the back of his brain. She was emerging whole, for the first time in her life; he felt it, and he couldn't let anything interfere with that, including his longing to be joined with her forever.

Leah had thanked him for helping her—more often

than he cared to remember. If he asked her to marry
him and she accepted, would it be out of gratitude?
Guy discarded the idea. She was as in love with him
as he was with her; that wasn't an issue. Her possible
desire to give up school and any attempt at autonomy
was. She'd already talked of dropping out. Their marriage might convince her she should give up on further
education. He'd seen her in the role of subservient wife
before; it was a natural position for her. He couldn't,
wouldn't, watch her slip into his shadow and stagnate.

"What do you think?" Leah breezed into the room,
still barefoot, and made a twirling circle for him to
view the dress from all sides. Her hair flew. Her eyes
picked up a violet hue from the vivid fabric. Some sort
of glossy stuff on her lips made them shine, and her
tanned skin glistened. As she moved, the exotic scent
of autumn roses in sandalwood floated to him. Every
sane thought fled.

"Well?" She stopped, breathless, arms outstretched.
"Do I keep it or exchange it for a pair of pruning
shears?"

"You, my comedienne, grab a pair of sandals and
anything else you need, then get me out of here before
I do something you could take me to court for."

"TLAQUE—WHAT?" Leah brushed hair from her eyes
and peered at a blue-and-yellow-tile sign set into a
white stone wall. Guy was edging the jeep into an im-
possibly small parking space crisscrossed with exposed
tree roots.

He reached to take several papers from the glove
compartment. "Tlaquepaque," he said, engrossed in
reading. "You say it, T-lockey-pockey."

Leah glowered at his nonchalance. "How do you know? I suppose you speak fluent Spanish."

He grinned, his eyes invisible through dark sunglasses. "My talents are endless." One long forefinger stabbed at the paper he held. "Actually, this is a pamphlet about the area, and it tells you how to say it."

"Fraud." Leah laughed and hopped to the dusty red earth. "What is this place, anyway?"

"You'll see."

Guy led her beneath a carved archway into a cobbled courtyard ablaze with beds of flowers and centered by a bubbling fountain. Through inner archways she could see similar courtyards lined by two-story buildings, lush foliage cascading from their upper balconies. "Guy, this is lovely. All the little shops. Feels very Mexican and foreign. I expected Sedona to be a sleepy backroads place."

He pulled her to his side to allow a horse and buggy to pass. The driver wore a top hat, and his cargo consisted of two laughing young couples. "I understand Sedona used to be pretty sleepy," Guy explained. "Some man bought this piece of land on the edge of town and turned it into an arts-and-crafts village with a purely Mexican flavor—even trucked in authentic village bells, wrought-iron railings and so on all the way from Mexico. People come from all over to visit the place."

Leah instantly fell in love with the quaint atmosphere. Every tiny shop, with its treasure of unique paintings, pottery or jewelry, beckoned her. Handmade quilts, extravagant blown-glass creations, crystal shapes faceted to catch ever-changing colors—the selection was unending.

"Look at that." She grabbed Guy's arm and pointed

to a window at a beaten silver necklace of interlaced hands, a continuous chain of touching. "What a beautiful idea."

"Let's get it" was his prompt reply, and Leah had to stop him from marching inside the store.

"I've had one fantastic present today, thank you," she insisted firmly. "If you're going to try to buy me everything I admire, I'd better keep my mouth shut. How about lunch? It's almost one."

He glanced back at the necklace, then reluctantly gave in. "I don't see why I can't give you some things if I want to. But okay, have it your way. Lunch. How's Mexican food sound, since that's the theme around here?"

Forty minutes later, full and deliciously mellow, Leah squinted at Guy over the salty rim of a margarita glass. "Rincon del Tlaquepaque Restaurante Mexicano," she announced with satisfaction, reading from the front of the menu. "How's that?"

"Perfect." Guy covered her right hand on the red-and-white checkered tablecloth. "Spoken like a native."

Leah chortled. "Practiced while you were in the bathroom. I've never had a margarita like this before."

"Mmm." He eyed her critically. "They say they put egg whites in them and that's why they're thick and creamy. But from the sound of you, two had better be your limit. Something tells me you aren't a drinking woman."

She waggled the fingers of her left hand airily. "Need a little practice, that's all." Their arms touched, and she leaned close to smile into his incredible eyes. "Have I told you—" Another swallow of the smooth liquor slipped easily down her throat. "Have I told you you have the sexiest eyes I ever saw?"

"You're tipsy," Guy whispered, and pulled her against his shoulder. "You must have the lowest tolerance for alcohol on record. Let's walk."

He was misreading the cause of her happiness, but Leah followed him obediently from the open-air terrace, back into a cool courtyard. Giant sycamores towered above them, and cottonwood and cyprus cast shadows over the paving.

"Feel up to a little hike?" Guy asked. "There are some easy trails we should be able to stroll up and get a good view of the whole area."

Leah nodded cheerfully, resisting the urge to tell him she'd follow him anywhere.

"Hey, look at that." He stopped so abruptly that she bumped into his back. They'd reached the shop where she'd admired the silver necklace. "See?"

Without giving her a chance to locate the object of his interest, he pulled her through the door into a dim interior.

As Guy spoke quietly to the clerk, Leah frowned. If he thought she would let him buy the necklace, he was in for a disappointment. She hadn't completely forgotten the rules of propriety.

He stood by the window until the case was unlocked and something small given to him. The ring he held up was gold, made like the necklace of hands joined in an endless circlet.

Leahs awareness cleared. Her heart contracted sharply, and the air around her took on the crystalline quality of high country's winter snap. She couldn't meet Guy's eyes.

He took her right hand and slid the ring on her third

finger; it fit snugly. "A bit tight," he said quietly. "But I like it. Will you let me give it to you?"

"Yes," Leah said, then added more loudly, "yes, thank you. It's lovely, the loveliest thing I've ever seen." The traitorous tears misted her eyes. In his own way, he was trying to tell her something, to give her a sign. And for now she needed no more.

Their walk back to the jeep was made in silence, as was the short drive to the outskirts of Sedona, where Guy parked again and came to help her down.

"Are you up to it?" He indicated a trail of switch-backs leading between jutting pink mesa scattered on their lower reaches with scrubby trees and tumbleweed.

Her answer was to set out, nimbly avoiding fallen rocks and larger boulders along the way. The ring on her right hand seemed a circle of cool fire. Every second she fought the impulse to stare at it. Her wedding band had been heavy platinum, studded with six diamonds and flanked by an engagement ring so massive it dwarfed her hand. Selling the set after Charles died had made her feel cynical, ungrateful, until she fully acknowledged her reduced circumstances and decided her late husband would have understood.

An unconscious gesture, left hand caressing right, savored smooth gold and found it more pleasing than any fabulous jewel. Goose bumps flashed across her skin. Was she disloyal to a kind man's good intentions? Guy caught up, towered over her, smiling down, and her doubt fled. There was a time to get on with life, and for her that time was now. He took the lead, and she followed in his footsteps.

They scrambled on; Leah's open sandals, although flat, were unsuitable for climbing, but she didn't complain. The rock face became shallow scarps, like terraced steps running in ridges around the closest mesa. "If we get to the other side of this," Guy shouted over his shoulder, "we should be able to see forever."

He was right. "Oh, Guy," she breathed, flattening herself against rust-colored stone. "The sky. It's so blue, it burns. And it's...infinite. This whole setting looks like something out of a Western movie."

"That's why they make so many movies here," he replied. "Can't you imagine wagon trains down in that gulch." Below, a sheer ravine plunged to a wide gap between mesa. "And men on horseback thundering past. Clouds of dust, sweat, leather chaps, lariats—"

"Yes," Leah interrupted, laughing, "and 'yahoos' all over the place. I've seen those shows, too. Right now I feel as if we're the only two people left alive in the world. It's so peaceful."

"Do you suffer from claustrophobia?"

Guy's left-field question startled Leah. "Why, no. What a weird thing to ask up here."

"There's a cave immediately above us." He was craning his neck, shading his eyes. "At least I think there is from the shadow. Stay here if you like. I want to take a look. Won't be a minute."

Being left alone in the middle of nowhere, even for a minute, didn't appeal to Leah. "Hang on," she gasped. "I'm coming. I love caves." *Liar.* She never even remembered being in a cave.

The shadow Guy had seen was cast by a jutting overhang above an aperture just high enough for him to enter upright. Inside was a smooth hollow, like a bowl lying on its side, the floor covered with a fine mixture of dusty silt and sand.

"This has to be the strangest cave I've ever seen," Guy marveled. He slowly paced the perimeter, running his hand over the walls. "Looks like some giant punched a hole when the rock was still soft, then rotated his fist back and forth. Hah! A prehistoric potter." He appeared enormously pleased with his analogy as he scanned every inch of his find.

Leah cleared her throat. "Your potter was kind enough to provide us with a seat—our own eagle's eye vantage point on the world." She sat on a slab in the cave entrance, swinging her feet and supporting her weight on her arms.

"In other words, cut the gibberish and come sit with me." Guy flopped down beside her and matched the rhythmic swinging of her legs.

"I wish we never had to go back." Leah tipped up her face and closed her eyes. "I like it here."

A sudden breeze whipped the light skirt from her knees, and Guy stilled her hand before she could pull it back in place. "That first night—in Texas," he said. "Did you know I'd been watching you for some time before you saw me?"

Her lips parted; then she swallowed. "No, Guy, I didn't know. I heard something and it frightened me. That's all."

He watched her mouth, then flicked his eyes to hers and covered her with a visual caress. "The lights in the water made your dress transparent around your legs. When the wind blew, I wished I was the wind and touching you."

Leah's chest felt compressed by some enormous weight. She breathed deeply, her bodice suddenly unbearably tight.

Guy turned sideways and stroked her bare thigh lightly, repeatedly, from knee to groin until she shuddered and arched her back. He kissed the hollow of her throat, and feathered tiny nips along her collarbone and up to her ear.

Leah bent her head, and he kissed the back of her neck. "You're driving me slowly—no, rapidly mad," he rasped. "I don't think I can take the waiting anymore."

Her heart made its own thunder. "You don't have to." He'd pushed her skirt high; his steady caress of her leg continued. His sleeve cuff was folded back. Vein and sinew, flexing beneath the tanned skin of his hand and forearm, the way his wide watchband rode low and caught the light—every minute detail about him fascinated her.

The message was clear. He wanted to make love to her, here, in this high place apart from the rest of the world. Leah reached for the buttons on his shirt and undid them steadily, feeling muscle jerk on contact.

"This isn't what I planned. I wanted to bring you somewhere marvelous for the first time we were together."

Leah laughed deep in her throat and pushed the shirt from his shoulders. "And this isn't marvelous?" She glanced at the breathtaking panorama.

Guy shifted and ran the tip of his tongue along the line of her parted lips. The heel of his hand made wide circles over her stomach and pressed downward, sending shards of primitive longing through her body.

Almost violently, Leah rained kisses over his torso, savoring the smooth, salty skin at his sides, and fingered his hair-roughened chest and the hard, contracted flesh of his belly above his jeans.

"My God," he groaned. "I'm scared."

Leah flinched as his fingers dug into her upper arms. "Why? This is right, Guy. I know it is."

He pulled his lips back from his teeth, squeezing his eyes tightly shut. "You don't understand, little one. You've talked to me a thousand times about remembering I'm only a man—and I am. Six years alone is a long time."

She covered his body with gentle, constantly moving hands. Could he think he'd be unable—? *Fool.* He was concerned about his ability to maintain control, nothing more.

"Don't worry," she whispered, kissing a flat nipple. "Everything doesn't have to be perfect at once. We'll make it right." He didn't know the narrowness of her experience or the length of her own abstinence.

"I don't deserve you." His kisses were instantly fierce, possessing her mouth, rocking her face with their intensity. Breathing heavily, he held her close in trembling arms, his lips tracing her brows, her closed eyes, her cheekbones and jaw.

The narrow straps on her dress fell easily from her shoulders, and Guy gave his attention to the hint of softly swelling flesh that rose and fell ever more rapidly above her neckline.

"Guy." She lifted his face. "I want to feel you against me. Undress me, please." A slight angling of her body gave him full access to the small buttons that closed the dress from neck to hem.

The sensation of the one finger he slid downward, between her breasts, brought her nipples to straining crests. He slipped each fastening open carefully, his restraint etched in the taut lines of his face.

Guy paused, nuzzling her ear. "Can I make love to you, Leah? Will you let me love you in all the ways I've dreamed of?"

She couldn't answer. Her voice seemed frozen in her

throat. Leah took Guy's hands and tucked them inside her dress to surround her breasts. Guiding him, she lifted herself to him, making his taking her giving. He rubbed tongue and lips back and forth over thrusting fullness, then pulled back long enough to tug the dress down to her hips.

Warm air, and Guy, caressed her naked flesh. Pressed to his body, Leah slid beyond choice, beyond decision, to a fury of passion from which there was no turning back. The contrasts of their skin, their textures, urged her on and drove her to rotate her breasts with wanton deliberateness against the stimulating roughness of his chest.

Their exploration was frenzied, insatiable, until their bodies took on a mutual heat, a delicious feverishness. "Stop." Guy panted, holding her wrists. "Where? Not here."

He looked around, eyes glazed, before pulling her to her feet and farther into the cave. Their discarded clothes made a tumbled heap on the sandy floor, and Guy quickly shucked jeans and underwear in one sweeping motion, before kneeling in front of Leah. Still clad in skimpy bikini panties, she took in his form, the symmetry of him, his complete arousal. Blood pounded in her ears.

"Guy." She tried to sink down with him, but he clamped her hips and held her fast. "Guy, I want you, now."

His hands slipped upward, curving across her back, bending her over him until he could take the tip of first one, then the other breast into his mouth. His gentle teeth and firm tongue weakened her legs until he had to stop her from falling.

Guy recognized her fervor but wouldn't surrender to

it. If he let go now, it would be all over before she could possibly be satisfied. She was so lovely—golden where the sun had touched her, ivory where a swimsuit had hidden her skin. Her breasts were full, with a tantalizingly translucent quality. Holding back was taking more of his will than she'd ever know.

He rubbed a cheek over her ribs and blew gently against her navel, then, with constraint that made his arousal a pain, slid down the skimpy white panties. He followed his spanned thumbs with his lips, down, down, to the center of her. And she cried out and drove her fingertips mindlessly into the rigid muscles of his shoulders.

"No." Her voice was small and distant. "What—? Guy, no." And when her perfect body convulsed, he eased her to the ground, smoothed her tangled hair from her face and kissed her lips.

"It's all right," he whispered. "With someone you love, anything that pleases you is all right."

Her eyes flicked open, wide and wondering, and her hands groped for him. She bent her knees and guided him between her thighs and inside her. "Don't wait any longer, Guy."

He'd allowed his own eyes to close. Now he stared down into her eyes and saw his own wanting, needing, mirrored in deep blue—a reflection of his own raw desire.

Their two bodies moved as one, the pace increasing until incoherent love utterings, dragged from their hearts, became a language as ancient and primitive as the dance of their joined flesh.

He lasted longer than he'd dared hope, and at their shared climax the outpouring of his continence purged him of tension and left him heavy, warm and infinitely calm.

"I love you," he heard Leah whisper very far away, and wrapped her close.

He muttered a reply but never knew what it had been. Their limbs remained entwined, and he rolled onto his back, pulling her on top of him. Leah's head fit perfectly into his shoulder. Her heart beat a rapid, answering tattoo to his own.

Languor threatened to take him into sleep. He forced his mind to hang on while he stroked her and kissed the top of her head. She needed to feel him still with her.

The sun had slid lower in the sky when Leah finally rolled away from him and dragged his shirt to the cave entrance, where she knelt, gazing out.

Guy turned on his side and propped up his head. She looked like a wood nymph, her hair a shimmering mass, her spine straight above a tiny waist and flaring hips.

"What do you see out there?" he asked, and smiled when she peeked over her shoulder at him. "Any giants making magic caves?"

"No," she replied, sighing. "There's only one magic cave, and we found it."

He laughed. "We made it magic, my love. Before us it was just a plain old hole in the wall."

Leah fell silent, and Guy reached for his jeans to retrieve his watch. Locating the wrong pocket, he found the long, official envelope instead and drew it out. Surely this was the perfect time he'd known would occur.

A rustle at the cave mouth made him glance up. Leah had turned toward him, the sun's back light hiding her face. There was a tenseness about her that suggested a welling up of emotion. "What is it?" he asked, forming the envelope into a cylinder.

"You make me whole, Guy," she said. "All I want is to be a part of you. Nothing else will ever matter again. Tell me you don't regret what's happened."

"I don't regret it." The inside of his mouth became as dry as the sand beneath his bare feet. "You make me feel wonderful, too. But don't say nothing else matters to you but me. That's a pretty big number for a man to carry around."

She stirred, her posture unyielding. "You don't have to carry anything. Just love me."

He did love her. God, he loved her—too much. He shoved the envelope away and searched until he found his watch. The right moment hadn't come.

"Guy?"

He had to answer her. "I do love you, Leah." Checking the time gave him a chance to hide the tears of frustration in his eyes. "Hell, look how late it got. We'd better get out of here if we're going to be through the mountains before dark."

Her awkward, hurried movements as she dressed wrenched his heart. He'd confused her, left her not knowing where she stood with him. But he must make sure she completed school and saw herself as a separate entity. If he told her now what he longed to share, she might stop growing. He had to wait a little longer—at least to get her over the one hurdle she'd started to jump. Then he could reassess what to do next.

Holding her hand, he led the way back down the trail. Neither spoke aloud, but their thoughts seemed to scream. Was he wrong not to tell her he was free and wanted to marry her? Guy agonized over the question with every footstep. He couldn't be wrong. Waiting would be as hard on him as it was on Leah.

He stopped abruptly and brought her fingers to his lips. "I love you, my darling." At his words, her features relaxed. He kissed her brow and then her lips before setting off again at a faster pace.

Just a little while longer, he reasoned with himself, but every atom of his being warred against waiting one more second to claim Leah.

CHAPTER THIRTEEN

THE ONLY LIGHT Leah could see at Guy's house came from the meager bulb beside the porch.

Tonight had been the first time he hadn't come to meet her since she'd started school. Even in the days immediately following their trip to Sedona, when the atmosphere between them had been charged and volatile, he'd still been there, lounging against the Bug, at the appointed time. As if by unspoken agreement, they had never mentioned the few hours of joy they'd stolen in a place and time that gradually took on an unreality for Leah. Slowly, they'd slipped back into their old routine—except for the probing glances that passed between them when they weren't wary and the occasional desperate kiss that left her throbbing and shaky.

She climbed from her car and hesitantly approached the rectory door. Why hadn't he come, tonight of all nights? She'd made it. So had Dan. They would receive their high school diplomas by mail within ten days.

In the parking lot outside the learning center, Dan, more carefree than she'd ever seen him, had guided her around in a sedate waltzlike dance before breaking into a wild, whirling jig. Afterward, they leaned on each other, panting and laughing and, Leah knew from Dan's searching eyes, both looking for and wondering about Guy.

She plucked an oleander blossom from the hedge,

stalling, and stepped back to scan the windows once more. Then she rang the bell, afraid if she let herself in and he'd fallen asleep, he'd mistake her for an intruder. Seconds tripped by, then minutes.

Leah checked the hood of the jeep and found it cold. He had left the rectory in the middle of the afternoon without warning or explanation but evidently had returned a long time ago. She tried the bell once more, then knocked before using her key to enter. Unfounded apprehension chewed at the pit of her stomach. What did his change in routine mean?

The dark hallway and the stillness intimidated her. Yet she couldn't bring herself to violate the gloom with light. Guy must have wanted darkness. He'd come back tired from wherever he'd been and fallen asleep. That was the answer.

But Leah couldn't go home without making sure he was safe. Her tennis shoes made faint squishing sounds on the terrazzo floors. The guest-bedroom door was closed, but the counseling-office door was ajar. She turned sideways, staring in as she passed, then walked backward to the corner.

Jumpy idiot. The pounding of her heart filled her throat.

Guy's study door was open, as was that of his bedroom, and she edged slowly as far as his desk. "Guy," she whispered toward the bedroom. "It's me, Leah. You okay?"

A sudden blast of air and the sound of rattling drapery hooks shocked her. Every nerve in her body jangled, and she approached the bedroom, forcing herself nervously inside on legs that felt as if she were dragging them through deep water.

The draft came from the open sliding door to the

patio and turned the single big curtain into an eerie, moonlight-filled balloon. Leah's attention flew to the bed, searching for Guy's shape, half convinced she would see him there, murdered by some mad stranger.

The bed was empty.

Relief was immediately snuffed out as she tried to decide what to do next. The patio. Guy wouldn't just open the door and leave it that way. He must be outside.

Walking on tiptoe now, she crossed flagstones to the edge of the pool and peered fearfully down into obsidianlike water. Good God, her imagination was on overload; she was a hair away from total panic.

"Anybody'd think you were in church."

At the sound of Guy's voice, Leah's body jolted with enough force to almost throw her into the pool. She spun around, her clasped fists knotted against her belly. Rapid swallowing was all that stopped her from throwing up.

He sat on a chaise longue, his legs outstretched. "You know how people always tiptoe and whisper in church?" he said hoarsely. "No, maybe you don't. Well, Leah, hi. Why are you creeping around in the dark?"

She couldn't believe what she'd heard or his behavior. And she was angry, suffocatingly so. "You scared me, Guy Hamilton, all you can do is make wisecracks. What are you doing out here in the dark?"

"I'm doing what I please. This is my house in case you forgot—or it is for the moment."

Leah neared him slowly, sniffing the air suspiciously but smelling no trace of alcohol. "I haven't forgotten whose house this is. But what do you mean, it's yours for the moment?"

"Nothing."

The moon glimmered on his hair as he turned his face away. Her irritation fled. Something was very wrong. "You weren't there to meet me tonight," she offered redundantly, and pulled a chair beside his. "I missed you."

"I forgot," he replied without inflection. "But I seem to remember your telling me you didn't want me there, anyway."

Irritation flickered again. "Guy, that was a long time ago, after the very first class. You didn't let what I said then stop you once afterward. Why tonight—the last night? Even Dan hung around pretending to be checking over that wretched old bike of his when I knew he only wanted to see you."

"The last night?" A clicking sound came from Guy's throat.

"Yes." Every muscle ached. "The last night, and we both found out we're getting our diplomas. Dan was talking about trade school or maybe even a community college. I was kind of wondering about college myself." Her throat closed, and she struggled for composure. "None of it means a thing without you. Without you I'd never have started or finished even this much of my education. And it was you who made it possible for Dan to carry on."

"I should have been there waiting," he muttered. "We should have celebrated."

A muffled sound snapped her upright on the edge of her chair. He couldn't be crying. "What is it?" She leaned over him, touched his cheek and found it wet. "Oh, please, Guy. Don't shut me out."

He covered his face with the splayed fingers of one hand. "I messed up, Leah. I didn't handle a single thing right. All these years I believed my own faith was strong enough to rub off on anyone I touched, carry them through—make them see each other the way I do. I accepted everyone else's weaknesses and failures, and I thought they'd do the same for each other and...and for me." The chair squeaked as he swung his feet to the floor and hunched over.

Instinctively, Leah reached for him, paused an instant, her hands hovering inches from his bent shoulders, then clasped him in a grip that made her arms ache. A sickening idea was forming in her brain. "Does this have something to do with us?"

He remained silent, his head heavy on her shoulder.

"It does," she said, sighing. "Someone's making trouble for you because of me. I knew this was going to happen."

"A petition," he muttered indistinctly. "They called me over to the McCleods' house and showed me this endless list of signatures they'd collected."

"Oh, Guy." Leah began to tremble convulsively. "I warned and warned you. You wouldn't listen to me. I knew there could be trouble. What did it say—this petition?"

"It doesn't matter. I should have been there to meet you and Dan tonight instead of sitting around her wallowing in self-pity. It's—"

"Guy, don't—" she broke in, but the glitter in his eyes stopped her momentarily. He was desperate. "It does matter. I care about what happens here, and so do you. I should have made you listen."

He held her hands. "This is your real beginning, Leah. You can go as far as you want to go now." His teeth glinted as he tipped his head up. "I dreamed of this for you, and I'm happy. Make the very best you can of yourself, my love.''

"My love." It was the first term of endearment he'd used in weeks, and Leah's thirsty soul drank it in. But he was skirting reality again. "We have to talk about what happened to you today," she said softly. "There's no way to avoid an issue forever. We talked about that once, Guy."

His forefingers rubbed the insides of her wrists. "Tomorrow I'll go to see Dan. Or maybe I'll call him and get him over here to talk. We've never discussed what he really wants. He's bright. He can do very well with the right chances, and I'd like to help him. I'd like to see him go to college."

"Oh, Guy, Guy." Leah shook her head slowly. "Helping every needing soul who passes your way won't shut out your own problems. Please—" Her voice rose. "Please tell me what happened today and what it means to you—to us."

He stood and faced the pool, his hands deep in his pockets. "I was informed that I'm a bad influence, a rotten example to my *good* people. More importantly, I don't give their children the right example."

"All because Elsie Culver saw you hold me that day?" Leah was outraged. "After a few months' imaginative embellishment, one tiny incident has mushroomed into some grand, illicit passion?"

"They have more than that to go on," Guy said. "Swimming together in this pool—"

"Once!" Leah interrupted. "And again, ages ago."

"Listen. You asked what they have on me, so hear me out. We were seen together having drinks. At least a dozen instances of the two of us together in your car—at night—were documented, and—"

"You driving back from school with me," she exploded.

"Listen, will you?" he ground out. "And think. We were 'observed' shopping at the Biltmore Fashion Center, where we appeared 'unsuitably animated' and 'unconcerned about the impression we created.' This, of course, shows my 'completely inappropriate tendency toward extravagance and materialism,' in addition to my 'lack of the decorum expected of a church minister.' Someone I don't know must have helped with the wording of that lot.

"And we left early one Saturday morning a few weeks ago, and I didn't get back to the rectory until the middle of the night," he finished, the words snapping through clamped teeth.

"We got back at nine." This was crazy, all crazy.

Guy flopped into the chair again. "You got back at nine. *I* didn't feel like coming here and thinking all night long, so I went for a drive. How was I to know my big-hearted flock had set up a surveillance system to monitor my movements?"

"They did that?" Leah breathed. "They've been watching you. Watching both of us all this time. What do they want you to do?"

Guy's laugh was bitter. "Ideally, I think they'd like to see me stoned and run you out of town. Or maybe the reverse. Failing that, it's shape up or ship out, Hamilton. I do things their way—to the letter—or their damned petition goes to my superior and I'll be lucky if I'm allowed to preach in some mission in Outer Mongolia. And you've been so fantastic with all of them. I can't believe it. I had to leave the McCleods' house without saying anything. I was afraid I'd lose it all if I opened my mouth.

"Poor old Wally was here when I got back, worried to death because he knew where I'd been. He wanted to help me. He'd come to warn me earlier, but I'd already left. I took his head off, darn it. I'll have to go see him."

Goose bumps had sprung out on Leah's arms and legs. She shuddered violently. "Then that's it," she said flatly, getting up.

"What?" Guy stared up at her.

"I've got to get out of here, of course. The decision's been taken out of our hands. I've said this before; now I've got to follow through. I won't be responsible for ruining your career." As she spoke, she backed away. She would cry soon, and long, but it mustn't be in front of Guy.

"No!" he shouted. The next instant he towered over her, his strong fingers wound around her elbows. "If you go, they've won. We'll be admitting everything they think of us is true."

Leah bent her head and said, "It is true, Guy."

She heard him swallow. "It's not the way they've made it out. What we've had isn't something obscene and unnatural. We—we care about each other, and that's beautiful. It would be wrong for you to go."

"If you thought all this, why were you sunk in some kind of black pit when I found you out here? You just said you have to do things their way."

He was quiet for a moment before kissing her forehead quickly. "I hadn't had time to think everything through properly. That, or I couldn't without having you here with me to make me realize I won't let anyone do this to us."

She wanted to agree, to throw herself behind him

and fight, but she didn't believe they could win. "It'll be easier on both of us if I leave."

"Stay, Leah. Please do it for me. I need you just to be yourself. Behave naturally and carry on. That way you'll be supporting me. If you go, I'm branded as some sort of monster, whatever I do. Surely you see that?" His breath escaped slowly. "I'm admitting to you that without you I'm not going to make it, anyway. Together we can weather whatever comes, and then I'll be able to get my own head together again and decide what to do next."

Leah carefully pulled free of his grip. "I'd better get home. Wally will be wondering where I am." They both knew she would stay in Phoenix as long as necessary. Why spell it out or dwell on the fact that they probably had no future together? "Guess I'll see you Monday. Have a good weekend."

"Thank you," Guy said quietly.

As soon as she was gone, he went inside and lay on his bed. He loved her so much. Every tiny detail of their lovemaking had flashed through his mind a thousand times since they'd been together. The weeks of not touching her or holding her had been hell, but the waiting should have been over tonight. Tonight he'd planned to ask her to marry him.

If his world hadn't suddenly been turned inside out, he would have met her and taken her somewhere quiet to toast the successful end of school and to offer her the sapphire engagement ring he'd bought. He reached up to lift the box from a bookshelf above his bed. Resting on one elbow, he popped open the lid. Ghostly light from the window bored laser shafts into the center of the three stones inside.

Her eyes were the color of these gems. Every day

since he'd bought the ring, he had studied it covertly, visualizing it on her slender finger. She'd never taken off the little band he'd found in Sedona. It sent a spear of happiness and longing into his gut every time he looked at it or saw her smooth its surface. But he had wanted to give her this real sign of his love and the life he planned for them to share.

For a few insane seconds at the McCleods', he'd considered announcing he was a free man and that he and Leah were to be married. Then reason had blessedly taken over. If he'd followed his instinct, then told her, perhaps just now, she would think he was using her to climb out of his predicament. She probably did think as much regardless. A sudden offer of marriage when his professional neck was on the line would seal her opinion, and he wouldn't blame her.

He was crying again. Hot tears ran down his temples, and he turned on his stomach, clenching the ring box in his fist. "Messed up" had been an understatement. He'd done a bang-up job of ruining both their lives. Why hadn't he told her the minute he received notification of his divorce and taken a chance on what she might do? Why did he always feel he had a clearer view of how others would or wouldn't react than they did themselves?

Guy didn't know the answers to any of his questions. He knew only that he loved his work—and Leah. And becoming her husband now would take a miracle.

Deep inside, he was convinced he could beat the threat to his job. An open discussion with his superior, and time, was all that should take. But Leah? She was unlikely ever to trust him again—or to take that step he so longed to see her take toward even a tentative faith.

The salt taste of his tears was in his mouth, and he ground his back teeth together. He couldn't give up on making it through with Leah.

CHAPTER FOURTEEN

THE PHONE RANG as Leah walked through her office door on Monday morning. She dropped her purse on the desk and leaned to pick up the receiver. "Good morning. St. Mark's."

She heard the caller breathing for several seconds before Elsie Culver's familiar, high-pitched voice scattered down the line. "Will you still be at the rectory tomorrow morning, Mrs. Cornish?"

Leah massaged her right temple. Three sleepless nights and the miserably confused hours between had left her with a constant, dull headache. Elsie Culver was all she needed right now.

"Mrs. Cornish," Elsie prompted, "are you there?"

A long, slow sigh flowed from the bottom of Leah's lungs. "I'm here, Elsie. And I'll be here tomorrow. What can I do for you?"

A muffled voice in the background, then a scraping sound, let Leah know Elsie wasn't alone and had covered the mouthpiece to confer with a companion. Leah tapped a fingernail on hard plastic and quelled the urge to hang up.

"Tomorrow's my day for cleaning," the other woman finally announced. Then, with a smug note, she added, "But under the circumstances, I'll put it off until I hear from the minister. I suppose he's talked to you about our little discussion on Friday?"

Leah's temper threatened to snap. "He did mention

something,'' she managed through gritted teeth. ''Don't give tomorrow another thought. We'll manage.''

As she dropped the receiver into its cradle, she sensed someone behind her and swung around to see Connie Ingalls hovering in the doorway. One look at the dark circles beneath Connie's blue eyes and the disheveled mass of her usually well-ordered black curls, shot fear into Leah. Mary and Anna stood each side of their mother, clinging to her hands. Their little faces were solemn.

Connie opened her mouth to speak but immediately choked on wrenching tears that shook her whole body.

''Connie!'' Leah sped to grab the woman's shoulders. ''What's happened? What's the matter?''

The ragged sobs only increased as Mary and Anna wrapped their spare arms around Leah's legs.

Helplessness overtook her. She needed Guy. ''There's no room to sit down in here. Let's go to the counseling office; then I'll find Guy.'' A sliver of apprehension invaded her at the thought of facing him, but she shoved it aside.

Connie let herself and the girls be led down the hall and settled in a huddle on a couch. Her tears had abated to irregular hiccups. ''I shouldn't have come here,'' she said. ''But I can't work at the nursery until I find out what's happened to Dan. And I don't know what else to do.''

Leah froze. ''Something happened to Dan? Oh, Connie, why didn't you let us know? Where is he?''

''That's just it.'' Connie's sobbing began again, but more quietly. ''I don't know where he is. He left yesterday afternoon, and he hasn't come back. The girls and I looked everywhere we could, but they're too little to walk far, and I ran out of places to go on the bus. Besides..." She trailed off, looking at her balled hands.

"Yes, yes, Connie. Besides?" Mary had toddled from the couch, and Leah swept the child into her arms.

"I didn't have any more money," Connie whispered, and hid her face in both hands.

Leah blinked rapidly. "Stay here," she told Connie gently. "Guy will know what to do."

She found him in the garden, attacking the soil with a spade as if pounding dirt would satisfy some deep anger. For a moment, she watched him, absorbing into her own heart the disappointment and agony she was sure drove him. Then the pressure of Mary's trusting little fingers tugging at Leah's collar broke the moment.

"Is Uncle Guy mad?" Mary asked in a loud whisper. She jammed a thumb into her mouth, and her smooth brow crinkled.

"No, just busy," Leah reassured, then shouted, "Guy, can you spare a few minutes?"

His head shot up, and his instant, welcoming smile made her swallow. He was relieved and incredibly happy to see her. The past two days had been hell for both of them.

"Coming," he called, sticking the spade upright in the earth before brushing at old work pants as he walked toward them. "Hi there, little Mary. How's my girl?" He kissed a dewy cheek and ruffled the girl's hair, but all the time he kept his eyes on Leah's. "It's so good to see you. If you hadn't shown, I'd have hunted you down. I don't know how I managed not to come to you over the weekend, but I figured I had to give you breathing space."

She hugged Mary tightly. "Not now, Guy. We've got trouble, and this time it isn't because of anything we've done. Come on! Connie's inside, and she needs you.''

Guy was strides ahead of Leah and Mary by the time they reached the counseling office, Leah having filled him in on what little she knew about Dan's disappearance.

Leah offered to take the two little girls away and leave Connie and Guy to talk alone. They both insisted she stay.

Guy made Connie repeat, word for word, what she'd already told Leah. She added that Dan had come home from the hotel job the previous afternoon, then left after an argument. Insistent prodding from Guy didn't produce more information except that Dan had walked out before, several times, but always returned after a few hours.

"Where would he go?" Guy repeated, talking to Connie but shooting a frustrated glance at Leah, who shrugged helplessly. "Please, Connie. If you won't give me anything else to go on, how can I help? I can go cruising around searching for him, I suppose. I will, anyway. But if I don't find him pretty quickly, we'll have to report him missing to the police.''

"No!" Connie exploded. "No police. He's always been such a good boy—a man now. I won't have the police putting his name in their books.''

"All right, all right," he calmed her. "But *help* me.''

"He likes the mountains." Total exhaustion had turned Connie's face gray. "And he took his bike. He could have headed out into the hills. I went all over the town, so I don't think he's here.''

"He likes mountains?" Guy lifted both palms. "Where would I start?''

Connie bit her lip. "We went to Squaw Peak for a

picnic once—when his dad was still alive. We've often talked about what a happy time that was. Dan would never go back afterward, but maybe..."

Guy leaped up. "I'll try there first."

"They turned off all the lights."

Anna's words, clearly spoken, gained her the attention of every eye in the room.

"Shh," Connie muttered, hugging the child. "She's just tired and confused," she added to Guy and Leah.

Guy frowned and went to kneel in front of Anna. "What do you mean, sweetheart, 'They turned off all the lights'?"

Anna curled her knuckles against her mouth, her face turned up to her mother's. "Mommie said not to tell. But they turned off the lights, and—" She began to sniffle. "We—we couldn't cook or use the fan. And when Mommie tried to call about it, the phone wouldn't work, either." Her voice ended in a shrill wail.

"Okay, Anna," Guy soothed. His features were a set mask. "We'll make everything all right again. Connie, they cut everything off for nonpayment of bills, didn't they? Why didn't you tell me?"

Perspiration appeared above Connie's mouth; she looked sick. "Because you've done so much for us already. Things got better for a while, but then our rent went up, and I couldn't make it."

"You could have told me," Guy said. "We'd have figured something out. I suppose this is what sent Dan running like some mad thing. He's had all he can take, poor kid."

Leah was clasping and unclasping her fingers, and both little girls scrubbed their eyes miserably. Guy surveyed them all and shook his head. "This is as much my fault as anyone's. If I'd kept my feet on the ground and my eyes open, I'd have realized you and Dan still might not make enough to get by. But I wish you'd come to me before things got so out of hand, Connie. Go home, please, in case Dan shows. Leah will call and arrange to pay your utility bills and get the power and phone rehooked. Later on, we can make some permanent decisions.''

"I left the McCleods' eldest girl in the nursery," Connie muttered. "I didn't know what else to do, and there wasn't anyone but you to turn to."

Guy helped her to her feet. "I'm glad you came to me. Try not to worry. I'll get someone over to the nursery, then run you home and see if I can find Dan. Leah will stand guard here."

He left, ushering the bedraggled little band ahead of him. Leah caught his brief backward glance and smiled encouragement. His job called for him to be all things—minister, mentor, the final straw to clutch when all else failed. A giant order for one man, too much for any man without human, as well as spiritual, support.

She made the necessary calls to the utility companies and wrote checks to cover Connie's outstanding bills. Then she began her vigil and tried, unsuccessfully, to work.

By midafternoon, the weather had taken on an unusually heavy atmosphere for the time of year. A pewter-streaked sky beyond the window suggested a rainstorm, rare for November.

Two calls from Guy, checking to see if she had any news, only deepened her gnawing dread. The house seemed to close in around her, and Leah wandered outside. An oppressive silence hung over the grounds and the buildings, and the palms seemed hardly to sway.

Useless. She felt absolutely useless. All she could do was hang around an empty house and wait. Dan's face, laughing as it had been on Friday night, came clearly into her mind. His happiness hadn't been allowed to last long. She wanted to see him, to make sure he was all right.

Guy's flower beds were still a blaze of color. Chrysanthemums and clumps of ice plant crowded each other out. They needed thinning.

Leah forgot her tailored gray slacks and went to her knees on the concrete pathway. After a half hour she had arranged at intervals several small piles of plants. She sat on her heels and regarded the uprooted flowers. Too bad to throw them out. Maybe she should make them into bouquets and give them away.

She had severed the stalks and filled her arms with blooms before she acknowledged the obvious. She had no one who would want her gift except Wally, and even he might find her offering strange.

A car sped by on Fan Lane. Its engine noise startled Leah, then plunged her into depression. If only Guy would come back and say Dan was safe.

Churches always had flowers, she thought. During her childhood, peeking into a church at the end of her street had taught her that. She looked at her gay armload, then at the white structure across the way. Funny, now that she thought of it, she didn't remember seeing any flowers the one time she'd been in the building.

Hesitantly, she walked down the path and beneath the palms to the wooden door of St. Mark's. She maneuvered her bundle from arm to arm to turn the handle.

Once inside, Leah had to locate the power panel to the left of the door. First she flipped on every lever, flooding the empty building with glaring brilliance. She turned off all but a few lights near the altar.

Finding herself on tiptoe as she moved along the

center aisle, Leah remembered Guy's comment about people's behavior in church. She immediately planted each foot with a smart click and dumped her burden beside the front pew. She grinned a little, and it felt good. Guy would smile, too, if he'd read her thoughts.

She hadn't been wrong; there weren't any floral arrangements. A cluster of green plants stood at each side of the altar, but there were no cut flowers in the church. Perhaps the parishioners wouldn't like it if she filled their place of worship with all this gaudy color. Guy might hate it, too. No, he wouldn't. Instinctively, she was sure Guy would love flowers in here, just as he loved them outside. She needed vases.

The first cupboard she checked yielded nothing but a stack of dusty old books and the guitar Guy had played. Leah ran a finger across the strings, winced at the discordant noise she produced and closed the door quickly. Three other cupboards failed to produce anything she could use. She was torn between abandoning her project and going back to the house for containers when she located a box of milk-glass vases and a metal jug in an alcove.

Further armed with a bucket of water from an outside faucet, Leah began to assemble cheerful, if not skillful, groupings.

While she worked, she thought of Guy and of Dan. If she were Guy, she'd be on her knees, praying for Dan's safety. Unconsciously, she threaded her fingers together. How did you pray? She glanced around the cool, pale interior. Peaceful. If she could pray anywhere, it should be here, but no one had taught her how. Maybe you didn't need to learn something like that.

"I just wish Dan would get back safely," she blurted out loudly. Then she added, "Please." It wasn't much, but it was the best she could do. This was a time when she couldn't afford to miss out on any possible help from anywhere.

Somewhere she'd heard the comment that God didn't make deals. But who knew what God did? If everything turned out all right for Dan—or even if it didn't—she might just start trying to be friends with Guy's boss.

She had just put two vases of flowers, one tall, one stubby, on the right side of the altar when the sound of the door opening was followed by squeaky steps on the linoleum floor. Leah was almost afraid to turn around. When she did, she hesitated long enough to take a deep breath and whoop before rushing headlong against Dan's tall, thin body.

"Where have you been, you little stinker?" She surrounded his ribs in a bear hug and felt his long arms awkwardly close across her back. Pounding him, keeping her head down on his chest, she started to cry. She'd cried more in the past few days than the rest of her life.

"Aw, hell, Leah," Dan pleaded. "Don't cry; please don't cry. I'm sorry I did this to all of you."

Leah released him and stood back to take in his length. "You look awful."

"Yeah." His wide mouth turned down. "That's what Mom said."

"You went home already? Good. Your mother was frantic. You should get back there to her, Dan—after you tell me where you've been." She pushed him into a pew and sat beside him. "Have you eaten?"

He smiled a little wanly. "I went to see my mother, remember. You think she didn't immediately start cramming food into me." The blue eyes, underscored with dark smudges, slid away. "Food Guy bought. We didn't have it yesterday."

The right words would never be more important with this boy than they were now. "It made Guy feel good to be able to help out. We both care about you all. You're very special to me, Dan. You know that, don't you?"

He shook his head and crossed his arms on the back of the next pew. "I don't know why. All you've done since you met me is put out. Now Guy's out there driving around for nothing. *I'm* nothing. I can't even try to let him know I'm okay."

Leah wiped slick palms on her pants. "Guy will be back soon, I'm sure. The last time he called, he said he'd give it another hour or so, then come home and decide what to do next."

"How long ago was that?"

"I don't know. An hour, maybe longer."

"Mom said he was looking in the mountains, Squaw Peak. But I'd never go there."

"No," Leah said. To deal with this situation, she needed wisdom, Guy's kind of wisdom.

"Leah—" Dan's throat moved, and he pressed his lips together. "Why do some people have nothing but rotten luck? My dad—my dad—" He covered his eyes.

She rubbed the sharp bones in his back. "Just say it all, Dan. Get it out. All the junk inside only grows until it chokes you."

He nodded, keeping his eyes closed. "My dad wasn't much older than me when he married my mom. They didn't have beans, but they were happy, and he was the kind of man who was always expecting good things to happen. When I remember him, I remember him laughing, not—not the way he was when he died."

He paused, and Leah saw him gathering together the

little pieces of his past and the confusion of his present and trying to fit them together. She knew there was nothing she could do or say to help him.

A shallow breath shuddered noisily past his lips. "He and mom went to church when I was little. Bob went with us, too. We were always so poor, but Dad gave to the church, and he prayed, and nothing good ever happened to him. I hurt him when I wouldn't go anymore, but I don't understand any of this." He made a wide gesture. "I can't feel anyone here. At least not anyone who gives a damn about me. On Friday night I thought I could see something worth having in the future. For about twenty-four hours I was just like my old man. Dreaming. There's nothing for the don't-haves in this world; only it takes some of us longer than others to realize it. My dad *died* without realizing it."

"Dan…" *Oh, God. The right words, please.* "Dan, you're no more of a 'don't-have' than I was. I don't even have a memory, any kind of a memory of a father to hang on to. He was a drifter, and one day when I was still a baby, he drifted right out of my life. My mother was…" The damn tears welled again, and she could hardly breathe. "My mother was a whore who worked in a restaurant and brought home a succession of men after she finished work each night. I grew up listening to them through the walls of a two-room apartment. Then, when I was nineteen, I married the first man who asked me. I was lucky. I'll never stop being grateful to Charles. He loved me. He gave my mother enough money to make some sort of new life. And he *never* threw up at me how I'd come from the gutter.

"I got a chance, and I'm not ever going back to the gutter. Now I've started making something of myself.

So have you. This thing that happened over money at home will pass; you'll see. You and I are going to be the best we can be, and we'll make our own good luck.'' She was weary, but she must press on. A flicker of light in Dan's lackluster eyes suggested she was making inroads. ''I never went to church as a kid. Although I often wondered about it. Charles and I went a few times. I didn't know why he wanted to go or what he thought about when he was quiet there. I just used to stare and wonder if I looked okay, because that was important to him. But this is a peaceful place, Dan. I still don't know what I believe, but I *can* accept that Guy's found something special I'd like to have a part of. Maybe it wouldn't be so bad to come in here sometimes to think. I might just try it one day. In fact, I'm going to do it for sure. Why don't you, the next time you feel like running away?''

He spread his arms along the back of the bench. ''I might. Know where I was?''

She raised her eyebrows.

His laugh was hollow. ''At the airport. I rode all the way out there just to sit and watch planes take off and land all night and wish I was on one of them going somewhere. It didn't matter where. I even thought of going to some railroad siding and jumping a boxcar, like you read about. Didn't have the energy or the guts. I fell asleep, and some guy picking butts from the ashtrays woke me up at about eleven. It took me the rest of the time I was gone to find the courage to go home.''

Leah laughed and blinked. ''If I cry much more, I'm going to flood us out. I'm so glad to see you, Dan. From the day we met, you've been like the brother I never had. Relax, kid. With Guy's help, we'll work it all out. Time you started thinking about more schooling, not skipping town.''

"Why don't you and Guy get married?"

Leah's insides dropped away. Her skin crawled. "That's a weird question," she managed around a pain in her throat.

"And none of my business, right?" Dan shrugged. "Only you two are obviously crazy about each other, and if you were married, we could all relax."

She tried to stand, but he held her wrist. "Mom and old Wally and me, and a lot of other people who think you're great, are getting pretty sick of worrying about the two of you. So why don't you just do it? That'd be the way to shut up all the rotten gossip."

She smiled tightly. How did you explain that you were willing but the other party wouldn't take the necessary steps to make it happen. "Don't worry about us. It's time you got back to your mother and the kids. But we'll talk tomorrow, okay?"

"Okay." His eyes were suddenly old, appearing to see deep inside her head. "Tomorrow."

"You bet it'll be tomorrow, kiddo." Guy had come beside them unnoticed and was gripping the end of the pew, glaring at Dan. "You've put your mother through hell, and Leah and me." He sat beside her and gathered her tightly against his side. He was filthy and wild looking, his pants spattered with mud.

Leah unthinkingly held his hand. "Go easy, Guy. Dan's had a rough time, and I understand. He's already talked to Connie, and he's going home again now. We all need to back off and get some perspective."

Guy watched her mouth as she spoke, then stared into her eyes. His fingers twined more tightly into hers. Leah wondered how long he'd been in the church, listening, before he approached them.

"Wise, as usual," he said. "When you start looking for someone to care about, Dan, one on one, try for a lady like this. Now get home. While I was running around like a dog after its tail, I came up with a doozy of a solution to your little financial foul-up. Working for me part-time. Wally should be doing less, and you can fill in. It'll work if it doesn't kill you in the process. Get some sleep and prepare for battle.''

All three slid to stand in the aisle, and Guy wrapped an arm around Leah's shoulders as they watched Dan leave. The door closed with an echoing thud. Their twin breathing was the only sound in the silence that rushed in.

''I'm bushed,'' Guy groaned. ''I went by Connie's on my way back and found out he'd shown. The electricity's back on, and they'll have the phone by morning. Sit with me a minute. My muscles are screaming for a hot shower, but all I want to do is be here with you for a while first.''

She made no attempt to stop him when he pulled her onto his lap and lifted her face to his. ''You're beautiful,'' he said. ''Have I told you that lately?''

''Not lately,'' she replied breathlessly.

''Well, you are. And I've decided what you should study in college.''

Leah leaned away. ''Oh, thanks. And what's that?''

''Crisis counseling, of course. You're a natural. I know that boy might still be gone if he hadn't wanted to come back and talk to you.''

''You give me too much credit, but thanks. He'd never have been able to walk away from his family.'' Guy's palm, massaging her shoulder, made thought almost impossible. ''You should get that shower and some rest,'' she added.

''Mmm.'' He looked past her, a speculative expression narrowing his eyes. ''Did you do that?''

''Do what?'' She craned around and instantly

guessed he was referring to the flowers. "The flowers? I hope it's all right. I had to do something, so I started thinning beds and couldn't bear to throw all of those gorgeous things away. Was it all right to put them here? I can easily take them—"

His hand, cupping her chin, immediately followed by a swift but intense kiss, cut her off. "They're lovely. Could be the loveliest thing I've seen in this building, next to you. I'll have to get you to do floral arrangements in here all the time."

He was avoiding the disaster steadily closing in around him. Leah followed Guy from the church, forming arguments, avenues to broach their dilemma, but discarding each one. She couldn't be the one to bring up the subject.

The rain she'd expected was falling steadily, and they ran to the house, arriving breathless and laughing, their shoulders damp.

Guy wiped moisture from Leah's face with his hand. "Don't go away," he pleaded. "I've hardly seen you today, and I can't stand to be alone again. If you leave, I'll only come and hammer on your door."

She flattened a palm on his chest. "I won't go yet. Shower; then maybe we'll talk for a bit."

"Why can't we talk *while* I shower." His eyes turned the color of green slate before he added, "Through the door, of course," and grinned.

Muscles in Leah's jaw trembled. "I guess we can." She was afraid, as much of herself as of him. They couldn't afford more mistakes, not now, not here.

He whistled as he led the way, then sang in an unusual grainy, intensely masculine voice that broke in a heart-twisting way. She closed her eyes fractionally and felt the magnetic force field between them. The heavy heat had started deep inside; the thrilling ache, in her thighs. She straightened and lengthened her steps. They were going to talk, nothing more.

"I'm going to strip off these disgusting rags," Guy announced, going into his rooms. "They may have to be burned later." His shirt hit the floor before he made it into the bedroom.

Leah automatically picked it up. "You are one of the most untidy people I've ever met," she remarked, thinking at the same time that it was totally true.

"I know," he replied complacently. "Guess I'm not completely perfect, after all."

She balled up the shirt and hiked it at his back, but he turned just in time to catch it. He'd tossed the crumpled checked cotton back before she had time to recognize the move as a diversion. Guy used the split-second advantage he'd gained to grab her waist and back her to the bed.

"Guy!" Her knees buckled, and she was flat beneath him, his face a few inches from hers. "We can't do this. I mean—you know what I mean."

"I know exactly what you mean." Firm lips covered and parted hers. His tongue found the farthest recesses of her mouth, teasing, until she began to relax and return his ardor. His naked chest and shoulders felt cool beneath her searching fingers, his muscles hard and his skin, when she lowered her face to kiss his neck, tasted deliciously salty.

His thigh pressed between her legs, and she turned her head sharply, the familiar wanting flaring out of control. She nipped his shoulders and arched her back when he stroked her breasts through her silk blouse and bra.

Abruptly, he seized her hands and captured them above her head. "Time out while we can still think. I'm going to shower. You can hide your face or watch, whichever appeals." He straight-armed over her, gazing down; then the bed rebounded with the loss of his weight.

"While we can still think." Leah lay very still, trying to form the simplest thought that didn't relate to the clamoring sensations in her body. Then she scrambled to sit cross-legged in the middle of the bed and propped her chin in the palm of one hand.

Guy aped a series of Adonis poses until she collapsed with laughter, which slowly subsided as he removed the rest of his clothes. He stood for an instant, his eyes silently telling her what he wanted, before going into the bathroom.

Leah was left with the mental vision of his straight back and wide shoulders, his tensile legs, like those of an athlete and sprinkled with blond hair.

The sound of dashing water, then the glass door bumping against rubber, was followed by Guy's voice, raised in song once more. By the time Leah reached the outside of the shower doors, she wore only her lace bra and panties.

His body was a tall outline, not moving, simply standing, head thrust back to allow water to jet against his face. She reached back to unhook the bra and dropped it on the counter beside the sink, intensely aware of the fullness and weight of her breasts. The panties followed, and she stepped into the enclosure behind Guy.

CHAPTER FIFTEEN

HE HADN'T HEARD HER. When she laid her palms flat
on his back, she felt muscle and sinew jolt. Guy stood
very still, elbows uplifted, his hands locked behind his
neck.

Leah smoothed his wet body. The steamy air filled
her lungs and shortened her breaths. She reached up to
trace his arms and shoulders. Lightly, she feathered her
fingers down his spine and fanned outward over his
ribs to the glistening skin at his sides.

"I love you," she whispered, and circled his narrow
hips, pressing her breasts to his back, massaging the
hard plane of his belly. There could be no more holding
back. This might be their only time together. Although
she cared with every tiny fragment of her being,
whether or not he loved her in return, she still savored,
reveled in, her own declaration.

Guy moved slowly and covered her hands, guiding
them over his groin to unyielding thighs and back to
his stomach. "I love you, too, Leah. So much it hurts.
Hold me, sweetheart."

Spray beat from his shoulders onto her hair and face.
He reached back, pressing her ever closer, and she
touched him with a total intimacy that sent a shared
tremor through their molded bodies. She touched him
as a woman in love and as a lover intent on pleasing
and being pleased. They loved each other, and the
knowledge set her free. Once, he'd told her nothing

could be wrong when given or taken by a man and a woman in love. Leah stroked and absorbed into herself the convulsive jolt of power from his muscle. He loved her, too. He'd told her once before. Now the knowledge filled her with voluptuous strength.

"Wait," he breathed, "wait, my love."

He faced her, his chest heaving, and Leah almost stepped backward, impaled by the intense light in his eyes. Slowly, he bent his head, and their mouths met, grazing tantalizingly back and forth. He braced his hands on the tile above her head, keeping inches between their bodies, until Leah unconsciously strained toward him, brushing erect nipples against wet chest hair.

Guy urgently thrust his hips into her belly, and they came together in a frenzied embrace that rocked her soul. His kisses inflamed her mind and her senses. She threaded her fingers into his hair and stilled his face, making him wait as she carefully ran a trail around his lips with her tongue before delving deep into his mouth.

"You're driving me mad," he muttered when she released his head and swept her hands to knead his hips. "And, little friend, the water's getting cold."

She burrowed against his chest, clinging, while they laughed. "Turn it off."

Guy held her away, his smile fading. "I want to make love to you, slowly, in my own bed." He cupped her breasts, his gaze flickering down to the softly swelling flesh beneath his hands. For seconds, he teased her nipples, watch them peak, then carefully tongued and took each one between his teeth.

Hot flashes of sensation coursed through her body. The nuzzling action of his cheek and the pressure of his mouth drove her against the cool wall of the shower. His hand went to her stomach, then swept down between her legs, and Leah had to clutch his shoulders as her knees turned rubbery.

By the time her mind gradually cleared, the water was icy. Guy held her tightly in one arm and reached to turn off the shower. His face grew darkly impassioned, and her renewed arousal was instant in flesh that still throbbed.

He carried her to the bed, pausing barely long enough to pull the covers partially back before they fell, wet, onto the sheet.

"I guess we can forget slow," he said against her mouth.

Leah urged her fevered lover's damp body over hers, gloried in his weight, received him, surrounded and fused with him. Their union, new again, as her brain acknowledged it would always be between them, created a heated place where skin and muscle, bone, breath and pumping blood, the life of two, became one. With Leah, Guy moved as part of her, faster, higher, the sounds of their lovemaking small and garbled. Then came the final, triumphant call at their climax, the tangle of suddenly leaden limbs and the sweet whisper of mingled breath over warm faces.

"My love, my love." Guy's voice broke. "You're everything to me. I never thought I'd get so lucky. It scares me."

Leah slid an arm around his neck and pulled his head against her breast. "Don't be scared—ever. Just keep on loving me and saying you do."

They nestled in a languid embrace until Guy began again to do as Leah asked. Hours passed before they fell into an exhausted sleep.

When Leah awoke, the room was dark. Blinking and yawning, she rolled beneath the weight of Guy's heavy

arm. She squinted. A muted gleam from a bedside radio's dial sent a faint shimmer over his tousled blond
hair.

Memories of their lovemaking flooded back in vivid
cameos. Guy murmured indistinctly, and his fingers
tightened around her ribs. Leah smiled, trying unsuccessfully to make out his features.

What were they going to do? The persistent question
wormed its way into the center of her happiness,
spreading its gray pall steadily outward. Leah pushed
back her hair and chewed the inside of her lip. Something bigger than either of them, or certainly her, was
going to have to sort this one out.

She slipped from the bed and went into the bathroom. With face freshly scrubbed, her teeth cleaned
with a new brush she found in a drawer and her hair
arranged into some semblance of order, she returned to
slide into bed.

"Hi, lady," Guy said from the darkness beside her.
Leah started and turned into his outstretched arm.
"Hi. Thought you were out cold for the night. I almost
wrote a note and snuck out of here, but you and this
delectable bed lured me back."

"Mmm." Guy's breath tickled her ear. "You'd better not sneak out. This is where you belong, and I don't
intend to let you get away again."

She frowned. "I don't want to get away, Guy. But
we both know I can't be here all night."

"Too dangerous for you?" he teased. "I'll behave
whenever you ask me to."

He couldn't be as wide awake as he sounded. "You
know what I mean."

For several seconds he stroked her hair and face.
"Leah—" he kissed her lips softly "—we have to
talk."

Hope made her heart bound. "I want to," she said. "I've wanted to for a long time."

"Would you consider marrying me next week?"

Leah's mind blanked. She must have imagined he just asked her to marry him. He wasn't even divorced.

Guy leaned away to flip on a small lamp, then propped his head and stared down into her face. "You do want to marry me, don't you?" He watched intently for her reaction.

Her body didn't seem to want to move. Her hand was a dead weight when she raised it wonderingly to the stubble along his jaw. "I want to be your wife, Guy. That can't be a surprise to you. But...yes, I'll marry you. As soon as it's possible. In the meantime, I can't stay here with you. I'll suffer every minute of the waiting, but we have to make sure we do everything right from here on out. I'm beginning to care almost as much about this place of yours as you do—and these people. Even the ones I shouldn't give a damn for. They'll be the biggest challenge."

His unwavering glance became disconcerting. Leah made herself keep her eyes on his.

"We don't have to wait, sweetheart. We can get married just as soon as we get the formalities out of the way."

Leah dropped her hand to his shoulder and let it slide down his arm. "I don't understand."

"My divorce is final." His nostrils flared. "I... Susan divorced me, and now I'm free."

"I see." But she didn't see, not quite. "Guy, do you mean that you've heard something from Susan and she's going to start a divorce?"

He shook his head. "No. Look, I intended to tell you this before. I'd planned to say it on Friday night, but I thought you'd get the wrong idea after the bombshell I got from the parish.''

Leah evaded the hand that tried to restrain her and sat up, pulling the sheet around her breasts. "Let me get this straight, please. You found out on Friday that you were going to be divorced but decided to wait until now to tell me? Is that the way it went?" A sickening knot grew in her stomach.

"Does it matter how it went?" He pushed fingers agitatedly into his hair. "We can be married. We *need* each other, and we don't have to wait."

Cold calm steadily replaced confusion in Leah. "Do you mind telling me when you found out Susan was divorcing you? I guess I'm a bit obtuse, but you've caught me off guard."

Guy sat up and wrapped his arms around his knees. "Yup. I guess this must seem pretty bizarre coming all at once. But it's not so difficult." He looked at her over his shoulder and smiled. "Several months ago I got notification from Susan's lawyers that she was starting divorce proceedings. Then I heard the thing had gone through. So you see, there's nothing standing in our way anymore."

The sick sensation in Leah's stomach rose to her throat. He couldn't possibly believe she'd accept what he said and fall into his plan for marriage simply because he'd finally decided to tell her the truth about what had been happening in his life for months. She stared at him, shutting her mouth deliberately when she realized it had fallen open. The full reality of what he'd said was seeping through her, leaving ugly disappointment in its wake. He hadn't lied to her, merely done what he'd done so many times before—failed to admit the complete truth.

"Say something, sweetheart." His skin looked

stretched over the bones, his eyes dark and troubled. "It's all right, isn't it?"

Begging. He was begging her to ignore how he'd punished her out of his lack of trust. "Did you know you were divorced the first time we made love?" She could hardly hear her own voice.

Guy scrubbed at his face with both hands. When he looked at her, anxiety had etched white lines from his nose to the corners of his mouth. "I found out the day before."

"Then you made love to me and let me feel guilty for making you compromise your principles?"

"It wasn't supposed to be like that—"

"But it *was* like that. And afterward you drew away from me and made me wonder why you were so cool. I accepted your behavior. I thought you were still fighting your conscience and you'd come around if I gave you more time."

"Please—"

Leah, scooting from the bed, cut him off. She grabbed her slacks and shirt, then remembered that her underwear was in the bathroom and disappeared into the smaller room, closing the door quietly but firmly.

Her fingers rebelled, fumbling with each hook and button, with the buckle on the belt of her slacks. By the time she reopened the door, she was shaking with hurt and self-disgust—and stinging anger.

Guy, wearing jeans he must have grabbed from the closet, grasped her arms as she emerged. "Listen to me," he implored. "You don't understand. And you won't if you refuse to let me explain."

She willed her heart to slow down and her voice to be steady. Neither plea was answered. "You lied to me. Oh, you didn't actually tell me things that weren't true, but you didn't let me inside your wonderful, private life. You made love to me in Sedona because you'd gotten word of the divorce. Don't ask me why you pulled back again afterward. Then—''

''Leah,'' he interrupted, trying to embrace her rigid body.

She shook free, backing away and holding out her hands as if to ward him off. ''No! No more, Guy. There was never meant to be anything between us. It's as much my fault as yours. I was the one who came chasing after you—and the one who made the first advances. Don't feel bad; just let me go and forget me. Please!'' The high, shaky note of her last word horrified her.

''I won't. You're going to listen.'' He stood between Leah and the door to the study. ''I didn't do things right, and I'm sorry. I made a mistake. Give me another chance and I can explain.''

Anger had already turned to panic. She *had* to get away. Dodging around him, she headed for the sliding door, clicked up the lock and slid the heavy glass wide.

''Damn it, Leah. Don't do this.'' Guy was behind her when she stepped onto the patio.

Rain was falling in diagonal sheets, slashing at her face, instantly soaking her clothes. For a second she was disoriented, unsure which way to run to reach the front of the house.

''I won't let you go like this,'' Guy shouted. His arm went around her waist, and she couldn't move.

In the glow from the bedroom, she registered his torso, naked and wet, his drenched jeans, the way his tousled hair curled in the downpour. Her own hair was plastered to her head and neck.

''Come back inside,'' Guy insisted, but she stood her ground.

''Why did you do it?'' she cried. ''How could you

when you knew how I felt and how I was suffering.''
The silk blouse adhered to her skin now, and rain
dashed in rivulets down her neck and dripped from her
hair to her face.

Guy laid his face on her shoulder, but she made no
move to hold him. "I thought I was doing the right
thing," he said hoarsely. "If you'll let me, I can make
you see it my way."

A bubble of blackness exploded in Leah's mind. *See
it your way.* "I don't think so, Guy," she said. She
was intensely aware of his proximity, the scent, the feel
of him. Her every emotion urged her to hold him, but
her mind argued, and it won. "You listen. Then maybe
one day you'll know how to give yourself completely
to…someone." She narrowed her eyes as she said
"someone." The rain would hide her tears, but she
didn't intend to cry yet.

He dropped his arms to his sides and stood there,
tall, muscles gleaming wetly. "I'm listening."

Her breath jammed in her larynx. "You felt you
could make love to me that first time because you
weren't married any longer. Then, for some reason, you
had a smattering of remorse, so you backed off. But
you didn't expect the congregation to come up with
their dirty little indictment. That triggered a whole different set of circumstances. They changed the rules on
you.

"I don't believe you intended to tell me about the
divorce on Friday or that you wanted to marry me at
that point. How can I believe that? What have you
really been afraid of with me, Guy? Commitment? If
you'd told me the truth, would you also have had the
guts to say you don't want to be permanently attached
to one woman again? Back in Sedona. What stopped
you from telling me then? Were you terrified I'd de-

mand too much from you?'' She was exhausted and weak. The scratching quality of her voice had to give away her tears.

Guy held out his hands, and she saw agony in his face. He was beaten, in pain. But only because he'd hurt her, and regardless of how wrong he'd been, hurting people was the last thing he'd ever plan or live with easily.

''Leah,'' he said. ''My love. Don't go away from me now like this. I didn't do things right, but we all make mistakes.''

The muscles in her face contracted. ''And how long before you do the same thing again?'' Her breath came in little gasps. ''Isn't this what happened with Susan? Different in some ways but the same. You shut her out, Guy, like you shut me out. I don't know if I'm wrong, but I think deep down you know you could do to me what you did to her, and that's what frightened you away from coming clean or risking another marriage.''

''Leah, please—''

But she'd started to run, sobs jarring her teeth together. The sound of his bare feet, slapping concrete awash with water, speeded her steps.

He caught her before she reached the grass and swung her around. ''I love you,'' he rasped. ''Damn it, Leah. I do love you.''

''You didn't care enough to let go of yourself and let me share all of your life. You manipulated me, and no one's going to do that to me again.''

''I *love* you, Leah.''

She wrenched her arm from his fingers and backed away, sobbing, doubling over to grasp her aching diaphragm. Every breath was torn from the bottom of her lungs.

''Not enough.''

CHAPTER SIXTEEN

GUY WALKED unseeingly past clusters of people outside the church. Only Providence had pulled him out of an exhausted doze in time to make it to the ten o'clock funeral rites for one of the parish's founding members.

"Nice eulogy, Guy."

He absently met the speaker's eyes. "Thanks, Wally," he murmured. What had he said about an ancient woman he'd hardly known? He didn't remember. Blessedly, there had been no call for music. He'd had difficulty concentrating on anything but Leah's bright splashes of floral color and the repetitive snatches of her accusations that bored relentlessly into his brain.

The sandy turf was still damp from last night's downpour, but he set out between the palms, avoiding the pathways along which parishioners always congregated to talk after services. They liked to shake his hand and chat. Guy didn't want to chat or touch, unless he could touch Leah. He should feel guilty about that, but he didn't. Since last night he'd been going through the motions of living, avoiding the decisions he must make. Now there could be no more avoidance.

"Hey, Guy!" Dan caught up with him, puffing slightly. "Boy, you were out of there like a jackrabbit from a trap."

Surprised at the boy's unexpected appearance, Guy frowned, slowly comprehending that Dan had been in church. He tried to rally enough reserve to do and say the right things. Holding on would be everything in the next few hours and days, for everyone concerned. At this moment, he had to forget himself and hold on for Dan.

"Man with a mission," he said with a brightness that threatened to crack his face. "Got a letter to write." Dan didn't need to know the letter would be Guy's resignation, addressed to his superior.

"We were going to talk, remember? I've been resting up since yesterday like you told me. Now I guess I'm about ready for that battle you've been planning for me."

Dan's blue eyes smiled into his, and Guy's stomach turned over. Before he left Phoenix, he must face the responsibility of completing some important projects he'd started. There could be no question of deserting the Ingallses. He rested a broad hand on the boy's shoulder. "I haven't forgotten, Dan. Can we get to it a bit later—say, late this afternoon?" He tried not to notice the disappointment that edged around the youth's smile.

"Sure," Dan said. "I'll come back about five on my way from work. Will that be okay?"

"Terrific. Five."

Guy had watched Dan sprint for his old bicycle and pedal away before he realized he hadn't given any positive reinforcement. Plainly, Connie had mentioned this morning's service, and Dan had ridden all the way from Indian School Road to attend, hoping to please Guy and to see him afterward. And Guy had hardly reacted; he'd allowed the boy to ride to work on the other side of town with the prospect of having to come all the way back again later.

Head down, Guy continued toward the house. He

ought to put in an appearance at the reception being held in the social hall. But the prospect of smiling and nodding, exchanging banalities with strangers, his declared adversaries, or even friends, was unbearable. A mixture of all elements had been present in force this morning.

I need you, Leah. The phrase had repeated and repeated in his head since she had run away. He'd blown it, made all the wrong assumptions and decisions, and now they would both pay unless his last-ditch effort worked. Guy didn't trust his own efforts anymore.

Not looking into her empty office as he passed took superhuman restraint. The whole house felt hollow, and he didn't want to be there anymore.

He'd spent the night's waning hours in one of the guest rooms, unable to face the bed he'd shared with Leah. After she'd gone, he had sunk into a chair by the pool and turned his face up to the beating rain, willing it to wash away the anguish that threatened to burst his skull. He didn't know how much later he'd found the courage to go inside, stepping over the tangle of sheets on the floor as he went.

The morning had brought no relief, only more wrenching questions about himself and the conviction that Guy Hamilton didn't know what was true about him, or best for him, let alone anyone else. He had no right to stay here, guiding, when he was lost.

"Guy! Wait up, will you, man?"

He'd left the front door open, and Wally was hurrying along the hallway.

"What is it with you?" Wally asked. "Deaf or something? I bin calling after you since Dan left."

"Sorry," Guy muttered. He wished the old man would go away.

Wally pushed his hat to the back of his head, then

hastily pulled it off. "Got something to tell you." A smile sent creases across his cheeks, but his eyes remained solemn as he studied Guy. "You okay?" He tapped Guy's upper arm.

Leaving this man would be hard, one of the toughest things Guy had ever done. "I could be better, Wally. But I think you know that. What's new?"

Wally took his elbow. "Where can we talk?"

Guy sighed. "I...do we have to do this now? There're some things I ought to get to right away." He felt sick.

"Won't take but a minute."

Defeated, Guy said, "In my study, then," and led the way. "I don't like putting you off, but I'm going through a rough time and..." His words fizzled away. He'd actually admitted everything wasn't coming up roses for him. He almost laughed in self-derision. *A bit late for mending fences, buddy.*

The door to his bedroom had been deliberately closed before he left. Showering in the same shower where he'd been together with Leah, dressing in a room that still held her fragrance, had left him shaky with longing. He had almost run from the memories, wishing he need never go back.

He slumped on the edge of his cluttered desk. "Shoot," he told Wally.

Ignoring his ungracious host's lack of manners, Wally lowered his rangy frame into a chair and leaned back. "You don't have a thing to worry about," he announced complacently. "Everything's taken care of."

Guy narrowed his eyes. "What's been taken care of?"

"McCleods, Culvers, Jenkins—the whole lot of them. They decided they didn't have so much they wanted to talk to your head honcho about. In fact, they decided they didn't have a thing they wanted to discuss, with anyone.''

Wally's expressionless gaze met Guy's uncomprehending stare. "*They* decided, Wally?" Guy asked softly. "What does that mean, you old goat? What did you do—hire the mob to strong-arm them?"

"In a manner of speaking." The tips of Wally's fingernails suddenly enthralled him. "There isn't one of those turkeys who doesn't have some goody tucked away in a closet." He looked sharply at Guy. "The kind of goodies people like to keep hidden, if you know what I mean?"

"Oh, I know what you mean," Guy said slowly, massaging his jaw. "You cagey devil. All these years you've been mooching around here, quiet, not involved in anyone's business. But you never missed a thing, and now you've put the thumbscrews on the poor devils."

Wally's grin was smug. "A fellow can't help what he hears. People tell things to someone who's almost invisible, someone who doesn't talk. And I don't talk, Guy. Still haven't and don't intend to. But it didn't hurt to remind a few people of a few things."

Guy couldn't help smiling. "I don't want to know what these things are, Wally. You wouldn't tell me, anyway. And, of course, I disapprove of your methods. But thanks. At least that's one less thing to worry about." Not that it mattered now.

"Yeah." Wally nodded his grizzled head emphatically. "And our Leah won't have to be putting up with any more nonsense around here. I couldn't have taken much more of that."

"No." Guy stood and moved around the desk. His chest tightened unbearably. "Leah won't be putting up

with any more...not now. Thanks, Wally, for everything. You're the best, I—I'm sorry I sounded off at
you on Friday. There's no excuse except I lost it there
for a while.'' If he didn't shut up, he'd probably cry
and embarrass them both.

He held out his hand, and Wally shook it. At the
door, he shot Guy a penetrating glance. *He knows,* Guy
thought, gathering his forces to respond to whatever
questions might come. But Wally silently inclined his
head before the sound of his boots clipped steadily
away.

So, his faithful flock had decided not to put him
through the hoop. Not because they'd changed their
minds about him but because they were afraid some
probably innocuous snippet of gossip about each of
them might be aired if they did. He fished around in a
desk drawer for a fresh sheet of letterhead and started
to write.

The words came slowly, and he tossed one piece of
paper after another into the garbage. What he had to
say was simple. He'd examined his conscience and
found it lacking. He wasn't fit to do his job and wished
to be released as soon as a replacement minister for St.
Mark's could be found. He was asking for an open-
ended leave of absence to decide on his career course.

Eventually, the sentences got his message across,
and he slid the folded sheet into an envelope.

Could he do what he'd planned? Could he go to
Leah one more time, as a plain man, unfettered by his
calling, and ask her to take a chance on a future with
him?

Exhaustion blurred his thoughts. If he went to her
now, he'd botch whatever he said. Best wait, at least
until he'd had some sleep.

He slammed a fist on the desk and buried his face

in his hands. If he were confident of Leah's reaction, he'd already be on his way to her. A man who couldn't believe in himself couldn't expect anyone else to believe in him. Maybe she'd be better off with someone else.

He heard a muffled noise but didn't raise his head. What did he have to offer her? Not even total security until he knew where he was headed.

A tentative brushing against his sleeve startled him, and he straightened. Dan Ingalls stood at his shoulder, one hand still on Guy's arm. The youth's face was streaked with what looked suspiciously like the result of tears mixed with dust.

Guy ran his tongue over dry lips. "I thought we said five." He checked his watch and was amazed it read a few minutes after one. "Shouldn't you be at work?"

Dan sniffed. "Don't you care?" His voice held a tremulous wobble.

Without knowing why, Guy felt his heart pump harder. "I don't know what you mean, Dan. Care? About you? Of course I care about you."

"I don't give a—I don't give a damn if you care about me. You know what I'm talking about."

The kid looked ill. "Did you lose your job?" Guy stood and tried to push Dan into his own chair. The youth wouldn't budge. He was angry—with him? "Did they fire you?"

Dan curled his hands into bony fists. "You son of a bitch. You don't care. I hate you. I hate you." One craggy set of knuckles glanced off Guy's jaw before he could react. A second blow connected squarely with his nose, and he felt a trickle of warm blood run into his mouth.

Guy saw Dan's right fist coming again and grabbed the wrist, twisting just enough to flop his weaker opponent into the chair. "Stop it," he ground out, wiping blood from his lips. "Stop it, you little idiot. Calm down and make sense before I knock some into you." He tried to pin Dan's hands together in one of his own, but the boy was too strong. It took surprising effort to subdue Dan's furious writhing and hold him until he sank back, head lolling, his breath coming in staccato bursts.

"She's worth ten of you," Dan gasped between gulps of air, and he began to cry, tears slipping from wide-open eyes. "She trusted you, and you've done something to make her go away. I knew everything had gone wrong from the way you avoided me earlier. When I couldn't find Leah in her office, I went over to her place to find out what was up."

Guy slackened his grasp on Dan's wrists. "What did she tell you?" The adrenaline that had pumped briefly through his body evaporated.

"Your lip is bleeding all over." Dan scrabbled in his jeans pocket and produced a grimy handkerchief. "I shouldn't have done that, but I believed in you."

Half-formed conclusions whirled in Guy's head. "I asked you what she said." He took the handkerchief and blotted at his face. His upper lip was swelling, and his head thudded sickeningly.

"Nothing!" Dan almost shouted. "You know her well enough. She wouldn't say anything against anyone. Least of all you. She even smiled and said she just reckoned it was time to make a change—to move on, get a new job and meet new people. But I'm not a little kid who can't figure out when someone's covering up. Leah loves you. I thought you loved her, too. But if you did and everything was okay, she'd be down there in that office where she wants to be most. Near you. I can't stand it if she goes away like this." Dan's crying became audible. He bent over, rocking. "She doesn't have anyone, anywhere. Why'd you do it?"

Guy's brain cleared. Unwillingly, he absorbed the message in Dan's disjointed accusations. "Listen to me," he demanded. "Look at me and listen." He waited until Dan met his glare. "Are you telling me Leah's getting ready to leave Phoenix?"

"Isn't that what you wanted?" Dan continued to rock.

"No!" Guy roared, thrusting the bloodstained handkerchief back into the boy's hands. "It's the last thing I want unless I'm with her. Go and lie down somewhere. Use one of the guest rooms and get some sleep before you collapse. I'll be back."

FOOTSTEPS CLATTERING up the metal steps to her apartment made Leah pause before stacking another saucepan in a cardboard box. It must be Dan coming back. She hadn't handled him well.

"Come in!" she called before he could ring the bell or knock. "It's unlocked."

The door opened behind her; then she heard it quietly close again. Dan was confused, wounded by what he saw as her defection. Leah couldn't bring herself to look at him.

"Glad you came back," she said. "I could use a strong pair of arms to help me with all this stuff. I think it grew since I got here, although I don't remember buying a thing—except plants."

He didn't answer. Her throat burned. She wanted desperately to make him feel better, but her own hurt was more than she'd be able to contain much longer.

"Dan." She turned around slowly. "I'll always... Guy!" Her mouth became dry at the sight of him. "Wh-what are you doing here?"

He leaned on the back of the couch, his head averted. "You'll always what? What were you going to say if I'd been Dan?"

She swallowed. "That I'll always keep in touch with him and let him know where I am."

"And me?" He jerked to face her. "Will you always let *me* know where you are? Or are you planning to disappear out of my life forever?"

"Oh, my God. What's happened to you?" She crossed the distance between them in a rush. Dried blood smeared his swollen upper lip and clung to the corner of his mouth. A reddened knot stood out along his jaw. "Guy, sit down. Did you crash into something?"

His mirthless laugh frightened her. "I always said you were bright. You got it right in one shot. I crashed into something. Or, to be more exact, it crashed into me."

She didn't know what to do first. "Shouldn't we get you to a hospital for X rays?"

"This sounds like a replay of something I remember," he said. "Stop wringing your hands. I'm not going to die. Not from this, anyway."

"Where's the jeep? Was anyone else hurt? Sit down and I'll clean up your face."

Guy dropped onto the couch and closed his eyes. "The jeep is in its usual mint condition. No one but me is hurt. And I don't want you to play Florence Nightingale for me. I want you to love me—as I am— for whatever I am. I just want you to love me."

Leah opened her mouth, but no sound would come. Yes, she loved him. She loved him more than she loved her life, but for a marriage to work, there had to be more than one totally committed partner.

She tore her gaze from his bruised face and went to

the kitchen sink. What had she done with the bowls? Sun, glancing off stainless steel, broke into blinding fragments, and she covered her eyes.

Guy's arm, circling her shoulders, jolted her. He pulled her back against his chest. "I'm sorry," he murmured into her hair. "I never meant to hurt you, Leah. Please believe that."

Hyperventilation must feel like this, she thought. She drew in a deep, slow breath. "I do believe it."

"Then will you give me a chance to spill all the crazy notions that led up to what I did?" He was trembling. "Let me talk for as long as it takes to get it out. Then, if you still feel the same way about me, I'll get out of your life. For good."

Leah rested her chin on his tanned forearm, registering for the first time that he wore his black shirt. She gently clasped his wrist and faced him. Blood stained the stiff white band at his throat. "How *did* this happen to you, Guy?" She touched his jaw lightly as he winced.

"Someone who cares almost as much about you as I do decided to wake me up. He seems to think I've done something to make you want to run away from Phoenix. I'm lucky he isn't better fed. He'd have killed me."

"Dan?" Leah's eyes widened. "Oh, Dan, Dan. That's got to be one of the sweetest kids around. We both know he is. And he hit you. He didn't mean it, Guy. He's just confused."

Guy gave a wry grimace. "I know. But for a sweet kid he packs quite a punch."

"And you let him do it. He's lucky he didn't pick on someone who'd hit back."

"What makes you think I didn't flatten him?" Guy tilted his head. He was very close.

Leah's nostrils flared. Her eyes prickled now. "I know you too well. You wouldn't even think of hitting him." She pressed her lips together. It would feel so good to feel Guy's arms around her.

"Right." Guy sighed. "You know me well enough to be sure I wouldn't hit Dan—even while he was destroying my face. Why don't you know all the other things that go on in my head? Like whatever I've done about us—however badly I've loused up—I always intended to do what was right. I'm only human, remember?"

Her legs quivered inside. What was she supposed to do, to say? She turned on the faucet and grabbed a wad of tissues from a box on the counter. "This has to be cleaned." The jerky pressure she applied to his upper lip brought Guy's swift intake of breath. "Plain old warm water will do for a start. Then I'll hunt for some antiseptic." She needed time to think.

Guy, removing the sodden tissues from her hand, cut off her mental flight. "I've had a little nosebleed," he rasped. "Not a car wreck resulting in multiple contusions. I don't need antiseptic. I need you—listening to me. And giving me a chance—giving *us* a chance."

He led her to the couch, and she settled wordlessly into a corner. Guy sat at the other end, leaning forward, his elbows on his knees.

"By the time you arrived here, I knew Susan was starting divorce proceedings," he said dully. "There was no reason to blurt that out unless I had solid evidence that you might be as interested in me as I was in you."

Leah tucked her feet beneath her and rested a cheek on the back of the couch.

"Then there was that night when I kissed you—"

"When I forced myself on you, you mean," Leah interrupted.

"No." Guy swiveled toward her. "It's impossible to force yourself on a man who's done nothing but dream of making love to you since the first moment he laid eyes on you. And it was that way with me, Leah."

"Guy—"

"Please let me get this all out. I kept trying to figure out what was best for you. That's where I went wrong from the word go. I fell in love with you when you were still another man's wife. I even detested him for having you. Seeing him with you made me feel pure hate for the first time in my life." Sweat gleamed on his forehead. "Then, when you came to me, I was determined that if you were going to really be mine, I wasn't going to make the mistakes Charles made."

Leah sat upright. "Charles was good to me."

"I know, I know." Guy reached for her hand and held it fast between both of his. "But he made you dependent. When I saw you there in that—that gilded cage he'd made for you, I felt helpless. And cheated. Even then I sensed what you *could* be if you had a chance to grow. Oh, I didn't know what your strengths were, but I knew you had them and weren't using them. And…" His gaze bored into her. "And I wanted you for myself, because you were also the most beautiful, desirable woman I'd ever seen. I went away from you with a hole where my heart used to be. Every night I went to sleep seeing those incredible blue eyes of yours and trying not to imagine how soft you'd feel if you were beside me. Leah, I made love to you in my mind, over and over, from the night we met. When we were finally together, it was the realization of a dream I'd lived."

The small voice that said, "I thought about you, too," didn't sound like her own.

"I'm going to say the rest of this fast, so listen closely." He stood with enough force to bounce Leah on the couch. "If I miss something, you can tell me when I've finished. I should have told you the divorce was in progress. I should have told you when it was final. A hundred times I intended to, but I was scared. I was terrified that you'd quit school and turn into my shadow, the way you were Charles's shadow. Having you do nothing but center your existence around me wouldn't exactly be hard to take, but it wouldn't be right. And I would never have felt right about it. I wanted you to be all you could be and still be mine.

"But I was wrong for not letting you make your own decisions. I kept telling myself I was helping you to be free when in fact I was controlling every move you made like a human puppeteer. I pulled your strings, sweetheart. And I don't blame you for being mad."

Leah dug her nails into the side seams on her jeans and waited. She'd know when it was time to say something.

He stopped pacing. "Last night you said I was afraid of permanent commitment. By this morning, I was so shaken up, I'd almost decided you were right. You weren't. I'm more than ready to commit myself wholly to you. And we would have a successful marriage, because I wouldn't make the mistakes I made when I was a kid infatuated with his own importance.

"Finally, I didn't ask you to marry me because I wanted to cut off parish gossip. I asked you because it's what I really want—have wanted—for months. And, in case you still have doubts about that, the parish doesn't figure in this anymore."

Leah's head snapped up. "The parish is always going to figure in what we…in what *you* do."

He turned the corners of his mouth down. "Wrong. I quit."

For several seconds, only the steady whirl of the air conditioner broke the silence. Leah slowly lowered her feet to the floor and stood. "Quit?" she said softly. "You quit. Guy, you resigned, officially?"

"I'm going to," he said firmly. "The letter's written. It would have been mailed if Dan hadn't decided to come for a chat. But I'm going to mail it, and if you'll have me, we'll get married, I'll start a new career, and you can carry on with your schooling. I thought—"

"You didn't think," Leah squeaked. "As usual, you made a snap decision on what was best for me, only this time you included you. You're getting worse, not better."

Guy's mouth fell open; then he sniffed and passed a hand across his face. A trace of fresh blood appeared beside his mouth. "You mean you won't marry me." It was a flat statement, and she saw him blanch. "There's nothing I can do to change your mind?"

"Oh, Guy. You dear, wonderful man. Lie down before you fall down." She pushed him onto the couch and maneuvered him into a supine position with a cushion beneath his head. Carefully, she lifted his lip and peered underneath. "There's a cut in here, too. That Dan may have missed his calling. We'll turn him into a professional boxer."

"I'll turn him into mincemeat when I get my hands on him again," Guy spat out.

"Shh," she ordered. "My turn. You aren't sending that letter."

"Why?" He frowned. "Because you're turning me

down? I can't stay here without you either, Leah. I don't think I'd be any good to those people after all that's happened. I need someone to guide *me* for a change.''

Leah sank down beside Guy, scooting him over to make room. ''When two people get married, aren't they supposed to do that for each other? Be guides, I mean?'' She didn't wait for his answer. ''Well, they are. So you're going to have a guide.''

He sat up and grabbed her. ''We're going to get married?''

''Unless you want me to sue for breach of promise. You asked last night, remember? And I accepted.'' She worked the gold band of intertwined hands from her finger and held it up. ''We already have the ring. The only wedding ring I could ever want. You even bought it to fit on my left hand.''

''Oh, thank God. And I've got an engagement ring I've been blubbering over for days.'' He tugged the box from his pocket and slipped the sapphire band onto her unresisting finger.

Leah stared at pinpoints of light in dark blue. ''It's beautiful, Guy. I'm going to cry again. But nothing would mean as much if we can't stay here. This place is my home now.''

He looked away. ''You want me to stay at St. Mark's?'' he asked, rubbing a hand over his eyes.

''Yes. I'll just have to remember to make sure I grab your attention every time you start getting too preoccupied.'' Leah bent to brush her lips across his temple. ''And do you think I could give up Dan now or Wally or good old Elsie? Everyone needs a challenge.''

Guy wrapped her tightly in his arms. ''I want to kiss you so badly. This damn mouth...'' He held her away, a tender glow in his green eyes. "What kind of things will you do to me if I get preoccupied?"

Leah smiled and kissed the undamaged side of his jaw. "I'll reorganize your study," she said, laughing. "But first, can you arrange for us to be married in St. Mark's?"

He buried his fingers in her hair. "St. Mark's it'll be. My good people wouldn't accept anything less."

HARLEQUIN®

AMERICAN *Romance*®

DADDY IN DEMAND

Muriel Jensen

MURIEL JENSEN

is the award-winning author of more than seventy
books and novellas that tug at readers' hearts.
She has won a Reviewer's Choice Award and a
Career Achievement Award for Love and Laughter
from *Romantic Times Magazine,* as well as a sales
award from Waldenbooks. Muriel is best loved for
her books about family, a subject she knows well,
as she has three children and eight grandchildren.
A native of Massachusetts, Muriel now lives with
her husband in Oregon, in an old Victorian home
on a hill overlooking the Columbia River.

HARLEQUIN®
Makes any time special ®

DADDY IN DEMAND
Muriel Jensen

To Cathleen Riley—
high-school buddy, long-term friend.

PROLOGUE

DORI McKEON STIRRED restlessly among the tangled sheets as the familiar scene played itself out in her recurring dream.

There was a small adobe church in a dusty little square in the Mezquital Valley in the state of Hidalgo, Mexico. Music rose from an old pipe organ, and the carved pews were filled with people dressed in bright colors, singing. In the front of the church was an ornate gold altar that had been brought from Spain in the seventeenth century intended for a church in San Antonio and "diverted" by enterprising bandits when the ship ran aground.

A couple stood at the altar exchanging vows—a small dark-haired young woman in a white cotton dress and the traditional mantilla, and a tall, smiling man in a dark suit. In deference to the bride, the service was being conducted in English.

She was the bride.

Dori could feel her joy, and just the smallest twinge of guilt that she was doing this without her family in attendance. But she and Sal had been apart so long, and he wanted to be married quickly, before anything could interfere. She'd agreed.

"Do you, Salvatore Mateo Dominguez, take this woman, Dorianne Margaret McKeon..."

The vows continued; they promised to love each other forever, as the scent of jacarandas wafted through the open windows.

She'd never been this happy, this sure of who she was in her entire life. She was a daughter, a sister, a teacher. She was the woman who loved Sal Dominguez—the woman *he* loved.

Then the carved double doors of the church burst open with a loud bang and four men hurried into the church.

"No," Dori said aloud. "Not this ending. I want the one where we leave the church and fly home to Oregon and build a house in Dancer's Beach! The one where we have six children!"

But her subconscious was intent on replaying the end of her wedding the way it had happened. She watched with a helpless sense of loss.

She recognized the two younger men as Miguel and Eduardo, Julie's brothers.

"It's Desideria," one of them said. "Paco's out of jail. There was an auto accident during a prisoner transfer, and he escaped. We came for you right away."

Sal said something in Spanish that brought a gasp from the wedding guests.

Dori always saw this part in slow motion.

Sal turned to her, his handsome features set in hard lines, love for her visible under the anger in his eyes. "I have to go," he said simply.

She'd stammered. "Wh-What do you mean? We're getting married!"

He kissed one of her hands. "We *are* married. I am yours and you are mine. You will wait here, and Diego and Manuela will take care of you until I return."

Diego was his right-hand man in the company he'd formed to build the hospital. Manuela was Diego's wife.

"I'm married to you, not to them," she'd said firmly. "I came all this way—"

He squeezed her hand and interrupted. "I know, *chica,* but this is important. A life-and-death matter. You must understand."

"I don't," she'd insisted stubbornly.

She'd met Desideria Cabral, a tall, slender woman with elegant features who'd been volunteering her decorating skills and consulting with Sal several times a day. The woman had smiled at him every time he passed her as he walked over the site. And on occasion, Dori had seen her touch his arm or his hand.

Dori had been grateful when Desideria had left for home several days before the wedding. She'd even wondered if it would have been too hard for the woman to watch Sal marry someone else.

"Then you will wait here until I return," he said with a charming smile, "and can explain it to you."

"Why—?" she'd begun, but one of the two older men with Julie's brothers had interrupted.

"Salvatore! There is not much time."

Sal had framed her face in his hands and kissed her.

She'd been too astonished by the turn of events to stop him.

Then, with a last look at her, his hand touching hers, he backed away until his fingertips were out of reach. He turned and ran with his friends out of the church. She heard the sound of horses galloping away.

Her own screech of anger woke her.

Dori sat up in the frail light of a June morning and blinked at the tiny dimensions of her blue-and-white bedroom in suburban Edenfield. She groaned and fell back against her pillows with relief—or disappointment. She wasn't sure.

Well. You couldn't expect happy endings when you married a thief.

She and Sal had a tempestuous history filled with strong attraction and intermittent hostility. His self-imposed role as her protector had embarrassed and annoyed her, and her resistance to his protection had surprised and angered him.

Their situation had been dangerous, unusual, and not at all conducive to romance.

Dori's friend, Julie Godinez, had been part of the same family of thieves that Sal had also belonged to. Dori and Julie had gone to college together, and Julie had explained that her father, her uncle, her brothers, and her cousin, as well as several friends, had banded together to form the Cat Pack. They stole jewelry from the wealthy, converted it to cash, then returned with it to Madre Maria to support the impoverished village.

Julie, who had also been part of the Pack, had eventually quit to pursue her education. Her father had been furious and they'd had a terrible row. One day Dori had found Julie sobbing over a newspaper headline that read, "Cat Pack foiled but leader at Large." The subhead said, "Godinez's daughter sought for questioning."

Julie suspected that the gang had been set up, and she feared that her father would think she'd done it because of their argument. She was going into hiding so that she couldn't be taken in for questioning about her father, but she wanted to contact him to tell him she had not betrayed him.

Dori had had a plan. "My brother Duncan's going to Mexico to do a film," she'd said. "And they need a translator to work with the extras. Is that perfect?"

Julie had hugged her. "Yes. If you can put me in touch with the right person, I'll be forever grateful. But, Dori, I need you to do one more thing."

That was the point at which she should have walked away, Dori realized now. But Julie was her friend. She'd wanted Dori to contact her cousin, Salvatore Dominguez, who was in hiding with her father in a place known only to the family and make it clear that she had not been the one who'd betrayed them.

While Julie was in Mexico with the film crew, Dori had been dealing with Salvatore Dominguez. He'd been autocratic and overbearing from the beginning, refusing to let her see Julie's father, who'd been injured escaping the police after an attempt to rob the penthouse of a New Orleans hotel.

Their haphazard communication had gone on for ten months, during which time she'd tried hard to focus also on her thesis on novelists of the nineteenth century for her master's degree in English Literature.

She'd been returning from Nova Scotia, where she'd been researching with the foremost expert on Jane Austen, and was supposed to take in a theater performance in New York, when Sal intercepted her at the airport.

She'd barely had a moment to express surprise that he was there before he told her someone would claim her luggage later and pushed her ahead of him into a cab. There was about to be a confrontation, he told her, between Julie's father and Suarez, the man they were convinced had betrayed him to the police. Sal thought it best to keep her out of everyone's reach until it was over. He had a plan, he said, to make it all end happily.

He'd hidden her in an elegant suite at the Plaza. She remembered plush white-and-gold rooms, and being worried about her family who might be worried about *her*, and being afraid for Julie. She'd shouted at Sal, flung accusations, vented her frustrations, and finally dissolved into tears—something she never did.

He'd caught her hand and pulled her into his arms. And that was when everything had changed. At least for her.

She still couldn't remember who kissed whom, but it had been a revelation. She'd stared at him in amazement, and he'd looked at her with a new possessive attitude.

Then there'd been the phone call, the sudden flight to Sandy Gables, Florida, and all the unreal events of the next few days.

When they'd finally returned to Dancer's Beach with

Duncan and Julie and her family, Sal had proposed marriage.

Dori had declined and they'd argued. He'd finally left for Mexico with a healthy contribution from her brother to enlarge Madre Maria's small hospital and add a children's wing, which the area needed desperately.

Her loneliness had been painful and had made every day seem interminable, even though she had earned her master's degree and had gotten a job teaching English at the local high school.

And then one day in late June she had caught a plane to Mexico City, and hired a private plane to Madre Maria. The pilot, who kept a beat-up old truck at the airport, drove her to the hospital.

The building had two stories and was modern in construction, except for several arches in the front and a bell tower. Inside was chaos. Wires dangled and plumbing stood up awkwardly where walls had been framed but remained unfinished.

Sal walked out of a side corridor, distracted by the contents of a sheaf of papers in his hand, and walked into her.

He'd grasped her arms with a smile of apology. "I'm so sorry, I..." And then he'd recognized her.

The moment had been electric. Possibly even nuclear.

They'd flown into each other's arms.

She'd agreed to be his wife.

She could remember now how she'd felt, standing at the altar, looking into his eyes. She'd never been that happy, that sure of who she was in her entire life. She was the woman who loved Sal Dominguez, the woman *he* loved.

"For all the good it's done me," she told herself now as she sat up again.

Two years of the wedding dream was enough! she decided. It was time to change things, to change herself. She couldn't alter the past. But she could darn well redirect her future—which at this point was going nowhere.

She liked teaching, but she'd always planned to write a book about the women of Georgian England. The events of her wedding day had taken their toll on her self-esteem and her trust in her ability to make sound decisions. So she'd stayed with teaching because it was safer than risking rejection from agents and publishers.

She threw the covers aside, climbed out of bed and went to the window. Edenfield, Oregon, stretched out before her, rooftops and chimneys and the tops of ash trees, cedars and Douglas firs.

She felt a longing for the coast and the peace she always found there—particularly when her family was somewhere else. Right now, she remembered as she warmed to the idea, her brothers and their wives and children were touring Europe for a month. Her father had just had knee replacement surgery, so he and her mother would be unable to follow her if she went to her brothers' summer house in Dancer's Beach.

That was it. The perfect place to turn her life in a new direction. She'd take her laptop, start her book, query several agents with the outline she'd prepared two years ago.

Then she'd hire a lawyer and get a divorce.

Pleased with her decision, she went into the kitchen to put on the kettle. As she filled it under the cold water faucet, she glanced at the calendar hanging on the side of the cupboard. Duncan and Julie had given it to her. Every month featured a different photo of their then two-year-old daughters.

This was Tuesday, June 26.

She gasped. How appropriate that she'd awakened with determination on this of all days.

She'd been married two years ago today.

CHAPTER ONE

"CONTAINS ISOFLAVONES." Dori read the nutrition panel on the back of the bag of toasted soy nuts. She couldn't remember what those were, but recalled that they had fat-fighting properties, and that they were a must for menopausal women. She dropped them into her cart.

At 26, she was far from that stage of her life, but fighting fat was something she should begin to consider, particularly if her book continued to go as well as it had been for the past three weeks. She'd done little but work and sleep, except for taking an occasional walk on the beach and a trip to town for groceries.

Last week, she'd run into Gusty and Bram Bishop, but had turned down their invitation to dinner, explaining that she was on a creative roll and was reluctant to distract herself in any way and risk a slowdown. Fortunately, they'd understood.

She phoned her parents every few days and was forced to endure the predictable lecture that a woman needed a healthy body as well as a healthy mind, and that she wouldn't be able to maintain either if she didn't get out into the fresh air and meet people.

By meeting "people," Dori knew, they meant "meeting men."

Her parents and her brothers had no idea she was married. In her family of charismatic, overachieving siblings, she'd always felt left out because of her gender, her inclination to be more academic than charming, and her place as the youngest child.

Her parents still thought of her as "the baby." She was sure it wouldn't matter how old she became, she would always be the baby. When she refused her mother's advice, the same guidance always came back to her in a chat with one of her brothers, or, since they'd married, one of her sisters-in-law.

She hadn't wanted to prove to any of them that they'd been right in their concerns about her ability to take care of herself. Or to let them even suspect that she was crushed by her mistake and didn't trust herself, either.

Though her mother had mentioned on more than one occasion that Sal had visited them, she'd never mentioned the marriage, and Dori had to believe he'd kept the secret also. If he had not, her mother would have interrogated her about it and reminded her that Dori had been warned against just such an error in judgment. Her entire family had liked Sal and would probably take his side, proving to her once again that she was the root of most of her own problems.

So, she'd been married for two years and no one north of the Mexican border knew, except the groom. According to her mother's report after Sal's last visit, he owned and operated a security company in Seattle. She'd provided Dori with the address.

That was good, she thought with brittle sarcasm as she snatched a bag of blue corn chips off the shelf. Then he could run to the aid of every beautiful woman who crossed his path, and even get paid for it—

"Dori!"

A cart collided with Dori's as she turned down the freezer aisle, studying a can of bean-and-cheese dip.

"Gusty!" she exclaimed. "Hi!"

The pretty redhead in a flower-sprigged sundress laughed. "No, I'm Athena."

Dori frowned apologetically. "I'm sorry, I'll never learn to tell the three of you apart." Gusty and her sisters were identical triplets who'd moved to Dancer's Beach the year before. The circumstances had been mysterious, but now the sisters were an important part of the community. Dori had met Gusty's sisters at Gusty's wedding nine months earlier.

"You're the lawyer?" Dori asked.

"That's right. I have an office in the Bijou Theater building."

"I was just thinking about making an appointment to see you."

Athena delved into the large purse in the baby carrier part of the cart and handed her a business card. "Please do. I can handle most things."

Dori lowered her voice. "Annulment? Divorce?"

Athena blinked and leaned across her cart. "I didn't think you were married," she said quietly.

There! She'd taken a giant step forward! "It's a long

story. We were married and separated the same day. My family doesn't even know. The wedding took place in Mexico.''

Athena had the grace to appear unaffected by what she'd heard. "In a civil ceremony?''

"No. In the Catholic Church.''

Athena hesitated a moment, then nodded. "Well, come and see me, and we'll get on it.''

"Thank you. When will David's book be out?''

She smiled broadly and patted a slightly paunchy stomach. "We'll both have a new edition out in November.''

Dori offered her congratulations. "That's exciting. Do you know if it's a boy or a girl?''

"It's a girl,'' she replied, clearly delighted. "We're raising David's two younger brothers, you know, so we're all thrilled, the boys included.''

They parted, with Dori promising to call Athena's office for an appointment.

Focusing on her groceries again, Dori inspected the fat content of the bean-and-cheese dip and retraced her steps to put it back. She examined the contents of her cart: sardines, a can of chili, several frozen dinners, a package of cranberry-nut English muffins, a box of English Breakfast tea, cheese, crackers, salsa, and the chips and soy nuts.

She'd almost forgotten chocolate. She picked up three Hershey bars, a bag of chocolate-covered peanuts and a box of chocolate-dipped shortbreads.

She had to give the isoflavones something to do.

Dori paid for her groceries and declined the box

boy's offer to take the single large bag out to her car. This summer was about doing things for herself. And so far she was pleased with her progress.

She'd written ninety pages of what she estimated would be a book of 100,000 words, or four hundred pages. If she could find a way to keep her brothers in Europe, her father in a cast, and herself working at her current speed, she could be finished by the end of the summer.

She'd called a plumber about a leak in the down-stairs bathroom faucet and had paid for the repairs. She'd watered the lawns and weeded the flower beds that surrounded the house. And she'd just spoken to a lawyer about getting Sal out of her life permanently.

She took a deep gulp of salty air as she stepped out of the market. Her life was on track. And it had only taken her the better part of twenty-six years.

She unlocked the door of her car and slid into her seat, the bag momentarily trapped between her chest and the steering wheel. She pushed up and sideways on the bag, managed to honk the horn, then leaned toward the passenger seat and deposited the bag.

She retrieved the blue corn chips and pulled the bag open. She put a chip between her teeth, her key in the ignition and started the car.

Yes, she thought. Her life was good. It was sort of a shame her brothers and her parents weren't here to see how she'd taken command of it. But if they were here, she'd be fighting for control of it—and probably losing.

So that would be counterproductive. She'd just have to be successful in silence.

She stopped the car at the parking lot's exit, looked both ways and pulled out onto Dancer Avenue.

The way her luck was running, she thought with pride, she should probably start planning her own autograph party. Nothing lavish—just a small champagne and gnoshes sort of thing, to which she would invite everyone who hadn't thought she had it in her.

Okay, now she was being a little too fanciful. She should probably try to find an agent or publisher first. Of course, if she got an agent, he'd want fifteen percent. But a publisher could take forever to respond to her if she *didn't* have an agent. It was a dilemma.

She should probably finish the book first, and then decide what to do.

She was startled by a loud sound of approbation from the back of the car. For an instant that seemed right—not at all unexpected. For all her family's interference in her life, there'd always been someone behind her encouraging her to "Go for it, Dori! Yeah!"

But she was alone in the car.

Her heart suddenly thumping, she looked into the rearview mirror, and saw... She stared, then blinked, then stared again. Could that be a cherubic little face looking back at her?

Her heart suddenly clogging her throat, she turned violently to the right, slammed on the brakes and brought her shuddering car to a stop on the narrow verge between the highway and the rocks rimming the cliffs outside Dancer's Beach.

The driver of a pickup behind her had to swerve to avoid hitting her, and leaned on his horn to tell her what he thought of her driving.

"It's an angel," she told herself, half amazed, half terrified to look again. "My family couldn't be here so they've managed to hire a special guardian angel..."

Another sound of approbation came from the back seat.

One eye closed, Dori risked another look into the rearview mirror. She saw the smiling fat-cheeked little face again, then the waving of a pair of pudgy little arms. Then she heard a high-pitched squeal.

She unbuckled her belt and turned in her seat. Her jaw fell open as she looked into the velvety dark eyes of a baby strapped into a car seat.

The baby raised both arms again and squealed at her, smiling broadly.

"Holy sh—!" She stopped herself just in time. Just in case this *was* an angel.

Apparently unhappy with the sound of her voice, the cherub's smile disappeared, replaced by a pout, followed instantly by a scream of displeasure.

Dori leaped out of the car as traffic zoomed past, ran around to the other side and opened the door. Now thoroughly displeased with her reaction, the baby screwed his eyes closed, opened his mouth wide and blared his unhappiness to the world.

He was plump with thick dark hair sticking up in spikes. He wore blue denim rompers over a white T-shirt, and tiny little brown suede hiking books.

"Oh, my God!" Dori whispered, fussing with the

car seat's protective bar. Her sisters-in-law all had babies and young children, and all the car seats worked
in a slightly different way. "No, you don't work for
Him, do you? You came to earth the normal way.
You're a baby, not an angel. Or maybe an angel-
baby."

Finally managing to raise the bar, she unbuckled the
protective harness that held the still-screeching baby in
place, then lifted him out of the seat. She rested him
against her shoulder and patted his back. He felt hot
and moist against her.

"Okay, sweetheart. It's okay, it's okay," she
soothed, walking to the back of the car with him, pacing as she tried to figure out what on earth had happened. "Mommy must have accidentally put you in the
wrong car," she said, then realized, even as the words
came out of her mouth, that that couldn't have happened. She'd locked the car when she went into the
market. Her brothers had drummed that safety precau-
tion into her head.

And she had no car seat. Someone had installed it,
then the baby, while she'd been in Coast Groceries.
But how had someone gotten into her car?

Okay, okay, she told herself as she continued to walk
back and forth, oblivious to the pale blue of the sky
and the darker, sun-embroidered blue of the ocean.
Think. Stay calm. There's an explanation.

Five minutes later, when the baby's wailing finally
began to quiet down, all Dori could think of was that
breaking into someone's car and installing a baby

seat—and a baby—were deliberate acts. This hadn't been done by mistake.

This baby had been abandoned.

No. That didn't seem like quite the right word. *Abandoned* created images of a Dumpster or a doorstep. But someone had left this baby in an up-to-code car seat, probably aware that the owner of the car would be out shortly. Maybe they'd even watched from the bushes surrounding Coast Grocery's parking lot.

The baby stopped crying and, with a ragged little shudder, grabbed a fistful of Dori's shirt. He had Latino features, she thought, as he dropped his head on her shoulder.

She stood still and rocked him, wondering what to do now. The only sensible course of action would be to call the police. She had a cell phone in her purse.

But she made no move toward the car.

She loved having her arms full of a baby. She'd helped her brother Darrick when the twins had been left at the hospital right after birth and he'd thought they were his. In the past two years she'd taken care of the entire army of McKeon children at one time or another, and had longed for the day she'd add her own brood to the new generation.

But thanks to her own abandonment on her wedding day, that wasn't going to happen anytime soon.

She sighed and walked reluctantly toward the car, thinking of how this summer was supposed to be about proving herself capable and competent, and about finishing her book.

The baby might have been left in her car because of

a squabble between his parents—one might have stolen him to hurt the other. His grandparents might be frantic, aunts or uncles worried.

At the car, she leaned into the back to put the baby back in the seat, resolving that she would drive back to town and the police station.

The baby screamed the minute she sat him down. Tears springing to her eyes, feeling like a monster, she buckled him in, secured the protective bar and backed out of the car to close the door.

That was when she noticed the diaper bag on the floor between the seats. It was bright blue-and-yellow plastic with elephants in party hats all over it. Two plastic baby bottles protruded from a compartment on the side, and a big front pocket bulged with something. She unzipped it to check, and found two disposable diapers.

A tiny pocket on the top flap yielded a pacifier, which she quickly offered to the baby. He took it in and began sucking, his screams turned off as though someone had flipped a switch.

Breathing a little sigh of relief, Dori unzipped the main compartment, hoping to find a note—any clue as to who the baby was and why he'd been left in her car.

And there it was, right on top, a piece of Garfield stationery folded in half. A very round handwriting filled the entire page.

"'Hi,'" she read aloud. "'This is Max. He's five-and-a-half months old and a very good baby. He's loving and cheerful. He wakes up a lot at night, but he'll fall asleep again when he sees your face.

'I love him, but I'm not a good mother. You don't know me, Dori, but you were once very kind to me, and I know you'll be kind to Max. Please don't take him to the police. The baby wipes will help you.

'Bless you.'"

Of course there was no signature.

"'You were once very kind to me,'" Dori repeated aloud, trying to remember. In Dancer's Beach, she wondered, or in Edenfield?

Since the baby'd been left here, she could only presume the act of kindness had taken place here. But what? When? She'd been raised to be kind, but she couldn't remember doing any good deed that would convince a woman to leave her her child!

She reread the note.

You don't know me. So it could have been an unconscious kindness she might never remember.

Please don't take him to the police.

She had to. It was illegal to simply pass children on to someone else like a hand-me-down.

She looked into Max's little face as she thought that, and he smiled at her around the pacifier, little arms and legs kicking with excitement at her recognition.

"All right," she said, rubbing a knuckle on his dimpled knee. "In your case, it's more like getting a precious gift than a hand-me-down. But I'm trying to prove something to my family this summer. Even to myself. That I can manage my life without everyone waiting around to lend a hand. And while I'd love to have you around, I'm afraid I'd consider you a handy excuse for not following through, you know?"

Max flailed and kicked again.

Dori rubbed his little knee and looked over the letter one more time, ready to fold it, put it back in the diaper bag, and take baby and bag to the police station.

The baby wipes will help you, she read again. That was a strange thing to write.

Dori dug past two baby outfits and a tiny blue knit sweater before she found the box of wipes. She opened it, wondering if Max's mother had stored in it tips on his care or a favorite toy.

She opened the lid—and stared in stupefaction at the contents of the box. Dead presidents! Grant! A three-inch stack of fifty-dollar bills filled the box.

With a gasp, she flipped through the stack and found that she was wrong. The bottom inch-and-a-half was Franklins! Hundred-dollar bills!

She quickly covered the box, looked around surreptitiously and, satisfied that everyone on the highway was traveling too fast to see what was going on in her car, stuffed it back under the baby clothes and zipped the bag shut.

With a comforting pat for the baby, she closed the back door, then ran around to slip in behind the wheel and lock all the doors. She sat for a moment, her breath caught in her lungs, which seemed to be refusing to do their job.

She made herself calm down. Draw in air, let it out. Breathe in, breathe out. In. Out. *There*. Oxygen was getting to her brain.

This wasn't so bad, after all, was it? Wasn't this just what she'd always wanted? A beautiful baby and

enough cash to invest some and play with some. It
wasn't an enormous fortune, but it was certainly
enough to keep a single woman used to economizing,
and a little baby.

She turned the key in the ignition and had to make
a decision. Which way? Back to town and the police
station? Or home?

McKeon morals flashed in her brain like a neon sign:
YOU CANNOT KEEP THE MONEY.

"I know that," she told herself impatiently. "But,
can I keep the baby?"

McKeon morals had nothing to offer in reply. They
were ambivalent. The McKeons were a law-abiding
family—but to the last person, they believed the good
of their children came first.

Dori turned onto the highway, headed for home.

CHAPTER TWO

DORI FED MAX a baby food jar of weenies and beans she'd found in the bottom of the diaper bag. It was a task for which she should have had Olympic training.

The loving, cheerful baby was a horror when it came to dinner. He grabbed the spoon from her, and when she watched, thrilled that at such a tender age he wanted to feed himself, she got an eyeful of its contents.

He did not want to feed himself, he wanted to decorate. He flung the orangey-brown mixture all over the kitchen in a style reminiscent of Paul Klee. Within minutes, Dori herself was a breathing canvas.

After dinner, she bathed him in the downstairs bathroom in a baby tub left over from Dillon and Harper's little Danielle, now two years old. By the time it was over, there was no water in the tub, an inch on the floor, and Dori was soaked to the skin. At least she was no longer covered in weenies and beans.

For an hour afterward, she watched Max at play on a blanket she spread out in the middle of the living room floor. He was working his way across the blanket in a sort of swimming, arching movement that was surprisingly efficient. Up against the bottom of the sofa, his progress blocked, he stopped, clearly trying to decide what to do.

He braced himself on his arms and looked around for her. Spotting her, he gave her a gummy smile.

That was when a very scary notion occurred to her. He was absolutely beautiful, with a dark-eyed look that was very Latino. He reminded her of…Sal!

She stood up suddenly, startling the baby. She picked him up as he began to cry, turned him around, and put him down on the blanket again. He was quickly off in the other direction, looking like a little seal on the sand.

Sal! she thought. *Of course!* Was this Desideria's baby? Or some other woman's? She'd scoured the newspaper earlier for an item about a missing baby, for some little blurb in the police report. But there'd been nothing. And nothing on the six o'clock news.

Sal. That was a much more reasonable explanation than the idea that a complete stranger to whom she'd once been kind had left her a baby.

But what about the money?

Max yawned and began to rub his eyes. Dori picked him up and moved to the rocker in her parents' bedroom, which was off the living room. It was spacious, with wonderful wicker furniture and a deep wicker rocker that had lulled many McKeon babies to sleep.

Dori rocked and thought about the money. Seeing that much cash hidden at the bottom of a bag had made her jump to the conclusion that it had been stolen.

The baby wipes will help you, the note had said.

Maybe the cash had been put there as an attempt—albeit a faulty one—to pay her to care for Max.

It didn't seem quite like Sal to have stuffed cash into a diaper bag. He'd have opened a bank account and stashed a debit card with its PIN attached in the diaper bag.

Maybe Desi had done this without his knowledge. The note had definitely sounded as though it had been written by the baby's mother, not the father.

And she doubted that Sal was much for notes. She hadn't received so much as a postcard from him since the day a week after the wedding when he'd come to her apartment and she'd refused to see him. If he'd had something to say to her, he'd have done it directly and without subterfuge.

Still, this could very well be his baby.

Dori stroked the glossy dark head and felt Max slump against her as he finally gave in to sleep. She'd brought a portable crib down from upstairs and now put Max in it. She covered him with a well-used baby quilt that one of Harper's aunts had made for Darlan. Its bright blues had faded with repeated washings, but the ducklings in each small square were snow white.

Dori breathed a small sigh of relief, unaware until that moment how tired she was. She went to the kitchen to retrieve the diaper bag, microwaved a cup of tea, and brought both back to the bedroom.

She closed the shade behind the sheer curtains then emptied the contents of the baby wipes box into the middle of the bed.

She counted $11,572. That was an odd amount. Perhaps Desi had simply cleaned out a savings account.

Dori didn't want to feel sympathetic, so she tried to stop thinking about it. About Desideria, anyway. She put the money back in the box and hid the box in the bottom drawer of her parents' dresser.

She had to talk to Sal. She didn't want to, but she had to. If this was his baby and he didn't know about it, there'd be hell to pay for everyone when he found out.

She turned off the lights, locked up the house, took a shower with the door open so that she could listen for the baby, then went to bed. But she stared at the ceiling for two hours, unwilling to go to sleep for fear of having the wedding dream again. If she was going to have to deal civilly with Sal, she couldn't do it with the fresh anger the dream always left in her.

She was about to doze off, when Max awoke. She fed him, changed his diaper and rocked him until he went back to sleep. She put him in the crib and climbed back into bed, this time determined to get some sleep—whatever she dreamed about.

SAL DOMINGUEZ LOOKED over Dominguez Security's quarterly report and was surprised at what a profitable three months it had been. Seattle was full of homeowners and commercial clients concerned about making their premises impenetrable, concerned about the safety of their cars and their commercial fleets, and concerned about their own personal safety.

It was his good fortune that one of the first clients

he'd served when he moved to town eighteen months ago had been a high-profile columnist for the *Post-Intelligencer* who'd offended a corrupt official and had needed a bodyguard. Though Sal had three other security agents, he'd taken the job himself.

He'd accompanied his client on a clandestine trip to the waterfront to retrieve vital documentation from a former aid to the official, when they'd been attacked by three men. Sal had sent one into the water, dispatched another after a brief altercation, then turned to see the third man draw a bead on his client, who was trapped in a corner.

Sal drew his own 9mm Smith & Wesson and fired as he ran toward his client, arriving just in time to take the third man's answering bullet in the shoulder as the man, too, went into the river.

The grateful columnist had had the forum through which to make sure word got around about Dominguez Security's dependability.

Sal handed the folder back to Diego Munoz, his vice president in charge of everything Sal didn't oversee— and his good friend. They'd met in Madre Maria when Sal was putting up the hospital and needed someone trustworthy and sufficiently obsessed with excellence to help him with the details.

By the time the hospital was up and running, they were friends, and Diego's wife, Manuela, was pregnant with their third child. It was no time to leave the man without employment. So, Sal had invited Diego to join him in the United States, where he'd open a security company.

Diego had the heart of an adventurer in a short, round body, and the sense of decorum of a butler. He was the one who'd insisted that the office look as if it belonged to a law firm rather than to a militia group.

He'd told Ben Richardson, a former wrestler, Los Angeles police officer, and now a bodyguard for Dominguez Security, to stop wearing camouflage on assignment.

"Unless you are guarding our client in a duck blind," Diego had said, "it is inappropriate."

Ben had taken offense, had turned to Sal for support, but had found none.

"He's right," Sal agreed. "Our clients go to the theater, the opera, fine hotels and restaurants, business meetings in important places. You function best if you don't stand out."

Ben had charged four three-piece suits to the company. Sal had paid for two.

"Excellent," Sal said now, leaning back in his chair. "We're in very good financial shape, and staffing's covered for the next two months. You and Manuela can take a vacation."

Diego, sitting stiffly in the client's chair, shook his head regretfully. "Miguel is on a baseball team, and Rosa is taking ballet lessons."

Sal envied the sparkle that came into Diego's eyes when he talked about his family. "Ballet lessons at four?" he asked in surprise.

Diego smiled. "She is a little butterball with the attitude of a lawn mower. We are hoping she will learn a little style."

Sal nodded. Perhaps that was what Dori lacked—ballet lessons. She was not a butterball, but she did have the attitude of a big-toothed, grass devouring, ride-on mower. He had to do something about her, he knew. He just didn't know what. And he seldom approached any task or brought on a confrontation until he knew he would emerge victorious.

Dori had so entangled things that no one could win at this point.

"Why don't *you* take a vacation?" Diego suggested.

Sal shook his head. "Where would I go?"

"Europe?" Diego suggested. "The Caribbean, the Mediterranean?"

"No. I have no desire to lay on a beach or to tour cathedrals."

"You're restless," Diego noted.

"I'm always restless." Sal grinned. "I need a twenty-story hotel filled with rich ladies with fine jewelry."

"Mmm. And what would you do when those ladies heard that a cat burglar was on the prowl and came to Dominguez Security for someone to protect them and their jewels?"

His grin widened. "Now, that's a profitable angle to the business I hadn't anticipated."

"As if you could steal."

"I *did* steal, Diego. I told you all about it."

"You gave everything to the village. You kept the school open, you got our goods to market, you put up the hospital."

"Duncan McKeon put up the money for the hospital."

"But you made it happen. Why are you so eager to dismiss your accomplishments?"

"Because at the bottom," he replied frankly, "I'm a really good thief. That's not precisely the legacy a man dreams of leaving."

Diego shook his head at him and stood. "You, *amigo,* need to see yourself through the eyes of a woman who loves you."

"Yes. Well. There is no such woman."

"There are many who would be willing."

"And they would flatter me in exchange for good sex and expensive baubles—but that's not what you're talking about, is it?"

"Good sex and expensive baubles?" a female voice repeated from the doorway. "I thought your business was alarms and bodyguards."

Sal leaned around Diego to see who was eavesdropping on their conversation. Had he not been as fit as his work required, he thought later, he might very well have died of a heart attack on the spot. Dori stood just inside his office.

She pointed into the hall. "I'm sorry for barging in. There's no one at the desk out there."

Diego, too, was speechless for a moment. Then he turned to Sal and said under his breath, "I've told you we should stagger lunch hours, but the girls like to go together and you let them. You will excuse me."

On his way out, he stopped and bowed stiffly in Dori's direction. He'd been her staunchest advocate before she'd left Sal. "It is nice to see you again, *Mrs. Dominguez.*" He emphasized her married name.

"And you, Diego," she said. "How are Manuela and the children?"

"They're well, thank you."

Sal had been so surprised by the sight of Dori's face, it wasn't until Diego touched the hand of the baby in her arms that he realized she wasn't alone.

He came around the desk, trying to strike an approach somewhere between collected and well-mannered. He found it hard to do, with his heart thudding against his ribs.

"Hello, Dori," he said, as she came toward him across the pale teal carpet. She wore white jeans and a simple rose-colored shirt. She'd cut her hair since they'd parted, and it was sticking up here and there and lay on her forehead in irregular wisps.

Her cheeks and her lips were the color of her shirt, and her eyes were dark and troubled, a curious overlay of anger snapping at him despite her courteous reply.

"Hello, Sal. I apologize if I interrupted a meeting."

"We were finished," Diego said, and left the office.

The baby in her arms smiled at Sal and waved his arms wildly. Sal felt a physical pain in his heart at the possibility the baby suggested. "And who's this?" he asked with pretended nonchalance.

"This is Max," she replied.

Max leaned away from her and stretched fat little arms toward him. Sal reached instinctively for him, unable to ignore the invitation.

"So, he *is* yours!" Dori said, anger now in her voice as well as her eyes.

Sal sat on the edge of his desk with the baby, not certain what she was talking about. However, he had heard that tone before and it put him on the defensive.

"What do you mean?"

She sank into the chair Diego had just vacated. She looked tired as well as irritated. "I mean that he just reached for you as though he knows you."

"Knows me," he repeated, waiting for the words to make sense. "How could he know me? You just walked in with him."

She appeared off balance, uncertain. "He looks just like you," she said.

He looked into the baby's face, wondering what on earth Dori was trying to say. "He could be a Dominguez," he said, as the baby tried to remove his tie through his neck. "But if you recall," he said, peeling back little fingers to free himself, "I haven't been anywhere near you in two years."

"Well, what does that have to do with anything?" she demanded, coming to help disengage the little fingers. "*I'm* not his mother."

"Then what are you doing with him?"

"Desideria put him in my car!" she said loudly, backing up with the baby, who was now screaming.

"Desi..." he began, mystified. He unfastened the tie and yanked it off, then took the baby back. Max stopped crying instantly. Sal felt a definite satisfaction that he didn't bother to hide. "Will you please sit down and try to make sense. What do you mean, Desi left the baby in your car? Where? You've been to Tucson?"

Dori fell into the chair, the tie held in her two hands as though she intended to garrote someone with it. "Tucson?" she repeated.

Sal nodded, quickly pushing his blotter away before the baby dragged toward him a variety of office supplies he could either choke on or use to ruin everything else on the desk. "She lives there with her husband."

"I thought her husband went to jail."

"This is a new husband."

Dori swallowed and seemed to collapse in upon herself. "You're sure?"

"I'm sure," he replied. "I flew there last weekend for Guadalupe's baptism."

She groaned and dropped both arms over the sides of the chair. "Well, damn," she said.

DORI TRIED TO THINK, but she was finding it difficult with Salvatore Dominguez a mere four feet away from her. He was still handsome, still had that calm assurance that made her feel innocent and incompetent. And he handled Max with easy confidence, though she knew he didn't have much experience with babies. At least, he hadn't two years ago.

And he was telling her he *wasn't* Max's father?

She was exhausted and confused. "I thought you and Desideria had a…" She wriggled her fingertips in explanation. His eyes went to her hands, then to her eyes. This was bringing them back to two years ago, and she didn't want to go there.

"A what?" he asked, his easy good humor changing suddenly.

The perceptive baby detected it and looked up at him. Sal smiled and pinched the baby's chin. Max laughed delightedly.

"A relationship," Dori replied.

He glanced at her but kept an eye on the baby's hands as they explored his watch. "We did. But it was not a sexual one. You'd have known that if you'd waited for me to explain."

"You're the one who left," she said, struggling to keep her voice down.

"I asked you to wait for my return."

"I came almost four thousand miles," she said, fighting for composure, "to tell you that I loved you. And you left me on our wedding day—not two minutes after the ceremony—to take care of someone else!"

"I asked Diego to explain, but he told me you refused to listen. You packed your things and flew home."

"I didn't want Diego," she said loudly. "I wanted you. I searched my soul and came all that way to find you!"

The baby moved on to study Sal's fingers. Dori noticed for the first time that Sal wore a wedding ring.

Something cold and hard rose to the middle of her chest and felt as though it cut off her air. "You're married," she said in a strangled voice.

He glanced up at her again, surprised by that observation. "To you," he said. Then, realizing that her eyes were on his ring, he added, "You gave this to me, remember?"

His eyes went to her left hand: it was naked. Brutally, she held it up for him to see.

"Well, I am not. We had a ceremony, but immediately after that the groom left. We never shared a bed or did any of the things that make a couple truly married."

"We repeated the vows," he pointed out.

She made a scornful sound. "Which you broke two minutes later. Hardly cause for me to consider myself Dori Dominguez."

"I came back to find you gone," he countered. "You're the one who decided you didn't want to be married, after all."

"I doubt anyone would be surprised about that, if they knew."

The look in his eyes disputed that. "You might be surprised," he said, "if you admitted your real reasons to yourself."

"What?" she demanded.

Max made a sudden grab for a letter opener that should have been out of reach. Sal pushed it farther away, then turned Max around and stood him on the desk. "This child will make a good outfielder one day. His arms are expandable."

"You're ignoring my question," Dori said.

Sal nodded. "That line of conversation never gets us anywhere. Let's forget that for the moment, and tell me about Max being left in your car."

She *wanted* to pursue "that line of conversation."

She'd driven six hours into Seattle and its horrible traffic, certain she had a case against Sal's old girlfriend, only to learn that she might be mistaken about their relationship. Not that it mattered. He'd still gone to Desideria the day he'd married Dori.

But, damn it, something inside her still responded to him in the same old way.

Then she noticed a photo on his desk. She remembered when he'd taken it, just two days before their wedding. Dori was pictured seated on his veranda, relaxed in a high-back chair, smiling. Clearly in love.

She wanted to run, but that was not the way to prove herself capable and competent.

With a sigh, she explained about the trip to the grocery store and the surprise she got on the way home.

"Someone broke into your car?" he asked with a frown.

She nodded. "Nothing was taken, just—" she indicated the baby "—deposited." She handed him the note.

She saw him read it quickly, then read it over more slowly. "A child's hand," he said. "What act of kindness did you do her?"

Dori shrugged. "I don't remember anything particular. Like most people, I try not to be *un*kind."

He glanced up from the note in dry amusement. "Unless, of course, you're dealing with me."

She let that pass.

"What does she mean about the box of wipes?" he asked. "What kind of help?"

She realized she'd been so involved with the baby

and their argument that she'd forgotten one of the more intriguing parts of the mystery. She reached into the diaper bag for the box, then stood and handed it across the desk.

Sal opened it and stared at it a moment, while Max was fascinated by a drawer pull.

"It's $11,572," Dori said. "I guess whoever left me the baby, left the money to help me take care of it. I was going to give it back to you or have you give it to Desi. But if it was neither of you…" She shrugged, unsure where to go from there. "Who do I give it to? If I take it to the police, I'll have to explain about the baby—and they'll take him away."

Sal frowned at the money, apparently thinking.

"Maybe I'll just wait," she went on, "and see what happens. It might turn up in the news. Dancer's Beach is a small town. There might be gossip about a theft or missing money. Then I can sneak it back to whoever lost it."

Sal gave her a quick look that was a clear negative. "No," he said, as though the look hadn't been clear enough. "You've obviously been watched and followed, if someone knows your name and waited for you to go into the grocery store before putting the baby in the car. Someone broke into your car and left you a suspiciously large amount of cash. This is not the behavior of a person on the right side of the law."

"I know," she said defensively. "But I don't think anyone intended me harm. I mean—"

"You may be right," he interrupted. "But what concerns me is where this money came from. It isn't wrapped as though it came from a bank. The way the bills are organized, largest to smallest, it looks like it may have been someone's bank deposit.''

''You mean a business?''

''Maybe. Or a bookie, or a drug dealer...''

''In Dancer's Beach?''

''Bookies and drug dealers,'' he said patiently, ''are everywhere. And you don't know where this person came from, do you?''

''No.''

''What if a desperate woman stole this money from her drug-dealing boyfriend, or her pimp? And he comes looking for it?''

She folded her arms stubbornly. He was right, but this summer was about... She knew what it was about. She didn't have to tell herself again. ''If that happens, I can take care of myself.''

''And the baby?''

That gave her pause. She'd taken self-defense courses. She could handle a mugger if she could see him coming. But if he took her by surprise, she had a tendency to hyperventilate and pass out cold.

She might be willing to risk herself, but Max?

Sal stood, transferring the baby to his hip. Max had his telephone receiver.

''Diego!'' Sal shouted.

Diego appeared in the doorway. He always reminded Dori of a very sweet undertaker.

''Yes?'' Diego asked.

''I'm going on vacation, after all,'' Sal said.

CHAPTER THREE

"WAIT A MINUTE." Dori stood, her chin at a stubborn angle. "You're not thinking you're coming home with me?"

"No." She looked relieved. He strode toward the door with the baby. "I *am* coming home with you." He enjoyed another glimmer of satisfaction at her annoyed surprise. "Will you bring the bag, please?"

She'd started to follow him, sputtering, then turned back to grab the diaper bag off the floor and sling it over her shoulder. "Sal, you're not coming home with me," she said, running to keep up with him, then colliding with his back when he stopped to talk to his secretary, who was just returning from lunch. "I'm writing a book this summer. I don't have time for continual arguments. And where do you think you're going to stay?"

Claudette Bingham, a tall, slender redhead with a photographic memory and a quiet nature that made even Sal seem frantic, had been with Dominguez Security since the day he had opened the doors.

She smiled at the baby in his arms and blinked at Dori. "*Mrs.* Dominguez?" she asked.

Dori put a hand to her forehead, "No, I..." she began hotly, then, apparently realizing the confusion wasn't Claudie's fault, drew a breath and started again. "Technically, yes. Actually, no."

Claudie raised an eyebrow at Sal.

"Don't worry," he said, bending over her desk to make a note on the calendar there. Max leaned out of his arms and reached for the large paper cup Claudie had just placed there. "We don't understand it, either."

She took the cup from Max and put the straw to his lips. "Can he have a drink?" she asked Dori. "It's juice."

"Sure," Dori said defeatedly. "Sal, we—"

"This man's name is in the file," he said, pointing with the tip of his pen to the name he'd written. "There are two addresses for him. I'll be at the one at Dancer's Beach. You can reach me there or on my cell."

"How long will you be gone?" Claudie asked, smiling as Max drank greedily.

"I'm not sure. We have a case I've decided to handle myself."

"We're not a *case*," Dori said. "I didn't come here to hire you, I came to ask you…Sal, no way!" She'd been reading Claudie's calendar upside down and suddenly realized he'd written her brother Duncan's name on it. "You are *not* staying at my brother's house in Dancer's Beach. *I'm* staying there."

Sal pulled a ring of keys out of his pocket and held up the one with the signature star bauble attached to all the keys to the McKeon residence. "I've been invited to use it any time I please."

"Well, presumably he meant when the house was empty. It's not empty now."

There was a loud noise as Max struck bottom in the cup. "All gone!" Claudie said and tossed the cup away.

Max protested with a shriek. Sal handed him to Claudie. "Would you watch him for a few minutes, please?"

"Of course. Come here, big boy."

Alissa, Diego's secretary, and Bianca, who kept the master schedule, all crowded around her desk.

Sal took Dori's arm and drew her into a small conference room at the far end of the hall. It had gray-and-burgundy padded chairs around an oval mahogany table, and formal burgundy drapes. Clients talking security seemed to relax here. He hoped the atmosphere would do the same for Dori.

"What do you think I intend in going home with you?" he asked. It always surprised her when an argument was placed in her lap. With three older brothers, she was used to having to fight even to be noticed, much less included. Sal wondered just how far that chin could angle up.

"You want to try to get back together," she said defensively.

He had to look into her eyes to spare himself the vision of neat little breasts covered in pink, of slender hips with just enough sway to them to be seductive, of graceful legs. Images of her had haunted his dreams—waking and sleeping—for two years.

He walked away from her toward the window, because now he was going to lie through his teeth. "If that was what I wanted," he said, "wouldn't I have tried to do that sometime over the past two years?" It *had* been what he'd wanted, but he'd had to make sure he had the business in order first. Then he'd waited for the right moment. And here it was.

There was a moment's silence as he stared out the window. He guessed he'd hurt her feelings. Perversely, she claimed to want nothing to do with him, but was probably upset that he'd suggested he wanted nothing to do with her. That was Dori.

"You didn't know where I was," she said finally.

"You went back to your apartment for a month after the wedding," he said, turning to sit on the edge of the deep windowsill. She stood and watched him from the side of the room, her arm resting on the curved back of one of the chairs. "You went back to England for research from August to November. You came home for the holidays. You spent Thanksgiving at your parents, where all the family collected. You joined the family at the summer house for two weeks over the Christmas holidays. Then you took a teaching job at Edenfield High during the second half of the year and were hired for the following year." Again, she was surprised. "I've known where you were every moment."

He couldn't tell what she thought of that. She folded her arms and asked calmly, "If you've known where I was, why didn't you serve me with divorce papers?"

"Because you're the one who wants the divorce," he reminded her. "Not I."

"Yet you haven't tried to change my mind."

He shrugged. "I know you to be a stubborn woman who wants things her way. My standing on my head to make you see things differently isn't going to help. I'm waiting for the day you come to your senses."

That nudged her temper. He'd known it would. Her anger was almost easier on him than that lost look that had come over her when she'd realized he'd known her every move over the past two years, yet had never approached her.

"I am being sensible," she said, dropping her arm from the chair and walking away from him. "What woman wants to be married to a man who runs out on their wedding day?"

"Then why didn't *you* file for divorce?"

"Because…"

There was a struggle in her eyes that she tried desperately to hide. If he hadn't once understood every subtlety in her, he'd have missed it.

"Because I didn't have the money," she said with sudden resolution. "But now I have, and I've hired a lawyer."

Now he knew he was the one struggling not to look desperate. "Then, there's nothing to worry about. In all this time, I've made no effort to reconcile, and you've started divorce proceedings. So there's little emotional danger if we spend time together in the same house for the sake of your safety and that of the baby."

She didn't look convinced.

"I'm Mexican, Dori," he said, getting up from the sill and going toward her. "Where I come from, women are buxom and warm with inviting eyes and smiling lips. They're not always sniping and turning away. Believe me. I have no desire to reignite an old flame."

She maintained her cocked-chin hauteur, but he couldn't tell if that was pain in her eyes. She turned away from him toward the door, her manner unhurried, but possibly…injured.

"But I don't want to see you in danger, either," he said briskly, reaching around her to grasp the doorknob. "Nor the baby. So let me keep you safe while we get to the bottom of this," he bargained. "Then your lawyer can prepare the divorce papers."

She turned to him. With his hand on the doorknob, they were mere inches apart, and history returned in a rush. Every stirring he'd ever had for her when they'd been meeting about Julie; every hot desire that had blistered the night they'd spent together during what her family now referred to as "the Julie incident," every dark and lonely moment since he'd yearned for even the scent of her—all rose up to pulse between them and make a mockery of his denial.

His impulse was to cup her head in his hand and kiss her senseless. But there was more at stake at this moment.

"Doesn't that make sense?"

She looked into his eyes. He had no idea whether she was seeing the logical reason that supported his Machiavellian plan, or the lust that had almost overcome it.

"Yes," she said finally. "It does."

He opened the door, trying not to betray his enormous relief. "Good," he said.

"I'm not cooking for you," she warned.

"I appreciate that," he replied.

DORI THOUGHT HER CAR seemed crowded with Sal in the passenger seat of her little red import. He drove an American luxury car, and she'd followed him from his office to his condo where he'd packed a suitcase and collected his laptop.

"You still drive like a wild woman," he said, though he appeared relaxed enough. "If you're going to be a mother, you're going to have to get that inclination under control."

She did like to drive—and the faster the better. Washington traffic encouraged her to indulge that habit. Everything else in her life—school, the Georgian women who so fascinated her, her family who were always watching— required that she be orderly, careful, controlled.

But pushing her foot down on the accelerator and controlling the maneuverable little car made her feel reckless, yet still in charge. And she liked that.

"You're safe," she told him with a quick side glance.

She caught his answering look. It told her he wasn't so sure. But he watched the traffic with no apparent concern. He didn't even make a sudden move of alarm when a truck cut in front of her to catch the freeway exit, and she had to slam on the brakes, then change lanes so the car behind them didn't drive over them.

Maybe, she thought, that doubtful glance wasn't referring to her driving. Maybe she made him feel unsafe in other ways.

No. He'd just told her in no uncertain terms that he no longer had feelings for her. And that was best. She was moving on this summer.

She glanced in the rearview mirror and saw Max sound asleep in his seat.

"I noticed that your accent seems less pronounced," she observed, remembering how his soft, round pronunciations and his elegantly constructed sentences had fascinated her.

"I issue a lot of instructions and orders on the phone and the radio in my work," he explained. "So I've been concentrating on making sure I'm understood."

A good point, she had to agree, but he sounded so…American.

The traffic thinned south of Olympia, but the road was dominated by large trucks; she had to pay close attention to the traffic.

They stopped for dinner in Longview, just across the river from Oregon. Max was refreshed by his long nap and drummed a discordant tune with a spoon on the tray of his high chair. Dori realized that she'd been driving all day long on four hours' sleep.

The helpful waitress brought a package of crackers to quiet the baby. "Bless you!" Dori said, opened the package, and broke off a small bite. Max took it in the palm of his hand and shoved it into his chin. His groping little mouth finally found it, and he chewed triumphantly.

"You're sure you want to do this?" Sal asked, as Dori offered Max another bite.

"Do what?" she asked.

"Raise a baby."

She was surprised by the question. "Of course I'm sure."

"Because your brothers all have families and you have to keep up, just like when you were children?"

Yesterday that question might have offended her, but she'd thought about it on the drive to Seattle and now it only amused her. "I don't think so. They left me behind ages ago when they all embarked upon successful and dynamic careers. No, Max is just for me. Or maybe for him. When I first discovered him in the back of my car, it took him a couple of minutes to calm down, but then he just melted against me—almost as though he was home. And that's how he felt to me. At last I was holding what I've always wanted."

Sal looked a little concerned. "But you look exhausted. Did you get any sleep last night?"

"Four hours," she answered. The waitress placed a burger and fries in front of Dori, and a Reuben and soup before Sal. "The exhausting part was driving in Washington. I don't know how you do that every day." She peppered her French fries and handed him the shaker.

Max studied their plates and stirred anxiously in his highchair. Dori took several small pieces of bun off her burger and put them on his tray. He began the laborious but clearly interesting process of getting them from tray to mouth.

"I'm used to it now. It hones both my killer and my protective instincts. Will you give up teaching because of the baby?"

She'd thought about that, too. "I don't think I'll be able to. Even if I sell my book, it'll have limited appeal, so I won't make enough to quit my job. But it'll probably pay for day care."

"How close are you to finishing the book?"

"Not very close. I've finished about a quarter of it, but it's going well." She dipped a French fry in the side of blue cheese dressing she'd ordered. "But you know, while I was driving up, I was also thinking that if I made some changes, I could turn it into a work of fiction and potentially make it more salable."

"Change a scholarly work to fiction?"

"Yes. It was supposed to be a book about how the personalities of the women of the period were affected by their clothing, their surroundings, and the very little that was expected of them besides attracting a man and bearing his children."

A quarter of Sal's sandwich was already gone. He waggled his eyebrows over the rim of his coffee cup. "My ideal of womanhood," he said, putting the cup down. "Go on."

He was remarkably easy to talk to, she realized, now that they'd decided they wanted nothing to do with one another. She suddenly felt more free than she had in the past two years. It was amazing.

"What if I made the heroine a seamstress of the period," she explained, "who'd always wanted to be a doctor or a lawyer or someone powerful. But she has to make her living in one of the few careers acceptable for women, dressing other women to help them attract men. She does so in the hope that those men will ultimately get her the things she wants. Until the women start dying and she's always the last person they've seen before they're killed.''

''Did she do it?''

''No.''

''Then, who?''

''I don't know.''

He arched an eyebrow. ''Isn't that a major problem for completion of the project?''

She laughed. ''Well, yes. But I'm feeling very enthused about it, and thinking that as I work along I'll come to a solution.'' Then she sighed ruefully as Max, finished with his pieces of bread, screamed again. ''Though how I'll accomplish that with Mighty Mouth, here, I'm not sure.''

''I'll watch him,'' Sal said, ''for as long as I'm at the house.''

She turned to him suspiciously, not entirely sure what to say. It was a generous offer, but she couldn't stop wondering if he had an ulterior motive.

''What?'' Sal asked with a half laugh. ''Are you going to second-guess my every effort to help you? I thought we had come to an agreement.''

''We have,'' she said, her tone subdued. ''I'm just a little surprised that you *want* to help me.''

''I'm thinking of you as a client.''

That made her a little nervous. ''How much am I paying you?''

"A no-charge client. We do that once in a while, if someone's in danger because they've stood up for something we believe in."

"But I haven't done that."

He pointed to Max. "You're looking out for a helpless baby. So, try to relax about this. I'll watch him part of the time so you can work, and you can spell me once in a while so I can explore Dancer's Beach. Julie's always telling me how much she loves it there."

"All right." His help would make a big difference to her ability to meet her goals for the summer. She was a little confused by it, despite his reassurances, but she would keep those concerns to herself.

"How is it that you're so good with babies?" she asked.

"Diego's children," he replied. "I've taken care of them for him and Manuela quite a few times. Delia, the baby, is just a year old."

"I see." So he would be an asset with Max. "Did I mention that I'm not cooking for you?" she teased.

"You did." He picked up the second half of his sandwich. "And I can only interpret that to mean that you do have some regard for me after all. I'll cook. You used to like my *frijoles* with chorizo and cheese, as I recall."

She'd stayed in his small rancho outside Madre Maria for almost a week before they were married. She'd worked with him at the hospital every day, and he'd cooked for her every night. Happy moments from that time rushed back to her, complete with the aromas and flavors of his kitchen.

"But none of that napalm-bomb salsa." She laughed. "You have to tone it down a little. And easy on the chipotle peppers in the chili."

"Sissy *gringa*," he taunted. "All right. I'll take it easy on the hot stuff."

Their eyes met and held as they shared the happy memories of those few precious days. And for one breathless moment, when she seemed to see all the way into his heart, she had a premonition that she was making a terrible mistake.

Then the shock of his defection and the long, lonely days that followed came back to her as well, and she knew she'd never be able to forgive and forget that. There was no danger here that she might fall in love again.

"Good," she said with sudden coolness. "Because that chili the night Diego and Manuela came made me sick."

"Three bowls of chili," he said, apparently aware that she was putting a damper on their memories, "on top of three margaritas, would make anybody sick."

She'd been deliriously happy and filled with the spirit of celebration, as she recalled, but she didn't want to admit that so she dropped the subject.

"I'll drive the rest of the way," he said, taking the keys from her as they walked across the parking lot to the car. Max, in his arms, made a grab for the keys and shrieked when Sal held them away.

"Our lives would be simpler," Sal said, unlocking the car with the remote as they approached, "if we tied his arms to his body."

Dori opened the back door behind the passenger side and took Max, then placed him in his car seat. "I know. He's like an octopus with extenders."

Max went peacefully, yawning as she strapped him in and lowered the bar.

Dori climbed into the passenger seat, finding it strange. She was seldom a passenger anymore, and the vantage point felt odd.

"Can I back-seat drive?" she asked, buckling her belt.

Sal put the key in the ignition and grinned at her over his arm. "The way you drive, I don't think it would be fair to tell *me* how."

She made a face. "Duncan taught me. I think the style comes from trying to outrun the paparazzi."

She fell asleep somewhere along the Columbia River, heading for Astoria, and didn't awaken until he stopped for gas somewhere south of Cannon Beach— still a good hour-and-a-half from Dancer's Beach.

"Want me to take over?" she asked, stretching her arms out ahead of her.

"No, thank you," Sal replied. "The road is quiet."

Dori suddenly remembered the baby, and turned in her seat to see him fast asleep, his head slumped to his left side. She unbuckled her belt, kneeled on her seat to turn around and tucked his blanket around him.

"Are you cold?" Sal asked, as she settled down again. "Manuela always puts a blanket on the baby when *she's* cold."

"When the baby can't tell you," she said, rubbing her arms in the sleeveless shirt, "how you feel is your only way to judge. It was such a beautiful summer day, I stupidly didn't think about a sweater."

Sal turned up the heat and reached behind his seat with his right hand, carefully watching the road. "I threw one back here somewhere. Ah. Here it is—" He produced it and put it in her lap.

It was a V-neck pullover in his favorite black—a throwback, he'd once told her, to his days as a thief. She pulled it on, catching a faint whiff of something subtle and herbal.

"Ooh." She couldn't help the expression of pleasure as she pushed her arms into the soft sleeves. "Cashmere?"

"Yes," he replied. "A gift from Diego and Manuela last Christmas. Warmer?"

"Yes, thank you." She reached into the glove compartment, remembering suddenly the Hershey with almonds she'd stashed there that morning. She unwrapped it, snapped it in half and handed half to Sal.

"What is it?" he asked, taking it from her.

"Chocolate," she replied. She bit off a chunk and let the delicious sweet melt on her tongue.

She heard his strong teeth snap off a piece.

"You still have that sweet tooth," he observed.

"I do." She took another bite and rested her head on the back of the seat. "Do you still make flan with that wonderful Mexican vanilla?"

"I can put it on the menu," he replied.

"I'll bet Max will love it."

"If you're willing to share."

"You could just double the batch."

"I'll consider that."

The chocolate made her feel, temporarily at least, that all was well with the world. The delicious soft sweater awakened the latent hedonist in her. She curled up, leaned against the door and was asleep in a matter of seconds.

SAL HAD A VAGUE MEMORY of the route to the McKeons' summer home, from his one and only visit there after he'd broken up the Cat Pack in Florida. While he was the McKeon's guest for several days, he and Dori had spent hours walking the beach and talking—and as usually happened when they talked, getting nowhere.

He'd proposed, tired of trying to make sense of their relationship and determined to simply let it have life. He was the kind of man who made things happen his way; he'd had to be. A life of poverty was not a happy prospect for the future, so he had changed things.

Dori, however, had dealt her entire life with older brothers who insisted she do what they considered to be in her best interest. Sal knew she didn't fully understand to this day that what governed her brothers was the notion that she was special, not that she was incompetent. A little sister in their lives, particularly after the loss of their brother Donovan, had given them a cause for the protective masculinity developing within them.

As they'd grown older, and she'd grown more beautiful, more intelligent, more eager to escape their continued protection, they'd become even more vigilant.

Dori, therefore, resisted everything and everyone

who presented a threat to her independence. And Sal thought the idea of marriage had done just that.

He'd gone home to Mexico with the funds Duncan had given him for the hospital, certain Dori would miss him and be right behind him.

But it had taken her a year of soul-searching to finally decide that being without him was worse than being with him. He remembered his excitement at the sight of her, his hope that finally he would have the family he wanted.

He remembered their wedding day and how beautiful she had looked as the sun filtered through her mantilla. Her eyes had been filled with love for him and her hands had been on his arm, his shoulder, as though she had to touch him to exist.

And he'd known that at long last, after all the control he'd exerted time and again to leave her untouched, she would finally be his. He could see them in his imagination, body to body in his bed, making love as he'd known they would from the first time he ever saw her.

Then his friends had burst into the church, right after the ceremony, with the news of Desi's husband—and everything had taken a sorry, sorry turn.

It had been a terrible thing to leave Dori, but had he not gone, Desi would be dead today. He'd gone to Dori after Paco had been returned to jail, and had tried to explain that to her, but she hadn't wanted to listen.

Finally, disappointed in her and angry at himself as well as at her, he went back to Madre Maria to finish the addition to the hospital. He'd expected to hear every day that she'd filed for divorce, but that news never came.

And then she'd shown up at his office this afternoon. Now their relationship had come full circle to the house in Dancer's Beach.

He passed the welcome sign and followed the highway to the road that turned up the hill. He was afraid he might not recognize the street in the darkness, but she'd left the porch lights on, and he saw the white farmhouse with its window boxes, front porch furniture and decorative columns backlit by the old Georgian coach lamps on either side of the front door.

He guided the car into the driveway, turning off the motor as he drew close to the garage.

He gave Dori a gentle nudge. "We're home, *querida,*" he said.

She emitted a soft little groan and, eyes still closed, turned toward him, arms unfolding to reach for him.

He remained still for a heartbeat, realizing she must still be ensnared by some dream that put that soft smile on her lips.

"Salvatore," she breathed with a little pout. "Come to me. It's been so long."

His breath left him, and he couldn't think. He shouldn't let this happen after what he'd promised, but he couldn't imagine why not.

He leaned toward her, and her smile widened as one of her hands went into his hair and the fingertips of the other explored the line of his jaw.

"Tonight, my love," she whispered, eyelashes fluttering. "Tonight at last!"

His temperature rose ten degrees when her lips parted and she leaned even closer. He knew he shouldn't do this, that he should wake her, but he simply didn't have the moral fiber. He opened his mouth over hers and let her have full rein.

Her tongue explored his, ran along his bottom lip, touched his teeth, then her lips moved on his with cleverness and ingenuity.

In silence, he responded with all the ardor she inspired. He kissed her throat as she nibbled at his ear, kissed her chin as she kissed his eyelids, and finally, in danger of really making this the night she saw in her dream, he tried to catch a fistful of her hair and pull her back, but her hair was now cut too short.

She woke up with a suddenness that startled both of them.

He watched the expression in her eyes change from languid desire to startled awareness to molten anger.

"Sal!" she said in accusation, pushing against him.

He caught her wrists and tried to be reasonable despite his disappointment. "Whoa. Think a minute. You were dreaming."

She looked around, and then he felt the tension leave her. "You beckoned me," he said, feeling obligated to explain. "You put your arms—"

"I know, I know," she said, pulling free of him. "It was my dream, after all," she added with a sigh. "I'm sorry."

He shouldn't say it, but he did anyway. "I'm not."

Even in the darkness, he could see the troubled look in her eyes.

"It was just a dream," she insisted, her voice a little rough.

He nodded. He could tell by the way she'd reached for him that it was the same dream *he'd* lived on for two years.

But she wouldn't want to hear that.

"Right," he said, reaching across her to push open her car door. "And we had a deal."

"I'm sorry if I...upset you."

She looked a little stricken, guilty. Upset him. Major understatement.

"Not a problem," he said, pushing his own door open. "You have a long history of upsetting me. It's a comfort that some things never change."

CHAPTER FOUR

TROUBLE STARTED right away. Dori took Max inside, hoping he would remain asleep. She was exhausted and troubled and thinking gloomily that she'd finally gotten the wedding dream to work out the way she'd wanted it to—the two of them going back to his rancho to finally make love—only to be awakened by rude reality before getting to the good part.

And now he probably thought she had designs on him, after all.

She carried Max into the downstairs bedroom that she'd been using and lay him in the crib.

"I would prefer that you and the baby sleep upstairs," Sal said from the bedroom doorway. "I'll sleep down here."

"Why?" she asked.

"Because you're out of the way, if anything happens."

She pointed to the crib and her small desk. "But the crib's down here and my—"

He cut her off with a nod, handing her the laptop off the desk, then picking up the small oak piece. "They're easily moved." And he carried it toward the stairs as he spoke. "I know you once occupied the attic room, but the stairs are too hard to manage with the baby. Which of the second-floor rooms do you want?"

She followed him as far as the stairs off the kitchen. "I was happy down here."

He went on up the stairs. "I'll pick one, then."

"Dillon's," she called after him, after a small growl of exasperation, "overlooking the garden. First one on the right."

A loud yowl came from the direction of the crib. She hurried back to find Max braced on his arms and smiling. He was not upset, simply vocalizing. And very wide awake.

Great.

As Sal carried the crib upstairs, Dori followed with the baby, thinking grumpily that only thirty-six hours ago she'd been congratulating herself on how well the summer was going. Now, a brief day-and-a-half later, she found herself in possession of a baby, eleven-thousand dollars and some change, the husband she hadn't seen in two years, and a headache so bad it was probably registering on a Richter scale somewhere. Another Dorianne success story.

Sal had placed her desk near the window, and the baby's crib in a dark corner of the room, leaving her nothing to complain about. "Thank you," she said stiffly.

Sal headed for the door. "I'll bring your clothes up," he said.

"No." She pointed to the room's tiny closet, packed with summer clothes and toys that stayed here when

Dillon, Harper and the children went home. "There won't be any place to put them."

He leaned against the doorway. "Would one of the other rooms have worked better?"

"Same kind of closets. I'll manage."

"All right." He came toward her, beckoning to Max, who almost leaned out of her arms toward Sal. "I'll get him back to sleep. You go to bed."

She turned away with the baby, who protested. "I slept most of the way home while you drove. You go to bed, and I'll get him back to sleep."

"Dori, why don't you—?" he began.

"You're here to protect us from crooks," she snapped at him, "not to save us from insomnia."

He raised both hands in a gesture of surrender. "All right. I'll get you the diaper bag."

She wanted to tell him she'd get it herself, but that would have been petty. She felt petty enough to do it, anyway, but Max was now screaming in her ear and demanding her full attention.

She paced the upstairs hall with him, wondering what had happened to his pacifier. It was somewhere in the back seat of the car, probably lost when he fell asleep in his seat.

She started for the stairs, not relishing the idea of searching for the pacifier with a screaming baby, when Sal reappeared with the diaper bag—and the pacifier.

"I noticed this," he said, handing it to her, "when I went back to the car to make sure I'd locked it. I rinsed it under the hot water downstairs." He walked around her and took the diaper bag into Dillon's room.

She offered Max the pacifier, and he took it eagerly. Blessed silence filled the hallway.

Sal emerged from Dillon's room, and they faced each other, several feet apart.

"Got everything you need?" he asked.

"Yes," she said, the silence suddenly deafening. She felt her entire body calm down a notch. She was even able to smile. "Thank you."

"Sure. What time do you want breakfast in the morning?"

"I'm usually up at seven. But there isn't much in the kitchen. I'll have to go shopping."

"I'll find something for breakfast. We can go shopping after you get your writing time in tomorrow. We'll need some things for Max, too, I imagine. Clothes, diapers, toys."

"Yes. Well." The corridor seemed to narrow as she walked past him to the bedroom. The warm air upstairs was growing heavy and humid. She had room to move, but it was as though she'd lost control of her body and something was pushing her toward him, and him toward her.

Suddenly she had a vivid picture of the very end of her dream. Of Sal and her in the middle of his bed, their arms around each other as they lay body to body, the knowledge that they would finally have each other intoxicating and thrilling.

Having to force herself, she moved past him and into the room. "Thanks for bringing everything up," she said abruptly. "We'll try not to keep you awake." And she closed the door.

The breath left her in a long, slow, slither of sound. Max now leaned against her, eyes heavy. She sat on the edge of her bed and rocked him, wondering how she was going to survive cohabitation with Sal. It had been less than an hour, and she was already prepared to throw in the towel.

She just needed a good night's sleep, she told herself bracingly. Max was opposed to that, of course, but if she could manage to rest between early-morning bouts of wakefulness, she would see things more clearly tomorrow.

Max was fast asleep in half an hour. She put him in the crib, then peeled down to her underwear and climbed into Dillon's and Harper's bed. She was asleep in minutes.

Max woke at two. Dori pulled on her shirt and wrapped Max in his blanket to take him downstairs with her while she filled a bottle. But they were intercepted by Sal, standing on the top stair with a plastic baby bottle shaped like a bear. He wore jogging shorts and a T-shirt.

She tried not to stare at the cotton pulled tightly across his shoulders. He seemed to be avoiding looking at her legs.

"I heard him," he said, "and remembered that everything was downstairs. I'm sorry it's all so inconvenient, but you're safer up here."

She couldn't help the smile. "If you keep acting as my personal servant, it'll be no problem."

He smiled, too. "I'm happy to fill that role—to a point."

"Oh, now," she teased, "if you're going to put qualifications on it, it won't work."

He handed her the bottle with a grin. "We'll discuss terms in the morning," he said, and ran lightly down the stairs again.

Dori put Max back to bed with his bottle, then went back to bed herself. She awoke at four, though Max didn't, and got up to stare into his crib in disbelief. He was sound asleep.

At five she woke again to silence. A glance into Max's crib showed him still fast asleep.

When she woke again, sunlight streamed through the window and made warm patterns on the bed. It was after eight o'clock.

Dori bounded out of bed and found the crib empty. She felt a moment's panic, until she became aware of the aroma of fresh-brewed coffee and...something else.

She padded halfway down the stairs in her shirt. "Sal?" she shouted.

"Yeah?" he shouted back.

"You have Max?"

"Yeah. He's eating Cheerios."

She frowned on the shadowy stairway. "I don't have Cheerios."

"I found a box in the back of a cupboard," he answered. "It's full of flour, oats. You know, the kinds of things you cook with. You probably never even looked in it."

She accepted that taunt with a "Cute, Dominguez!"

"There's a sausage omelette waiting for you, and a croissant," he cajoled.

That sounded promising. Fattening, but promising. "I'll be right there!" She ran back upstairs, found a blue-and-white checked cotton robe among Harper's things, and carried yesterday's clothes down with her to put them in the laundry later.

Max sat in a high chair, Cheerios all over his tray.

He laughed as Dori approached, kicking excitedly and moving the little circles of cereal around with the sweep of a tiny hand.

She leaned over him to kiss his cheek. "Hey, big guy," she said, helping herself to a Cheerio. "I didn't even hear you get up."

"I was up early, checking the cupboards and making a grocery list," Sal said. He folded an omelette in a small frying pan, then took the pan off the burner and angled it to cook the still-liquid part of the egg. "I heard him talking to himself and went up to investigate." He flipped the omelette onto a plate, added two pieces of toast and handed it to her. "When I saw that you were still asleep, I brought him down with me."

"Thank you," she said, putting her plate on the table, then pouring coffee into the two cups he'd set out. "But I was kidding about the personal servant remark last night." She replaced the pot and took her chair.

He retrieved his own plate from the oven and brought it to the table, then sat opposite her. Max's high chair was pulled up at a right-angle to their chairs.

"You sure?" he asked, handing her a jar of apricot jam. She took a bite of the omelette. It contained broccoli and cheese, and was delicious. "Well, maybe if you'd consider being a kitchen servant."

"Sure. But the galley's going to need a few supplies. Want to go shopping first thing, then I'll watch Max and get things organized in here while you work on your book?"

"I need something from the library." She spread jam on a piece of toast and put the jar within his reach. "Why don't I go there and meet you at the market? I'll take Max with me."

Sal shook his head. "I don't want you and Max alone."

"It's just a block…" she began to argue.

He shook his head. "Sorry. It's a principle of guarding someone. You never leave them alone."

She sighed. "You mean we're going to have to spend every waking moment together?"

"Not together," he placated, "but in the same place at the same time."

"We're going to get awfully tired of each other," she warned. She wasn't entirely sure that was true. He did look rather fascinating this morning in black cotton slacks and a black T-shirt.

"That'll help us remember our deal," he said, picking a wayward Cheerio off the table and putting it on Max's tray.

Her conscience pricked her, and she took offense. "Is that a reference to my kissing you while I was dreaming?" she asked coolly.

"No," he replied with a quick smile across the table. "It was a reference to my response when you kissed me."

That deflated her sense of indignation. He'd turned

it all around on her. She felt like a woman in a spin—
disoriented, confused.

GOOD WORK, *Dominguez,* Sal praised himself silently,
happy with the uncertain look in Dori's eyes. Considering what she'd put him through since he'd known
her, and the past two years particularly, he liked knowing she was feeling off balance.

She dropped the conversation to concentrate on her
breakfast, then washed Max's hands and face and took
him into the downstairs bedroom to get him ready for
the trip to town.

Sal cleaned up the kitchen, then waited for her in
the living room.

The house had a comfortable beachy feel that he
remembered from his brief visit three years ago. There
were hideous antiques all over—a clock set in a horse
collar, and a lamp with ruffles too ugly to describe.

But there were also lovely country crafts the Mc-
Keon women had made—a curtain of ribbon and shells
in the kitchen, a window frame decorated with moss
and dried flowers. These, along with the toys and baby
things scattered around the house, all conspired to cre-
ate a welcoming coziness.

"We're ready," Dori said, coming out of the room
in stone-colored shorts and a dark blue shirt. Max, in
her arms, wore yellow overalls and a white-and-yellow
striped shirt. She pinched Max's cheek. "Isn't this the
cutest baby you've ever seen?"

Dancer's Beach was a carefully preserved example
of small-town America, Sal thought, as Dori pulled into

a parking spot in front of Coast Groceries. Up and down the street, postwar storefronts with large plate-glass windows were interspersed with late-nineteenth century buildings with wood trim and small-paned windows.

There was an old hotel, the Buckley Arms, named after the founding family of Dancer's Beach, three brothers who ran a mill on a knoll overlooking the ocean. A ship carrying dancers from San Francisco, heading for the mining camps in the Klondike, ran aground off the coast. The brothers rescued four of the women, who gave the town its name.

A small, picturesque church with a spire stood in the middle of everything and opposite a park bordered by a library and a playground. City Hall stood just beyond it. Sal remembered with a pang that he and Dori had met several times in that park to talk about Julie. Beyond the park was an Italianate building that housed a theater and office space.

There were hanging baskets of flowers, larger than he remembered them, and park benches in the middle of every block for sitting and soaking up the charm of the small coastal town.

While in Seattle with its traffic, congestion and hurried pace, he'd dreamed of this place with its intimate little downtown and its sense of neighborly cooperation.

"First thing I have to do," Dori said, interrupting his personal analysis of Dancer's Beach, "is buy one of those strollers where the seat comes off to be a carrier."

He took Max from her as she hauled him out of the back. "I didn't know there was such a thing."

She pointed up the street. "There's a shop called Baby, Baby! that has everything. I'm sure my family won't mind my using the crib and the high chair, since they're always passing such things around, but the strollers always go home with them." Then, noticing unusual activity as merchants began to pull tables and racks out onto the sidewalk, she smiled delightedly. "Sal, there's a sidewalk sale today."

"Do we need a sidewalk?" he asked gravely.

She gave him a look of mock disgust, her eyes alight with amusement. "That joke is so old, it probably came over on the ship with the dancers!"

"And I thought I was being clever. It looks like an old Mexican marketplace."

"Come on. Let's see if Baby, Baby! has anything on sale!"

"Remember, that the eleven-thousand dollars doesn't belong to you," he said quietly as he followed with the baby. "I seem to recall your overspending considerably when I took you to Mexico City to shop for the wedding." She made her way around several other shoppers who apparently weren't moving fast enough. "Don't be silly," she said, with a smiling glance over her shoulder. "That's only because you'd driven me all that way. I felt obligated to buy."

Dori found the stroller-carrier combination she wanted right away. It had a dark blue pattern with cheery-faced suns, moons and stars, and it was twenty-five-percent off. She was beside herself with excitement. "Now I can buy him some clothes!"

In a section devoted to tiny designer garments, she bought several rompers, shirts, footed sleepers—because Max had a tendency to throw off his covers—and more socks. She also couldn't resist a little white cotton hat with a soft brim decorated with embroidered animals.

Sal put Max in the stroller, and Dori put the hat on him.

They waited for a reaction. But Max simply lay back, studied the new pattern above his head, and waited patiently for whatever would happen next.

"I thought babies always ripped their hats off," Sal observed, as Dori pushed the stroller.

"He obviously has more fashion sense than other babies. A white hat in the summer is the sign of a gentleman."

"Really. Even with bears and tigers on it?"

"Especially with bears and tigers on it."

"Life is full of mysteries."

Sal thanked the fates that had made him a patient man. Well, perhaps not patient precisely, but tolerant. While Max dozed, Dori stopped at every table and rack on Dancer Avenue.

She looked everything over, compared one item against another at a different shop, then finally made a decision, occasionally to change her mind and decide against it altogether.

Fighting boredom, Sal bought an Americano at the coffee bar on the bottom floor of the hotel.

"But I don't want coffee," Dori objected.

"I know," he replied, pointing the clerk to a piece of chocolate in the shape of a mouse with a licorice tail. "But if I have to follow you around, I have to have something to keep me awake. And I'm not leaving you alone. So put your shopping frenzy on pause for just a moment."

Accepting that mild reprimand, she laughed lightly and punched his arm. "There are purses on sale across the street, and I'm standing in line for coffee!"

"It's not coffee," he corrected, accepting the confection the clerk handed him and giving it to her. "It's espresso. A double shot."

"Yum! Thank you, Sal," she said, admiring the beautifully crafted little mouse. Then she heartlessly bit his head off.

Sal pretended horrified disapproval. "You murderess!" he accused, as she chewed with relish.

The clerk handed him his drink.

Dori shrugged. "It was that or pull off his tail, and that seemed cruel. This way, he never knew what hit him. *Now* can we shop for purses?"

"Lead the way," he said, taking a sip of his drink through the lid's narrow slit. "I'll be right behind you."

Purse shopping took an hour, though there were only thirty-one purses on the rack. He'd had time to count. And many of them were the same style, but in different colors.

She finally stood back and stared dispiritedly at the rack.

He pointed to the one she'd studied the longest. "What's wrong with that one?" It was a simple, square style with a front pocket and many separations inside.

"No pocket for my keys," she said.

"Your keys can't go into one of the twenty-two pockets inside?"

She made a face at him. "There are only five pockets inside, and no, they can't. I like a small pocket on the outside. They have to be accessible in the dark, or when my arms are full. Like when I'm carrying the baby."

"If it'll help you decide," he bargained, "I promise to always carry the baby."

She made another face. "What about when you're not here?"

"I told you, I won't leave you alone."

"I mean, when this is over," she clarified, "and you go back to Seattle."

She said it quickly, noting nothing significant in it until she heard the words lingering in the air. Then she looked for a moment as though she didn't know what to do. She seemed flustered, upset.

She took that purse in a dark blue and paid the clerk. "Darrick's always telling me I should have my keys in my hand when I step out of the car, anyway." She spoke cheerfully and pushed the stroller toward a stationery store.

Sal wandered after her, pleased at visible proof that she didn't like the idea of their eventual separation any more than he did.

After leaving the stationery store, they had started

for the car, when Sal saw something that made him stop in his tracks. It was a hammock—an Adirondack hammock on a stand so that it didn't have to be tied to trees or poles.

The McKeons had had a hammock in the backyard when he'd visited after the Julie incident. He'd noticed when he and Max had taken a stroll through the garden before breakfast it was still there, but that it must have been left out all winter; it was mildewed and rotted in places, and looked as though it would split under a child's weight.

Sal had precious memories of a hammock in his childhood. There'd been one strung between two jacaranda trees at his grandmother's in Mazatlan. He'd liked it there, but his mother's mother hadn't liked his father, so they seldom visited. When they did, he spent time in the hammock every morning watching the birds and the clouds; then every night, watching the stars appear, searching for the constellations.

Then his mother had died, and life had changed dramatically. His father had joined his uncle and some friends to form the Cat Pack, and Sal and Julie had learned to steal.

Sal caught Dori's arm and pulled her toward the sporting goods store and the camping display.

"Oh, Sal, I'm not much of a camper," she said, frowning dubiously at the camp stove and the dried food display. "I can't cook indoors, much less over an open fire. I mean, if—"

"*Querida,*" he said, putting a silencing finger to her

lips. "You do not have to go camping. And, anyway, this is for me."

"What?"

He pointed to the hammock.

"We have a hammock in the backyard," she said.

He walked around the one on display. "Have you looked at it lately?"

"Oh, yeah." She nodded. "Dillon and Harper were the last ones there before winter. They were supposed to bring it in, but Dillon and the Northwest Medical Team got called to some disaster, and they ended up leaving in a hurry."

Sal bought the hammock.

Dori smiled blandly. "It's neat, but how are we going to get it home?"

"Do you have rope in the car?"

She folded her arms. "Of course not. I don't go to many lynchings."

He rolled his eyes at her. "To tie the stand to the top of the car."

"Ah." She'd been teasing him, but he'd been so wrapped up in his memories, he'd missed it. It was unlike him not to catch a joke. "Certainly these guys must have rope."

She rummaged through a bin and emerged with a thick loop of bright yellow cord. "Will this do?"

"Beautifully. Do you have a tarp or a blanket in the trunk?"

She shook her head.

"What would you do if you were ever stranded?"

he asked, looking through a stack of tarps leaning up against the side of a table.

She blinked at him. "How would a rope and tarp help me?" she asked. "I could shinny down a cliff, then spread the tarp in case I wanted to paint something?"

She was being smart, as she often was, and there was something exasperating and somehow endearing about it. He took her chin in the *V* of his thumb and forefinger, and pinched gently. "The rope would have a hundred uses, and the tarp would keep you warm and dry at night."

"But, so would the car."

"What if the car was no longer habitable because of a crash or a fire, or you'd simply left it to explore and gotten lost?"

She patted her purse. "I always have my purse with me. I'd call for help on my cell phone."

"One of your brothers, no doubt."

"Probably."

"I thought you resented their interference in your life?"

"Well...saving me from death isn't really interference, is it? It's rescue. Unless you think I could fashion a rope and a tarp into a car or a magic tarp or something, and drive or fly back to civilization."

He dropped his hand from her and sighed. Explaining danger to a woman accustomed to being protected was hopeless.

"If I hadn't forced you into a decision about the

purse," he reminded pointedly, "you wouldn't have had it to put the cell phone in to call your brothers."

"That's reaching, Sal," she said with a giggle.

He didn't know why he wanted to kiss her.

He bought the tarp.

"So, what did you want it for?" she asked. "Are you going to leave me stranded somewhere?"

"No," he said, scolding her with a look. "I wanted to protect the roof of your car from the hammock stand."

She patted his shoulder. "Well, that's very considerate. Once you get it attached to the roof, I'll take you to lunch."

It was simply done, Max offering encouragement from the stroller.

Dori stood back to admire the tarp-wrapped stand securely fastened through the open windows. "Ah..." she said. "How do we get back in the car? The doors are tied closed."

"I put you in through the window," he explained, "then hand you the baby."

Her eyes went up and down his long body. He felt as though she'd touched him from head to toe.

"Can *you* get in through the window?"

"You forget what I used to do for a living," he said with a grin. "I can get through any window."

She studied him for a moment, then arched an eyebrow. "Maybe I'll make one of my characters a jewel thief," she speculated. "Maybe even the hero." Her eyes lost focus as she considered the idea. Then they fixed on him again, bright with excitement.

"I wonder if a reader today would consider a thief-hero sympathetic?" she asked, unconsciously hooking her arm in his. They'd stowed the stroller frame, and he carried Max in the carrier. "I mean, would they love him, anyway, even if he steals?"

"I suppose it depends on why he steals."

"True. If I made his motivation something noble. Like yours was."

He was happy to know she thought that.

"But he'd have to reform in the end."

"Of course."

"But..." She still sounded troubled. "Would a reader love him?"

"You did," he reminded her.

CHAPTER FIVE

DORI WAS CHATTY and cheerful through lunch, feeding Max tiny bites of cottage cheese with one hand while picking at her fruit salad with the other.

She kept up a stream of conversation about their purchases, thoughts about her book, questions about Sal's business. Inside she was wondering why she felt stricken at the thought of his return to Seattle.

She was still angry with Sal, still resentful that he'd left her at the altar after their wedding; hurt, now that she thought about it, that he hadn't made more of an effort in the past two years even to talk to her about what had happened. But this strange situation with the baby and the money was forcing her to be civil and to cooperate with him until they solved the mystery.

That was all that was confusing her, she thought with some relief. When a woman was angry, she should be able to behave angrily, not be forced to pretend everything was fine. That was unnatural and bound to blur what she really felt—even in her own mind.

Feeling better now that she'd reasoned that out, Dori pushed the cart in Coast Groceries, while they talked over meal possibilities and Sal tossed food into the cart.

Car loaded with food, they headed home, where Sal

set up the collapsible playpen, then sent her upstairs to write.

Dori made every effort to clear her mind of all her concerns and concentrate on the book. This was what was going to set the direction of the rest of her life, she told herself as she spread out her notes on the scholarly work she'd intended to write and restructured them to form a novel.

She had to accept that the process would set her back three weeks, but now that she had a child to support, she had to give thought to the book's marketability rather than simply her own sense of accomplishment in producing it.

She had to call Athena Hartford, she told herself, making a note on a Post-it that she attached to the shade of her lamp.

It was almost six o'clock when Sal called her to dinner. The sun remained high and bright, and they ate outside at a picnic table under an old ash tree. Max, already fed, played with a rattle in the playpen.

Sal had made taco salads, a favorite of hers, with the added touch of a large Anaheim pepper stuffed with cheese, then rolled in eggs and cracker crumbs and fried.

"It's wonderful," she said simply. "You must have girlfriends all over the place who adore you for your cooking."

"Of course I don't," he said, holding up his left hand with the ring she'd put there. "I'm a married man. How'd your afternoon go?"

"Good," she said, ignoring that remark. "I have

enough of the plot in mind to be able to convert some of what I've already done to background and also use it to give substance to my heroine's work. I've just gotten started, of course, but I've written a couple of pages and I'm excited about it.''

"I'm sure that'll help carry you through." He pointed across the lawn to where the hammock was set up in a pool of sunlight. "Max and I mowed the lawn and assembled the hammock before we made dinner.''

"Have you tested it yet?"

He shook his head. "I thought I'd do that after dinner. You are going to reward me by doing the dishes?''

"Of course."

"Good. Then I don't have to withhold the flan I made for dessert.''

She paused, a forkful of flavorful beef, cheese and lettuce halfway to her mouth. "You didn't!''

"I did. Couldn't find Mexican vanilla, but it should be palatable all the same.''

"You are a treasure.''

"I know,'' he said modestly.

"In the kitchen, anyway.''

He gave her a quick, suggestive look as he took a sip of wine. "I'm a treasure in a lot of places,'' he said, "but you didn't hang around to find out.''

She was determined to maintain peace. "Let's not talk about that,'' she said, putting the bite in her mouth.

"We have to sometime,'' he persisted.

She shook her head as she chewed and swallowed. "No, we don't. It doesn't matter now. If we intended to stay together, maybe we'd have to straighten it out. But since we don't, it doesn't make any difference."

He shook his head. "That's your usual illogical assessment of things," he said, his words sharp but his tone mild. "It's the *reason* you left. Don't you think your attitude might change if you really understood what happened?"

"No," she replied candidly. "I know all I need to know. And let's not pollute this wonderful dinner with discussions of the past. It's over."

"Maybe for you," he said quietly.

"Take the ring off," she advised. "Let it be over for you, too."

He took another sip of wine, a long one. "I'm not running away. I made promises, took vows."

"That you ignored two minutes after the ceremony was finished!" She slammed a fist on the table. Crockery shook, and Max looked up in alarm.

"But you don't want to know why?" Sal asked.

"No." She swung her legs out from under the table and began to gather up dishes. "I remember how much it hurt. I don't want to hear you validate that with some charming explanation that still won't justify the past two years."

She marched into the kitchen.

When she went back outside with a tray to carry in the leftover food and the dishes, Sal and Max were lying in the hammock. The baby was on Sal's chest, Sal's brimmed hat protecting Max from the sun. Max was babbling, and Sal replied as though he understood what the baby was saying.

'I am never speaking to him again,' Dori told herself as she covered the salad bowl with cling wrap and put it in the refrigerator. She spotted six clear glass cups of flan and took one. With the can of whipped cream from the shelf in the door, she created a tall column of topping and stood at the counter to enjoy the dessert. She was aware of the wonderful taste and texture, but her mood made her unable to enjoy it.

She cleaned up the kitchen, started the dishwasher, and went back outside to bring in the tablecloth. Max was banging on Sal's face and squealing with delight. *Men,* Dori thought in disgust, and went to put some things in the washer. Then she headed for Sal's room, tiptoeing as though he might hear her from outside, and took a change of clothes and underwear for herself and Max for tomorrow.

Maybe one of those bars that fit over the top of the door with a clothes hanger attached would simplify her life. Then she could have a few changes of clothes in her room upstairs.

Looking for underwear, she opened the drawer in which she usually kept it, only to find it filled with briefs and T-shirts. She stared at them in surprise.

"I've heard of panty raids," a lazy male voice said from behind her, "but never a briefs raid."

She turned to find him standing just inside the room, Max on his hip, a pudgy arm hooked around Sal's. They were quite a picture, handsome man and beautiful child, dark features and Latino good looks making them appear related.

Mine, she thought in a moment of painful longing. *That's what I could have had if he hadn't left me.*

She knew that thought to be counterproductive, and pushed it away. "I was looking for my own underwear," she said. "Did you move it?"

"Next drawer down," he said, coming to pull it open and show her. "This is the only drawer I've taken."

"It's all right." She quickly snatched two pairs of panties, a bra and a couple of pairs of socks. She scooped up the clothes she'd dropped on the bed. "I'll take these upstairs," she said politely, determined to put their personal issues aside, "then I'll watch Max while you relax."

"I have a few phone calls to make, but that's about all."

"I'll be right down."

When Dori returned, Sal took the cordless phone into the kitchen while she spread a blanket on the floor for Max, then found a sitcom on television.

One eye on the TV and the other on the baby, Dori sat on the edge of the blanket and leaned against the bottom of the sofa. Max turned and rolled and "swam" his way across the blanket. Dori turned him around, and he eventually worked his way back. He inspected one toy after another, dropped them and picked them up, and occasionally threw them at Dori.

Sal returned, phone in hand. He placed it on the coffee table a few feet away from her. "Want some popcorn?" he asked. "Or coffee and flan?"

She met his eyes, refusing to look guilty. "I've already had my flan, thank you. I'm sorry I didn't wait for you, but I wasn't speaking to you at the time. So I ate it all by myself.''

He laughed. "No need to explain. Also no need to feel limited to one. You want another?''

It was an agonizing decision. While she was making it, the phone rang.

As though in slow motion, she saw Sal reach for the cordless, and realized what she would be put through if that was her mother on the line.

She leapt across the edge of blanket and grabbed all she could reach of Sal—his pants leg. "No!" she shrieked, reaching for the phone with her free hand. "No, don't answer it!''

He looked down in amused disbelief at her hand clutching the fabric of his pants just above the knee. "Why not?''

"It could be my mother!''

He looked down at the readout and read the number aloud.

"That's her!" Dori whispered harshly. "Give it to me!''

He held it out of reach. "Why?''

She tugged on the material she held, as the phone continued to ring. "Because if she hears your voice, *I'll* never hear the end of it! She'll be ordering wedding invitations and hiring a hall!''

"But she's too late for that.''

"She doesn't know that. Sal, give me the phone!''

"Deception," he said didactically, "is its own trap.''

"Don't preach to me!" she snarled. "Just give me the phone!"

He finally handed it to her.

"And don't say a word while I'm on the line!" she ordered in a loud whisper, then pushed the talk button. "Hi, Mom," she said pleasantly, still glowering at Sal. "How's Dad doing?"

With an indulgent shake of his head, Sal went into the kitchen.

"Oh, you know your father," her mother said with acceptance. "He can't dance the jig, so he's discouraged. The doctor told him it'll take time, that he has to do his exercises—but all he does is complain and watch ESPN. I thought maybe you could talk to him."

Peg McKeon was in her early sixties, a short, round woman with a charming but bossy disposition, and a particularly aggressive approach to Dori's love life.

Charlie McKeon, on the other hand, was laid-back and sweet, and Dori missed his sudden appearances on her doorstep with care packages from her mother. He was tall and barrel-chested, and had had bad knees since Dori entered college. When they finally prevented him from getting on the floor with his grandchildren, he decided to do something about it.

"Put him on," Dori said to her mother.

"Hey, sweetheart," his gruff, strong voice said.

"Don't 'sweetheart' me," Dori scolded firmly. "I want to know why you aren't doing your exercises."

"Because they hurt," he replied. "I do them, just not as many as I'm supposed to."

"And that's probably why you're not recovering as quickly as you want to."

"I'm slow recovering," he said with significant emphasis, "because I'm being nursed by Nagging Nellie! 'Do this. Don't eat that. Walk around. Don't sit there. Are you watching that again?'"

"She's just trying to take care of you, Daddy," Dori placated, secretly grateful she wasn't the one confined with her mother. "She wants you to get better. And if you don't promise me you'll do *all* your exercises, I'll call Dillon."

"He's still in Europe," her father said with a sigh. "Or I'm sure your mother would have him here. Why she had to call you today, I'll never know."

Dori laughed. "You know Mom. She's not happy unless she has the entire family turned against the evildoer, whichever one of us that is at the time. That's what she thinks family is for—not to support you, but to gang up against you."

He laughed. "You've got that right."

"But I mean it," Dori said, firming her voice. "You do what you're told, or I'll come over there myself and cook for you."

"Now, there's no call to get mean," he admonished. "Peg, she's threatening to come and cook for us."

"Well, promise her you'll be good," Dori heard her mother say in the background. "There's no reason I should suffer, too."

"Bye, baby," her father said.

"Bye, Daddy," she replied. "I don't want to hear any more bad reports on you."

There was a rustling on the other end of the line as the phone changed hands. "Dori," her mother said. "It would be lovely to have you visit. And you don't have to cook. Really."

"I will, Mom," she promised. "Maybe in a week or two. I'm doing really well on the book, and I hate to lose momentum."

"That's wonderful," Peg praised. "Are you remembering to eat?"

Remembering to eat. She'd eaten more today than she usually ate in a week. "I am," she replied.

"Are you sleeping well?"

That was a hilarious question, considering Max's presence in her life. But her mother didn't know about him, and Dori had to keep it that way if she didn't want instant and major interference.

"I'm doing fine," she insisted. "Coming here was a great—" Before Dori could finish the thought, Max, trapped against the sofa and unable to move, shouted his need for assistance.

"What was that?" Peg asked.

Dori picked him up, turned him around and set him down again.

"What was what?"

"That squeal. Like a baby."

There was no use denying what her mother had heard. "I'm baby-sitting for the neighbors," she said.

"The Fishers?" her mother asked. "They're our age."

Dori knew the Fishers. They were on a cruise at the moment, but her mother didn't necessarily know that.

And Dori knew they had a daughter who had a young baby.

"Their daughter's visiting with her baby," she said. "They were going to a movie, and I was just going to hang around and watch television, so..."

"As good as you are with babies," Peg interrupted, "you should have your own, you know."

"Mom, don't start," Dori pleaded.

"I'm not starting, but neither are you. You should think about that. You're getting up there, you know."

"Twenty-six isn't 'up there.'"

"It isn't eighteen."

"Mom."

"Well."

Dori recognized that tone of voice. Her mother was giving up, but not without audible signs that she was the misunderstood and mistreated victim of the conversation.

"When you feel inclined to visit, we'll be here."

"I'll call first."

"We'll be waiting."

Dori turned off the phone, exhausted.

"Why didn't you tell her about the baby?" Sal asked, handing her a bowl of popcorn. "Yes, I was eavesdropping."

"When I tell her," Dori replied, "she'll be here like a shot, Dad on crutches or not, and I don't want that to happen while *you're* here. She'll think it means there's something going on between us again."

"And you're afraid she'll find out we're married."

He put a can of cola down beside her popcorn. "Why didn't you ever tell your family?"

"You know why," she said, reaching for the baby as he hoisted himself toward her leg. She stood him on his feet on her thighs and smiled into his bright-eyed little face. "It'll be just one more thing that proves to them how incapable I am of managing my life, or attracting a man, or carrying through with anything but education."

He looked confused as he went to the kitchen for his popcorn and coke. When he returned, he sat beside her. He took the clicker off the coffee table and muted the sound on the television.

"I don't understand," he said. "Isn't marriage proof that you *were* able to attract a man?"

"When he left me immediately after the ceremony? I don't think so."

"Ah." He took a sip of his drink and put the glass on a coaster on the coffee table. "I hadn't thought that through. You did turn our marriage into something you didn't have to finish."

"You," she said pointedly, "turned it into something I *couldn't* finish. And why didn't you tell them?"

"To help you out. I could tell you hadn't."

"Since you'd ruined my life, that was very considerate of you."

He groaned. "Let's not go through that again. The point is, someday she will have to know about the wedding, and you won't be able to hide the baby forever."

"I don't intend to. Just for the time being. Put the

sound back on, please—this story was just getting interesting.''

A COUPLE ON TELEVISION were kissing. Sal would have preferred to watch baseball or the news or anything other than a man and a woman locked in a passionate embrace. Living in close proximity with Dori was taking its toll on him.

He thought about making love to her all the time. When he'd gone to Desi's rescue, when he'd put himself between her and Paco and taken a bullet in the shoulder, and the police had hauled him away and he'd been driven to the hospital in an ambulance that hit every pothole, he'd been sustained by the knowledge that when he got home, he would make love to Dori at last.

And instead, he'd found her gone. The bullet wound had been a nuisance compared to the ache in his heart.

But he sat without complaint, telling himself that if he just stayed with it and did his best to see this through, he'd find his moment. She'd loved him once; he could make her love him again. But she wasn't a woman one could push or force. She had to come to him in her own time.

All he had to do was remain sane that long.

The love scene over, she lifted Max up and down. He giggled happily, catching a fistful of her bangs and pulling.

"Ah! Sal!" she pleaded.

Sal put his popcorn aside and turned to free her hair

from the baby's fingers. It was as silky to the touch as he remembered, but he wasn't wild about the new style.

"Thank you," she said, turning Max around so that he faced the television while she bounced him. He seemed pleased with the new distraction.

"Why did you cut your hair?" Sal asked.

"It was part of the new me. It helped me change direction." She put a hand to it with a side-glance of self-deprecation. "You should have seen it at first. It was a buzzcut. About half an inch all around."

"Aerodynamic, at least," he said.

She laughed. "Yes. It cut my morning getting-ready ritual in half."

"And why did you need a new direction?"

"After dreaming about..." she began, then apparently changed her mind. "I decided it was time I went to work on the book instead of just talking about it. And that seemed to require that I streamline everything. Even my hair."

"Did you like teaching?"

"Sometimes. The kids were great, but there's a lot of politics going on in a school, a lot of things taking place behind the scenes that I'm not crazy about. But I may have to learn to live with it, with a child to support." She turned to him, her eyes lively with interest. "What about you? Are you enjoying the security business?"

"Yes, mostly. Every once in a while there's a client I'd be happy to abandon to whoever's after him, but I try to remember that I don't have to like everyone."

"Your secretary's very pretty."

She made that observation while pretending to peer around the bouncing baby at the television, as though his reply didn't matter. Did he detect jealousy?

"Yes, she is," he replied simply.

"She seems to like babies."

"She has three of her own."

She turned to him. "Really."

He nodded. "All girls."

"So she's married."

"Widowed."

"Oh."

She said it casually, but he heard the subtle sound of disappointment. "He was a cop. Died in a car wreck while in pursuit of a robbery suspect, just before she came to work for us."

"Poor thing."

"She seems to be coping well. She looks like a fashion model without a care in the world, but she's really all soul and substance."

Max started to fuss, and she turned him around and put him on her shoulder. "I think he's winding down. Time for his bottle."

Sal put a hand to her shoulder when she tried to get to her knees to stand.

"I'll get it for you. Do you want to sit with him in the rocking chair in my bedroom?"

"You don't mind?"

"Of course not." He took Max from her and helped her up. He handed the baby back, then went to the refrigerator for a bottle, while she went into his room.

He ran the bottle under hot water and tried not to

think about her sitting just a few feet away from his bed.

He took the bottle in to her and saw that Max already had his head on her shoulder, eyes glazed with weariness. But the baby straightened at the sight of the bottle. When she repositioned him he lay back eagerly and put both hands up to help hold it.

"One more thing, please?" she asked.

"Yes?"

"His blanket. I think it's still in the playpen in the kitchen."

Sal retrieved it and tucked it between the baby and Dori's arm. His fingertips brushed the tip of her breast, startling both of them. For an instant, he didn't move, and she stopped the rocking that would have taken them out of contact.

They looked into each other's eyes, remembering, imagining.

Then he remembered his decision to be subtle and cool, and asked, as though nothing had happened, "Anything else?"

"Nothing, thanks," she replied in the same even tone.

He left the room and went to turn the television to a news channel.

She emerged about ten minutes later and carried a sleeping Max upstairs. She was back down in a few minutes and went to open the front door.

"Paper's here," she said, bending down to retrieve a thin newspaper rolled up tightly and secured with a rubber band. "It's just a weekly, but it's full of local news and gossip. The new television schedule for the week is in it tonight."

She closed and locked the door, slipped off the rubber band and unrolled the paper as she walked toward the sofa. She stopped halfway into the room and gasped. "Sal!" she exclaimed.

"What?"

She peered at him around the side of the newspaper. "I think I've just solved the mystery of Max's money." She walked toward him and sat cross-legged on the floor beside him. "You won't believe this," she said, reading an article on the front page.

He muted the television. "Believe what?"

"Faith Community Church had an auction to raise money for their new roof."

"Yes?"

"The Sunday School Mothers got donations from all the merchants in town."

"Yes?"

"Burgers by the Sea catered a prime rib dinner at cost."

"Generous."

"The choir entertained during dinner with a medley of pop tunes from—"

"Dori! The point?"

She sat down beside him and put the paper on his lap. "'Pastor Price took the evening's earnings home with him to the parsonage,'" she read aloud, "'and, lacking a safe in which to protect the cash overnight, locked it in the drawer of the desk in his office. When he went into his office the following morning after breakfast, he found that the lock had been broken and the drawer stood open—empty.'''

She pointed to the last paragraph of the story.

"'The auction's take,'" she read, "'was $11,572.'''

CHAPTER SIX

"WE KNOW who to return the money to!" Dori said excitedly to Sal. "I'll do it first thing in the morning."

He shook his head. "I don't think so."

She huffed with impatience. "Why not?"

"Just a hunch," he said. "I don't think that Max's mother is the one who stole the money in the first place."

Dori nodded. "I know, I know. You think it's her boyfriend, or pimp, or whatever. But what difference does that make to returning the money?"

"If you return the money, there'll be press coverage," he said. "Or, even if there wasn't, this is a small town. Someone will remember you walking into the parsonage."

"So?"

"I'll bet they'll conclude that if you had the money, you also have the baby. Right now, they don't know who has either. When you and I are out with Max together, we're just another family and nobody notices, but once everyone knows you had the money…"

He was right. But she didn't like it.

"So the poor church has to go without a roof?"

Sal shook his head. "I'll have Diego make an anonymous donation right into the church account."

She brightened. "You'd do that?"

"First thing in the morning."

She studied him for a moment, remembering the kind but tough and unyielding man he'd been during the Julie incident.

"You were always a sensitive man," she said, noticing for the first time a subtle change around his eyes and in the line of his mouth. "But I don't remember this sweetness in you before. And I don't understand how you've managed to acquire it while operating a security company."

He put a hand to his eyes as though trying to hide. "Dori, I don't think it's acceptable to tell a bodyguard you consider him 'sweet.' I'm sure there's a law against it somewhere. In fact, the law enforcement world calls us 'hard men.'"

She was amused by his embarrassment. "Well, you don't define yourself by your work, do you? You're also a man who helped a criminal reform so that he could be a grandfather to his daughter's babies.... You were so efficient and innovative in supervising the addition to and renovation of a hospital that your plans are now a model for similar constructions funded by charity.... Max thinks you're wonderful...."

It occurred to her that she might have gone a little over the top there. She understood why he didn't want her to return the money, but the idea that he would anonymously restore the cash himself, so the church wouldn't suffer while he kept her safe made her completely forget the animosity between them.

He smiled. "One wonders then, why *you* have no use for me."

She began to wonder herself, but she wasn't willing to admit it. So she fell back on the old argument.

"The last time I had use for you, you weren't there."

"And there's no forgiving that?" he asked quietly. "Ever?"

Saying no would make her sound selfish and heartless and open a whole area of discussion she couldn't even think about at this hour. And so would saying yes.

"I have to go," she said instead, avoiding his eyes, knowing she was being cowardly as she backed toward the kitchen and the stairs. "Next time we go to town, I have to get a baby monitor so that I can hear him and know what's going on."

His eyes told her he knew precisely what she was doing. "Hmm," he said. "I wonder if they'd have a Dori monitor to help me know what's going on with you?"

She turned and headed for the stairs. "Good night," she called.

"Yeah," he replied.

THEY HAD CEREAL, fruit and yogurt for breakfast, and steered clear of all contentious topics of discussion.

"You're sure there isn't something *you* want to do this morning?" Dori asked Sal, as she fed Max baby cereal and bananas. Fortunately, Max was hungry and used only a few spoonfuls to decorate the room.

Sal shook his head. "I'm going to call Diego, but I can do that while Max and I are getting some sun."

"I feel guilty," she confessed.

"Good," he replied, clearing the table. "I'll have a chip to use in my favor one day. Are you wide awake enough to work? I heard you get up with him a couple of times."

"I think so. He went right back to sleep twice, so I managed almost five hours."

He handed her a thermos. "Made you some tea. And if you tell me that's sweet, I'll get very upset."

She laughed. "Can I say it's thoughtful?"

"Thoughtful's acceptable. And if you'd like to reward me for it in any way..." He let the suggestion trail off, his expression blandly innocent.

But she knew what he had in mind. And the very thought of kissing him made the blood rush to her cheeks. It was a stupid schoolgirl reaction that she couldn't stop because a kiss suggested intimacy, and two years ago they'd both eagerly anticipated an intimacy that had never happened. An intimacy that was now probably on his mind as much as it was on hers.

She saw him note her blush as she stood and pushed her chair in. "I could make you a character in my book," she said, pretending to be unaware of her own reaction and his surprise at it. She held up her cup. "I'll take this with me for the tea."

"Good idea," he said, apparently willing to let the moment pass. Proving that he could be thoughtful *and* sweet.

Feeling as though the world was a very confusing

place, Dori wiped off the baby's face and kissed his cheek. Then she hurried upstairs to spend the morning with the fictional people she was beginning to understand more than real people.

She went downstairs for a snack and to stretch her legs at a quarter to eleven, bringing the already empty thermos with her. In the quiet kitchen she filled the kettle and put it on to boil. Then she looked out the window to see Sal, the baby on his hip and the cell phone to his ear, pacing the backyard.

She felt herself smile. She was amazed and frankly touched by how easily he'd taken to the baby. She would miss him when it was time for them to go their separate ways.

She could forgive him for having left her on their wedding day to run to Desi's aid, she realized now, but she could never love him again with the wholehearted devotion she'd felt at that time.

The kettle having boiled, she filled the thermos, dropped in a tea bag and went back upstairs to work.

At a quarter to one, she copied her work onto a disk, expecting Sal's call to lunch. When it didn't come, she worked a little longer.

At one-fifteen, she turned off the computer and chased down a detail she needed in her source materials.

When he still hadn't called at one-thirty, she went downstairs to investigate.

She found sandwiches and fruit salads on covered plates in the refrigerator. Peering out the screen door, she saw the picnic table set and the playpen covered with a bedsheet, Max fast asleep inside. Sal was asleep in the hammock.

Dori went out into the lazy afternoon, the sun warm, insects droning, and felt herself drawn to the hammock.

It was safe, she told herself. He was asleep.

A little breeze ruffled his thick black hair, and his dark, straight eyelashes gleamed in the sunlight. His mouth and the line of his jaw were relaxed—something she never saw during the day—and his fingers were laced together over his flat stomach. He'd kicked off his tennis shoes, and his white stockinged feet were crossed at the ankles.

She couldn't count the number of times she'd dreamed of him lying beside her. Or the number of times she'd awakened in the night so sure that she had only to reach out to touch him. But the sheet beside her had been cold and empty.

And now here he was, warm and vital, even in his sleep. Longing escaped her in a gasp that hurt as it left her throat.

His eyes opened lazily, slitted against the sun. He saw her, caught her wrist and pulled her down beside him.

"No," she began to protest. "I have to..."

"Shh," he whispered, putting his fingertips to her lips as he fitted her against him.

The hammock swayed with the action. She knew she should fight this, but she'd wanted it for so long.

She flung an arm across his waist, searching for steadiness in the swaying hammock. He covered it with his own, his palm closing around her elbow.

She opened her mouth to speak, but he shushed her again. "Rest," he said softly. "The sun is very restoring. It feels like Mexico this afternoon."

Mexico. She could remember his rancho and the bed she'd dreamed of sharing. They'd have lain just like this, bodies touching...

She resisted her body's willingness to relax. This was trouble. She shouldn't...

He stroked gently up and down her upper arm. "Easy, *querida,*" he said, his lips in her hair. "Be easy."

And suddenly, fighting it was just too hard, too contrary to everything she felt, everything she wanted. She let her body relax into his, curves and hollows finding their place against his hard planes.

She hiked a leg up over his, felt the sun massage her body as though it were a soothing hand, and fell asleep.

"GOOD ONE, *muchacho,*" Sal told himself, as her knee brushed up his thigh and settled right where she would probably have liked to put it two years ago. The pressure was gentle and wouldn't have been painful if he hadn't wanted her so much, hadn't imagined them lying just like this—only without clothes to hamper their explorations.

In his imagination, she was awake and eager for him. But right now he'd settle for this pale imitation of his dreams.

And if he were honest with himself, it wasn't so pale at all. Loss and time had taught him that the passion he'd thought so essential to his existence two years ago was no longer as important as a softly whispered *I don't remember this sweetness in you.*

She'd found something to like in the man he was inside. And for now, that, and an armful of her even though she was fully clothed and fast asleep, would keep him going.

SAL AWOKE to a sense of being smothered. Remembering instantly that Dori had been lying in his arms when he fell asleep, he tried to assess whether she remained.

If she did, he didn't want to make a sudden move and frighten her. If she didn't, it was entirely possible that she was taking advantage of his being asleep to finally do him in, as she'd threatened when he'd left her at San Ignacio's.

He opened his eyes slowly, almost afraid of what he'd see. A pillow pressed to his face? A blanket?

It was fur. Orange fur. In July? Dori hadn't been wearing fur.

Without warning, the fur shifted. Sal drew a long, welcome breath and looked into a pair of round gold eyes—eyes with elliptical pupils. Cat's eyes.

The nature of the owner of the fur was confirmed an instant later when a scratchy tongue slurped his nose.

He put a hand up to assess the size and shape of the cat.

As though reading Sal's intention, the cat stood on his chest, straddling Dori's arm, and stretched a striped, orange body until he was up on the tips of four white feet, his white-tipped tail curling and uncurling. White-tipped ears pointed straight up, and preposterously long whiskers seemed to curl in, then roll out like party favors.

The cat settled down again, purring, looking very much as though he intended to spend the afternoon.

"Well, hello, Cat," Sal said, scratching him between the ears. The cat closed his eyes and purred more loudly.

Sal had had a cat as a child, but it had been left with a neighbor when he'd followed his father and uncle to embark upon a life of crime.

Since then, he'd been in Texas part of the time, in Mexico part of the time, and now he lived in a condo that didn't allow pets.

Dori raised her head and opened her eyes, looking disoriented and still sleepy.

She looked at the cat, then at Sal. "Who's this?" she asked.

He was pleased that her interest in the cat had forestalled any embarrassment she might have felt at waking up in his arms. "Ah...I'm not sure," he replied. "He hasn't told me."

The cat licked the underside of Dori's chin.

She smiled and stroked the cat's head. He leaned toward her and pressed his body into hers.

She giggled and looked at Sal to share the moment. She was propped on an elbow that was digging into his chest, but he wasn't about to complain.

"Well, he's a cutie." She scratched his neck. "He doesn't have a collar."

"A lot of cats don't wear one."

"True."

"He might live anywhere around here."

"But he's chosen to spend the afternoon with us. I'll get him some milk." She pushed herself up, apparently forgetting that they lay in a hammock, shifted her weight as though to stand and, before he could shout a warning, dumped the three of them onto the grass.

The cat screamed and shot away as though from a cannon, and Sal and Dori landed in a tidy pile, Sal uppermost, braced on his forearms.

"Well, this is only fair," he said, stroking her short spiky hair back from her pink and flustered-looking face. "You slept on me for about an hour."

"You...invited me," she said, sounding breathless.

"I did." It was going to take superhuman effort to let her up, and he was beginning to believe he wouldn't be able to, when there was a shriek from the playpen.

Sal rolled off Dori, and she was up like a shot, her concern for Max turning to laughter. His cry had been excitement, not alarm or distress. The orange cat looked at him through the nylon mesh of the playpen.

Dori pulled the sheet off the top of the playpen and lifted Max into her arms. Sal scooped the cat up with a hand under his belly and brought him toward the baby. Dori took Max's hand and stroked the cat's fur.

"This is a cat, Maxie," she said. "And if you treat him nicely, he'll be your friend."

Max shrieked again, and the cat, unsure of the baby's intentions, leaped down and watched him from behind Sal's legs.

"Would you get him a saucer of milk?" Dori asked

Sal. "I'll put Max back in the playpen. He might enjoy just watching the cat long enough for us to eat our sandwiches."

Max was fascinated with the cat. And, apparently, the cat was fascinated with Dori and Sal, or at least with their ability to provide milk and chicken, because he was still there when night fell. He made himself comfortable in the basil, oregano and thyme Julie had planted in the window box outside the kitchen window.

"Should I let him in?" Dori asked Sal, peering back at the cat, who looked in at her. It was an I'm-starving-and-lonely-and-have-no-one-but-you look.

Max leaned out of Sal's arms and stretched both little hands toward the cat.

"It's your house," Sal reminded her.

She made a face at him. "That's the point. It's not. It belongs to my brothers, and there's no one here a lot of the time. And I live in an apartment in Edenfield. What'll happen when I have to go home?"

He shrugged. "Maybe we'll just have to stay married so you'll have somewhere to put the cat."

He said it easily, thinking it was time he started preparing her for the fact that ultimately, that was what was going to happen.

He expected hot and instant denial, but she was apparently more worried about the cat at the moment than the future of their relationship.

"That would be no help at all," she said. "You live in a condo where you can't have animals."

Okay. He'd push this a little farther. "When we decide to stay together," he said matter-of-factly, "we'll buy a house here."

"Really." She was beginning to catch on. She turned from the window and leaned back against the counter, folding her arms. "Where?"

"There's a great old house just up the hill behind the Bijou Theater building," he said. He'd noticed it one afternoon three years ago when he'd been exasperated with Dori and had gone for a walk. It was straight up and down, and three stories tall, set up on a bank and back from the street. It had looked freshly painted then, pale blue with dark blue trim and oyster-colored columns supporting a front porch. Children had been playing on the porch, and their laughter had caught his attention.

He described it briefly and told her how he'd found it. "I noticed yesterday when we went to town that it's for sale."

Her eyes lost focus, and he wondered if she was imagining the house filled with their children. That was probably wishful thinking on his part, but he'd been an optimist all his life.

She finally refocused on him, her expression filled with reprimand. "When you came back here with me, we made a deal."

He nodded. "Two years ago we made another deal." He raised a hand to stop her before she could reply. "Yes, I know. And I broke it." He sighed. "But that was because of another deal, and...I can't ignore that one any more than I can ignore the one you and I made."

She opened her mouth, a bitter reply on the tip of her tongue, if he could judge by what he saw in her eyes. But she sighed and bit it back.

"We were talking about the cat," she said, deflecting a quarrel.

He couldn't believe she'd done that with all the weight of it on her side.

"I'll let it in," he said, going to the door to do just that. The cat darted in. "When the time comes to leave, we'll worry about what to do."

Smiling, she scooped the cat up into her arms and stroked him. His purr was loud and rumbling, his gratitude apparent.

"What'll we call him?" she asked. "What's orange besides marmalade. Everyone names orange cats Marmalade."

Max reached toward the cat, arms swinging excitedly. Sal wisely kept his distance.

"Uh...apricots, cheese, poppies, goldfish..."

She looked at him in exasperation. "You can't name a cat Goldfish."

"I'm trying to help," he said. "I don't hear you coming up with anything."

"Sunset?"

"Those are also pink and purple."

"Pumpkin?"

He thought about that. "That's a possibility."

"Peaches?"

He frowned his disapproval. "Please. He's a guy."

She rolled her eyes. "I know!" she said after a moment. "What about Cheddar?"

He liked that. "Cheesy," he replied, "and a little sharp, but I like it."

She shook her head at him. "I don't remember you being corny, either," she said.

"Are you beginning to wonder," he asked, "if you really knew me at all?"

She looked stricken for a moment.

Max had leaned so far out of Sal's arms trying to reach the cat that Sal had to reclaim him and settle him back on his hip amid loud protests.

"Maybe you've just changed," she observed quietly.

"Maybe," he replied. "Isn't that what time and new experiences are supposed to do to you? Make you different than you were before?"

She stared at him as though trying to decide. "I don't feel different."

He nodded grimly. "Well, maybe that's more our problem than the fact that I do." He indicated the squirming, fussy baby in his arms. "I'll get a bottle and see if I can relax him for bed. You find the cat a cozy spot."

DORI PREPARED A BOX for Cheddar, which she lined with a soft old towel from the linen closet. She placed it in a warm corner of the pantry near the water heater.

Then she picked up the cat and put him in the box. He sniffed it carefully and jumped out.

She put him back in, hoping to relay the message that it was where he belonged at night.

He did a turn in it, then jumped out again.

She hoped that when the lights were out, he'd remember the box.

Max fussed until after ten. They took turns walking him, bouncing him, playing with him on a blanket on the floor. He would be distracted for a few minutes, then whine and cry again.

"A tooth, probably," Sal guessed as he lay stretched out on the sofa, while Dori paced. "I was vacationing with Diego and Manuela when Rosa was teething. I suppose it won't make you feel any better to warn you that there'll be no peace for months?"

"Thank you," she said with an amused glance at him. She turned and paced in the other direction. "No, it doesn't. I was hoping maybe he just got overly excited about the cat. I remember Mom telling Skye that babies sometimes get themselves so excited and overtired, they don't know how to calm down." Skye was Darrick's wife.

"And whiskey is not the answer?"

"No, it isn't. It's being calm and calming them."

"I'm calm," Sal said, "but he's still fussing."

Dori laughed. "I have about two more minutes of calm left, then I'm going to start screaming myself."

Sal swung his feet to the floor. "Then, it must be my turn to pace."

"Oh…oh…" she said quietly, stopping in her tracks and looking over the baby's head at Sal. "Look," she whispered.

Max's head lolled against her shoulder, then finally fell back into the crook of her arm as he went to sleep.

She remained where she stood and rocked him back

and forth for a few minutes until satisfied that he was well and truly asleep.

She smiled wearily at Sal. "Thank goodness," she said softly. "I'm going to bed, too. See you in the morning."

"Okay." He blew her a kiss.

She responded with a tilt of her chin in his direction, wondering, had her hands been free, if she'd have blown one back.

Max slept until just after three.

"Almost four hours' sleep in a row," Dori thought, reaching for the bottle of juice she'd placed in a small cooler under the bedside table.

Then she remembered that during their frantic effort last evening to calm Max, she'd come upstairs for the bottle of juice because there had been none left in the refrigerator.

She picked Max up, wrapped him in his blanket and went quietly down the stairs to the kitchen. She took one of the bottles Sal had run through the dishwasher that afternoon, filled it with milk and ran it under the hot water tap.

Max took it eagerly, wrapping both little hands around it. She walked around the side of the kitchen and into the pantry to check Cheddar's box and was disappointed to find it empty.

Where had he gone? she wondered, hoping he wasn't scratching furniture or doing other rude things in her brothers' house.

It was as she turned back to the kitchen that she saw the face in the window. It was peering in the top half of the back door. If it weren't for the whites of the eyes, she thought as she stared, horrified, at the picture it made framed by the window, she might not have noticed it. The face looked as though it had been blackened. The eyes had a wide, frenzied look.

She watched in terror as the doorknob turned, first one way, then the other. She opened her mouth to scream—at that moment, Sal flew out of the bedroom, yanked the door open and ran out into the night.

"Sal, no!" she shouted after him, but he was already gone.

With shaking fingers, she dialed 911. A young man's calm voice told her help would be there soon.

Sal was back in two minutes. "Are you all right?" he demanded, putting one hand to her face and the other to Max's.

"He didn't get in," she said, her voice trembling. "Did you see him?"

He shook his head. "He jumped the back fence, and I didn't want to get too far away on the chance there was someone else with him, just waiting for me to disappear."

The police arrived a moment later. Sal took one of them outside to show him the path the "face" had taken, while Dori told the other officer what had happened. He took notes, then excused himself to return a call from the station on the radio transmitter clipped to his shoulder.

"Apparently one of your neighbors a block down the hill just called in a prowler." He smiled sympathetically. "He's probably looking for an unlocked door," he said. "I know that was frightening, but now that he knows there's a man in the house, I doubt he'll bother you again. Most prowlers get off on scaring women alone."

Dori nodded politely, thinking it probably hadn't been a simple prowler, but proof of Sal's theory about someone wanting their money back. But she knew she couldn't say anything about that.

Sal walked in from the back with the other officer.

"And your name?" the officer who'd questioned her asked.

She suddenly realized that she was dealing with legalities here, with someone who would probably track records down and learn things she'd never told anyone.

"Dorianne McKeon..." She hesitated a moment as she caught Sal's eye and added with a sense of having just turned her entire life upside down, "Dominguez."

Sal raised an eyebrow.

"And you, sir?"

"Salvatore Dominguez," Sal replied.

"I'm glad you're vigilant, Mr. Dominguez," said the officer who'd followed him outside. "But it might be a good idea to call us first, before you follow a prowler into the night."

Sal nodded agreement, never mentioning what he did for a living.

"I told your wife," the other officer said, "that prowlers seldom come back when they know there's a man in the house. And we'll keep driving through the neighborhood during the night."

"Thank you," Sal said, walking them to the door.
"And we appreciate your quick response."

"Sure. Good night, now."

"Good night."

Sal closed and locked the door, hooked the chain in
place, then turned to Dori with a smile. "I'm sorry you
were frightened, *querida*," he said, putting a hand to
her cheek. "But that was the first time I've been able
to enjoy hearing you call yourself by your rightful
name. Come." He put an arm around her shoulders.
"I'll make you some tea."

CHAPTER SEVEN

"WHERE'S CHEDDAR?" Dori asked, trying to avoid a discussion of her name.

Sal pointed to the open door of his room as he passed it on his way to the kitchen. Dori peered inside and saw Cheddar on his side on the bed's second pillow, one paw over his eyes, the toes on his hind feet curled in.

"It's a good thing we didn't take him in hoping for an attack cat." Dori looked around for the bottle of milk she'd prepared before she'd been frightened by the face.

It lay in the middle of the kitchen floor, still tightly closed. She picked it up, and Max reached for it, screeching his disapproval when she put it in the sink and started over with a fresh bottle and more milk.

She finally sat at the kitchen table with it, Max in the crook of her arm sucking hungrily.

She was trembling. She felt it inside, a sort of quivering in her stomach that seemed to grow with her memory of the face in the window, until her whole body was shaking.

She couldn't remember ever feeling so frightened. But then, she'd never been responsible for the safety of a baby before.

She rocked Max, hoping the action would hide from Sal that she was quavering.

"What made you come running?" she asked, mistakenly thinking that making conversation would contribute to the illusion that she was fine despite the scare. "I never got a chance to scream." She was pleased. The question came out sounding strong, interested.

"I heard you come downstairs," he replied, pulling cups down from the cupboard as water began to heat in the kettle. He reached for her box of tea. "Then I heard him outside. I've been expecting some kind of…"

He glanced in her direction as he held up a box of cookies, apparently to ask her if she wanted one with her tea.

She tossed her hair back, a casual gesture that might have worked had she had hair to toss. As it was, it just seemed to punctuate her fear with a giant exclamation point.

He put the box down on the counter and walked past her into the living room, then returned with a cotton throw that he wrapped around her shoulders, tucking the back in between her and the chair.

He fell to one knee in front of her to adjust it around the baby. Then he looked into her eyes.

"I promise you," he said earnestly, "that I won't let anything happen to you or Max. This is what I do, Dori. You're safe."

She nodded, fighting the need to burst into tears. But that wouldn't advance her plan for the summer. Not that anything that had happened in the past few days was doing anything at all for the plan.

"I know," she said, her voice strained. "It's just that the face in the window was…scary." She held the baby more tightly. "I wonder how he knows I have the money?"

"Did you see one face or two?" He wiped a tear away with his thumb.

She hadn't realized she'd let one fall.

"Just one. Why? Did you see two people?"

"No, I chased just one," he replied. "But I heard something in the bushes on the other side of the yard. Could have been raccoons, or possums."

"Or Max's mother is hooked up with her boyfriend again," Dori speculated, "and wants her baby back."

"Anything's possible. But for now, you just have to relax. Sit tight, and I'll put some brandy in your tea."

She watched in perplexity a few moments later when he carried the tea into his bedroom rather than to the table.

"Come on into my room," he said, returning to turn off the kitchen light. "I'll feel better if the two of you are in sight."

She followed him a little hesitantly, not sure this was a good idea. It was also contrary to what he'd said in the beginning—but he probably guessed that she did not want to be alone with Max upstairs.

He had propped up the pillows, and now pointed her to the side away from the window. Cheddar had been moved to the seat of a wicker chair and didn't seem to mind.

"You have your tea, I'll finish feeding Max." Max never missed a beat with his bottle, while Sal took him from Dori. "When you're finished, I'll go get his crib and bring it down here."

They sat leaning against the headboard, Sal with the baby in his arms, Dori sipping her tea, and talked about everything but what had happened tonight.

She didn't care for the taste of the spiked tea, but it did blaze a nice warm trail into her stomach, where that betraying tremor originated. It was quieting now. She was still afraid, but better able to cope.

"Have you called the lawyer?" Sal asked.

Max had finished the contents of his bottle and yawned mightily. Sal put him to his shoulder and patted his back.

"No," Dori admitted. "I got to wondering what the law would require her to do if she knew I had a baby that wasn't mine. Maybe she'd have to tell Adult and Family Services."

"I'm not sure," Sal replied, "but I think if you'd hired her, that's privileged information. And considering how you got him—I mean, you've got that letter with your name on it that proves the parent intended you to have him—I think you'd be safe."

She might be, but she didn't want to take the chance.

"I'll just wait until this is all over." She turned to Sal, comforted by the muscular arm wrapped around the baby, the strong, bare legs in jogging shorts stretched out atop the covers. "But how are we going to get to the bottom of it?"

"I'm working on it," he replied. The baby belched

loudly, and Sal turned to grin at Dori. "I hired a private detective," he added.

She blinked at him. "Why didn't you tell me?"

"Because everything was fine, your work on your book was going well. I didn't want you to worry if you didn't have to."

"Did you hire someone from town?"

"Yes."

"Not Bram Bishop?"

"Yes. Husband of a friend of yours. He told me." He laughed lightly. "Small-town life. Everybody's connected somehow. Which worked in our favor, because it turns out that *his* brother-in-law, who has a photo studio, was taking a passport photo for a couple that provide flowers for the church—and they told the photographer, who told Bishop, that the young housekeeper who was just hired at the church in February has been missing since the theft. So he's on her trail."

"Do you think it's Max's mother?" she asked.

"I don't know. We'll have to be patient and see what he comes up with. I'll call him in the morning and tell him about tonight."

"But it was a man's face I saw in the window," she insisted.

"Which proves my theory that she's probably working with or for a boyfriend."

Max belched again and began to make little melodic sounds, as though wanting to be part of the conversation.

Dori put her empty cup aside and turned toward Sal

to rub Max's back. "I wonder if he's trying to tell us he thinks his mother is innocent."

"Guys always think their mother is innocent."

Sal smiled, a little ruefully, she thought.

Dori tried to remember what little she knew about Sal's mother. She'd died very young, and her absence had been Sal's father's impetus to follow his brother-in-law into a life as a jewel thief.

"You were twelve when your mother died," Dori said.

He nodded, stroking the baby's back.

Dori waited for him to volunteer more. He didn't.

Suspecting there was something important here, she persisted gently, "You've never talked about her very much."

"I know." He sighed. "I discovered she wasn't perfect one day when I was about ten years old, and in my foolish youth, that was hard to take."

"Another man?" she guessed.

He leaned back against the pillows and stared at the ceiling. "My father's friend, Mateo Salvatore. She had his baby when I was eleven."

"You're named after him?"

"Yes."

Dori leaned her cheek against his shoulder, wondering why he'd kept that from her all this time. Then she remembered that it wasn't the kind of thing one shared on first meeting. Their early relationship had consisted of quick, clandestine rendezvous, and that night at the Plaza when things had been passionate one moment, then frantic when they'd made the quick flight to Florida.

They'd quarreled and separated. Then she'd run to him in Mexico—and those days before the wedding had been spent catching up, making promises, planning the future. Not resurrecting the past.

"If it still hurts you," she encouraged softly, "it might help to share it."

"It's been over a long time," he said.

"But you sound as though it still matters."

He closed his eyes and drew a deep breath. Max rose and fell with Sal's chest, now fast asleep against him.

"She was very beautiful and very gentle," he said, slowly reeling out the memory, "and later, when I understood him as a man, I realized that my father was strong and did his best to provide for us. But he was very exacting, sometimes to the point of forgetting that children learned by making mistakes. And people, too. I think my mother's life must have been dull and hard and without much laughter."

He paused and patted Max when he wriggled, then settled down again. "One day my mother wasn't there when I woke up, and my father told me what had happened, that she was expecting Mateo's baby and they had run away together."

"Oh, Sal." She wrapped her arms around him.

"Mateo left her destitute somewhere in Juarez some time later. He was smuggled over the border with a dozen others and died in the back of a pickup in a traffic accident."

"What happened to your mother?"

"She came back to us, about to have the baby. To my father's credit, he let her stay, but he refused to raise the baby. When the child was born, my mother turned it over to a priest, who found an adoptive family in Mexico City. She was broken in spirit and lived with the guilt of what she'd done every day. She died the next year."

"Sal, I'm so sorry." She hugged him, trying desperately to find some hope in that sad story.

"But...you might have a brother somewhere," she said. "Have you looked into it?"

He smiled a little grimly. "I have a sister," he said, then added quietly, "Desideria."

Dori started upright, unable to believe she hadn't seen that coming. *Desideria.* She felt as though she'd been punched hard, then dunked in cold water.

She'd left her husband because he'd gone to the rescue of...his sister, she thought in disbelief.

"She was raised by a wealthy family who were happy to receive my letter, explaining who I was and that I thought I was their daughter's brother. I promised that I wouldn't intrude, that I just wanted to know that she was well."

He smiled. "Her mother wrote back that she was not only well, but beautiful, intelligent and prone to be wild. Desi's adopted father had died, and her mother was worried about her. She invited me to visit.

"I did, we all got on famously, and I became a part of Desi's life. She unfortunately had a predilection for falling in love with dangerous men and eventually married a man who conducted just the kind of business that had killed Mateo.

"I received a frightened call from her one day when she suspected what his export business truly was, and together we alerted the border guards and finally sent him to jail. At the time of our wedding, he got away during an accident while he was being transported from one prison to another, and he headed back to Laredo to exact revenge against Desi for sending him to jail."

Dori looked into his eyes and saw no anger there, no resentment, no grudge against her, just fear at the memory of the danger his sister had faced.

I left him, she thought in disbelief, *because he went to save his sister's life.*

She sat still, trying to absorb what she'd done. Anguished over his perception of her as someone he could walk away from, to run to the rescue of a beautiful young woman she'd heard was reckless and spoiled. Dori had fled. And she'd refused to listen to the truth when he'd followed her home—she'd been so sure she knew all she had to know.

Oh, God.

SO. THE TRUTH was out. Sal looked into Dori's face and suspected that this wasn't necessarily a good thing. She'd finally asked to hear the truth that he should have shared earlier, the truth he had tried to explain when he'd come home from Texas, then had given up on for the two years he and Dori were apart.

But judging now by the astonished, guilt-ridden look

in her eyes, it was going to do him more harm than good.

"I'm sorry," she said finally, her dark eyes wide and stricken. "You didn't tell me..."

He nodded. "Before we got married," he said, "we had so many other things to talk about. And afterward, you wouldn't listen."

"I thought she was a friend," she whispered. "She was introduced to me as a friend of yours! No one in Madre Maria knew she was your sister."

"She wanted it that way. In the States, when her husband was arrested, there was a lot of scandal attached to their name. She wanted to help out at the hospital, but she didn't want any of that notoriety to touch the project, so she came with a phony last name—and as a friend."

"She looked at you with such adoration!"

He shrugged. "The way you look at Duncan or Darrick or Dillon. They've loved you and rescued you, and you love them for it."

She put both hands to her face.

Sal put the baby down on the bed between them and swung his legs out of bed. "I'll go get the crib. If we don't get some sleep, we won't even hear him wake up."

He ran lightly up the stairs, wondering how best to handle this. If he was forgiving and understanding, she would slip deeper into that well of guilt and self-flagellation.

But he didn't have the heart to remind her that she'd robbed them of two years of their life together. It would certainly make her feel anger rather than guilt, but he couldn't do it.

He picked up the portable crib from the room she occupied upstairs and carried it down. There had to be a middle ground, he thought, between rubbing it in and letting her off.

When he walked into the downstairs bedroom, Dori sat in the middle of the bed, Cheddar in her lap, the baby beside her still sound asleep.

Sal scooped Max up, lay him in the crib and covered him with the blue blanket. He turned off the light and climbed into bed beside her with a casual ease he was far from feeling.

She didn't move. "Sal?" she asked after a moment. "Yes?"

"I don't want this to be my fault." Her voice was tight and high. "I...was so sure it was yours."

"I know. Forget it."

"How can I forget it? I cost us two years of our marriage!"

And that was where he found the solution. It was drastic, and it would hurt, but it might also work. And it would take the pressure off and give them time.

"Doesn't matter anymore," he said genially. "You said so yourself, and I'm beginning to think you're right. Now that we've both decided there's nothing left, it doesn't really matter how it fell apart. Relax. I've got my business, you've got your book."

There was a long, heavy silence from her side of the bed. Then she slid down under the covers. Her heel collided with his hip as she lay down, and he felt a very familiar twang of desire.

"Sorry," she said.

"No problem," he assured her. Oh, yeah. This was another one of his good ideas.

"Good night," she said.

He turned onto his back. "Bacon and eggs for breakfast?" he asked.

"Sure," she replied in a small voice.

Something touched his arm, and he had an instant of hopeful expectation. Then he heard the rumble of an enthusiastic cat purr and was suddenly trod upon by four padded feet. They did a circle on his chest and suddenly sat, sharp little teeth biting his chin in a cat kiss.

"Your cat's on me," he said.

He heard Dori's sigh in the darkness. "He must have liked the sound of bacon and eggs for breakfast, too."

"We have to get some cat food tomorrow." She sounded grim, and he thought a simple domestic conversation might lighten her mood. "And litter, probably."

"Yeah. And I have to find something for my mom's birthday. She'll be sixty-three next week."

"That should be easy. There's that big antique shop downtown. They're still collectors, aren't they?"

"Yes, but you know my parents' reputation for falling in love with ugly stuff. We may have to travel around to find something bad enough for Mom to appreciate."

"We'll do that. It's good to have a purpose."

There was no response from her side of the bed.

Sal closed his eyes and tried to sleep, not an easy task with her just a hand-span away.

Without warning, she sat up again. "What do you mean, we've decided it doesn't matter?"

Cheddar, startled by the sudden movement, leaped off him.

Knowing this was a critical question, Sal considered his answer.

Dori poked his shoulder, apparently wondering if he'd heard her. "Are you awake?"

"Of course, I'm awake." He propped up on an elbow, facing her. He couldn't see her in the darkness, but all his radar told him she was there. "I didn't say we decided it didn't matter—I said it didn't matter because we've decided there's nothing left."

"Who's decided?" she demanded.

"I believe it was you," he replied. "You couldn't love someone who took vows one minute and walked away from them the next, so—"

"But I didn't know the truth when I said that."

"Not my fault. I asked Diego to explain it to you. But you didn't listen. Then I went to your place when I came home, to try to tell you about it, but again, you—"

"You'd left me on our wedding day!"

"Here we go again." He flung a hand out in exasperation and made contact with her bare arm. He drew his hand back, everything connected to it pulsing in reaction.

"I'm sorry about what happened," she said plain-

tively. "You just don't understand what I was feeling
when you left. You just know you had a noble reason
and that makes you right, and I'm just a selfish brat
because I was hurt."

"No, you were a selfish brat," he amended carefully, "because you wouldn't listen to an explanation."

"Fine." He felt her slam back against her pillow. "I
don't want to talk about it anymore."

Maybe letting her be eaten by guilt, he thought with
fresh frustration, wouldn't have been so unpalatable,
after all.

The next three days passed in the same way. They
were polite and considerate of each other. He prepared
meals and watched the baby in the morning so she
could work, and she cleaned up and watched Max in
the afternoon so Sal could check with the office, do a
few chores around the garden, and lay out in the hammock, nothing more productive on his agenda.

They slept side by side at night, never touching, and
Cheddar slept between them on the pillows. Max woke
only once a night, and whoever was awake responded.
They had domesticity down to an art. They just
couldn't find the bliss.

IT DIDN'T MATTER.

There was nothing left.

When she wasn't writing, Dori played those lines
over and over in her head. The basic truth was that it
was all *her fault* that it didn't matter and that there was
nothing left.

She spent long hours in the afternoon thinking about

it, Max in the playpen while she cleaned house. She'd tried to remember every detail so that she could put the blame elsewhere. But it stood squarely with her.

So it was up to her to fix it.

But how did you re-engage the affections of a man whom you had alienated sufficiently that he could finally bare his soul—then tell you the loss of your love didn't matter because there was nothing left of his?

Then the obvious occurred to her.

It was early Saturday evening and she'd just put Max down after a napless day. Sal lay in the bathtub soaking away an entire afternoon of mowing, trimming, pulling weeds and filling a large terracotta pot with pink begonias, while alyssum and blue lobelia. The flower-filled pot was a gift for her mother that she intended to deliver the following week when she visited for her birthday. The search for the perfect "ugly" antique continued.

Sal had emerged from the garden, moaning. Dori had helped him off with his shirt. "You're a little rickety for thirty-six, aren't you?" she teased.

He groaned as he pulled his arm out of a sleeve and gave her an injured look. "I've been spending a lot of time at a desk for almost two years."

Her eyes roamed over his shoulders as she prepared to tease him again, then she saw a ragged scar on the front of his right shoulder and an elongated one from collar bone to rotator cuff on the left. The long one was still thick and corded, and looked as though, whatever the cause, it had been painful.

She put her fingertips to the ragged scar. "What happened here?" she asked.

"A bullet," he replied, his voice a little weak.

She remembered reading about his defense of a newspaper man who'd uncovered corruption in Seattle's City Hall. He'd defended the man, she remembered, by blocking the bullet. "That newspaper man?"

"No, that's the other shoulder. This one is from Paco."

"Who's Paco?"

He answered cautiously. "Desi's husband."

She'd seen him without his shirt during those days before the wedding. He'd worked bare-chested in the hospital, and he cooked that way at home in the intense heat. She remembered what a flawlessly beautiful specimen he'd been. It wasn't that she considered him diminished by the wounds, but she felt personally affronted that such a thing could have happened to him, that someone else would have deliberately hurt him in such a way. It made her feel vengeful and darkly angry.

"Well, goodness, Sal," she said, trying to force lightness into her voice. "Certainly you must have another technique for protecting people than acting as a shield? You're out of shoulders. What will you sacrifice next?"

He struggled with a smile, apparently amused by her reaction. "I don't know," he replied. "What do you think I could do without?"

She stood on tiptoe to rap her knuckles lightly on his head. "This doesn't seem to be doing you much good. Climb into the bathtub, and I'll bring you some wine.''

That was why it had taken him seven days to come home from Desi's, she thought as she went into the kitchen. He'd probably spent that time recovering from the wound.

She took a bottle of Reisling from the refrigerator and filled a wineglass three-quarters full. She put Max in his carrier and walked wine and baby upstairs, then put Max near the bed in the room they'd occupied across the hall from the bathroom.

Wine in hand, she rapped lightly on the half-open bathroom door.

"Come in," Sal said, the tone of his voice suggesting uncertainty.

She walked in and handed him the glass. He was covered to the middle of his chest in the aromatherapy suds she'd put into the water, and he raised a bubbly hand to take the glass from her.

"Thank you," he said. He took a sip and leaned back with an appreciative sigh.

"You want me to fix dinner?" she asked, reaching for the loofa and the soap on the dish near the faucet. She dipped the sponge into the water to get it wet.

Eyes closed, he smiled. "Please, *querida*. Haven't I suffered enough?"

"I should splash you," she replied, coming around behind him, "but you don't look as though you could defend yourself. Want your back scrubbed?"

He was still for a moment, and she thought he might

refuse. Then he sat forward and allowed her access. "Where's the baby?" he asked.

"In his carrier right across the hall," she replied. "Fast asleep."

She rubbed soap onto the wet sponge and began to work it slowly from shoulder to shoulder. Neither bullet, she noticed in relief, had penetrated his back.

"Then going out wouldn't be wise. We could call for pizza, or I could get Chinese takeout."

"Pizza's a good idea," she said, a little distracted by the definition of his back muscles. She watched them move as he brought the wine to his mouth.

She worked the sponge in circles down his spinal column, dipping into the water to follow the ridges of vertebrae.

The man she'd teased just a moment ago about being defenseless turned and caught her arm and hauled her across the tub so that she sat suspended over the water, her legs straight out ahead of her and resting on the rim.

She squealed in surprise.

"Would you like to get wet?" It was a threat, not a question. The look in his eyes said she had his complete attention.

"Depends," she replied, relaxing in his arms. "What's in it for me, if I do?"

His voice lowered an octave. "What are you after, *corazón*?"

She met and held his gaze. "You, my love."

There was surprise in his eyes for an instant, then

passion ignited there. "You have always had me. You just kept too great a distance between us."

"That's not a problem now," she pointed out.

He lowered her into his lap, put a hand behind her head to protect her from collision with the wall, and kissed her soundly while his free hand unfastened the buttons of her shirt.

Warm water soaked through her clothes from her bottom to her breasts.

She had him now.

HE SHOULD ASK QUESTIONS, he thought drunkenly, as she returned his kisses with ardent eagerness.

There was something in her eyes that troubled him, something that didn't seem entirely...spontaneous. Not that there was anything wrong with a planned seduction. He just couldn't help wondering what had changed her mind so completely.

If this was sympathy over his wounds, or some kind of compensation for having left him, he didn't want it. Oh, hell, who was he kidding? Of course he wanted it, whatever motivated her.

Once he had her buttons undone, he sat her forward to help her pull off the shirt. Her sports bra came off right over her head, leaving two perfect little globes, rose-tipped and beading, as he leaned down to kiss one and then the other.

He turned her lengthwise atop him so that she could shed her elastic-waisted shorts and panties, then he cradled her again. But before he could claim her mouth, she smiled and pointed to her shoes and socks.

"You can drown in the water—" she giggled "—wearing shoes and socks."

"Don't worry," he said, his brain barely functioning enough to form words now that her bare flesh was against his, "we'll keep you on top."

She toed off the shoes, and he reached a hand out to pull off the socks. Then he turned her onto her stomach atop him.

For a moment they simply held each other. Then she squirmed against him, as if to get closer still, her arms tight around his neck as though he was the answer to a prayer.

He framed her face in his hands and saw the love in her eyes, the small smile. She put her hands over his and said with a wince, "I should probably tell you..."

He put a fingertip to her lips. "No confessions. I've done things I even prefer not to know."

She kissed his fingertip, then lowered it, a little frown still in place. "I was just going to confess virginity," she said.

CHAPTER EIGHT

THERE'D BEEN MOMENTS before they were married when he'd suspected that. She'd had a kind of innocence in her glance and in her touch that he didn't think would be there if she'd had experience.

But then he'd told himself he was imagining things. She'd been the protected younger sister of three watchful brothers, but she'd been abroad to school, she'd traveled extensively on her own doing research for her work. And she was beautiful and desirable. There had to have been someone.

"At twenty-six, *querida?*" he asked.

Arms wrapped around his neck, she sat sideways and brought her knees up so that she was curled in his lap.

"I was a serious scholar, with brothers who looked over my friends and checked out my boyfriends. Those brave enough to date me a second time were not brave enough to do anything but kiss me good-night—and usually on the forehead."

Sal smiled at that. He'd been investigated, he knew. Despite his background as a thief, the McKeons had approved him. It was Dori who'd been the holdout.

"Then I met you," she went on, "and even though you went back to Mexico and things looked impossible for us, you were on my mind all the time.'' She smiled. "Then I chased you down, and we planned to get married in the Church and that meant we had to wait to make love.''

That had been torturous because he'd insisted that Dori stay at his home where conditions were more comfortable than in the little cantina in town.

"My housekeeper watched us like a hawk,'' he recalled with a light laugh. Then he grew serious again. "But that was two years ago.''

"Yes,'' she admitted, "but I've been a married woman since then.'' She tucked the tip of her slender index finger into the center of the small hoop earring on her left ear. "Doesn't this look familiar to you?''

He took it in his hand, careful not to pull. His heart punched against his ribs when he saw the thin inscription inside it. *Mi amor,* it said simply. My love.

"This is your wedding ring!'' he said, freeing her ear and turning her chin toward him. "Why?''

"Because I loved you,'' she said grudgingly, "but I was so angry at you for leaving me. I didn't want to wear your ring, but I couldn't put it in a drawer, either. So I found another hoop that matched and made my wedding ring into an earring.''

He'd intended an impromptu lovemaking in the tub, thinking the unorthodox setting would be part of the fun of finally coming together.

But she was a virgin. And she'd always loved him. He'd be damned if her first time would be in a bathtub.

He lifted her out of the water again, propping her

bottom on the rim. "We're rethinking this," he said, pulling himself to his feet.

"I don't *want* to rethink it!" she complained. "I've been planning this all afternoon!"

He snatched a towel off the rack and handed it to her, then took one for himself. "I've been planning it longer than that," he said with a quick kiss. He dried himself off, then wrapped the towel around his waist. "I don't mean we aren't going to make love. We're just not going to do it in the tub."

He took the towel from her, dried her back and her hips, almost driving himself over the edge when he wrapped it around her and tucked it above her breast.

He lifted her into his arms and walked across the hallway with her into the bedroom she'd occupied with the baby. Max was still asleep in the carrier.

"Do you think we could pretend," she asked as he set her down by the side of the bed, "that two years *haven't* passed, that it's our wedding day and we've made it all the way back to your place where there's the scent of jacarandas coming in through the window?"

He tossed the covers back on the bed, then hooked a finger in her towel to pull it off, dropping his own as well.

"We can pretend whatever you want," he said, lifting her again to place her in the middle of the bed. "But this is very nice." He pointed to the lace curtains blowing into the room on an early evening breeze. "I smell roses and the salty fragrance of the ocean. And you."

Sal lay down beside her and nuzzled her throat. "That complicated fragrance that haunted my place for weeks after you left. Lavender and..."

"Vanilla," she whispered.

"Mmm. It's in my black sweater now," he said, turning onto his side and wrapping her in his arms. "You're all over me, Dori. Inside, outside, everywhere."

"Good." She kissed his throat as he began to explore the line of her back, the flare of her hip. "I want us to be forever entangled. Not a fairy-tale romance, but the real thing—where you're so close you're not entirely sure who's who, and it lasts forever."

He caught the back of her thigh and pulled her leg over him so that he could chart her from knee to torso. "It's been the real thing for me since the first time I saw you."

She tipped her head back to smile at him. "I thought you were gorgeous but autocratic."

"I was trying to protect Julie's father."

"And I was trying to explain Julie's position."

"Then their relationship was restored thanks to us, and *we* couldn't get along."

"We're getting along now," she said with a little sigh as she dropped her head against his shoulder. "Tell me what to do for you, *querido*."

He held her closer, loving the sound of the old endearment on her tongue. "Do whatever occurs to you, my heart, and I will love it."

WHAT SHE WANTED TO DO, Dori thought, was to learn everything about his magnificent body. She touched him everywhere, letting her fingertips trace the outline of his shoulders and arms, follow the ridge of his collar bone and ribs, explore the tangled pattern of chest hair that ran down his chest, past his waist, over his flat abdomen, to the juncture of his thighs.

He caught her hand before she could touch his manhood. "Not yet," he said with a self-deprecating little laugh, "or there won't be time for all I want you to know."

He pushed her gently onto her back, his hands doing just what hers had done to him, except that he seemed inordinately skilled—everywhere he touched seemed to acquire a life she'd never been aware of. Her breasts tingled; shudders rippled under her rib cage and inside her belly.

His lips followed his fingertips, and her body arched toward him of its own volition, as though it no longer needed instructions from her.

The notion was both liberating and alarming. But he made her feel too wonderful for her to be afraid of anything. Her only regret was that she'd missed two whole years of this!

He tucked her into his arm and reached gently inside her. She lay very still, focused on the exquisite rightness of his tender invasion. As his hand moved gently and her body accustomed itself to his exploration, the scholar in her thought to analyze the nature of a woman's react—

A tight spiral of feeling began deep inside, and she lost all powers of analysis. Thought fled. That tight little feeling began to grow and recede, grow and recede, until she felt a sort of frantic desperation to catch it, to know what it was.

"Easy," he coached quietly. "Just be easy."

"I want to touch you!" she said urgently. It would help. She knew it would help.

"Not yet," he insisted. "Focus on you. Think about you."

She opened her mouth to protest, but only a small, startled gasp escaped, as pleasure darted at her one more time, then broke over her in a shockingly intense wave.

She felt powerless to move, pinned against the mattress with pleasure. So that was the truth everyone else knew. The magic wasn't just in that star-shower of feeling, but in the fact that a loving and caring man could give it to you.

As her pleasure subsided, what occurred to her first was the need to return that unutterable sense of well-being. "Salvatore!" she whispered earnestly, running her hands down the middle of his stomach.

"No," he cautioned, trying to stop her. "Not until— Ah!"

She closed her hand over him with a reverence for all he'd just given her.

"Dori, I said…" He sat up again to try to stop her, but she pushed him back, her forearm leaning on his chest as she said sweetly, "Easy, *querido*. Focus on yourself. Think about yourself."

Caressing him was all new to her, but there was clear evidence that she could be very good at this.

She was just beginning to feel confidence when he caught her by the waist and lifted her astride him.

"All right," he said, his voice strained. "I wanted to give you more time, but if you insist on being in control, you must now be in control of all of me."

He caught her hips in his hands to brace her as he lifted up, poised to enter her.

She smiled. "Then let me have all of you. I've waited forever."

He thrust upward, and they came together at last.

For just an instant the pressure felt like more than she could bear. A metaphor for their lives, she thought. She'd always felt as though he filled her life too full, as though she couldn't contain him without losing herself.

Then, as had happened when he'd first come home with her, a certain satisfaction in his presence eased the discomfort, then the satisfaction turned to contentment, the contentment to happiness and the happiness to a joy so profound that she could hold him easily. And she wondered how she'd managed this long without him.

Then clever metaphors fled, basic thought fled, as pleasure came at her again—bigger, deeper, more sweeping.

She began to move on him, some instinct making her sway in a little circle.

He laced his hands in hers to give her leverage. Then they were moving together, and this time she didn't have to pursue fulfillment—it hit her broadside so that her head fell back even as she tightened her knees and her fingers to hold on.

SAL HAD NEVER had an experience like this, in which a partner's pleasure gave him the delicious thrill he felt now. She'd been so determined to be in control, and was now enslaved to him.

Of course, he was securely bound and shackled himself, as she seemed to dissolve with pleasure, arch backward with release, then collapse atop him with a long, ragged sigh. He freed himself, lifted her off him, then gathered her in his arms.

"Oh, Sal," she groaned against his chest.

"I know," he said, still adjusting to the miracle of having made love to her. "Tell me we weren't destined for each other."

"I hate to think of the time wasted," she said regretfully.

"Then, don't." He gave the back of her hair a little tug. "Think of all that lies ahead. Babies, that house up the hill from the theater, growing old together—"

There was a sudden scratching on the other side of the bedroom door.

Dori looked up in the direction of the carrier. "What is that?" she asked. "Max is still asleep."

"Cheddar has found us," Sal guessed. "Now we not only have to contend with making sure the baby's asleep so we can make love, but we have to sedate the cat."

"About more babies…" she said, obviously not concerned about the cat.

"You don't like the idea?" he asked worriedly.

"Oh, no. I love it," she assured him. "But I was thinking about Max. I mean, that's okay with you, isn't it? Keeping him? Adopting him?"

"Of course. I love him as much as you do."

She sighed and rested her head on his shoulder again. "Good. I'll be so glad when we know where we stand there. I hope Gusty's husband finds out something soon."

"Oh. Forgot to tell you," he said, wondering how he'd managed to do that. Although, as he remembered, he'd been one very frustrated man this afternoon. Hence the over-the-top yardwork. "Bram called while you were writing this morning, and we're invited to their place for lunch tomorrow."

"Really?"

"Really. He has some answers for us, and his wife's been cooped up with the baby all week. She thought it would be fun to have us over so that we can eat while we talk business, and the babies can play together."

She smiled, clearly pleased with the idea. "That sounds like fun. And Max will love it."

"All right. I was supposed to let him know. I'll call him back, then I'll call for pizza."

His timing impeccable, Max began to stir and shout to the world that he was awake. Beyond the door, the scratching grew frantic.

Dori groaned and pushed up on Sal's chest. "Darn it. Back to our real lives."

He pulled her back down for a quick kiss. "From now on, this *is* our real lives."

DORI LIVED in a state of wonder. They made love when they went to bed. They made love after getting Max back to sleep after a four a.m. feeding. They drove to Mass in Lincoln City, had brunch at the Shilo Restaurant, then came home to relax for a few hours before going on to lunch—and made love again when Max dozed off.

If she'd known her marriage would be like this, she thought as she mixed a salad in Gusty's garage-apartment kitchen, she'd never have left for home two years ago.

Sal was turning out to be everything she'd ever prayed for in a husband. Though it was early yet, though the circumstances were unusual, and though she'd finally seen the light only one day ago, she had a good feeling about this. The marriage could work.

They ate steaks and salad at the Bishop's dining room table, while Max played with little Sadie on a blanket on the floor just beyond the table.

Sadie had the advantage. She was a mature nine-month-old who could sit up by herself, could use the bead rung on the side of the playpen to pull herself to a standing position, could take what she wanted to examine it, and could say "Mama." She was beautiful and seemed to delight in all she could do.

Max complacently allowed her to take his toys, and simply rolled and twisted away from her when she became too much of a pest.

"Brenda Ward, 18, is Max's mother," Bram said, consulting a sheet of notes near his plate on the table. "He was born on Valentine's Day in Lincoln City to

Brenda and her boyfriend, Will Valdefiero. Valdefiero is a small-time hood who's always getting caught and doing time. He and Brenda met when they both worked for Burgers by the Sea."

Dori frowned over Max's sad beginning. "What's his full name?"

"Maximiliano Felipe Valdefiero," he replied, smiling. "Very important name for such a little guy. Police have been tracking the two. Brenda hasn't been back to work at the church since the theft."

"Are they sure *she* did it?"

"She probably just let the boyfriend in. His fingerprints were on the base of a lamp on the desk where the money was kept. He must have moved it for fear of knocking it over in the dark. The police are thinking they might still be around. The boy's car is still parked at Burgers. Nobody's seen the girl."

"Why would she help the boyfriend steal the money," Gusty asked, "then give it to Dori along with her baby? They must have had a falling out or something. If that's true, she has to be in big trouble with him."

"I hope he hasn't hurt her," Dori said, a little surprised that she'd said the words aloud. She smiled apologetically at her companions. "I think she cared for her baby."

"This note suggests that you know her," Bram said, as Gusty stacked plates.

Dori pushed her chair back to help, but Gusty gestured for her to remain seated. "You talk, I'll clear."

Dori focused on Bram. "I know, but I don't remem-

ber doing anything for anyone that would so convince
them of my generosity that they'd give me their baby."

He held up a photo. "Does this jog your memory?"

She was shocked to recognize the face instantly. "It
does!" she whispered in surprise, taking the photo
from him and studying it. The memory unfolded easily.
"But I only saw her once. In the rest room in the library. She had everything she owned in a backpack
and she was washing her face." She could see the image as though it had happened that morning. "She must
have been embarrassed to be caught doing that, because
she told me she had a job interview at a church!" She
turned abruptly to Bram, feeling mingled excitement
and trepidation for the girl. "At a church!"

Tears sprang to her eyes, and she felt Sal's hand in
the middle of her back, rubbing gently. "I heard her
stomach growl," she continued, "and I gave her the
chocolate bar I had in my purse." She was surprised
by the wrench of emotion she felt. "That's all I did.
One eighty-nine-cent chocolate bar."

"Street people," Sal said, "don't experience a lot
of kindness. You touched her life, and for that moment
you made a difference to her."

"And when she needed someone who'd love and
care for her baby," Gusty said, her own eyes pooled
with tears. "She thought of you."

"But I don't even live here," Dori said, surprised
that the girl had found her. "I mean, I come and go a
lot."

Bram shrugged. "You were here at the right time—
both times."

Gusty hurried to retrieve Sadie as the baby ventured off the blanket and headed toward the television. "Anyone for dessert?" she asked, picking up Sadie and placing her inside the playpen. "Chocolate torte with coffee ice cream. Show of hands."

Dori, thinking about Brenda Ward, missed the instructions. Sal raised her hand for her.

Sadie screamed a protest at being confined, while Gusty went to the kitchen. Gusty returned with a teething biscuit that she broke in half, giving one to each baby. Sadie began to munch, and quieted instantly.

Max fussed. Dori picked him up and gave him a bottle that kept him quiet while she ate dessert.

"Cliffside," Gusty said, pushing her dessert plate away and dabbing at her lips with a napkin, "is going to be crawling with babies by Christmas. Literally."

She referred to the property on which their garage apartment stood. It included the big house where Athena and her husband David and his brothers lived; a guest house once occupied by Alexis, the third triplet, and Trevyn McGinty, her husband, but now empty since they'd bought a house on the cove; and this apartment above the three-car garage.

"Athena told me she's pregnant," Dori said, pleased at the idea. It might make the attorney more determined to help her adopt Max.

"She is," Gusty replied. "And so's Alexis. They're due two weeks apart in November. Be ready to come to a baby shower sometime early in the fall." The sisters had married friends of Bram. The men had all once worked together in high-security government jobs.

"I'd love that," Dori said. "Our family's just blossoming with children. It's so much fun when we all get together to see who looks like whom and who's at what stage of development. My parents are so thrilled with their growing brood."

Gusty smiled wistfully. "Ours are gone, unfortunately. We have Bram's sister, though, and Trevyn's father, and, of course, David and Athena are raising David's younger brothers. Then we'll be adding two. Maybe the triplets and the McKeons will have to take a count and see who's ahead."

Dori thought about that remark later that night when she, Sal and Max had returned home. Sal walked the floor with the baby, who was fussy from all the excitement. Dori sat cross-legged on the sofa with McGinty's photo of her family in her lap. He had a photo studio now in the Bijou Theater building.

It had been taken on the beach just before a rainstorm. They'd all worn red and white, at her mother's request, and they were laughingly arm in arm, expecting to be rained on at any moment. There were children, babies, dogs—and a real air of happiness.

She counted heads.

"You don't have to bother," Sal said, pacing toward her with Max, who stood up stiffly in his arms, crying pitifully. Sal raised his voice to be heard. "We've got the numbers hands-down. You've got—what? Twelve, thirteen there?"

"Thirteen," she replied.

"Then Max and me. Fifteen."

She nodded. "Even with the babies coming in November, the triplets only have twelve counting Dottie."

"Dottie?"

"The housekeeper. I'm sure they'd count her."

"Then we're way ahead." He lifted the still-whining baby up in front of his face. "I'll bet you're crying because your mother looks so depressed. Maybe if you cheer up, she'll cheer up. What do you say?"

Max's response was to kick his feet and scream more loudly.

"That's what I thought." Sal put the baby on his shoulder again and continued walking. "I continue to be the only cool head around here."

"I was worrying about Brenda Ward," Dori admitted, holding the family photo to her chest. Her throat was thick, her eyes burning. "I want to keep Max more than anything, but what if she just made a stupid mistake and got hurt for it by the boyfriend? Or what if they find her and she wants Max back. Should she have another chance?"

Sal came to sit beside her, angled one leg on the other knee and placed the baby half on his thigh, half on the sofa. Max grew quiet, surprised by this new position. He took a fistful of Sal's pants leg and inched himself forward.

"You're asking big questions, Dori," Sal said, keeping a hand on Max's diapered bottom to steady his progress. "If she's committed a crime and has to go to jail, she'd lose the baby, at least for a time."

"I know. But what if she wants to straighten herself out? Maybe she regrets giving him to me."

Dori placed one of Max's toys on Sal's other knee, and the baby reached for it. "He's learning something new every day," she said, grimly thoughtful as she moved the toy within his reach. "He should have a good home. But should his mother lose everything because she screwed up?"

"You're wondering whether, if the situation comes up, you should go to court for custody," Sal spelled out for her.

She rested her cheek on Sal's shoulder as they played with the baby. "At first I thought I would. Now I wonder if it'd be the right thing to do."

"I guess you won't know that until she's found and you see what kind of young woman she is. If she put him in your car, it's entirely possible she's given him up in her heart, whatever happens."

"Yeah," Dori said. "'Cause I've accepted him in my heart."

"I know. And he adores you."

"And you. We'd be the perfect family."

He kissed the top of her head. "Let's not get upset about anything until we know for sure what we're dealing with, okay?"

She sighed. "I'd like to agree to that, but I know I'll worry, anyway."

Max managed to turn himself sideways, grab the front of Sal's shirt and grin broadly, pleased with himself.

"Whoa!" Sal said, sitting up and standing the baby on his knees.

"What?" Dori demanded worriedly, wondering what he'd seen. "What is it?"

Sal put an index finger to Max's bottom lip and drew it down until Dori saw the tiny rippled little bud of a tooth in the middle of his bottom gum.

She shrieked excitedly. "A tooth! He's got a tooth!"

Max, upset by her scream, began to cry again.

Sal turned to her with a teasingly condemning look. "Thanks, Mom. I've only been working on calming him down for an hour-and-a-half."

"Sorry," she said penitently, and took the baby from him. "Maybe a bath will do it. I did it, I'll fix it. You relax."

"You are a genius," Sal said half an hour later, when Max, bathed and toweled off and rocked, lay fast asleep in the crib in Sal's room.

She smiled. "Thank you. I've always maintained that myself, but I've had three brothers trying for years to prove me wrong. How about a cup of tea?"

"Already made," he said. He pointed to the teapot and cups on the coffee table.

They sank onto the sofa, sipped tea and watched television, all curled up together.

"I thought only old folks did this," she said tiredly.

He laughed. "I think children make you old."

"But you were talking about having more."

"I happen to like sitting with your legs in my lap and watching the Spice Channel. So I'm okay with it."

She backhanded him in the chest. "We're not watching the Spice Channel."

He held his cup of tea a safe distance away. "I was

fantasizing a little. Want to go to bed and make my fantasies come true?''

"This would be the fourth time in the past twenty-four hours.''

"Hah," he said. "That's why the triplets and their husbands will never catch up to the McKeon-Dominguez family.''

"Oh, all right.'' She put her cup down, pretending reluctance. She stood and caught his hand. "If the honor of the family is at stake.''

He went willingly. "Honor above all,'' he said heroically.

An hour later, Dori lay in his arms in the darkness and thought how lucky she was that Brenda Ward had put her baby in the back of Dori's car—because that had led Dori to contact Sal, which had led to this time together and finally to the rebirth of their marriage.

She owed Brenda a lot.

Dori had a second chance to rebuild her life after having selfishly almost destroyed it.

But didn't Brenda deserve a second chance as well?

CHAPTER NINE

MONDAY MORNING, Dori glanced at the calendar near her computer and noticed the big red circle around August third. Her brothers and their families would be home from Europe.

They had talked about using the beach house for a few days as a sort of leveling-out place before going back to their busy lives. They had also discussed celebrating their mother's August fifth birthday while here, and had told Dori that since she'd refused their invitation to accompany them to Europe, she could be in charge of preparations for the celebration.

She had to do something about that, she thought. And she had to brace herself to explain what Sal was doing here with her. She wondered if the living-together concept might not be easier to explain than the fact that they'd been married two years ago in a ceremony to which her family hadn't been invited.

She raised her hands from the keyboard and put them to her face with a groan. And then there was the baby. She could just imagine her parents' and her brothers' reactions to her decision not to go to the police.

She dropped her hands, squared her shoulders and focused on the hope that Bram would find Brenda by then. That way the entire matter of the money and the baby would be resolved.

And then she got the phone call. The voice was a raspy whisper. "Dori?"

She'd been rereading a line of dialogue as she picked up the receiver, but at the sound of the voice, she gave the call her complete attention. "Yes?" she asked.

There was a hesitation. Her heart began to race. "Brenda?" she asked.

A gasp sounded on the line. "How did you know it was me?" Then a little more pointedly, the woman added, "How did you know my name?"

Not a good move, Dori realized. Would Brenda suspect that she was being investigated?

She thought quickly. "I read the article in the paper about the theft from the church. It was exactly the same amount of money you left in the diaper bag. And no one's seen you since then, so that suggests you were involved." That detail hadn't been in the newspaper, but maybe Brenda wouldn't notice. "And it's clear from the note you left that the same person who left the baby, left the money."

Another pause, then a long breath. "How's Max?" the woman asked in a strained voice.

Dori felt everything inside her tense at the thought of the possibility that Brenda wanted Max back. "He's fine," she replied calmly. "I'm taking good care of him." She didn't want to ask, but she made herself do it. "Are you regretting giving him up?"

"No," Brenda replied with a quickness and sincerity that relieved Dori's mind. "I didn't like being a mother. He's a sweet baby, but I don't want him back.''

That was chillingly firm.

"Do you still have the money?'' Brenda asked her.

Dori tried to remember all Sal's cautions, but she couldn't help but worry about the frightened young woman on the phone.

"Did you steal it," she asked, "from whoever stole it from the church?"

There was another pause, then she replied in a frail voice, "Yes."

"Your boyfriend?''

"Yes.''

"Does he know?''

There were sniffles, sighs. "He figured it out. Do you still have it?"

"Why?'' Dori asked.

"Because if I can get it back," Brenda said, "and give it to the police, then maybe I won't have to go to jail when they catch Will. And I'll sign the release form so you can adopt Max without any trouble.''

Dori's mind leaped ahead to the day Max did an adoption search and discovered that his mother had gone to jail for stealing from a church. She could protect him from that and secure his adoption at the same time.

"Where are you?" she asked.

"You still have it?" Brenda asked anxiously.

"Yes," Dori replied. "Where are you?"

"Can you meet me," Brenda asked, "in the corner

of the park where that little bench sits under the big maple tree?''

Dori knew the one. It was concealed by a high hedge on one side and playground equipment on the other.

''What time?'' Dori asked.

''Three o'clock?''

Dori looked at her watch. It was two-fifteen. ''I'll be there,'' she said.

There was a pause, then Brenda said in a choked voice, ''Thank you, Dori.'' And the line went dead.

Dori thought she knew just how to handle this.

She couldn't tell Sal what she was doing; that was clear. He'd be opposed to it, and either refuse to let her go or insist on coming along. Either reaction would result in her losing the opportunity to help Brenda.

But Sal worked in the yard every afternoon, with Max in the playpen under the shady ash. If Dori did this correctly, he wouldn't even know she was gone.

She hated to deceive him, but she knew he'd respond like the protector he'd made himself—and she had to do what she had to do.

She went downstairs on the pretext of filling the tea-kettle, an afternoon ritual. She stood in the doorway with it in hand and pushed open the screen door.

''Hi!'' she called. ''How're you two doing?''

Max, sitting up with a soft toy in his hand, squealed at the sight of her.

''Good.'' Sal looked up from the picnic table where he was working on his laptop, Cheddar curled up in a tight ball beside it. ''Are you going to join us for an afternoon break?''

She shook her head regretfully, ignoring the little pinch of guilt. "Sorry. I'm on a roll and I should probably stay with it. I just came down to refill my thermos. You want anything?"

He shook his head. "Not yet, thanks. Who called?"

"My mother," she replied, the pinch of guilt turning into an outright burn. "If I bring you the cordless, would you mind answering the phone for the rest of the afternoon, so I won't be distracted?"

"Of course not," he replied amiably.

She went back into the kitchen, put the empty kettle on the stove without turning on the burner, picked up the cordless phone from the kitchen counter and carried it outside.

Sal caught her wrist to pull her down for a quick kiss. "So your plot's coming together?" he asked.

She nodded, looking into his warm eyes and feeling suddenly fidgety and certain that the whole fake scenario showed in her face.

"Yeah," she replied, drawing away and taking a few backward steps toward the kitchen. "I'm fighting with the middle, but I think it's happening."

"Good." A very small wrinkle formed on his brow. "Don't fall over the playpen."

She turned to find the backs of her legs almost up against it. She rolled her eyes in self-deprecation, reached into the playpen, tickled Max—who giggled infectiously—then hurried back into the kitchen.

Her heart was pounding. *Good grief,* she thought. *Remind me never to embark on a life of crime.* She simply didn't have the temperament for it.

She ran upstairs, retrieved the box of cash in the diaper bag in the bottom of the closet and stuffed it into her purse.

Then she tiptoed halfway downstairs, stopped to listen to make sure Sal and the baby were still outside, then hurried the rest of the way down and out the front door.

She couldn't start the car, or he would hear her. She glanced at her watch. She had thirty-five minutes to walk to town.

SAL WATCHED Max try to throw his toy and succeed only in dropping it into his lap. It seemed to thrill him, anyway, and he giggled.

This life was a miracle, Sal thought. His marriage with Dori resurrected, this beautiful baby in their lives. He'd feel better about everything when he knew they could keep Max, but they couldn't be sure of that until Brenda Ward was found. And Bram had had no luck so far.

The telephone rang, and Sal picked it up, recognizing Peg and Charlie McKeon's name and number on the small display screen. Knowing Dori would be upset if he answered it, he walked as far as the open kitchen door, his eyes on Max as he listened to the answering machine.

"Hi, Dori," Peg's voice said. "It's Mom. Dad and I just got in from the doctor's, and I wanted to report that he's doing better this week. The doctor was pleased, so thanks for talking to your father so sternly.

I think the threat to come and cook for us is what turned him around. Love you. Mom.''

Now that was strange, Sal thought. That message didn't sound as though Peg and Dori had just talked. He went back to the table, pushed the caller ID button and flashed to the call before Peg's.

He frowned as he read the name: Voicestream, and a 555 number. A cell phone. He hit the flash several more times on the chance there'd been a call he hadn't heard. But there hadn't.

He lifted Max out of his playpen and went to the foot of the stairs. "Dori!" he shouted. There was no answer.

An awful suspicion formed in his mind. He ran upstairs and pushed open her office door. The room was empty.

Swearing and hoping Max was too young to pick up bad language, he sprinted out to the front door. He half expected to see the car missing.

Then he realized he would have heard her if she'd started the motor. So that meant she *really* hadn't wanted him to know she was leaving.

He checked the geranium on the porch under which she usually left a spare car key—and found it. He pulled the door closed and ran down the porch steps to the car, fumbling a little as he stuffed Max into his car seat.

Then he ran to the driver's door and let himself in, thinking gratefully that there was only one route to town. And if she'd left on foot, she had only a ten-minute head start on him.

He was sure this had something to do with Brenda Ward. Dori knew he would never let her meet the young woman without him, so she'd put on that performance to keep him out of her way. He didn't know what he was more furious about—the lie or the potential danger in her going off alone.

He spotted her halfway to town, khaki shorts and pink T-shirt swaying in a seductive quick-step as she hurried along, her purse over her shoulder.

Traffic was light, only a log truck far ahead of her and an SUV some distance behind him. He accelerated and reached her just as she turned to cross the highway, probably to walk the rest of the way in the shady shelter of a long line of hawthorne trees.

He pulled up in front of her, just as she stepped off the curb. She looked first startled, then exasperated, then reluctant to get into the car when he leaned across the front seat and opened the door.

"Get in," he ordered quietly.

She seemed to square her shoulders. "I have every—"

"We're not having this argument in the middle of the road," he said. "Get—in."

"If I get in," she asked, remaining stubbornly where she was, "will you just pull over and let me explain?"

He drew a breath for patience. "Your getting in is not negotiable. If I have to get out and put you in the car, neither one of us is going to like it."

She gave him one last defiant look, which he met intrepidly, then climbed in and closed her door. He took the first turnoff to the beach and pulled onto the far end of the pavement where the road met the deep expanse of sand.

He turned off the motor and angled his body in his seat, waiting for her to explain. Max, mercifully, had been mesmerized by the short ride and had fallen asleep.

She glanced at her watch. "Please, Sal," she said urgently. "I have only fifteen minutes left to get there."

He ignored that. "Your mother called," he said. "She and your dad were just back from the doctor's. He's doing well. She credits your threatening to cook with turning him around."

She had the grace to look sheepish.

"So, who called," he asked, "when you told me it was your mother?"

She sighed. "Brenda Ward," she replied, then glanced at her watch. "I have fourteen minutes left." She looked up at him imploringly. "Please let me go."

"Sorry. Where were you meeting her?"

"The park. Sal…"

"Where in the park?"

"The bench behind the playground under the maple tree. Sal…"

He pulled out his cell phone and began to dial.

She reached across him to catch his arm. "Please, don't! I was bringing her the money so she could turn it over to the police. Then she'll sign the release form for me to adopt Max."

He hit the cancel button and started over, giving her a doubtful look.

She caught his arm again. "Sal! If she turns over the money, she might not have to go to jail when they find Valdefiero. But if she finds she *can't* trust me, she might change her mind about Max."

"She let a hoodlum in to steal money from a church!" he reminded her a little hotly. "And you can get Max in court."

"She's trying to right the wrong!"

He shook his head at her. "Or she's trying to lure you there so she can simply get the money back."

"Well, let me find that out for sure!"

After Sal finally dialed the number, Bram Bishop answered. Sal explained the meeting place Dori and Brenda had agreed upon.

Dori slammed back against her seat, tears of temper streaming down her cheeks.

"They were to meet at three o'clock," Sal said. "I'd meet you there, but I don't trust her to go home if I don't take her there myself. So you might want to bring back up. I have a feeling the boyfriend's either involved in it with her, or forced her to set up the meeting. And he was part of a gang, remember, so he might not be there alone."

"I've got it covered," Bram promised. "I'll let you know what happens."

"Thanks."

They drove home in silence. When they arrived, Dori took the baby out of the back of the car, then put him in the crib in the downstairs bedroom and pulled the door partially closed.

Sal went into the kitchen to fill the kettle.

"I thought I'd make tea," he said as she stormed in, "since you only pretended to the last time."

"I am an adult!" she said, so angry that she was on tiptoe as she pointed to herself. "I have every ri—"

"Adults don't lie to one another," he returned calmly, setting the filled kettle on the burner and turning it on.

"Oh, well, that must be why I thought Desideria was your friend and not your sister!"

She had him there, but he wasn't giving an inch on this. He reached above him for cups. "I wasn't the one who introduced you," he reminded her.

"You also never corrected the impression!"

"It was her wish."

"Well, it was Brenda Ward's wish that I meet her at the park!"

He turned to her, hands on his hips, her attitude doing nothing to quiet the temper he was trying very hard to control.

"I can't believe," he pointed out reasonably, "that if you're such an *adult*, it didn't occur to you that meeting her could be dangerous. What if her boyfriend put her up to calling you just to get the money back, and he and his friends were waiting for you at the park, instead of her?"

THAT HADN'T OCCURRED to her until he'd brought it up. It sounded logical when he suggested it, but she simply hadn't thought of it. "She said she wanted to give it to the police," she said stubbornly.

"But she would, wouldn't she? Particularly if she's dealing with someone gullible enough to believe her."

She folded her arms. "Well, it sounded reasonable to me."

"Did it?" he asked pleasantly, leaning back against the counter. "Then why didn't you tell me where you were going?"

She knew this was a trap, but she answered just to show him she wasn't intimidated. "Because I knew you'd tell me not to go."

"Now, why would I do that?" He watched her innocently, setting her up.

"Because you'd get all paranoid and feel sure it was somehow dangerous."

His temper flashed at her reply, but his voice remained quiet. "And whose instincts would we trust on this? Yours, as a writer and a teacher of English Literature, or mine, as a bodyguard and former thief?"

Her argument lost, she was so frustrated that all she could think to do was turn up the volume. "I just wanted to help her! I know what it's like to have everyone misjudge you!"

"I presume you're talking about the way your family tends to hover over you," he said coolly. "Well after your behavior this afternoon, I don't think you've been misjudged at all. In fact, I don't think it would be out of line to fix you with one of those monitoring anklets."

"Pardon me," she retorted, lowering her voice as she heard the baby stir, "but I don't think you're in a position to judge me, considering you married me, then abandoned me for two years.''

He closed his eyes and groaned. ''*Dios,* Dori. I think you really having nothing to complain about in your life, so you bring up the old stuff over and over. You're the one who resurrected our marriage by coming to find me, by seducing me, by saving yourself for me. So don't blame *me* because you're too much the baby of the family to know what to do with a real relationship!''

She was so outraged that she sputtered. ''I knew what to do with it! You just weren't around to do it with!''

''I'm here now!''

She walked up to within an inch of him and glared up into his face. ''Well, I don't need you now. If all you're going to do is tell me what I can and cannot do, then you can get the hell out of my life.''

He leaned down to her until they were nose to nose. ''Don't lie about it, Dori. You're not upset because you feel overprotected. You're just mad because I stopped you from doing what you wanted to do. I think that's the same problem you have with your brothers. You're just ticked off that you can't do whatever you damn well please. Well, let me tell you, *querida,* it doesn't work that way. Everything you do affects everyone who cares about you. You're not in this alone.''

''Well, I'd like to be!'' She unscrewed the back of the earring that had once been her wedding ring, and slapped it on the counter. ''Hopefully Bram will solve this thing this afternoon, and you can go home. I'll call my lawyer in the morning. I'm going back to work. Call me when Max wakes up, and I'll come down."

She turned with great dignity and walked out of the kitchen, shoulders straight, step resolved. She was only three steps out of the kitchen, when he caught her arm and turned her around.

"You're running away from us again?" he asked, his fingers biting into her arm.

She tried to break free of him, but he held on. "Well, it doesn't seem to be working, does it?"

There was genuine puzzlement in his eyes, as though he couldn't understand why she thought that. "Of course it's working. You just don't want to do what it requires."

"Accede to *your* wishes, you mean?"

"Yes!" he replied hotly. "When that wish is that you don't get yourself hurt, or worse!"

"I've managed for twenty-six years, thank you very much."

He dropped her arm with a resigned expression. "Yes, with an army of McKeons to keep you from harm. Go back to work. Two-hundred-year-old literature seems to be all you have the capacity to understand."

Now no longer concerned with dignity, only escape, Dori hurried up the stairs.

She put Sal out of her mind as she sat stiffly in her chair, trying to remember what she'd been working on when the call had come from Brenda.

Bram called at four forty-five. Dori reached for the

phone, but Sal had already picked it up. She ignored it until Sal rapped on her door.

"Bram wants to talk to you," he said, then walked away.

Dori picked up the receiver. "Hi, Bram," she said.

"Dori, hi. I'm sorry, but we weren't able to grab Brenda. She wasn't on the bench at all, but in a van waiting on the street. I ran the plates, and it's registered to her boyfriend."

Dori hated to believe that strained voice hadn't been genuine. "He probably forced her to call me."

"That's possible," Bram said. "But had you gone, the result would have been the same whether he forced her or she did it on her own. He was there with several friends."

"Thank you, Bram."

"Sure. I'll be in touch."

She hung up the phone and went downstairs. She found Sal in the kitchen. The aroma of chili wafted out of a big pot on a back burner, and the room was filled with the smell of baking cornbread.

He usually cut up jalapénos in it, she remembered absently.

Max sat in the high chair with a handful of Cheerios. Dori went to him when he uttered a shrill sound and reached for her. She lifted him onto her hip, loving the way he bounced in her arms, clearly happy to see her.

Sal turned from chopping green onions, probably for the salad in a bowl on the counter.

"The boyfriend was there," Dori said.

Sal nodded. "Bram told me."

"So you were right and I was wrong." She knew her tone was not at all conciliatory.

He nodded again. "The world will not collapse."

"But it doesn't change anything," she insisted stiffly. "I'm calling my lawyer in the morning."

"So you've said."

"We've always been a mistake."

He shrugged a shoulder. "So it would seem."

Dori was a little startled to hear him admit that. He'd always been so insistent that it would work out, if she would simply listen, or change, or something.

It seemed to burn a little hole inside her. It must really be over if he thought so, too.

Suddenly her brain was filled with memories of the past several days, of their happiness together and their delight in Max's tiny bud of a tooth, in his ability to sit up, memories of the lovemaking that made her forget everything for a time, except how perfectly she and Sal fit together, and how wonderful she felt in his arms.

She made herself nod amiably. "Well. This should be easier to deal with now that we're in agreement."

He turned back to the chili. "We can only hope. Are you ready for dinner?"

"Are you ready to serve?"

He grinned at her over his shoulder as he checked the cornbread. "Don't be too agreeable. Then the world might collapse, after all."

She listened to the local radio station while preparing for bed that night, and heard the pastor of Faith Community profusely thank the anonymous donor who'd replaced the stolen roof-fund money.

"Our entire congregation will pray for you," he promised. "Whoever you are."

Feeling oddly defeated, Dori got into bed. How did a woman stand up against the man who'd just earned the prayers of hundreds of God-fearing people?

CHAPTER TEN

DORI STUMBLED DOWN to breakfast at seven. Max, riding her hip, was far too lively for a baby who'd been up most of the night teething. The companion tooth to his first was breaking through, and he'd been up every hour on the hour. Or so it had felt.

Sal had offered to relieve her twice, but she'd turned him down politely, determined that she was going to learn to function without the man coming to her aid all the time.

But she hadn't expected to have to do it without breakfast. The table was set with silverware, and a nice aroma lingered, but the kitchen was quiet.

Sal's bedroom door had been open when she'd passed, and she'd seen that his bed was made. Had he left already, she wondered? Had he decided not to wait until the issue of Brenda and her boyfriend was resolved?

She had a brief mental image of that face in the window the other night, of her planned meeting with Brenda's boyfriend yesterday—which hadn't happened but might have—and realized for the first time what it would have felt like to be alone through all of that.

Was she about to face the rest of it alone? As fear

threatened to overwhelm her, she reminded herself that this was what she wanted. She could do this. At the moment she didn't particularly want to, but she could.

The back door was open, summer fragrances wafting through on a breeze. She went to the screen door and looked out. There was no one at the picnic table, and only Cheddar occupied the hammock.

Everything inside Dori seemed to sink to her toes.

"I guess it's just you and me, baby," she said to Max, putting him in his high chair and going to the cupboard for more Cheerios to keep him happy until she could mix baby cereal.

There was an odd pressure in her heart and in her throat. But she'd be fine. Fine.

She put a bright yellow plastic bowl with the Cheerios on Max's tray, then went to the refrigerator for the carton of eggs and the gallon of milk.

When she turned around to bump the door closed with her hip, a man stood there, startling her out of her wits. She managed to juggle the egg carton, but the milk fell like a stone. The wax container exploded, and milk flew everywhere.

Max, apparently of the opinion that she'd done it just for his entertainment, laughed gleefully.

Sal, momentarily unfamiliar in a white T-shirt and jeans, arched an eyebrow at her violent reaction.

She closed her eyes as her pulse dribbled back to normal. When she opened them again, she saw that the basket he held contained black cherries, half a dozen navel oranges, several fat, glossy plums, and a bunch of green grapes. The spray of milk had fortunately been close to the ground and had missed her shorts and his jeans.

"Sorry," he said. "Mrs. Fisher up the hill came over with these. She and her husband are just back from a cruise, and bought these at a roadside stand yesterday on their way home from Portland."

Once Dori got over her alarm, a sense of relief and renewed security filled her, despite the milk mess. But she tried to act casual.

"*I'm* sorry," she said. "I got very little sleep."

He nodded, stepping carefully over the little white river to put the basket on the counter. "I heard you. I'll get the mop."

"I'll clean it up." She, too, moved cautiously to put the eggs on the counter. "It's my mess."

She stopped arguing when she heard him fill a bucket in the service porch. She got a colander from a bottom cupboard and put the fruit in it to rinse.

"I'll start breakfast," she said, as Sal reappeared with the sudsy bucket and a sponge mop.

He frowned at her as he set to work. "I've eaten. Your breakfast is in the oven."

"It is?" She peered in, surprised, and found a plate of golden-brown French toast and a pipkin of syrup warming. No wonder the kitchen was aromatic. She reached for a pot holder and pulled them out. "Thank you."

"Sure," he said as he worked. "I presume that part of the deal remains in effect? I cook while you work?"

Before she could answer, there was a firm, even authoritative knock on the front door. Hoping that didn't mean her brothers were home early, Dori went to answer it.

"Wait!" Sal shouted.

An impatient retort came to her lips, but she bit it back and spread her arms in an exaggerated gesture, ushering him before her.

"Stay in here with the baby," he said. "Eat your breakfast."

She rolled her eyes. "You know, one day you're going to need me to defend *you,* only you won't call for me because it won't occur to you that I'm competent enough to help."

He'd started toward the door, then turned back to her, apparently surprised by her remark. "How have you gotten that so twisted?" he asked.

Now she was surprised. "What?"

"The concept of man and woman," he replied, as another series of loud raps sounded on the door. "We protect you not because you're incapable, but because you're precious to us."

He strode toward the door, and she remained where she stood, made boneless by that explanation.

Sal opened the door.

Dori couldn't see beyond him, but she didn't have to. She recognized the gasp instantly, and the shrieked "Sal! Oh, my God, it's true! I can't believe it!"

Her mother. Dori put both hands to her face and thought that if anything could worsen a morning that had started with a sleepless night and spilled milk, it was the arrival of Peg McKeon.

"Peg. How nice to see you." Sal leaned down for

her mother's hug, then drew her into the house. He turned to Dori with a bland look that she interpreted as barely concealed delight over her impending doom. "Dori, your mom's here."

Dori came forward to hug her mother. Meetings among the McKeons after a separation of more than a day always began with a hug, whether the purpose of the meeting was friendly or hostile.

Her mother returned the hug, then stepped back to shake her finger at her. Peg's eyebrows converged, her cheeks pinked and her mouth had a definite downward curve.

"Dorianne Margaret McKeon!" she said as though Dori were four years old. "You are in so much trouble!"

Tell me about it, Dori thought. This confrontation with her mother was probably going to be worse than anything Brenda's boyfriend could have conceived.

"Would you like some coffee, Peg?" Sal asked, leading her to the sofa. "A cup of tea?"

"I'll have two fingers of brandy," Peg replied, settling into the middle of the sofa, her arms crossed over the purse in her lap. "And please don't dawdle. Charlie and Dori's aunt Letitia and cousin Natalie are on their way. Well, they're not on their way, they're waiting for me to get back to the restaurant, but they'll *be* here today—and we have to clear up a few things before they arrive."

That didn't entirely make sense to Dori, but she felt a very lively sense of panic, anyway. For a woman who was created from the same gene pool as Dori's father,

Aunt Titia had none of his endearing qualities. She was pushy, condescending and forever putting her children forward as superior to her brother's—something that had always entertained the McKeon boys because they'd all been overachievers and hadn't cared. Dori had laughed, too, because it was expected of her.

Gordon Browning was a physicist, and Chase Browning had something to do with software at the Pentagon. Dori hadn't cared much about the successes of her male cousins. No one really compared her to them. But Nattie was an anchor on the KRTV Philadelphia evening news. Natalie was five foot nine, golden blond, with wide gray eyes and delicate features in a face that was a perfect oval.

"How is little Dori?" Aunt Titia would usually preface an interrogation. "She must have a boyfriend by now! Does she have that degree yet? Has she started on *the book?*" Titia always verbally italicized *the book.* When the book was finished, Titia was definitely one of the people Dori intended to invite to her autograph party.

"What is she doing here?" Dori asked now, sitting in a corner of the sofa, reminding herself that this summer was about taking control. It's a shame it wasn't about telling lies and springing surprises, she thought in a state of mild hysteria. She'd have that one sewn up.

Peg waved a hand dismissively. "I don't know. Nattie's getting some honor or other in San Francisco, and Titia's riding her coattails. But that's not what I'm here to talk about!"

Dori accepted that with a nod. "What are you here to talk about?"

Peg yanked her purse open and removed a copy of the local newspaper, folded in four. Dori knew her mother and father subscribed to the paper and had it mailed to their home in Edenfield so they could keep abreast of Dancer's Beach happenings.

"I was reading this last night, when your aunt called from the Portland airport and said she and Nattie were on their way to San Francisco and thought it would be nice if they dropped in on the relatives on their way."

Her mother made a face and added as a personal aside, "You know. Spread a little cheer among the peasants. Let them see how the other half lives. The only one of you children she's ever had any respect for is Duncan because he's a big star, but she told me just last night that he'll finally get somewhere when he gets a television series. It made me want to put her head in the microwave on defrost at the first opportunity!"

The image almost made Dori smile, but she was pretty sure that wasn't the right move at the moment. So she just listened.

"'Nattie would love to see her cousin,'" Peg quoted Letitia. "Of course, I interpreted that to mean that Nattie wanted to come and gloat that she has a three-carat diamond, and that little Dori is still single and living alone in a beach house writing a book."

"I'm—" Dori attempted to interrupt but was turned off with a dark look.

"So, I promised we'd come. They can only stay one night because they have to be in San Francisco the day after tomorrow. Well, your father's going stir-crazy in the house, so I thought, wouldn't it be nice if we all paid a surprise visit to Dori? So we pile in the car early this morning, and I'm telling them that you now have your degree and you *are* working on the book, and Nattie says we should plan to take you out to lunch since you probably won't want to cook—at which point Titia reminds everyone of the potato salad incident at the family reunion…"

"I explained," Dori said with a sigh, amazed that Aunt Titia still remembered, "that lots of people have made the sugar and salt mistake."

"I know, and we all understand because we love you—but we're talking about your aunt Titia."

"So, to continue…?"

"Right. Well. Because I'm driving, I ask your father to look in the paper, which I've brought along because there was a coupon in it for twenty-percent off anything at the antique shop, and I wanted to check to see if Burgers by the Sea has anything but burgers. I know you kids go there all the time, but your father and I usually eat at home when we're here."

She accepted a jigger of brandy from Sal, took a swig Dori was sure would cause her to turn purple, then continued with barely a grimace. "Then your father says, 'Peg, let's stop at Burgers and see for ourselves what's on the lunch menu.'" I look at him to tell him we can just call from your house, and he's wearing this odd, desperate look. You know your father. He doesn't know how to panic."

Dori nodded. Everyone knew that.

"He insisted we stop for coffee and check it out. Your aunt said she was tired and needed a bathroom, and why didn't we go straight to Dori's, but Nattie said it'd be a good idea to check it out and she could use a cup of coffee. So we stopped." Peg drew another breath, took another deep swig, then shook the paper to unfold it. "And while Titia and Nattie are in the bathroom, your father shows me *this!*"

She handed the paper over. Sal leaned over the back of the sofa to read over Dori's shoulder. It was the editorial page, where Burgers by the Sea always had an ad.

And then she saw the column entitled "On the Public Record." The third item was about the prowler at the beach house, and all the information was correct—including the names of the residents with whom the police had spoken: Salvatore Dominguez and Dorianne Dominguez.

"So, on the pretext of not being able to reach you by phone to tell you we were coming," her mother said, "I left them at the restaurant and came to see if you were home while they're relaxing with coffee."

It was a plot worthy of the CIA, Dori thought.

"Dominguez?" her mother asked, her voice rising an octave and a decibel. She finished the brandy. "Dorianne *Dominguez?*"

Dori folded the paper and handed it back. "We were married," she said, knowing she was going to have to be firm if she was going to take control of this situation, "in Mexico."

"What?" Peg demanded. "When did you go to Mexico?"

Dori enjoyed her mother's shock. Peg was usually so unshockable. And then Dori remembered that she had to tell her how long ago it had been.

"Two years ago," she replied with a matter-of-factness that was completely bogus. "I'd just come back from England and I'd been thinking about him all the time and I decided that maybe I was wrong about us and that I should see if he still felt the same."

Her mother looked up at Sal. "And you did?"

"I did," he replied.

"Well, pardon me for wanting to murder both of you!" Peg shouted. "But why wasn't her family invited to the wedding?"

Dori opened her mouth to reply, but Sal cut her off with "I take responsibility for that." He looked properly penitent. "I insisted that we get married right away. I didn't know what had changed her mind, or what might change it back, so we were married within a week of her arrival in Madre Maria."

Peg looked from one to the other in astonishment. "And you've been married for two whole years, and no one told us? How can that be?"

Dori sighed. This was going to be grizzly. "Because we've been married for two years but we haven't lived together since our wedding day."

Peg picked up the jigger, now empty of brandy, and looked as though she might chew the glass. "Why?"

Dori explained.

Peg frowned at Sal. Dori waited for her to lay into

him for leaving her daughter on their wedding day, but all she said was "I can't believe we weren't invited."

"I'm sorry," he said.

Then there was a loud, prolonged shout from the kitchen and the banging of little feet against the high chair's footboard.

Peg lifted her chin, and Dori knew she was scenting the air, like a predator that had found new prey. "What is that?"

Dori put both hands over her eyes.

"I'll show you," Sal said, and disappeared into the kitchen.

Dori concluded later that Max was the only reason her mother didn't kill them both. Sal put him in Peg's lap and she was transformed instantly from an angry goddess to a besotted earth mother. Max responded brilliantly to her effusive attention.

"So, he was conceived in that week before your wedding day?" her mother considered. "We can pass that off to Aunt Titia as a wedding-night home run."

Sal now sat in a chair opposite the sofa and met Dori's eyes. His gaze said she had to take responsibility for this one.

"Mom, Max was left in my car," Dori began. At her mother's shocked expression, she explained about finding the baby, about going to Sal, about his insistence on returning with her. But she left out the face at the window and the aborted meeting with Brenda.

Peg dandled the baby on her knee and made funny faces at him, while he watched in fascination. "Sal," she said, her tone of voice not at all in line with her comic expressions. "Are you telling me you're here only to keep them safe until this mystery is solved?"

Dori suddenly saw a way to redeem herself. "Actually," Dori said, willing him with her eyes to understand her course of action and follow it, "we've fallen in love again since we've been here together."

"You have?" Peg glanced away from the baby to catch Sal's eye. Hers were hopeful.

He was still staring at Dori, his expression telling her she couldn't throw him out of her life one minute and expect him to act the lover the next.

She pleaded with a look. "Haven't we, *querido?*"

SAL ENJOYED THE MOMENT. She was wheedling—and charming about it—but he had to have more than that.

He looked away from her to smile at her mother. "Spending time with your daughter is always an experience."

Peg rolled her eyes. "I raised her. I know that. But do you love her, after what she's done to you?"

Dori gasped. "What *I've* done to *him?*" she demanded. "He left me on—!"

"Your wedding day," her mother nodded. "The same thing your brothers would have done for you had *your* life been in danger. And don't forget that he saved you from Suarez."

Dori fell back against the sofa with a groan. "Mother, I—"

Peg didn't even hear her. "I want to hear you tell me that you love her," she insisted to Sal.

Well. That was true enough. "Yes, I do love her," he said.

Peg hugged the baby to her and nibbled on his neck. He laughed in hysterical little hiccups. "Thank God! Then we can bring Titia and Nattie here, and everything will be fine!" She waggled her eyebrows greedily. "And my daughter's married before hers to a handsome man in a sexy and dangerous business. Oh, this is almost too good! And a baby to boot! Nattie's going to be so jealous of you!"

Dori almost felt sorry for her cousin. They'd always liked each other well enough, but though Nattie had never precisely bragged, she'd been happy to list each new accomplishment at family gatherings. Dori had been delighted when the Brownings moved to the east coast when Nattie was in high school. They'd seen each other only occasionally since then.

"Okay! Sal, come and take this baby so I can get back to the restaurant and report that you're home and eager to see us."

Dori saw her mother to the door, then returned at a run, picking up toys and fluffing and redistributing pillows.

"DID MAX EVER have anything but those Cheerios?" Sal asked her, keeping his voice and his manner deliberately polite.

"Uh, no." She dropped the toys into a laundry basket she kept in a corner.

"Okay." He carried Max back into the kitchen, put him in his high chair, and found the baby cereal and the bowl Dori had taken down for breakfast. He mixed the cereal up while Max protested the delay. Then Sal sat beside him and concentrated on spooning in one bite after another.

Dori flew into the kitchen a few minutes later with teacups she tended to hoard upstairs. She put them into the dishwasher and chewed on one of her now cold pieces of French toast while she added other things to the rack. After she closed the washer, she poured out the last half cup of coffee in the carafe and made another pot.

"What'll we do for dinner?" she asked anxiously, wiping off the counters. "When did you finish mopping up the milk?"

"When I got your mother's brandy. And don't worry about dinner. I'll make cheese enchiladas, rice, beans and salad."

She looked doubtful. "This is my aunt Titia. She hates everything."

"Then it doesn't matter what we prepare, does it?"

She came to sit in the chair on the other side of the baby so she could look at him. Her eyes were dark with worry and uncertainty. She tried to smile. "Thank you for saying you love me. Otherwise, my mother really would have freaked."

He didn't look at her, but spooned baby cereal into Max's open mouth. Max kicked and banged his hands on the tray, clearly enjoying it.

"I didn't do that for you," he informed her.

She looked momentarily upset. "Then why did you do it?"

Max reached for the next bite, but Sal held firmly to the spoon. "Because it was true," he replied, holding the baby's free hand down. "But she doesn't have to know that between us love isn't everything."

She looked as though she wanted to argue, but she knew there wasn't time. Still, there was obviously something else on her mind.

"What?" he asked. When Max started to wrestle him for the spoon, he gave it to him and capped the baby food jar.

"I just want to...to make sure..." She was having trouble getting out whatever it was. He didn't feel inclined to help her.

"To make sure," she repeated, "that you—you know—sort of...*act* like you love me."

She heaved a sigh once that was out.

He put the baby food jar in the refrigerator, then wet a paper towel and dabbed at the baby's face. The action required the speed of a quick-draw artist.

"You intend to choreograph the action?" he asked, untying the messy bib.

She sounded offended. "No. So that I won't be humiliated in front of my aunt and my cousin. Having a handsome, sexy, dangerous husband who could care less about me would be worse than being single and all by myself, working on my book."

He met her eyes. "And why does what she thinks matter?" he asked.

She shrugged. "Because Nattie's always been better at everything than me. Because everybody's always known she's special, and I've just been 'little' Dori, who always had her nose in a book when everyone else was doing something big.''

He shook his head at her. ''I think you wish you were different, more than your family wishes you were different. I don't think they compare you with the boys or your cousins—I think *you* do. And for reasons I don't understand—unless you consider how bad you are at being in love—you don't think you rate well by comparison.''

She looked desperate. The subject was a little heavy for the ticking clock.

''Just tell me,'' she pleaded, ''that you'll act like a loving husband.''

''What's in it for me?'' he asked brutally.

She played with her fingers. ''What do you want?''

''You'll have to sleep with me tonight,'' he said, ''if you want me to look like a loving husband.''

''I know. I've thought about that.''

''Well, I've spent enough nights in the same bed with you without touching you. I want to make love to you.''

She looked troubled. He couldn't decide whether she found the idea distasteful or simply surprising. ''All right,'' she finally replied.

''Then you've got a deal.'' He offered his hand across the table.

She reached over to shake it. Then she sighed dispiritedly. ''I hope it works better than the last deal we made.''

''The promise to love each other until death do us

part?'' he asked. ''Or the one we made on the way over *not* to love each other?''

She stood and spread her arms helplessly. ''We haven't successfully completed either one.

''Yes, we have. The only problem is, you kept one promise and I kept the other.''

CHAPTER ELEVEN

DORI'S AUNT TITIA was tall and angular and very elegantly dressed. She wore pants and a loose shirt in a silky gray fabric that billowed out behind her as she moved, a little like royal robes.

She had side-parted, chin-length gray hair that curved around the strong bones of her face in a flattering frame. A wave at her left temple was streaked with white.

She was perfectly put together, Sal thought, but without the spark of warmth and humor that made beauty live.

Her daughter Natalie had it, he noticed. She was as tall as her mother and slender, but more shapely than angular. She wore the large diamond Dori had talked about, but there was a sweetness in her smile that couldn't be manufactured.

"Well, there's little Dori," Titia said, gathering her niece into her embrace. Dori became lost in the woman's height and voluminous shirt. "How are you, darling?" she enquired in the tone of voice with which someone might ask *Did anyone come out alive?*

Natalie rolled her eyes in an expression of amused sympathy. Then she hugged Dori herself.

"Hey, Dori!" she said, holding her cousin away to look at her. "I love your hair! I've always been so jealous that you have that great brain, yet you'll always look sixteen. It isn't fair, you know."

"Yeah, right." Dori laughed. "You're such a mud fence with only two million viewers every day."

Sal, with Max on his hip, moved up behind Dori.

Titia turned from a smiling perusal of her daughter and her niece, and noticed Sal for the first time. Her eyes went from him to the baby to Dori, then back again in growing puzzlement.

"Titia, I'd like you to meet my son-in-law," Peg said with obvious relish, "Salvatore Dominguez. Sal, this is Charlie's sister, Letitia Browning."

Sal shook Titia's hand. She stared at him and said nothing.

"And this is our niece, Natalie. Nattie, meet Sal."

Natalie smiled warmly at him and gave him a quick hug. "Well, how wonderful! I don't mean to be rude, Sal, but you don't look like someone she met in a library."

"He's the one who kidnapped her at the airport during the Julie incident," Peg said, clearly enjoying herself. "Remember, we talked about it on the phone the Christmas after it happened and you said it sounded so romantic? Well, apparently it was. Sal now has a security firm in Seattle."

"My goodness." Natalie sighed. "Well, now I'm even more jealous than ever. A husband who looks like a mature Ricky Martin, and a baby?"

"The baby, Max, is going to be theirs eventually,

but that's rather a long story. Why don't we all get comfortable, first?'' Peg prepared to shoo everyone into the living room, but a frowning Titia stopped her with a "Well!"

"Mom," Sal heard Natalie warn her mother under her breath.

"I don't remember hearing about a wedding," Titia insisted. "And I do not remember receiving an invitation."

"We were married in Mexico," Dori said. "Kind of quickly. My parents didn't even know until...later."

Titia looked Sal over again. "Mexico? I suppose your family's there?"

Sal put a hand on Dori's shoulder and drew her just a little closer. "No. They're gone. This is my family."

Natalie held her hands out to Max, who leaned toward her, showing his obvious good taste. She took him into her arms and sat with him in a chair.

Titia frowned. "Well, what ever happened to big family weddings where everyone was invited? Chase and his fiancée tried to pull one of those elopement things on me, and I said, 'Absolutely not!' Why not tell the world you're getting married, unless you have something to hide?"

"You mean, like our criminal pasts?" Dori asked her aunt seriously.

Sal was happy to leap into the middle. "Or the two children we had out of wedlock?"

Peg's eyes widened. Charlie turned away with a cough and limped toward the sofa.

Titia blinked. "I wasn't suggesting..." she began, her voice a little high.

"Good," Sal said, "because we weren't hiding anything." He wrapped his arm around Dori's shoulders and pulled her against his body. "We're just very independent people who knew we wanted to be together. We just couldn't decide on whose terms. So when she came to visit me in Mexico, I didn't want her to have a chance to change her mind. So I married her as quickly as I could."

Titia blinked again. "I see."

"He's a man of action, Mom," Natalie said from the chair, where she lifted the giggling baby up and down and laughed at his delight. "You just haven't known any of those. Come and sit down."

Titia frowned at Peg. "You were going to explain about the baby."

"Yes." Peg led her to the sofa. "Get comfortable. It's an interesting story."

"I'll get us something cold to drink." Dori slipped out of Sal's arm and went into the kitchen.

"Charlie, if you give me your keys," Sal said, "I'll get your bags out of the car and take them upstairs."

Charlie struggled off the sofa, as the women began to talk. "I'll give you a hand."

Sal started to tell him that wasn't necessary, thinking of his new knee, but Charlie gave him a look that told him they had things to talk about.

Once outside, Charlie didn't pull any punches. "You married my baby without telling me," he accused.

"Yes, I did," Sal admitted, as he walked and Charlie hobbled to the van.

"I got a very garbled account of what happened from Peg after she put Titia and Natalie in the van and got me aside on the pretext of making reservations for lunch at Burgers by the Sea. Reservations! At Burgers! Do you see the level of subterfuge she's sunk to!"

Sal found all of that more comic than upsetting, but then, he didn't have to live with Peg.

"I'm sorry," he said again.

"I don't want you to be sorry," Charlie said querulously. "What's done is done, and I always liked you. But from what I got from Peg in a shouted whisper behind the Dumpster at Burgers, you two quarreled again the day of the wedding and have been separated all this time and just got together again because of the baby—" Charlie winced "—that was left in her car?"

"That's right?"

"My God."

"I know."

"And you've fallen in love again?"

He didn't want to lie to Charlie, but found a way to tell him the truth. "I never fell *out* of love with her. She's just stubborn and hardheaded and wouldn't listen to reason."

Charlie laughed mirthlessly. "We all know where that comes from."

"Her mother and some throwback to her aunt Titia?" Sal guessed.

Charlie smiled, his mood lightening. "You got that

right. I just want some reassurance that you're making her happy."

Again, the truth just had to be carefully put. "When she lets me, I make her happy."

Charlie sighed. "And does she make *you* happy?"

Sal thought that through and finally sighed. "She makes me crazy," he replied candidly. "She makes me question everything I know to be true, including my own sanity. She doesn't do anything the way I would or see anything the way I see it. Sometimes she makes me feel as though I'm speaking Martian. But somehow she reaches me here—" He put a hand over his heart. "She bypasses my brain altogether, but I feel as though my heart doesn't beat without her."

Charlie patted his shoulder sympathetically. "You poor devil. If it's any comfort, it evens out a little as you mature, but you're never going to belong to yourself again, and the world will always be a little off-kilter."

Sal nodded, accepting that. "Thank God for gravity."

Charlie laughed. "And whiskey."

DORI INSISTED on helping Sal with dinner. He wore a white apron over a black shirt and pants, and grinned at her over the steam rising from sauteeing onions.

"Have you suddenly learned to cook?" he asked.

"Ha, ha," she said, refusing to take offense. Then she added softly, "I just think it'll look better if I'm helping."

"Won't it 'look better' if you're out there entertaining your aunt?"

She shuddered dramatically. "Please don't make me go back out there."

"Your choice. Want to make the salad?"

"Sure." She was capable of washing lettuce and chopping vegetables. She pulled the greens and other makings out of the crisper. "Ah, lettuce in a bag," she said, finding the scissors to cut it open. "I'd be such a happy camper if you could buy stuffed pork chops in a bag, or chicken Kiev."

"You can probably find those things frozen."

"I know, but that's not the same."

"Then you have to move to the big city where you can be closer to a good delicatessen."

She emptied the lettuce into a large stainless steel bowl, then dropped radishes, green onions, red and yellow peppers, and tomatoes into a colander and rinsed them.

"I was just beginning to think I might move here full time," she said, smiling in his direction to show that she had no hard feelings about what had happened. She would have loved to live in that old house behind the Bijou.

"This place does grow on you," he said, adding chopped garlic to the pan.

"But you like the big city." She dried off vegetables with paper towels and put the green onions on a cutting board.

"I do. And it would be difficult to find enough clients to sustain a security firm in Dancer's Beach."

"So, what would you do if you had to decide upon a second career?"

He smiled. "It would be a third career. I was a thief first, remember?"

She stopped chopping onions to frown at him. "Why do you keep bringing that up? Do you miss the life, or wish you could erase it from your past?"

His smile waned just a little, and he turned back to add tomato puree, bouillon, and other herbs and spices to the pan. "I guess since we've had Max around, I've been thinking that it's not a very good thing for a child to have a father who was a thief."

"He'd have a father," she reminded him, "who helped his family support a village that otherwise wouldn't even have had basic education and health services."

"I think we need some juice," Natalie said, walking into the kitchen with a wailing Max. "Or milk, or something. I've been doing pretty well with him all afternoon, but either he's decided that I'm not the woman he wanted, after all, or he's hungry."

Dori laughed. "Guys react pretty much the same way to either problem. Here, I'll take him."

"No, you look busy. I can give him a bottle, if that's what he wants."

Dori got one out of the refrigerator and ran it under the hot water. "Maybe if we're lucky, he'll go to sleep with this, and we'll have a peaceful dinner. Do you need something to munch on until then?"

Natalie shook her head. "I'm still stuffed from our burgers at lunch."

Dori handed her the bottle, then a clean tea towel to put over her shoulder. "Now that he's getting teeth, he's droolly. Does your fiancée like children?"

Natalie frowned. "Actually, we've been arguing about that. When we first got engaged, he was just a bit actor on a soap. Now he's on the short list for the starring role in a new sitcom that's going to film in Malibu. He's saying we have to put off the baby because he'll have too much to worry about."

She sounded troubled, and Dori felt sorry for her. When they were young, they played dolls together all the time. Natalie had always wanted babies as much as Dori had.

"Well, how do you feel about it?"

Max had already helped himself to the bottle, and Natalie settled him in the crook of her arm. She made a face. "I don't think it would be wise to coerce someone who doesn't want a baby into having one."

"Sounds to me," Sal contributed, "as though you need to put off the fiancé, not the baby."

Natalie turned to him, new interest in her eyes. "I thought most men were eager to avoid the responsibility of children."

He shook his head. "Not the ones I know."

"Or forget the fiancé altogether," Dori said, "and have the baby without him."

"Without him?"

"Sperm banks are one way to go if you want a baby but don't necessarily want to deal with a man."

"Hmm." Natalie smiled over that. "Now, there's

something to think about. This guy's getting heavy. I'm going to go sit down.''

"I like her," Sal said, as Natalie walked into the living room. "She's very elegant. And there has to be the right man for her somewhere."

"I know," Dori said mournfully. "I've always wanted to look like her. Then I wouldn't be 'little' Dori."

He laughed lightly. "No, you'll always be 'little' Dori because you're small and petite, and because you always look a little lost, as though you're not sure where you belong. So there's a tendency to think of you as someone who needs protection."

"Great." She chopped vigorously. "It isn't likely that I'll grow any more, or that I can change my facial expression, so I'll probably be 'little' Dori forever."

"Enjoy it," he advised. "I'll bet there are lots of people who'd love to have someone worry about them."

Everyone enjoyed Sal's enchiladas. Dori watched her aunt try to needle him, but he remained resolutely polite and charming.

"I can't believe you kept a baby that you found in the back of your car!" she said, turning to Dori when she couldn't upset Sal.

"I didn't want to turn him in to the police," Dori said calmly. "I just fell in love with him."

"We have a detective looking for his mother," Sal added. "When we find her, we can formally file for adoption."

"I don't understand why you just don't have your own."

"We'll do that, too."

Titia shook her head. "You don't tell anyone you're married, you keep a baby that isn't even yours. I don't understand this generation."

"Love makes him theirs, Mom," Natalie said. "And the wedding was their business. Family is wonderful, but sometimes you just have to do what you have to do."

Titia turned on her suspiciously. "If you got married and didn't tell me, I'd never forgive you."

"Then, I guess I'd have to live with that," Natalie said.

Titia turned to Peg and Charlie in horror. "I can't believe what this generation is coming to."

Sal calmed the atmosphere by serving flan for dessert. The conversation turned to the accomplishments of Titia's two sons, and everyone listened dutifully. It was after nine when she pleaded weariness and excused herself to retire for the night.

"Thank you for a wonderful dinner," she said politely to Sal. "I don't understand why little Dori married you without inviting her parents and her family, but I do understand *why* she married you."

Sal bowed modestly. "I appreciate that. Thank you."

When Titia's back was turned on her way to the stairs, Peg gave Sal a thumbs-up.

"Sal and I have been using your bedroom," Dori explained to her parents, "because it was more convenient with the baby. You'd probably like to sleep upstairs tonight, because he's up a couple of times a night. You'll get a better night's sleep."

Peg nodded. "Whatever's more convenient."

"But can your father do the stairs?" Sal asked.

Charlie nodded. "I'm supposed to work out a little on them, so that'll be fine." He asked with an interested twinkle, "What's for breakfast? We have to be at the Portland airport by eleven a.m."

Peg backhanded him in his paunchy stomach. "Cereal and fruit. You ate enough tonight to put your cholesterol in four figures."

Sal leaned toward him conspiratorially. "I'll see what I can do for you," he whispered.

Dori wasn't sure why it pleased her that her father liked Sal—and that Sal liked her father. She would have to call her parents when they got home from the airport tomorrow afternoon and explain that her story about the rebirth of their marriage had been for the benefit of Aunt Titia—and that she was getting a divorce.

But Dori enjoyed watching her mother hug him good-night. And Dori liked the sparkle in Peg's eyes when she smiled up at Sal and told him how much she'd enjoyed dinner and how valuable an addition he was to the family, with his suave good manners and his cooking skills.

She also enjoyed the new respect in her mother's eyes when she hugged Dori good-night.

"I'm upset that you didn't tell us you were married all this time," Peg scolded gently. "But I do applaud you on your good taste and your good sense. I don't think your father and I could have done a better job of finding a man for you than you did yourself. Congratulations.''

That was high praise, indeed. She basked in the glory of it, while Sal helped her father upstairs. Natalie loaded the dishwasher, while Dori wiped off counters and filled the coffeepot for the following morning.

"Now, I'm more jealous than ever," Natalie said, redistributing cups to make room for one more.

"He is a great cook," Dori said.

Natalie nodded. "He is, but I'm not talking about that. I'm talking about the way he looks at you and touches you. As though you'll never have anything to fear again.''

Dori made a face. "Because I'm 'little' Dori.''

Natalie frowned over that. "No. It's more than just protective, it's…possessive. That's what I'd like to see in a man's eyes, but the twenty-first century really doesn't allow for that—unless you're lucky enough to find a man raised with Old World ways. And he looks at the baby the same way, even though Max isn't his biologically.''

Dori pushed the filter basket in place and filled the water well with filtered water. "Your fiancé…''

"Is wonderful in many ways.'' Natalie pushed the dishwasher door closed, then studied the controls. "Shall I leave it the way it's set?'' At Dori's nod, she started it, and they moved by mutual consent to the table and sat down.

"It's just that he's a very contemporary man. I loved

that, at first. My work is all very immediate and I thought I was, too. Until he told me we had to put off having a baby. Then I began to have very old-fashioned feelings about motherhood and home and hearth.'' She smiled across the table at Dori—a smile of congratulations.

''We're all trying so hard to be in the game, you know what I mean? To show how sophisticated and independent we are. And I wonder if we aren't completely losing the ability to live for each other—to know how to love wholeheartedly.''

She leaned her chin on her hand and laughed at herself. ''Listen to me. I don't know what's gotten into me lately. I've always been fairly self-confident and comfortable with who I am, but suddenly I'm questioning everything. I'm wondering if it isn't nature's way of telling me that I'm on the wrong road or something. That I should stop and think before I take another step.''

Dori nodded. ''Stopping to think would never be a bad move, would it?''

''No, I don't think so.'' Natalie straightened in her chair and heaved a sigh, as though she'd come to a decision. ''And now that I've seen what you have, I want that, too.'' She laughed again. ''Sal's yours, I know. But I want someone like him. Someone who looks at me as though I'm his everything.''

She reached across the table to cover Dori's hands with her own. ''I'm so glad I got to see you. I remember what fun we used to have as little girls, before my mother's competitive syndrome took over my life.''

Dori turned her hands to squeeze Natalie's. "I think you should go for whatever it is you want. Maybe there's something in the air, because that was my plan for the summer, too. I wanted to gain my independence and write my book."

"Is it working?"

"I'm not sure." Dori grinned wryly. "It's hard to assert your independence when your life is filled with a demanding baby and a...a possessive man."

"Yeah, well right now I'd kill for either of those. Preferably both." Natalie stood and hugged Dori. "Thanks for your hospitality. We'll have to keep in better touch. You must have an e-mail address?"

"I do." Dori retrieved a business card from her day-timer on the edge of the counter.

Natalie looked at it as though it were precious. "My cards are upstairs. I'll leave one with you in the morning." She hugged her again. "You love that man—and fight for that baby."

"I will," Dori promised. "Good night."

As Natalie went upstairs, Dori stood alone in the middle of the kitchen, feeling as though her entire world was off balance, slipping on its axis, spinning out of control.

Possession meant ownership. How could that be a good thing?

Not that Sal treated her in any way like a slave or a piece of property. However, he did seem to feel entitled to affect or even change some of her decisions, usually in what he considered her best interest. That resulted in her losing control, didn't it?

She heard Sal's footsteps on the stairs; then he walked into the kitchen, unrolling the sleeves he'd folded back while cooking.

"Your parents are settled," he said, his eyes going over her face. "Is something troubling you? I thought the evening went well. We all managed to blockade your aunt so that she couldn't ruin things."

She had to agree. And looking into his face when night had fallen and the house was still always made her wonder why she worried about their relationship in the first place. His quiet, intelligent eyes watching her, his smile always ready, made her feel as though she had slipped into a harbor where she was safe.

But the same thing that comforted her also worried her. He offered safety—just as her brothers had always done. Still, life was supposed to be about risk, adventure and exploration.

"It was a lovely evening," she said, deciding that she didn't feel like any of those things tonight. Right now, she wanted the harbor. "Dinner was wonderful."

"Thank you," he said. He continued to scan her features, as though looking for an answer he couldn't find. He came closer to take her chin between his thumb and forefinger. "Did someone upset you?"

She rested her hands lightly at his waist. "Yes, but not deliberately. It was Nattie."

He raised an eyebrow. "Nattie seems to have great affection for you."

"She does. She said she was jealous of the way you look at me."

"And what way is that?"

"Possessively."

He pinched her chin and then released it. "And you're resenting that because you've decided that it's over between us?"

She retained her hold on him. "No," she replied candidly. "I guess I resent that because I know it *isn't* over."

He frowned and looped his arms loosely around her. "I don't understand."

She sighed and leaned in to him. "Neither do I. Shall we just make love and try to understand it later?"

HE DIDN'T HAVE TO THINK about that twice. He lifted her into his arms and carried her off to bed.

Hours later, he lay with her wrapped in his arms, her bottom tucked against him where he still ached for her, and wondered what had possessed her tonight. She'd made love to him like a woman trying to assume control.

Part of the time, he'd fought her for control because he'd taken charge of things his entire life. But the rest of the time he'd enjoyed the test of wills and the occasional surrender to a fate that was deliciously predictable.

And she had seemed to take pleasure in everything— the battles she'd won and the battles he'd wrested from her. He wondered if she understood that there had been no loser tonight.

CHAPTER TWELVE

SAL DIDN'T UNDERSTAND why Dori seemed even more troubled the following morning. She usually glowed after their lovemaking, but today she was all business in a buttoned-to-the-neck robe she'd borrowed from Harper's closet. She fed the baby, poured coffee for her family, and brought him a cup, as he turned pancakes on the griddle, unable to send Charlie off with just a bowl of cereal.

"Thank you," he said, taking it from her.

He didn't think she'd heard him. Because when she wasn't all business, she seemed completely unfocused. He didn't know what to think.

She'd admitted last night that she still loved him, but she hadn't seemed entirely pleased about it.

There were hugs and goodbyes after breakfast. Natalie teased them by carrying the baby out with her and pretending to put him in the car.

"Give me back that baby!" Dori teased in return. They'd hugged each other, and then Natalie had climbed into the van.

"We'll see you next week for my birthday," her mother said. "You are coming to Edenfield, aren't you?"

Dori looked stricken for a moment, then smiled widely and hugged her mother. "Wouldn't miss it. You drive safely, Dad."

"Always," he said.

Sal stood with his arm around Dori and Max, as they waved her family off.

"Mom's birthday!" Dori said urgently the moment the van was out of sight. "I was supposed to plan a party and I forgot! What'll I do?"

"You mean a party at a restaurant?"

"I don't know. It was supposed to be up to me."

Now she looked distressed. He followed her back into the house. "I was supposed to write my book, assert myself as an independent member of the Mc-Keon family, and I end up with a baby, a husband and terminal confusion!" She glowered at him as though it were all his fault. "And no party!"

"We can pull it together in a week," Sal said bracingly. He could see that she wanted to believe him.

"You think?" she asked.

He was about to reassure her that he did, when the phone rang. She picked up the cordless from the coffee table. Max was pulling at Dori's hair, so Sal took the baby from her, put him in the playpen in the kitchen and handed him one of the soft toys he loved to examine.

Sal was clearing away the table when Dori appeared in the kitchen doorway, her distress hiked up a notch.

"What?" he asked, preparing himself.

"Duncan's been asked to replace Harrison Ford in

the fourth *Raiders* movie," she said tightly. "So the family had to come back from Europe early."

"All of them?"

"Every last one. They called from Chicago. They'll be here tonight, and they asked me to see if I can get the folks here for the next few days, because Duncan has to leave for Africa on Sunday. So we're moving up the birthday party."

"Can you reach your parents?"

She held up the cordless phone. "I called them on their cell phone. They'll come right back after they drop my aunt and my cousin off at the airport."

"Uh-oh."

"We're not going to get it pulled together in eight hours, are we? And I still don't have a present!"

She ran from the room, sobbing.

He stared for a moment at the spot where she'd been. Then he moved Max and the playpen out into the living room and within sight of Cheddar, who slept on the back of the sofa and could always entertain Max, even in his sleep. Sal went toward the bedroom and the sound of sniffling and hiccuping.

He peered around the half-open door and saw Dori standing in simple white bra and panties, slapping through the things in the closet.

"You want to talk about it?" he asked, leaning against the doorway.

She yanked out a sweater and pair of jeans. She sniffed and drew a breath probably intended to help her get control. "No, thank you," she replied with stiff courtesy. "Talking only makes it worse."

"Makes what worse?"

"The confusion." She pulled the sweater over her head. Her short hair stood up in spikes.

"Which confusion?"

She gave him a quelling look as she fell onto the edge of the bed and pulled on her jeans. "Sal, this is talking."

"True. It's just hard for me to stand by, while you're clearly upset, and do nothing."

The jeans pulled up as far as she could manage sitting down, she stood, fitted them up to her waist and zipped the fly. "Well, there's nothing you can do about this," she said, sitting down again to pull on a pair of ankle socks. "I'm just disappointed in myself. And much as you'd like to protect me from everything, there's nothing you can do about that."

"You know," he said, trying to sound reasonable when he really wanted to shake her, "I can't see where you have any reason to be disappointed. You might not have gotten as much work done on your book as you'd planned, but you had a baby in the house, one you've kept and cared for by choice."

"Actually, you did most of that," she corrected. "And I'm not disappointed about the book or the baby, or anything." She pulled on a tennis shoe, stomped her foot to the floor and leaned over to tie it.

"Then what's left?" he asked.

She pushed herself up and hobbled toward him, one shoe on, one shoe off, a storm raging in her eyes. "*You're* what's left!" she said. "I was going to have my life under control by September, but I'll never accomplish that if I don't have my feelings for you under control!''

Ah. He liked the sound of that. He knew it was important to remain cool. "But feelings can't be controlled, as a rule. We can control the way we react to them, but we can't control *them*."

She spread her arms and let them fall to her side. "Oh, don't get technical! I don't care! I just want to feel that at twenty-six years old I know what I'm doing with my life."

"What do you want to do with it?"

She went back to the bed and sat down to put her other sock and shoe on. "I want Max, but I don't want to stomp all over Brenda Ward's rights if she simply screwed up one time."

"Well…that's noble."

She was silent while she put on and tied her second shoe. Then she stood up, folded her arms and looked at him defensively from the middle of the bedroom. "And I want to live with you, but I don't want you to feel possessive about me."

He could say something conciliatory, but their life together was at stake. "Well. There we have a problem," he said.

She turned to the mirror over the dresser and ran her fingers through her hair. Some of the spikes lay down and others sprang up. "I know. And I want personal freedom to do as I please without recriminations from anyone. I want that more than I want anything."

"Then I guess we're at an impasse."

She looked away from the mirror and snatched her purse up off the bed. "I guess we are."

She looked weary, but not entirely defeated. He took that as a good sign.

"I have to go shopping for a birthday present, get some party stuff, lay in some groceries. I suppose you're going to insist on coming."

He smiled. "You're not suffering confusion on that score. Let me make sure everything's turned off in the kitchen."

DORI GRABBED the diaper bag, the money safely stashed in a shoe pouch in the bottom of the closet, pulled Max out of the playpen, and carried him out to the car. Sal followed.

She put Max into his car seat, while Sal stashed the stroller frame in the trunk.

"If you're in a temper, maybe I should drive," Sal suggested, grinning at her over the top of the car. "Anger and your lead foot are not a good combination."

He was teasing, she knew, but she wasn't prepared to be charmed out of her depression. "Fine," she said. "I want to go to the antique shop. Maybe they'll have some really ugly new stock."

"We can only hope."

"Miss McKeon!" the clerk said, familiar with her now that she'd been back several times in search of the right gift for her parents. "We have a new shipment from a dealer in England. There might be something you'll like."

He walked her around the large room, while Sal stayed nearby with Max.

The clerk showed her beautiful jewelry that was not only too beautiful to appeal to her parents, but too costly for her budget. There was a piece of art deco glass that was interesting but a little austere for her the-more-ruffles-and-doo-dads-the-better parents. She studied a regimental helmet that was beautiful, but too significant, and an ugly dish stand worth considering if she couldn't find anything else.

And then she saw it.

"It's a Mayan jaguar head from Mexico," the clerk said, embellishing as he noted her excitement. "About 600 AD."

"Stone?" Dori asked, running her fingertips along the small figure's large ears and the sharp teeth visible in the open mouth. He was ugly, but somehow appealing.

"Yes," the clerk replied. "It was found outside Mexico City, I understand."

"Sal!" Dori called, taking the stone head carefully into her hands. "Look at this. It's a jaguar from Mexico."

He nodded over the find. "He's ugly, all right," he agreed. "But have your parents ever collected anything that wasn't American or European?"

Dori ran through a mental list of everything in her parents' home, things that had been given to her and her brothers, and things they'd brought to the beach house.

"I don't think so," she replied, "but it wouldn't be bad to start them on something new, would it?"

"Not at all."

Dori handed it to the clerk, elated. "I'll take it."

The clerk wrapped the head in bubble wrap, then tissue, placed it carefully in a box and gift-wrapped it.

The treasure clutched in her arms, Dori led the way out the front door. I'll buy you an espresso," she said to Sal. "Then I have to get some paper plates and napkins, order a cake and buy lots of groceries. We have a lot of people to feed."

"I'm at your service," Sal assured her. "See? You're not the only one enslaved."

She gave him a stern look. "No smart remarks, okay?"

"Sorry." He followed her into the coffee bar at the Buckley Arms and settled her at a small round table. "You seemed a little more cheerful. I thought you were feeling less confused."

She sat with the baby in her lap and pushed everything within reach to the other side of the table. "I think this is just a shopper's high. I'm still confused about us."

"I see. You want a mocha?"

"Please? And one of those little chocolate mice things you bought me the last time."

"Are you going to bite the head off again?"

She nodded. "And I'll probably mutilate the licorice tail, too, so you might want to sit at another table."

"Remember that the baby's impressionable."

With a grudging smile, she put her fingertip to the

baby's nose. He caught her hand in his two and pulled her finger into his little mouth.

As Sal went to the counter, she rocked the baby gently, trying to ignore the little saw-teeth working into her knuckle. She couldn't believe how much she'd come to love Max in such a short time. She had what Sal had termed the "noble intention" of making certain Brenda had a fair chance when she was found, but Dori truly didn't know what she'd do if Brenda wanted the baby back.

And then there was Sal. She watched him waiting at the counter, his eyes scanning the street beyond the window, ever the bodyguard.

She loved him desperately. Now that she understood why he'd left her on their wedding day, she could understand and accept his actions. She could even accept the blame for their two years apart.

She also knew that he loved her; he'd been the perfect father to Max, and the perfect husband since they'd come back from Seattle together. Except for that possessive quality that made him second-guess her decisions, and even reverse them if he felt he should.

After finally ridding herself somewhat of the yoke of her brothers' protection, she didn't think she could live with that again.

Sal returned to the table with her drink and his, a white paper bag trapped between his fingers and her cup. A curious prickling took place throughout her body as he placed her cup at the farthest reach of her hand and out of the baby's way. He never forgot to think about Max.

He put his own cup down right near hers, handed her the bag, then took Max from her as his grasping little hands reached for the paper.

She pulled out a sugar cookie.

"That's ours," Sal said, reaching across the table for it.

Her chocolate mouse was on the bottom. She ate it slowly, with relish, deliberately biting the head off when Sal glanced her way. He laughed and shared tiny bites of the cookie with the baby. Max's feet kicked and his hands pounded the table in his excitement over the treat.

They stocked up on an enormous amount of food, for which Dori knew her brothers would reimburse her when they arrived. She ordered a cake in the market's bakery, bought paper goods and found a card to go with her gift.

Shopping took several hours, and finally Max, who'd grown tired and fussy, was fast asleep on Dori's shoulder. Sal pushed a large cart filled with their purchases across the street to the parking lot behind the antique shop.

"I hope there's enough room in the car for all this," Dori said. "And, please, no cracks about strapping me to the roof."

He grinned as he pushed the cart. "You'd make a very seductive hood ornament."

"Sweet of you. If there isn't enough room, I'm leaving you with the baby, hauling everything home, then coming back for you. And I don't care about your bodyguard rule about never leaving your cli—"

At that very moment, a dark van pulled up right in front of them with a screech of tires.

Sal turned her and the baby in the other direction. "Run!" he ordered, as four young men and a young woman leapt out of the van. Brenda and her friends.

Dori didn't remember ever feeling so torn in her entire life. She wanted to protect the baby, but she didn't want to leave Sal.

"Go!" Sal shouted at her again, pushing her, trying to cover her retreat.

She made the decision to stay. She wrapped her arms around Max and stood her ground, in the belief that Brenda would never hurt her own baby.

WHEN THIS WAS OVER, Sal thought, he and Dori were having a firm talk about the principle of cooperation in a crisis.

He should have been more watchful, he berated himself as he got squarely in front of Dori and Max. But he'd been worried about Dori's mood, worried about what she was thinking, worried that she'd decide it really was over between them, and that he'd have no recourse but to tie her up and take her home with him and Max as freight on a flight to Seattle.

The four young men fanned out, street punks with baseball hats on backward and sleeves rolled up to show off tattoos of a shark's head.

The young woman ran around them to take the baby from Dori. She was pale, with yards of dark hair and an expression of hopelessness. She wore pencil-slim jeans and a short-cropped leather jacket.

"Brenda!" Dori whispered as she clutched at Max. "Get Max out of the way!"

"Dori." Brenda hesitated as though she would have said something, but Dori pushed her to the side.

"Get out of the way!" the tallest of the young men barked at her. Valdefiero—he'd been the face at the window, Sal guessed.

Brenda backed away, stopping several yards away from them, the baby clutched to her.

Sal had the Smith & Wesson in his waistband, but there had to be a better way out of this. "What do you want?" he asked.

Dori had moved to stand beside him but he pushed her back behind him.

"You know what I want." The kid came to stand right in front of him. Dark hair stuck through the sizing hole in his hat, and he had a silver stud in his nose. He had a baby-fine mustache and sloping shoulders under a Grateful Dead T-shirt.

The punk was measuring him, Sal decided, as shoe-button black eyes roved over him from head to toe. He was trying to decide if the eighteen or twenty years Sal had on him would make the older man tired and weaker, or stronger and more experienced. He didn't seem to be able to decide.

"What you *should* want," Sal said, indicating Brenda, "your girlfriend has already taken."

Valdefiero shook his head. "I want the money."

"I understand the church got the money back."

"Yeah, so the way I figure it, you'd better come up with $11,572 for *me*."

Dori peered around Sal. "You stole from a church!" she accused.

The punk blinked. "Of course I stole from a church. No security guards. Now, give me my money."

"What do you intend to do with it?"

The kid rolled his eyes. "Mend my ways and start over," he said in tones of bored sarcasm. "Maybe go to college. Establish a fund for underprivileged children. What do you *think* I intend to do with it?" His voice rose and his indolence took on a dangerous edge. "My friends and I are going to drink and bed girls until it's gone."

Brenda took a step toward him. Dori moved around Sal, presumably to reach for the baby, but Sal caught her arm.

"You told me we were going to California," Brenda said.

"And you told me," Dori said to Brenda, "that you were going to turn the money in to the police."

Valdefiero shook his head pityingly. "That's what I told her to tell you." Then he turned on Brenda. "You stole my money!" he roared at her. "Did you really think I'd take you anywhere? We only brought you along because you know this chick's car."

"You were wrong to take the money," Brenda said, tears in her voice, "and I took it from you to make a better life for our son."

"How many times do I have to tell you? I don't want a son. I don't want a woman. At least, not a woman who hangs on."

"Brenda," Dori called, reaching an arm out to the girl. "Come here and stand with us."

Brenda looked from the man she'd trusted to Dori and Sal.

"Come on," Dori encouraged. "Someday you'll be proud you took the stand."

Brenda, looking uncertain, came to stand beside them. Dori put an arm around her. Max, now awake, leaned out of Brenda's arms and cried for Dori, but Brenda held on to him.

"What is this?" Valdefiero demanded. "Some stupid line in the sand crap? You got two women, a baby and an old guy against the four of us. What do you think you're going to do with that?"

Apparently impatient with the turn of events, he swung at Sal. But it was the "old guy" crack and not the swing that did it. Sal knocked him out cold.

The other three punks looked at each other. Before they could decide what to do, a Jeep pulled up behind them, and they scattered.

Sal tackled one, and Bram, leaping out of the Jeep, chased the other one down. The third one got away.

Bram tossed Dori a cell phone as he struggled to cuff his quarry. She dialed 911 and told the dispatcher that they had three of the four men who'd stolen the money from Faith Community Church.

WHEN DORI LOOKED UP, Brenda was gone.

She felt her heart snap in two. Oh, God. She'd known she was taking a chance, but she'd wanted to believe that Brenda had the baby's best interests at heart—and that Brenda knew giving him to Dori was in Max's best interest.

She started to cry, large gulping sobs that came from deep inside and felt as though they churned up everything in her chest.

Sal came and caught her arm, drawing her with him toward the red car. "Come on. We'll find her," he said.

She wanted to do just that, but she really understood for the first time what it was like for a mother to have her child ripped from her arms—either physically, or by circumstances she was powerless to prevent. Still, the baby wasn't safe with a biological mother who couldn't make sound decisions.

The police arrived, and Will Valdefiero was put into the back of one police car, his two companions into another.

Bram came to them. "We have to go to the station," he said, frowning in concern at Dori. "Did she get hurt?" he asked Sal.

"Brenda took off with the baby," Sal explained. "Take Dori, I'm going after—"

Bram shook his head. "The police are putting out an APB for her right now. They'll find her. I followed them here and was just waiting for someone to make a move."

Dori pulled herself together, discovering that "together" wasn't quite the same as it had been just half an hour ago. Now there was a hole where her heart had been.

She leaned in to Sal, and they started for the car.

"Oh, wait." Sal pointed to the cart. "The groceries.

Bram, can we drop those off at Dori's first? The whole family's coming home tonight, and we've got a couple of hundred dollars' worth of food here.''

"Uh, sure. Just get there as soon as you can." He leaned closer to say quietly, "And you'd better bring the cash. I know you replaced it, but the police will…"

"Sure," Sal said. "See you at the station."

They had stashed groceries everywhere—the trunk, the floor and the back seat. Dori burst into tears anew at the sight of the empty car seat.

She sounded as though she were going to die, and Sal thought the sound of her grief would kill him, too. His own distress over Max was eating away at him.

When they arrived at the beach house, Dori's parents, home from the airport, came out to help with the groceries. Sal explained briefly what had happened, while Dori fell apart in her mother's arms. Peg wept with her. Sal and Charlie, jaws set, made a dozen trips from the car to the kitchen and back again.

All the groceries finally stowed, Dori washed her face and, composed again, went with Sal to the police station. They told their stories in a small, pale-green office, where they were given paper cups of strong coffee. When they were finally finished with their reports, an attractive young woman in a dark blue suit stepped inside the office.

"Mr. and Mrs. Dominguez?" she asked.

Dori's eyes were glazed, but Sal responded, "Yes."

She smiled. "I'm from Adult and Family Services," she said. "May I speak to you when you're finished here?"

"They're finished," the officer said. "Here. You can have the office. I have a few calls to make."

"Good. Well." The young woman put her purse on the desk, then smiled at each of them in turn. "I'll be right back. I know you've had a long afternoon, but I'll be very quick."

Dori put a hand to her forehead. "I have Riverdance going on in my head," she said to Sal with a wince.

"You have Tylenol in your purse," he reminded her, going to a water cooler in a corner of the office. "You gave me one the other day."

She located the bottle in her purse, then fumbled, seemingly unable to open it. He handed her the cup of water, took the bottle from her and handed her two pills. She popped them in her mouth and drank. "I suppose she needs information on Brenda," she said.

"I suppose," he replied.

Sal had the selfish thought that, because Dori seemed so distraught, she might decide that she needed him, after all, whether or not he was possessive.

Then he knew with certainty that if it was a choice between that or getting Max back for her, he'd find the baby.

With that in mind, he thought he was hallucinating when the office door opened again and the AFS woman walked in with Max in her arms.

Dori, even with her back to the door, sensed Max's presence immediately and ran to him with a cry of delight. "Max!" she squealed, taking him from the woman. "What happened? Where's his mother?"

"Brenda Ward has been an emancipated minor for

the past year," the woman said. "Her mother died, her father's alcoholic, and she was better off on her own, or so we'd hoped. The boyfriend wasn't a good choice, but she came to me about an hour ago with Max, here, and gave me instructions to take him to you and Mr. Dominguez. We'll be filing release papers tomorrow, and she wants you to adopt him."

"She's...sure?" Dori wept, hugging Max, who squealed in protest.

"Positive. She recognizes that though she loved him, she was a poor mother. We'll have to see what the judge says about her letting Valdefiero into the parsonage, but she wants to get her GED, go to college, and be smart—like you are." The woman delivered that last with a smile. "She admires you. She says you were kind to her."

"I gave her a candy bar," Dori said, taking the handkerchief Sal handed her. "Such a small thing."

"To a person who has nothing," the woman insisted, "that's a big thing. So I've arranged for Max to stay with you until you can get his adoption under way."

Dori nodded. "I'll see an attorney tomorrow."

The woman turned to Sal. "I guess we're just presuming you're in agreement with all this."

"I am," he said, striking a tone intended to convince her that he figured in the decision.

"Good." She handed him her card. "If there's anything I can do, please let me know. And keep me apprised of the adoption proceedings."

"We will," Dori promised.

Max reached for Sal. He took him and, with an arm around Dori, walked out to the car. During the entire ride home, Dori peered around her seat and stared at Max.

At home there were Airport Rental cars everywhere and a virtual tide of humanity ran out of the house to greet them. Her parents and her brothers, looking worried, came first. At the sight of the baby in the back seat, there was an urgent discussion.

Dori opened her door before Sal turned off the motor, and her mother demanded, "The mother brought him back? Do you get to keep him?"

"I do!" Dori shouted. "She gave him up to me. She's signing release papers tomorrow, and I'm getting a lawyer to file for adoption."

There were shouts and screams of excitement and congratulations, hugs and tears.

Sal wanted to skulk away and find a way to stay sane until he knew for certain whether the adoption was all she was going to have the lawyer file for tomorrow. He couldn't possibly ask her tonight, with her whole family here to celebrate her mother's birthday.

But Skye and Harper, Dori's sisters-in-law, were upon him, offering their congratulations. Peg had apparently explained about the baby and about his spending the last week-and-a-half with Dori. And she'd passed on what she thought to be true—that Sal and Dori had rediscovered their love. Everyone seemed happy about that so he could find no escape.

Tall, brunette Skye, and small, blond Harper each caught one of his arms and led him around the car to their husbands. Darrick and Dillon had the dark, handsome stamp of the McKeons.

Darrick shook his hand and frowned. "You married our sister without inviting us to the wedding?"

Before Sal could explain, Dillon also shook his hand. "Thanks, buddy. I'm getting to hate weddings. And Mom assures us that Dori looks happy, so you must be treating her well."

"Doing my best," he assured him carefully.

"Sal!" Julie, his cousin, small and dark-haired, flew out of the crowd and into his arms. They'd been carefree children together, then budding criminals, then young people forced to make a choice between their families and their futures. She'd bravely chosen her future, and he'd done his best to see that she didn't lose her family.

"I can't believe this!" she squealed in his ear. "You're married to my best friend! And you're my brother-in-law!"

The family was all crowded around, the children in a second layer like the exotic undergrowth in a forest. Max was being passed around. Sal caught Dori's pleading eyes in the middle of the group.

"Yes, I am," he agreed. "And I've had a very trying afternoon. If anyone has a lead on a Bloody Mary, I'd be very grateful."

"Come with me." Duncan, Julie's husband, put an arm around Sal's shoulders, led him into the living room and pushed him into an overstuffed chair. "I understand you've been cooking since you've been here. Well, you just relax, because Dillon and the ladies are now in charge.'' He pinched Dori's cheek as she passed him. ''The ladies who can cook, that is. Sit right here—someone will bring you a drink. And dinner will be ready in under an hour.''

''Madre de Dios,'' he said. ''I'm home.''

DORI WAS QUIVERING. She remembered that the same thing had happened to her the night she'd seen Valdefiero's face at the window.

They'd had dinner, and then they all sat around in the living room, adults on sofas and chairs and on the floor, children on the backs and arms of sofas and chairs and in the laps of aunts and uncles. They'd talked about the trip to Europe, about Dori's book, about the hospital in Madre Maria, about the big birthday bash tomorrow. Cheddar, delighted with the new variety of laps, large and small, tried them all.

Dori had been keeping a low profile, not wanting anyone to know that she was jelly inside. Fortunately, she was holding Duncan and Julie's three-year-old twins, who were sprawled all over her in a sleepy stupor and didn't seem to notice.

She was going to have to admit that she hadn't planned anything. But before she could, Julie, sitting on the arm of Duncan's chair, said, ''Why don't we just have it here? I mean, Dori wouldn't have had time to plan anything with the baby and the worry about the thief, and we can't make reservations for so many of us at the last minute. Can't we just have it in the backyard and be gluttonous and noisy?''

"That sounds wonderful to me," Peg said. "Doesn't it, Charlie?"

"Of course it does." Charlie sat with his leg propped on an ottoman, Harper and Dillon's Darian and Danielle asleep in his lap. "But it's your birthday, Peg."

"We missed beer and brots for the Fourth of July," Dillon said. "And Mom likes that as much as we do. Why don't we do that?"

Dori congratulated herself for having bought ten pounds of brot.

Peg led the unanimous cheer of approval.

"A few salads," Harper added, "a few desserts. It'll be a feast!"

More cheers of approval. Then the adults began to gather up children and wander off to bed. Darrick had to peel David, ten, and Drake, five, from Sal, who sat on the floor with one boy asleep against each shoulder.

"Since you've got the baby and you need access to the fridge," Julie said to Dori, trading her a sleeping Max for one of the twins, "Duncan and the girls and I will sleep in your attic room, the folks can have our room, and you two can still have the downstairs bedroom."

Duncan came to get Gabrielle. Everyone involved in the game of musical rooms nodded approval.

Dori took a hot shower, while Sal put Max down in the crib. She'd hoped the heat would calm her, but nothing seemed to help. She needed...something.

Sal was waiting outside the shower in his nighttime attire of jogging shorts and T-shirt, with a towel and a brandy.

When she looked surprised, he handed her the brandy and wrapped the towel around her, rubbing her dry through the thick folds. "I was afraid you were going to fly apart while we were discussing the party," he said. "Fortunately, everyone was too excited and too happy to be together to notice."

"I don't know…what's the matter with me," she said, her teeth now chattering. "Max is fine. I'm…I'm fine."

"Just post-crisis reaction," he said. "Drink that, come to bed, and you'll be fine."

"You're sure?"

"I'm sure."

She drank and coughed, drank and choked, and drank and finally enjoyed it.

"That's the trouble with brandy," she said, handing back the glass and pulling on her cotton nightshirt. "By the time it's sedated you enough for you to enjoy it, it's gone."

"Very philosophical," he said. "I suppose life's a little like that."

She climbed into bed as he turned off the light. He gathered her into his arms, pulled her back against his chest and burrowed his nose in her hair. Somewhere above her on the pillow, Cheddar purred like a little engine.

"Everything's all right, *querida,*" he said softly. "You have what you want now. Be easy. Everything's all right."

It was. She knew it was. Everything was all right.

But something was missing.

She wanted to understand about…about a man owning a woman. How ownership could possibly relate to love. But she couldn't focus, couldn't remember…

She held on to the arms wrapped around her and fell asleep.

CHAPTER THIRTEEN

DORI'S FIRST THOUGHT upon awakening the following morning was, did she *have* to understand it? Sal loved her, and she loved him. She enjoyed his company so much because there was friendship as well as passion in their feelings for each other.

She just wondered if she could adjust to that possessive quality in him, or if he'd be able to cope with her resistance to it. Many marriages based on love in the beginning eventually fell apart because of some difference that hadn't been addressed. And the last thing she wanted to do was fail at marriage, when everyone else in her family was so good at it.

Sal was already up when she climbed out of bed, and Dori discovered that Max's crib was empty. Cheddar had also left her. The buzz of conversation came from beyond her closed bedroom door. Apparently most of the family were up and having breakfast.

The first thing Dori did was call Athena Hartford's office and schedule an appointment for the following afternoon to talk about Max's adoption.

"Adoption?" Athena asked in surprise. "I thought we were going to talk about divorce."

Dori groaned. "It's complicated," she said. "I'll see you at two-thirty tomorrow."

"Okay," Athena agreed. "I'll be ready."

Dori showered quickly and dressed in jeans and a light blue camp shirt. She made the bed and tidied the bedroom, realizing grimly that she was reluctant to go out and be with her family.

She squared her shoulders and looked at herself in the mirror. "You had been getting it together," she told herself firmly. "It isn't your fault that a baby and husband slowed you down. Well, the husband might have been your fault, but his reappearance wasn't. Well, not entirely. You did go and seek him out, but that was because of the baby. Okay, let it go. You're starting to confuse yourself further. And confusion's the whole issue right now, isn't it?"

It was hard not to be confused around her family. They were charming but forceful people. Just like Sal.

A quick rap on the door was followed by Sal's entrance. "Eggs?" he asked, "or French toast—since you didn't really get to eat yours yesterday? Harper's asking."

Dori felt contrary. Not quarrelsome precisely, because she didn't want to fight with anyone, but she didn't feel like doing things the way they were usually done. If she was feeling confusion, she may as well go with it.

"Is there ice cream?" she asked.

He arched an eyebrow. "Uh, I think so. Coffee-fudge something."

She smiled as she came toward him. "Coffee sounds like a good breakfast flavor. I'll have two scoops, please."

"Of ice cream."

"Yes."

"For breakfast."

"Yes." She stopped in the doorway, a hand on her hip. "You're not going to try to countermand that, are you?"

"No. I wouldn't think of it." He held the door open and stood back to let her through.

The house was in a kind of cheerful chaos. Most of the children were sitting at the kitchen table, except for David, who was watching baseball in the living room with his grandfather.

The cousins were having a riotous time. Max was kicking and squealing and trying to feed himself crumbled pieces of scrambled egg. Skye and Julie were attempting to maintain some sort of order.

The three-year-old twins in matching pink shorts sets, with tea towels tied around their necks, sat in kitchen chairs, their little heads barely visible above the table. It didn't stop their enthusiastic devouring of toast and jam and milk in cups with training lids.

Danielle sat in Skye's lap messily eating a banana, and it was Skye who wore the tea towel. Drake and Darian ate Cheerios in milk, Darian holding two of the little disks up to his eyes and delighting his cousins.

Harper, manning a frying pan, greeted Dori with a cheerful "Good morning. What'll it be?"

"Ice cream," Dori replied, going to the freezer for the carton.

Darian looked at his mother as though his faith in adults had just collapsed. "How come Aunt Dori gets to have ice cream for breakfast," he demanded, "and we gots cereal?"

"Yeah!" Drake supported his protest.

Harper sent Dori a reprimanding glance. "Thanks, Aunt Dori," she said, then added to the children, "Aunt Dori is a grown-up and doesn't have to worry about building strong bones and teeth. When you're an adult, you can have ice cream for breakfast if you want to. But Uncle Sal's going to have a healthy breakfast, aren't you, Uncle Sal."

"Yes, I am," Sal replied stoutly. "Eggs and toast and orange juice."

"*We* couldn't have any juice!" Drake reported in an affronted tone.

"Ixnay on the uicejay," Julie said, holding up the empty carton. She added in a whisper, "One too many screwdrivers last night."

"Ah. Just coffee, then," Sal conceded.

"Good man." Julie pulled a cup down and poured it for him, while Dori pulled an ice cream scoop out of the drawer.

"There's apple juice concentrate in the freezer," Dori said to the boys, momentarily abandoning her ice cream. "Want me to make you some?"

The boys chorused an affirmative.

She mixed it up quickly, stirred vigorously, then poured juice into glasses for Darian, Drake and the twins, and into the bottles for Danielle and Max.

She poured the last few ounces in the pitcher into a glass for Sal. "There you go. You'll have to pretend it's orange."

"I can do that," he said quietly. "We've been pretending a lot of things since I've been here."

She didn't want to get into that. She put the pitcher

in the bottom of the dishwasher, scooped up her ice cream and wandered out into the backyard.

Her brothers had carried chairs outside, and Darrick was scrubbing the picnic table, while Dillon and Duncan hauled the second one out of the garage.

"If you got another scrubber," Darrick said to her, indicating the second table, "you could clean off that one and help me put up the umbrellas."

"I could." She ate a spoonful of ice cream and went to sit in the middle of the hammock, legs folded pretzel-style.

He stopped in his work to lean both hands on the table and look at her. "But, you're not going to?"

She turned to him, dipping her spoon into her cup again. "That's why you're such a good administrator. You're so quick."

"I'm a good administrator," he said ominously, "because I don't take guff from anyone."

"Except Skye," Dillon replied, as he and Duncan crabwalked with the table past the hammock.

"He has to be nice to her," Duncan explained, grunting as they set the table down. "She once crashed him in an airplane and keeps threatening to do it again. Dori, go get us something to clean this off with."

"You go get it," she said, scraping the last little bit of ice cream out of the bottom of the cup. "You've been on vacation for a month, while I've been writing a brilliant book."

"What," Duncan asked in surprise, turning to his brother, "has happened to our sweet little sister?"

Dillon frowned at him. "What family do you belong to? We've never had a sweet little sister."

"Well, she used to be willing to help us."

"When was that?"

"Not since she was little," Darrick put in. "Since she turned twelve, she's been nothing but mouth and attitude."

Dori lay back in the hammock with a contented sigh, letting her hand with the cup fall over the side until she could drop the cup to the grass.

"I had three very bad examples," she said, getting comfortable. "So there's no way you can blame me."

"We know Sal didn't make her this way," she heard Duncan speculate. "He's the epitome of suave good manners."

"Well, she is half Mom, you know," Dillon said.

"We all are," Duncan argued, "and we're not spoiled rotten like she is."

"Ha!" Dori exclaimed without opening her eyes. "You have to see the three of you from my perspective—always calling the shots, always getting in my way, always terrifying my boyfriends."

"I think we did pretty well on that score," Duncan said. "We did approve Sal, and he's the one you finally chose—even if you didn't tell us about it for two whole years."

She opened her eyes and sighed. "Well, we got married and then he was gone. For two whole years it was like we weren't married."

"But your marriage is working now." It wasn't a question. Dillon said it as though he wanted reassurance that it was true.

She sat up again and folded her legs. The hammock swung gently. "Mostly," she replied.

Darrick came closer. "I don't like the sound of that. What do you mean, mostly?"

The three of them were now lined up beside her in various poses of fraternal displeasure—Dillon leaning on the base at the foot of the hammock; Duncan, arms folded, frowning near her feet; Darrick right beside her, hands in his pockets.

"This is precisely it!" she said with sudden vehemence, angry that they'd messed up her contrary but mellow morning. "He's just like the three of you. And he does exactly this same thing when he doesn't agree with something I've done. He's always convinced that *I'm* wrong, and that he can explain to me how it should be, or fix it for me, whichever course will bring about the least argument."

Darrick frowned at her as though trying to figure out how that was bad. "So, yours is the only opinion allowed," he asked, "and presumed to be right?"

"No. But I'm *allowed* to be wrong without someone having to fix it."

Dillon, the doctor and a scientist at heart, didn't understand that at all. "Why would you want to remain wrong, if someone could help you make it right?"

She closed her eyes in exasperation. "Because I have the personal freedom to *be* wrong. It's my right! And my point is that I'm not *always* wrong! But if you don't agree with me, you presume I am."

Duncan narrowed his eyes. "I don't think that's true. The only time we interfere is if we think you're in danger. And that whole mess surrounding the Julie incident should have proven to you that you should have come to us for help in the first place."

She growled, too exasperated to form words. "I didn't come to you," she said slowly, as though to simple children, "because Julie didn't want you to interfere—and I knew that was exactly what you'd do. I can't believe that even now, three years later, you still don't see that!"

"What I see," Darrick said, "is that you seem to think brothers and husbands should sit around like potted plants and stay out of your life because you don't want interference. If you help us because you're a woman, it's okay. But if we help you because we're men, we're taking over."

"Help and interference are not the same thing," she pointed out.

"So, we've interfered with you more than we've helped?" Duncan asked.

She was beginning to regret the entire conversation. "Can we just drop it?" she asked. She lay back again and closed her eyes. "I came out here just to mellow out a little and think things through."

"Really." She heard Duncan sigh, his voice moving slightly away from her as he said to Darrick and Dillon, "No small surprise her marriage is only *mostly* working."

She ignored the jibe and her confused, hurt feelings and kept her eyes closed, hoping her brothers were moving toward the house and would leave her to her thoughts—

A moment later, the hammock made a wide swinging motion. She opened her eyes and tried to sit up, but she was rocked backward as the woven rope suddenly surrounded her.

DORI WAS GOING to torture and then kill every one of her brothers before they went home tomorrow. She'd been hanging in the ash tree for the past five minutes like some trapped jungle creature in *Hatari!*, a good six or seven feet off the ground. During that time she'd been carefully making plans. Fraternal retribution was one thing, but they'd gone too far this time.

She refused to call for help for fear someone would come and see her humiliation. So she sat silently, trapped in her net prison, brooding, one foot caught in the mesh.

"Oh, no." She heard the screen door slam and dropped her head on her arms, which were folded over one bent knee.

"You're lucky I don't call Harper to immortalize you in a photograph," Julie said, looking up at her.

"If you're going to gloat," Dori said, "go away."

"I'm not gloating." Julie sounded offended. "Duncan sent me out here to talk to you. He said you wouldn't resent it because I'm another woman."

Dori did feel resentful but couldn't determine whether it was because she'd have resented anyone trying to change her mind about anything, or because she was hanging in a tree.

"So, what's the problem?" Julie asked. "Why have they hung you in a tree like an old float from a fishing net?"

Dori relayed most of their conversation. "Does Duncan interfere with what you want to do all the time?" she asked. "And if he does, how do you stand it?"

"Hmm." Julie sat down on the grass as though she were simply having a conversation with someone sitting across from her at a kitchen table. "Subordinating your will is always an adjustment. And I never do it on big things. I fight for what I believe in, but I also believe Duncan has the right to argue for his point— even if it differs from mine. But if we're dealing with nothing really significant, I sometimes do what he wants just because I know he'll be more peaceful about it, and I love him, and peace is what I want for him."

Julie laughed lightly. "But being the scrapper that you are, you probably don't get that, do you."

"I don't know," Dori admitted. "I'd like to, but why shouldn't *he* give in? Why don't you get to be the one at peace?"

"Because when you love each other, one of you is always conceding to the other. It's what makes a marriage work. When you intertwine two lives, someone has to give, otherwise the connection is broken. Or you can live parallel lives like some people do and get along just fine, but then I don't think you ever really get to grasp the depths of real love. Giving is the only sure test of it, and when your lives intersect only occasionally, you never know what that other person is willing to do for you on a day-to-day basis—or you for him. Giving builds on itself time after time. But I think if you just walk along side by side, one day you're going to go off in different directions."

Dori found some sense in that. "I resent Sal's strength because I'd finally broken free of my brothers." She shook her net cage and made a scornful sound. "Or thought I had."

Julie shrugged. "I think love and personal freedom are mutually exclusive. If you want to answer to no one, my advice is don't get married and have children. But I'm a little late with that, I think."

"Julie?"

"Yeah?"

"Can you get me down from here?"

Julie got to her feet and dusted off her hands. "I'll have to get help. Hold on."

"Oh, good advice. I'll just *hang* here until you get back!"

Okay, that all made sense to Dori. Love made its demands. But from what Sal had taught her of love, it was usually well worth it. And maybe she could concede her opinion on minor points if it helped their relationship and his peace of mind.

But...

The back door slammed again, and Sal came sprinting out to stop stock-still in the middle of the yard, staring.

"DORI?" he asked, not quite able to believe his eyes. His wife hung in the ash tree like a queen bee in a hive. "What happened?"

He grabbed a chair and placed it under her.

"A little sibling humor," she said, sounding less annoyed than he'd expected her to be. "Can you get me down?"

He stepped onto the chair, balancing himself by looping his fingers in the netting. He pushed her protruding foot back inside the netting and was about to free her by reaching for the long ends of the hammock looped over a thick branch—when he realized his advantage here.

"Depends," he replied, figuring he had nothing to lose by interrogating her while he had the upper hand, so to speak.

"On what?" she asked in disbelief.

"On whether you made plans to file for divorce as well as adoption when you talked to Athena Hartford this morning."

She sighed. "I'm not filing for divorce."

He felt relief, but only a little. She didn't sound happy about not filing. "Why didn't you?"

"Because I'm not sure it's the right thing."

That wasn't the answer. He'd been a patient man, considering, but that was about to change.

"Then, if you're not sure divorce is the right thing," he concluded, "you're also not sure staying together is the right thing."

"I'm confused!" she shrieked at him. "Aren't you ever confused?"

"Not about you," he said, reaching up to hold on to the branch above her head as he worked the loop on the front part of the net trap toward the end of the branch.

"Reach your arm out the side," he ordered, "and put it around my neck. Hook your other arm in the netting behind you."

She did as he asked, her floral scent wafting around him, trying to dim his billowing temper. But he was beyond being seduced by a fragrance.

"All right, hold on." He freed the loop, and the front part of the hammock fell between them in a pile. She tipped her face back as the netting slapped her in its fall.

Holding on to the branch with one hand, he moved
her to his side with the other arm until he could kick
the end of the hanging hammock off the chair. Then
he set her down again, leaped to the grass and reached
up to swing her down in front of him.

"What is it about us," he asked, "that you don't
see working?"

She looked wide-eyed and startled, as though surprised to be finally free of her net. "We've had this
argument over and—"

"Well, let's have it one more time," he insisted.
"What is it?"

"You're not only autocratic," she accused. "You're
possessive! Even Natalie noticed it."

That surprised him. "I thought Natalie and I got on
well."

"You did." She angled her chin. "She thought it
was a good thing. I don't. A woman wants to be allowed to be who she is. No one wants to be...owned."

So that was it. He'd never quite understood the problem before. And as he saw it now, it was probably
worse than he'd thought.

He caught her upper arms and, exerting great control, gave her just a small shake. "That, *necia,* is because she seems to understand that a man who is possessive about his woman..." He shook her again. "Are
you paying attention?"

She was frowning at him and her lip was quivering.
"What is *necia?*"

"It means 'silly,'" he explained tightly. "*Stupida*
also came to mind, for which you wouldn't have
needed a translation, but I chose to be the gentleman."

She firmed her lips to stop the trembling. "Go on, then."

"Natalie knew," he said, "that a possessive man doesn't want to own a woman's body or her soul—he wants her love."

He dropped his hands from her, suddenly worn out with loving her.

"But I'm thinking your love has too many conditions and sub-clauses," he said, climbing back up onto the chair to free the rest of the hammock. "You give very carefully, and I'm not sure I like that."

"That's because you have a history of taking what you want," she retorted.

She'd intended it to hurt, and it did. He'd been taken in to the criminal world as a child, but he'd chosen to stay as an adult—until he'd had to decide to make everyone stop during the Julie incident. He could live with what he'd done, but he hated that to be part of his child's background.

"You're right, *querida*," he said, reattaching the hammock to its base. "Maybe that's why you hold your love so tightly. I'm not the one you want to give it to." His task completed, he turned to her, a carefully controlled expression hiding the pain in his gut. "I came out here to tell you that Diego called and there's a problem with one of our clients. I have to go back."

"I see." The sound of her voice was liquid, as though it had emerged through tears.

"I'll simplify things for you," he said. "I'll file for the divorce. I'll assume the blame. And I'll see that you and Max are comfortable."

COMFORTABLE. Without him?

Dori watched Sal walk back into the house and experienced a sudden two-part epiphany.

First, she understood his point about being possessive. He'd wanted to own her love and he'd committed every kindness in the book to get it. She'd just been confused by vocabulary.

Second, it just occurred to her that the only way a woman could hold her own against a man who was just too much of one, was to be even more of a woman.

And she'd learned through her study of women of the past that strong women weren't always ladies.

Dori pushed her way into the kitchen and stormed through a crowd of sisters-in-law who were peeling, mixing and cooking.

Julie caught her eye. "So?" she asked.

"So, I'm sorry I've left Max to you all this time," she replied, looking around the kitchen for him. All the children had left the table, and Max's high chair had been wiped off and placed in a corner. "Where is he, anyway?"

"Sal took him," Skye replied. "Mom and Dad are hosting a cartoon marathon with the rest of the kids."

"Good." Dori pushed up her sleeves. "Excuse me a few more minutes."

"Go," Julie said.

"Don't panic if you hear shouting," Dori warned.

Harper rolled her eyes. "We live with McKeons. Our ears are set at a higher register."

"Where are they, anyway?"

"They went to pick up the cake."

"All of them?"

Julie smiled. "I think they feared someone's retribution."

"Smart guys."

Dori hugged each of her sisters-in-law in turn and headed for the closed bedroom door.

Her mother looked up from the living room sofa and waved at her. Dori blew her a kiss. Her mother looked surprised.

Epiphanies all over the place, Dori thought.

She didn't bother to knock; Sal was her husband, after all. She had to clarify that.

She closed the bedroom door behind her and leaned against it, her knees weakened by the sight of Sal filling a suitcase. Max was sitting up, surrounded by pillows propped against the headboard. Cheddar lay curled up a safe distance away.

"Okay," she said. "That was rude and rotten and I'm sorry. I've never thought of you as a thief. Even the police didn't, because, when restitution was made, they let you all go."

He gave her a look that was weirdly disconnected, as though he'd somehow managed to cut himself off from her—from them.

"No need to apologize," he said, putting a stack of T-shirts into the bag. "I've often thought I wouldn't want a child to have that in his family."

When he turned his back to return to the dresser, she removed the stack of shirts. "That's ridiculous. To a child, that'd just give him status among his friends."

He had two handfuls of socks and, apparently prepared to stack them on top of the shirts, looked around as though he'd lost his mind. Then, seeing her replacing them in the dresser, he made a face.

"I'm not in a playful mood, Dori," he said, dropping the socks into the bag.

She ignored him. When he went to the closet, she removed the socks and put them back in the drawer. "What are you doing with Max?" she asked.

"Explaining to him why I won't be..." He stopped in front of the bag with several pairs of slacks and noticed the missing socks. "Are you campaigning to end up back in the hammock trap?" he asked threateningly.

She shook her head. "That was very uncomfortable, but very enlightening. It was like a metaphor for the trap in which I'd put myself. My whole life, I wondered how to fight my brothers, and then you came along— a man just like them—and you presented the same problem, only worse, because I loved you and wanted to bear your children."

He looked puzzled. She liked that because he was always the one who had the answers.

"That must be why you kept us apart for two years," he said, his expression still uncertain but curiously removed, as though he wasn't sure he cared.

She had to do something about that.

"I kept us apart because I was selfish and...and *necia*," she said.

He dropped the slacks in the suitcase, then leaned back against the dresser and folded his arms, nodding at her use of his word. "So you do sometimes listen to me."

"I always listen to you," she corrected. "I just don't

always agree. And, *querido,* we're looking at a lifetime of my not always agreeing with you. But I won't let you overrule me every time. Because I've finally realized that the only way to hold my own with a man who's just too much of one is to be more of a woman than I've been so far."

WELL, THAT HAD interesting possibilities, Sal thought. But he was still afraid to hope that this was going to work out, after all. So he simply listened. Behind her, the baby shouted and waved his arms, wanting someone's, anyone's, attention.

"No more whining and railing against you," she said, going to pick Max up. "No more running away, pouting or otherwise behaving like a jerk. I will love you to the absolute best of my ability, but I will not lay down or roll over for you."

That was the point at which he lost his reserve. Laying down and rolling over were some of their best moves. "Ever?" he asked with a grin he was sure revealed every lascivious thought in his head.

She smiled, too, obviously chasing the same memories. "Well, maybe sometimes."

He drew a breath. Max reached for him, and Sal took the baby, thinking how much he loved the weight of him in his arms, his funny face now full of recognition and budding intelligence.

But he had a position to state here, too. "I understand and appreciate your declaration," he said, looking her in the eye. "I even applaud it. But please don't expect me to be any less your protector and defender because you've decided you're invincible. I've been around longer and in more dangerous places. I know you're not. You may consider yourself free as a bird, but in matters of personal safety, you will accede to my advice.'' That point made, he smiled again. "And I will lay down and roll over any time you ask."

She threw her arms around him and the baby, laughter deep in her throat.

"Did I mention that I love you?" she asked, looking up into his face, while the baby pulled at her ear.

Sal worked to extricate it from the grasping little fingers. "You did say something about wanting to bear my children. I think Max should have some company."

"Absolutely. A brother and a sister, at least."

"I like that."

Something seemed to occur to her suddenly, and she took a step away, looking unhappy. "Your trip..." she began.

He shook his head. "Was a fabrication. Diego didn't call me. I just didn't think I could stand to be in this den of deliriously happy McKeons if we were over."

"Oh, my darling," she said, holding him tightly again. "We are finally beginning."

She kissed him with what felt like complete conviction.

He kissed her with the promise that she was right.

Cheddar, as though understanding that all was resolved, moved to sit in the suitcase.

"What'll you do about the business? Do we have to go back to Seattle? I mean, I will, I just...wondered."

He'd given that some thought. "No. We'll look into the house behind the theater. I'll move our business headquarters here and Diego can manage the Seattle office. With computer hook-up and faxes it should be easy.''

She hugged him fiercely again. ''Oh, I'd love that,'' she whispered. She finally drew away and sighed. ''We'd better go lend a hand out there. I've done nothing to help all day.''

''Okay.'' Reluctantly, he backed toward the door and turned the knob.

As the door opened, Peg and all her daughters-in-law stumbled into the room. The brothers and Charlie, at the back of the small crowd, smiled innocently.

''Did I mention,'' Dori asked Sal dryly, ''that there's no privacy in this family?''

Peg took Max from them and pulled Sal down to kiss his cheek. ''But there's more love than you'll ever find anywhere.''

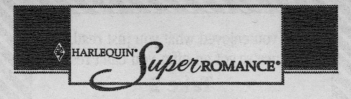

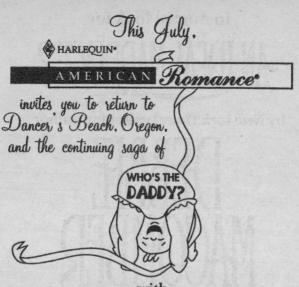

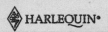 **HARLEQUIN**

AMERICAN *Romance*®

Heart, Home & Happiness

Save $1.00 off the purchase of any 2

AMERICAN *Romance*®

series titles.

$1.00 OFF!

any two American Romance series titles.

RETAILER: Harlequin Enterprises Ltd. will pay the face value of this coupon plus 10.25¢ if submitted by customer for this product only. Any other use constitutes fraud. Coupon is nonassignable. Void if taxed, prohibited or restricted by law. Consumer must pay any government taxes. Nielson Clearing House customers submit coupons and proof of sales to: Harlequin Enterprises Ltd., 661 Millidge Avenue, P.O. Box 639, Saint John, N.B. E2L 4A5. Non NCH retailer—for reimbursement submit coupons and proof of sales directly to: Harlequin Enterprises Ltd., Retail Marketing Department, 225 Duncan Mill Rd., Don Mills, Ontario M3B 3K9, Canada. Valid in Canada only.

Coupon valid until December 31, 2001.
Valid at retail outlets in Canada only.
Limit one coupon per purchase.

52602968

Visit us at www.eHarlequin.com
T5V3CHARCAN
© 2001 Harlequin Enterprises Ltd.

 **HARLEQUIN**®
Makes any time special®

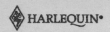

HARLEQUIN·

AMERICAN *Romance*®

Heart, Home & Happiness

Save $1.00 off the purchase of any 2

AMERICAN *Romance*®

series titles.

$1.00 OFF!

any two American Romance series titles.

RETAILER: Harlequin Enterprises Ltd. will pay the face value of this coupon plus 8¢ if submitted by customer for this product only. Any other use constitutes fraud. Coupon is nonassignable. Void if taxed, prohibited or restricted by law. Consumer must pay any government taxes. For reimbursement submit coupons and proof of sales to: Harlequin Enterprises Ltd., P.O. Box 880478, El Paso, TX 88588-0478, U.S.A. Cash value 1/100¢. Valid in the U.S. only.

Coupon valid until December 31, 2001.
Valid at retail outlets in the U.S. only.
Limit one coupon per purchase.

107427

5 65373 00033 5   (8100)0 10742

Visit us at www.eHarlequin.com
T5V3CHARUS

HARLEQUIN®
Makes any time special ®